The Witch Wars
As featured in the War N' Wit novellas

Gail Roughton

Print ISBNs
Amazon print 9780228627104
BWL Print 9780228627111
Ingram Spark 9780228627128
Barnes & Noble 9780228627135

BWL Publishing Inc.

Books we love to write ...
Authors around the world.

http://bwlpublishing.ca

Dedication

To Magic – Wherever we may find it!

Table of Contents

Chapter One

No lightning bolt streaked from the sky the day my life as I knew it began to end. There was no warning at all. Nothing. There I was, sitting at my desk, minding my own business, doing my job. My official job title is "legal assistant." The more exotic sounding title is paralegal. In the old days when folks called jobs what they actually were, the title was "legal secretary." Me? I answer to any of the above. Or just to Ariel. That's my name. Ariel Anson.

Now, I know the general public thinks a law office is an exciting place, full of fascinating cases and esoteric points of law highlighted with flashes of legal genius, something different every day. Not. Trust me on this. You seen one accident case, you seen 'em all. And corporate law? Business law? Wills and estates? Oh, man, you don't even want to go there. Domestic law? Right. The only thing worse than a divorce case is an estate fight. At least folks involved in a divorce are supposed to hate each other whereas a fight over Daddy's will? Oh. My. God.

Anyway, that's what I was doing. Just minding my own business in the course of my humdrum day and doing my job at the century-old, prestigious central Georgia law firm of Baker, Lawson, Abercrombie & Hunter, where the partners walk around in blissful ignorance of the fact the firm is referred to in legal circles as BLAH. All us legal assistants think that's a hoot.

I was the only legal gal who worked for three partners. Some of the girls had just one, most had two. Sort of gave me a certain mystique of extreme competence, you know? In all honesty, most of the time the three attorneys I had were cakewalks, though I wasn't about to announce such to the powers-that-be lest I end up with four attorneys to babysit. It all depended on who the three partners were. And mine were hand-picked, a luxury I had because I was good, good enough after eleven years in the business to pick and choose the attorneys I worked for. Diplomatically, of course. So diplomatically that nobody knew that but me. And my little sister.

Stacy, whose given name is Anastasia (our parents swore they hadn't smoked a lot of pot during the early years of their marriage but given our names, we didn't believe them), was following in her big sister's footsteps more or less by accident. I'd gotten her the office runner job one year during her summer break and she'd gotten the legal-eagle bug. She worked down at the other end of the firm for Calhoun Spencer, one of the more senior partners who specialized in insurance defense. Believe me, nobody working for Cal could have handled anybody else. I knew. I'd done it for six years myself before impending carpal tunnel syndrome had me scrambling to move to another location within the four hallowed halls of BLAH. I still felt bad about hi-jacking Stacy into my vacated seat but she claims she's forgiven me. I still have my doubts about that sometimes.

For the past three years, I'd been taking care of Ashton Davis, litigator 'par excellence' and the only attorney in the firm who liked criminal work, Mark McCray, who specialized in complex business litigation, and Anderson Halloway. Anderson was 74, the number one name on the letterhead. He did pretty much whatever the hell he wanted to.

Ash and Mark, being in their mid-thirties and thus computer literate, did a lot of their own typing because it was easier for them to think and type than to think and dictate. A generation thing. Since I didn't have to be their typist, I was free to organize, clean-up and grind out those standard, rote legal pleadings the public thought attorneys drafted and everybody in the legal field knew damn well the secretaries did. Anderson was a different story. He could barely turn on a computer and used his to check the stock market. In his current exalted position and with his history—the man had an unbelievable trial record—he only took the cases he wanted and spent a lot of time at his mountain house in North Carolina and even more at his beach condo at Hilton Head.

All in all, I considered my set-up ideal and considering the six years I'd spent in the halls of the firm back forty turning out hundred page pleadings for Cal Spencer, I didn't feel guilty at all when I grabbed a spare thirty minutes or an hour to indulge in my private hobby of writing. I'm a closet writer. I write books and put 'em in the closet. Nobody ever suspected except Stacy, of course, because nobody believed that with three attorneys I had time to breathe, let alone write a book.

And so the earth was turning in its proper orbit and all was right with my world when I returned from lunch that fateful day after meeting my fiancé, Scott Newton, at a local sandwich shop. Okay, Scott wasn't what you'd call glamorous or exciting, but he was steady. An upcoming CPA with a good practice that was getting better. Good husband material. Good father material. Future Little League coach. I'd had exciting and it hadn't worked out well. Steady was fine. Steady was good. If I could just teach the man how to kiss. Well, time to work on that, I supposed.

I stuck my head in Mark's door to check on the progress of a new complaint arising out of a case we'd gotten from a firm in Philadelphia because three Georgia corporations were involved. Mark's my complex commercial litigator.

"So—you ready for me to file?" I asked. Since this was a federal case, all pleadings were filed electronically. Usually that's great, since it circumvents time deadlines of racing to the courthouse before it closes at 5:00 o'clock, not so much when you're racing the clock at 11:45 p.m. to get something filed before the date changes at midnight. Oh, yeah, I'd been there, done that, and Ashton Davis owed me big. It's always nice to have something to hold over your attorneys' heads.

"Yeah." Mark pushed his chair back and sighed. "But they want it served yesterday. Get the summons and all the other stuff ready, okay? I got the name of a good process server from one of my buddies down in South Georgia. Dude we got to serve lives in Tifton. Already called him and he says he can get it served this afternoon. Get it together for me and then shoot it to me so I can get it down to him"

"Sure," I said, and proceeded to do so, which was accomplished in something under twenty minutes, with the majority of the time on line spent in negotiating the credit card payment for the filing fees. That part was always a bitch. Then I hit "send" and shot the whole kit-and-caboodle over to Mark. Not as efficient as just letting me sent it to directly to the process server, but whatever kept my guys happy, thereby making them keep me happy, was fine with me.

"Thanks!" floated back down the hall from two doors up. I sat in front of Anderson Holloway's office. If Mark and/or Ash lasted till they were 74, they could fight over which one of 'em got their secretary in front of their office. "Hey, check my voicemail if you're away from your desk, okay, make sure that complaint's served? I'm leaving in a minute, Jenny's got something at school this afternoon."

"Sure. What's your server guy's name?"

Mark came down and stood in front of my desk. "Name of the company's Warnwit, Inc. I sort of assumed his, too. First name's Chad, I think. Call me when he calls, and email—"

"Philadelphia," I said, scribbling "Chad Warnwit" on the steno pad I kept by my phone. Nobody'd really used a steno pad in 40 years, but I did like the split lined pages and spiral flip top for keeping notes together. "Yeah, got it, run along now."

"Thanks, Ariel!"

"No problem," I said. With Mark gone and Anderson at Hilton Head, and Ash in the library trying to back-track the financial goings on in an ugly estate fight, my afternoon was gravy. I pulled up my latest venture into fantasy land and reminded myself not to zone out to the extent I didn't hear the phone.

Two hours later I did hear the phone when it rang, but it was a near thing. Mark's line. I pulled my brain back into the real world. Oh, yeah. The case from Philadelphia. Probably Mark's South Georgia process server.

"Mark McCray's office," I said crisply.

"But not Mark McCray, I'm guessing."

"No, sorry. Just his secretary."

"Well, I'm not."

"Excuse me?"

"Sorry. I'm not sorry you're not Mark McCray. Though I do need to let him know his guy's served."

His voice surprised me. It wasn't what I'd expected from a South Georgia process server, there was no real southern accent, Georgian, South Georgian or otherwise. Rather, it was accent-less, the accent of Florida.

"Mr. Warnwit?"

"That's the name of the company. Mine's Garrett."

"As in Pat?" I asked before I could stop myself. My brain was a hodgepodge of collected bits of totally useless information, including the name of the lawman who'd brought down Billy the Kid by allegedly shooting him in the back. I grimaced to myself. He'd think I was crazy. Nobody but Stacy ever got my private wise-cracks.

"As in Chad. Can't say as I've brought in anybody comparable to Billy the Kid lately. Haven't shot anybody in quite a while, either, and never in the back that I recall. That'd cause too many legal problems."

Some damn. He got it!

"How reassuring. So, you got our boy for us, did you?"

"At 16:12 hours. Sorry, that's –"

"Four twelve. Got it."

"By service on the wife as she was pulling out of the driveway to soccer practice with the two girls. Casey Douglas, 5-7, 145 pounds, blonde, glasses, not contacts, social security—"

I laughed in delight. "Did you copy her driver's license, too?"

"I always write down a description so there's no question of who got served. And I always have them sign the Return of Service, too, so they can't claim they weren't really served. Got some pictures of the house. If you're going after a judgment, there's money there, very up-scale neighborhood. Pulled the property assessment from the Tax Commissioner's Office, I'll send it back with the return of service when I get back to the office. To you or Mark McCray?"

"Either," I said. "You already have Mark's, though."

"Yeah, but I like you better."

I laughed again and gave it to him. And then, because I couldn't stop myself, I asked, "If your name's Garrett, who's Warnwit?"

"Not Warnwit, like a name or one word. It's W-a-r Capital N W-i-t," he spelled out. "War-N-Wit. Inc., to be official."

"That's unusual. Who's War?"

"Oh, that's me."

"Who's Wit?"

"Silent partner. But I'm expecting an appearance real soon now. Much sooner than I'd figured, I think."

"Oh, I see," I said, not seeing at all. "Well, that was great service. Well above and beyond the call of duty."

"Just earning my lunch with you at Carrabba's," he said cheerfully. "Keep me in mind if anybody needs to find somebody. Or any other type of PI service. I'm based in Quitman, right above the Florida line, center of the state, real near I-75. I do Alabama, Florida and Georgia. You'll get your money's worth. I don't deliver, I don't charge."

"For real? How do you stay in business?"

"I'm good. I'll send you some cards and fliers with the bill."

"For sure. I'll spread the word. Thanks for your help."

"Anytime," he affirmed, and hung up.

I stared thoughtfully at the phone. Damn. Intelligence. Humor. *Just earning my lunch with you at Carrabba's.* Nothing like a charming flirt who knew how to do it perfectly to make a girl's day. I had no idea in hell that my life as I knew it had just begun to end.

Chapter Two

October moved to November and the beginning of what was usually a busy time in a law office. I'd never understood it, never will, but let Thanksgiving and Christmas and year-end loom on the calendar, and damn near every attorney I've ever known decides to start working cases they haven't touched in six months. My current three weren't so bad about that, especially Anderson, who certainly didn't plan to be in the office much at all during either Thanksgiving or Christmas, but there're always attorneys on the other side of the case.

True to form, one of Anderson's car accident insurance defense cases reared its head—or rather, the plaintiffs' attorneys did—and started yelling for the deposition of the driver's passenger. A deposition is where the attorneys for both sides get in the same room with whichever witness whose story they want to hear in front of a court reporter and swear to tell the truth, the whole truth and nothing but the truth, just like in court, except there's not a judge.

Sounds easy, I know. Not. Depositions are a pain in the ass to schedule under the best of circumstances since nobody's ever available at the same time. Every deposition has to be scheduled at least five times. It's a law. This one was worse. We didn't know where the hell our insured driver's passenger was. We did know if we found said insured driver's passenger, she probably wasn't going to talk to us since ex-boyfriends and ex-girlfriends tended to be pissy. Which meant she'd talk plenty if the plaintiffs' attorney found her first.

Plaintiffs and their attorneys had one thing in common. They really liked to settle their cases near Christmas. It's like extra money from Santa Claus. And this particular plaintiffs' attorney was a bitch to deal with, both in gender and personality. Had a good case, though, and she knew it.

"Well, we just have to find that passenger," Anderson pronounced in typical Anderson fashion, leaning back in his chair and gesturing grandly. "Get some of the young boys on the internet looking."

"We've already done that, Anderson, they can't find her."

"Sure they can. Anybody can be found in this day and age—"

I put my brain in neutral and let it cruise and hit on the solution to the problem at the exact time he finished up with his standard, "—and all we can do is all we can do. And if we can't find her, then we might just have to hire a private detective. 'Cause I can't let Sandy Rozier find her before I do and talk to her without me, our insured says she hates his guts. She'll crucify us, policy limits here we come, get out the checkbook."

I chewed my lip a bit. "Actually," I said "I've got just the man for the job. But I'm not sure how much it'll cost."

"Well, let's see. Insured in this case is a doctor. With an umbrella policy. Sandy Rozier's got three clients in that car, one of 'em's an eggshell plaintiff. We got well over a million dollars sitting on the table. I don't think a PI'll cost us nearly that much. Whoever it is, get me the number. And any last known addresses we have. Handle it!"

"I'm on it!" I exclaimed, fleeing his office and running for the file. And one of Chad Garrett's cards, patiently waiting in my desk drawer.

I flew back in and deposited all on Anderson's desk. Ash's line started ringing so I missed Anderson's conversation with can't beat the price Chad Garrett. I hung up just as Anderson called through the door.

"Hey! Here's the email address. Send him the addresses we have, he's waiting on it!"

I went in to collect the material, sat back down, proceeded to forward it to war@war-n-wit.com and was rewarded with an almost immediate reply: "Got it. When I find her, do I use kid gloves or brute force?"

Cocky much? "If you find her," I sent back, resisting the urge to italicize or underline the 'if', "kid gloves please. You did a job for us, well, me and another attorney, a few weeks back. I told Anderson how you went above and beyond, don't know if you remember it or us. Did Anderson explain she's probably going to be a fairly hostile witness and won't be very cooperative?"

The response came within seconds. "I remember you. *When* I find her," it read, and he hadn't resisted the urge to italicize, "I'll have on my best pair of kid gloves and charm her right into cooperation. Report later."

Well, alllllriiighty, then! I smiled and turned to the massive pleadings indexes waiting to be updated in one of Anderson's medical malpractice defense cases. I wouldn't hear from him for a few days. I gave it a fifty-fifty shot either way. And wondered how his voice would sound if he had to call in and concede defeat. I didn't think that happened often.

The email came in something slightly under an hour. "Got her. Back at the Shellman's Bluff address you had for her before she flipped up to Ohio for a while, but she's pretending real hard not to be. Headed there now. I'm about two hours away and then I'll have to work the charm. Please make sure I have a phone number that'll get Mr. Halloway. I'll put her on the phone with him."

Holy. Hell.

"Anderson!" I called through the door, while hitting the reply button to supply Anderson's cell number. "He's got her! Be sure you keep your cell phone with you! And on!"

Anderson came and went with impunity. And he used his cell phone like he used his computer. Only when he wanted to. He was forever leaving it in a coat pocket or turning it off. His voice mail wasn't even set up. It was already four o'clock. By the time Chad of War-N-Wit had her on the phone, he'd be long gone. It was unusual for him to be here this late. "Says he'll have her on the phone with you in probably three hours."

"Well, if he's got her, why doesn't he just give me the number and let me call her?"

"Had a lot of luck with that so far, have you?" I asked. "You wanta' spook her so he'll never convince her to talk to you?"

"Hell, no!"

"Then let the man do the job we hired him for, why don't you?"

Anderson came out of his office with his coat, grumbling mildly as he passed my desk.

"Gets real annoying, you being right all the time, you know," he said, adjusting his hat.

"Dirty job but somebody's got to do it," I responded. All my guys were special, but Anderson Halloway was a legend, the last of his breed of gentlemen attorneys. The legal world would be the poorer when he departed the practice of law, which I was sure wouldn't be until he departed this world. "Now, do you have your cell phone and is it—"

"Yes, I've got it, and yes, it's on, and yes, I'll keep it with me."

"Good man. Can't wait to hear how it goes."

Chapter Three

I didn't even have to ask. Anderson was gushing when I came in the next morning.

"I don't know where you got that guy's name, Ariel, but he's a miracle worker. Had a real long talk with the girl, she's cooperating about the deposition, won't hurt us too bad. Sure as hell not as bad as she'da hurt us if Sandy Rozier'd gotten to her first."

"Good to know," I replied, stashing my purse under my desk. "What time did he call you?"

"'Bout 9:00 last night, I think. Get this—major problem we had with getting her to talk to us is she's gotten married. So with an ex-boyfriend in the mix and all, she didn't want her husband upset and the new husband doesn't want her upset. So our guy sat with the new husband for an hour and a half while the dude grilled hamburgers before he'd let him talk to her!"

"Well, I did tell him to use kid gloves," I said. "Must have a really soft pair." The mail hadn't been distributed yet, so I pulled up Outlook and started through the emails. War@war-n-wit wasn't too far down in the mix:

Our Ms Tiffany Leigh Andrews Hartwell, date of birth 8/12/78, social security no. xxx-xx-8723, 5-3, 120, blonde with help as evidenced by the dark roots, no glasses, don't know about contacts, is back at the 1380 River Cliff address in Shellman's Bluff, Georgia. She works at one of the local restaurants and I would imagine with the tourist trade coming, does pretty good on tips. Home phone 555-8742, cell phone 555-3815. She has a new husband of a little under a year and believe me when I tell you he is very protective of her and very resentful of the way the insured driver in *this case treated her and I will leave to your imagination the descriptive phrases utilized in expressing that resentment. I sat on their patio handling with kid gloves while he grilled hamburgers and hotdogs for an hour before he would consent to permit her to come out of their bedroom where she was watching television. I then called Mr. Halloway on his cell and handed it over to her. Consequently, this assignment is complete with this report to Anderson Halloway and his secretary Ms Ariel Anson. Invoice to follow by mail for one skip trace in the amount of $200.00 and one service for $175.00, for a total of $375.00. Please note that War-N-Wit, Inc. stands ready for the next assignment. Have a good day.*

Was this man real? Obviously. But maybe I could fictionalize him, and my fertile brain which had not so sub-consciously stored him away as the base for a future character back during Mark's case went into overdrive. I hit the reply button.

Did they at least offer you a hamburger or a hotdog? You are awesome, and they should do a reality show on you! Anybody in the firm needs anything doing in South Georgia, believe me, you da man! (And we're a big firm, look us up. I'll see what I can do about getting business your way for sure.)

I went through two more emails before his response popped up. And this time, it wasn't from War@wit-n-war.com. It was from chad7777@hotmail.com. He'd switched me to his personal Email?

Yes, actually, they did offer me a hamburger, but I declined as I felt it breached the level of professionalism I was trying to maintain. Besides, I didn't want the kid gloves to get dirty. Please note that War-N-Wit, Inc. services all of Georgia, Alabama and Florida, not just South Georgia. You can run but you can't hide. Thanks for the kind words, but I was just beefing up my chances of lunch with you at Carrabba's.

I'm a closet writer, remember ? I'm going to pass up the chance to chat with a guy with a sense of humor, an obviously high IQ, a made-for-television career, and enough charm to blow the top off a charm-o-meter? Give me a break. I don't think so.

Of course they offered you a hamburger! Southern hospitality dictates that you offer a burglar a glass of ice tea. I stand corrected, your area of service is noted, and if anybody needs anything doing in the firm, I'll certainly steer 'em your way. You can run but you can't hide is what I tell my guys when I track 'em down in the men's room, by the way. (Not really, but they're not too sure I wouldn't if I really needed 'em.)

Well, that was fun, I thought. That was the last one, of course, he'll get on to work and so will I. Brightened the day though, sure enough. It took about five minutes for the next one to come in.

If you're going to track a man down in the men's room, we definitely need to form a partnership. So, what about the chances for lunch at Carrabba's the next time I swing up I-75?

Yet again I asked myself if this guy was real. But I sure as hell intended to enjoy the exchanges for as long as they lasted. I hit the reply button.

Be warned. And be careful what you wish for, you might get it. You're a character just waiting to be put in a novel, and I'm a closet writer. I write books and put 'em in the closet. My sister gave me a T-shirt for Christmas that says "Watch out or I'll put you in my novel."

I hit the send button before I realized what I'd said. I did *not* just tell a perfect stranger that I wrote novels. I didn't tell close friends that I wrote novels. What the hell was the man doing to me?

If you're serious about writing, we definitely need to corroborate. Everybody tells me I should fictionalize my cases and write a book. I would love to

*see your closet. And send me something, I'd love to
read some of your work.*

I chewed my lip before replying. Well, in for a
penny, in for a pound. And anyway, this was just an
email flirtation. I'd never meet the man anyway.

*I'm serious as a heart-attack about writing. I have
seven novels in my closet, though actually, I had to
move them to a file cabinet. But you don't need any
help writing. You're a great writer yourself. And I
don't believe I'm telling you this, I know you don't
believe this the way I'm gushing, but I don't tell
anybody I write. Only my sister knows.*

It didn't take but a minute this time for the
response to arrive.

*So where's my sample? Do you really write that
much and just put it aside? Surely you've given
publishing a shot?*

He must be having a slow day. My morning wasn't
all that heavy either. I could take the time to play for a
minute or two or ten. I pulled up the excerpt from my
last completed novel that I'd culled and prepped for
submission to a couple of agents and looked at it
thoughtfully. Stacy thought I didn't try to submit much,
which drove her crazy, but in actual fact, I tried rather
frequently. I just didn't tell her about it because the one
or two times she had known about it, the rejections
upset her a hell of a lot more than they did me. Well,
hell. Why not? I repeated to myself I was never going
to actually meet the man anyway.

*Well, I told you to be careful what you wished for.
Pulled this out of my last one as the requested first
pages and sent it to a few possibilities. But writing and
publishing's not what people think. In actual fact, you
can't get published if you don't have an agent and you
can't get an agent unless you're published. I think it
was Stephen King who said that by the time you could
get an agent, you didn't need one. And you can use
brute honesty, I don't need kid gloves. Wouldn't have*

survived in a law office for eleven years if I did. You're under no obligation to ask for any more of it.

And with that, I hit send and turned sideways from the screen to get back to the massive pleadings waiting to be indexed in Anderson's med mal defense case. Certainly he wasn't going to read that sample, certainly if he read it, he'd think it was juvenile beyond belief, and almost certainly he wasn't going to hurt my feelings by telling me so, both because he was a natural charmer who liked the ladies and because the firm was a new and potentially quite lucrative client for him and I was its contact. No joke, we were big, at one time the biggest in the state outside of Atlanta and if we were no longer the biggest, which I wasn't sure about, we were pretty damn close.

Then I sat bolt upright. Shit! That particular novel had an undercover agent, drug-running, dirty rural county plotline. The man was a private detective, and most private detectives had a law enforcement background. Oh, my Lord, he'd think it was worse than juvenile, he'd think I was a complete and total dumbass! Maybe his law enforcement background wasn't that extensive though. I flew into Anderson's office. The secretaries had email access but not internet access for fear we'd play on Facebook or shop on line all day, and in all fairness, insofar as some of the girls, they were probably right. No problem for me in any event. I just used Anderson's. I Bing'd War-N-Wit, Inc. to see if it had a web site.

Oh, yeah. Sure as hell did. And Chad Garret was ex-Fort Lauderdale PD and ex-Florida Bureau of Investigation. Well, that explained the accent or lack thereof. And I'd just sent an undercover, drug-running plot to an ex-Florida drug-capital-of-the-world Bureau of Investigation agent. Way to go, Ariel! I hated feeling like a fool.

I didn't want to even glance at the computer screen as I sat back down, but of course, I couldn't stop myself. Why do all humans just have to stop and look at car wrecks? And there was another, and this time I was sure it would tell me he had to go to work on something right now.

Okay, so you mean to tell me the love of Billy's life thought he was dead for 25 years? Billy is probably helping out his own son he never knew he had which made Mom marry Joe asshole in the first place. OMG maybe it will turn out better if I get the rest of the story. It's great thus far, but please don't leave me hanging like this!

He was just being charming, of course, and wasn't he just about the best at being charming I'd ever run across? I certainly wasn't going to send him anymore of that one, thank heavens what I'd sent him was set up so that it didn't get into the inner plot. Maybe I could end this little email flirtation without him knowing what a complete idiot I was.

Since Billy's been gone 25 years and the kid's 17 that'd be a little difficult. And besides, I'm not that obvious, the son he never knew he had's been done to death...

And for the moment, I surrendered completely to the pull of that powerful personality sitting at a computer screen down in South Georgia near the Florida line. Responsible, conscientious, what are the day's deadline's Ariel Anson disappeared. I didn't care what needed to be done today (unless it was a deadline that was going to get us sued for malpractice, of course, and I never let anything like that get remotely close). I didn't care which attorney needed how many copies; I didn't care if Scott needed me to pick up his dry-cleaning on my lunch hour or what he wanted me to fix for supper that night. I'd care if Stacy needed me, of course, but for the first time in I didn't remember when, that was about the only thing I cared about other than the computer screen in front of me and the emails that never seemed to stop.

Chapter Four

By mid-afternoon, I'd received his picture. I looked at the strong lines of his face, the dark hair already heavily threaded with pure silver, the eyes emphasized by laugh lines and the Florida sun. "Reciprocation requested," read the subject line. Like most women, I didn't like too many pictures of me and went out of my way not to collect them. I didn't even have—oh, wait a minute! Yes, I did. I had a picture of me and Stacy from last Easter that wasn't too bad. I attached it to the email and advised that at least that would have the effect of putting a stop to the increasingly not-so-subtle requests for a definite lunch date.

I didn't realize until after I'd sent it that I hadn't specified which figure in the picture I was. I shrugged. Just as well. He'd write back gushing about the glorious hair and the sparkling eyes and of course he'd be referring to Stacy. Little sister was a fox, her hair an unusual blend, not a red-head, not a blonde, not a brunette. Just a cloud of shimmering brightness. And she'd modeled for GAP at some local modeling shows at the mall when she was a teenager, too. Well, all good things came to an end, and then I could reassure myself that he was, after all, just a man, and men went straight for looks.

If you want me to stop pushing for lunch, you shouldn't have sent that picture. Why on earth would you think that would send any man running anywhere except towards you? My God, that dark hair and those slanting, mysterious eyes, that long jaw line...how 'bout yesterday? No? Tomorrow? Tonight?

What? I clicked the picture back up. There was no way he'd mistakenly referred to Stacy's hair as dark, nor anyway he'd refer to her eyes as slanting and mysterious.

Say what? I'm the bright-haired gal with the bright blue eyes, there's nothing dark and mysterious about me.

The response was instaneous, blunt and to the point.

Bullshit.

I might be in serious trouble here. I was beginning to believe that if I told him to meet me in two hours at the Perry Motel, he'd be there. No, I wasn't beginning to believe that. I *believed* that. And all good things come to an end.

Okay, I'm the dark and mysterious girl, though I don't recall anybody ever actually referring to me that way. The usual description boils down to, "she's okay." So what is it about a few emails that's got you in such hot pursuit? And actually, it seemed a little irrelevant under the circumstances of me being here and you being down next to the Florida line, but I'm engaged. I'm getting married in six months. And I've enjoyed today tremendously but I'm not exactly in a position to meet you anywhere tonight. Or any night. I didn't mean to come on like a tease, I really didn't think you were serious and actually you probably aren't, which means you really think I'm stupid, it's just—you're so easy to talk to. Really, it was a great day.

Pleasant interlude over. Back to reality. And boy, did I screw that one up, way to seem like an insecure teenager.

If you're willing to wait six months to get married, it means you're definitely not so overwhelmed with your significant other that you can't live without him which tells me something's missing on your end, something our on-line flirt session today makes me bet you're missing badly. Think about that before you completely dismiss the possibility of an actual meeting. And much as I hate it, the day's drawing to a close and I have a dude about to get off work that I've got to go corral. But I'll be around. Remember, you can run but you can't hide. And you are well beyond being "okay". You're more special than you know.

That was a perfect sign-off. And that was that. I was engaged. I was going to marry a good steady man who'd be a good husband and whose passwords on all his bank accounts would be some combination of sensible numbers. I wondered what Chad Garrett used as a password with such an unusual business name as War-N-Wit. I wondered again what War-N-Wit stood for. And if and when he'd be "around" again and if it would be as soon as Monday.

Then I remembered I wouldn't be here Monday. I was going out of town this weekend with Scott to visit his parents. I almost send a final email to let him know should he drop in for a flirtation and then I stopped myself. He wasn't going to be back Monday. He'd had a slow office day and I'd provided entertainment. End of story. But maybe I'd come in Monday at least around lunchtime, just to take care of the email. Emails got backed up on the weekends, always took a while Monday morning to clean them out and it'd take a lot longer if I let them go till Tuesday. And then, just in case he'd dropped back in, he wouldn't think I was ignoring him. I shook my head firmly, called myself a total idiot, and started clearing my desk for day's end and weekend's start.

Chapter Five

I didn't go in Monday, though I won't lie and say I didn't want to. By Monday night I was in a foul mood, slamming around my kitchen and throwing together the meat loaf recipe Scott insisted I get from his mother. I'd promised to fix it tonight. We didn't live together, although we swung back and forth frequently overnight. I suppose the living arrangement was telling, at least on my part. For Scott it was just a comment on his personality and frugal nature. We'd both just signed year-long leases on our respective apartments when we got engaged and he didn't want to risk one of us sub-letting to a tenant who might trash the place and thus circumvent refund of the deposit. Since the leases were for a year, we set the wedding date for a year. Romantic, huh?

I was in a foul mood for more reasons than one. In one of those serendipitous things that sometimes happen, I was a good cook though I really didn't like to cook. Most folks who don't like cooking don't do it and aren't good at it, but somehow I seemed to know instinctively what went with what, how to modify a recipe to make it better, adjust cooking times up or down. Stacy could do it, too, but she actually did like to cook. Scott was the only person on earth who always tried to improve on my cooking skills, probably because his mother sucked as a cook and he had no idea how things were actually supposed to taste.

In any event, he didn't like my meatloaf. This recipe, however—oh, my God. This was going to taste like crap, way too much sour in the mix, meatloaf needed brown sugar mixed with tomato sauce, sweet and tangy, not this—nauseating blend of mustard and garlic. And then there was that little niggle in the back of my mind, the urge to run to the office right now and see if Chad Garrett had made an appearance.

Needless to say, the evening was not a spectacular success. Scott's frequent exclamations confirming that this was how meatloaf was supposed to taste didn't help things a damn bit.

"What's the matter?" he asked, rinsing the plates and loading the dishwasher. He was good about that, I had to give it to him.

"Got a headache," I said.

He gave his imitation of what he thought was a sexy sneer. "No room for headaches tonight, I've got plans for you."

"Change 'em," I said quickly.

He looked startled. "You mean you really have a headache? Sorry, hon, I thought you were just playing around. Here, go sit down and I'll give you a neck rub."

"Hell, no!" I exclaimed, before I could stop myself. "You hurt when you rub my neck or my back, you do it way too hard."

"Just trying to get the kinks out of the muscles," he defended himself. "Men want the best for the women they love."

Where it came from, I don't know. But I couldn't have stopped myself if my life depended on it. "Yeah, well, I don't even like you."

I had such a reputation for straight-faced kidding that it didn't even phase him. I could and actually did say some absolutely outrageous things at times, at home and in the office and everybody was sure I was kidding, because nobody ever said exactly what they were actually thinking, now did they? I found it a very handy skill.

"I know, honey, I know. I don't like you either, you know." He glanced at me appraisingly. "Hey, you want me to go home and let you take some Tylenol and go to bed?"

"Yes, actually, that would be lovely," I said, plastering on a pitiful expression and rubbing the back of my own neck.

"Well, okay. If you're sure. Call you in the morning, honey."

"Fine," I said, locking the deadbolt behind him. I stared thoughtfully at the door. You know what? Maybe I really didn't like him. And maybe he didn't really like me either.

Chapter Six

I had a bad hair day the next morning, and then I changed clothes three times because I had a bad outfit day too. So I was a little bit later than usual when I blew into the office. The mail was already there, so I made myself go get my coffee and open the mail before checking the emails, and yes, between the Saturday and Sunday spam and junk mail and Monday's real emails, there was a long list waiting. And I purposely made myself not look down the list first to see if there was one from war@war-n-wit or chad7777@hotmail. This served the purpose of keeping me in a very heightened state of anticipation. Nothing.

Of course there wasn't. What had I expected? See, it was a very good thing I hadn't ruined my day off by running into the office to check, now wasn't it? I put thoughts of Chad Garrett out of my mind and turned back to business.

When there was still nothing by Friday, I clicked for a new email and sat looking at the blank screen for a while before typing.

Oh, I see. You've found another email flirt to catch your fancy. Well, come back and visit if you get bored, it breaks up the day.

Then I hit the send button before I could change my mind. The next week passed. Nothing. What a very good thing I was such a sensible girl because of course he just been flirting on a slow day. What a very good thing I was engaged to such a steady, reliable man.

It was the next Wednesday when I found a chad7777 in my inbox. Heart racing, I clicked. An internet link? Two and a half weeks and he sends me a freakin' internet link? I forwarded it to my phone, it was probably just spam and no way could I risk exposing the office. I pulled up my gmail and debated. What if it was a virus and I blew my phone. I pulled it up anyway and was rewarded with an advertisement for Viagra. *Whoopee. Shit.*

I went back to my desk. He'd gotten a bug in his computer and it was spamming. And yeah, I was disappointed he hadn't returned to flirt, but he was a PI and one thing he didn't need was a bug in his system that he didn't know about. I clicked the reply button.

Darlin', you got a bug in your system or you tryin' to tell me you need Viagra?

I went back to work. After lunch, chad7777 made an appearance.

I'm really sorry about that, I've been on a couple of very tough, very long skip traces and I seem to catch all sorts of crap when I have to flip around so much on the internet. Nothing on this one, is there? No, there's no flirt can touch you, girl, just had a mass of work out of the office I had to take care of. I'm about done and then I'll be back for some serious flirting. P.S. Do I need Viagra?

I laughed. I couldn't help it. Even though my first thought was to wonder if he thought I was so stupid I hadn't caught the "Sent from my iPhone" on the bottom of some of the emails from that marathon email day.

You'd know about that better than me. Certainly you don't need it on my account. But I know in your business you don't need a bug you don't know about and I didn't know how long it'd take you to trip on it if somebody didn't tell you.

There was nothing for the rest of the week. And then, on Monday morning, as though he'd never been gone, he was back. In full pursuit. I could always tell when he was actually in the office because those emails were long and conversational, and when he was in a tearing hurry he let me know he was around with the funny little emails that proliferate along the internet, including one or two that were more than a little off-color and had me hitting the permanent delete code in a red-hot hurry. All office email's subject to being monitored, you know. Though all the emails had a remarkably similar and repetitive theme, they also ran the gamut of ordinary conversation, current events, the state of the world. However, that remarkably similar and repetitive theme was enough to make me hit the permanent delete code on anything he or I sent. After I'd printed them for re-reading, of course.

And they began merging to reveal the inner soul of a unique individual; kind, intelligent, charming, funny, discerning. And after saying that, this sounds as though I'm blowing my own horn and I'm really not—but he reminded me a lot of me. In male form, of course. Any thoughts of writing fiction flew out of my head; I sent him an email of my day during pretty much every lunch hour, along with thumbnail sketches of my sister, my friends, the folks in the office I didn't consider my friends, the attorneys—whatever happened to be going on that day.

What I didn't do was admit why I was doing it. Not to him, of course, though it's kind of hard to lie to yourself about a fascination rapidly becoming an obsession. And I wasn't about to admit I had an obsession. Been there, done that, not going back. I'd had obsessive exciting and it hadn't worked out well. And that, friends and neighbors, is the understatement of the century. It damn near killed me and left me virtually numb for at least five years, which is why it was so important that—go ahead, speak the truth and it will set you free—why it was so important that I marry a good, steady, boring, man like Scott who would never make the top of my head explode when he kissed me, but wouldn't tear my heart out while it was still beating and throw it away, either. He was safe. I cared about Scott. Well, I thought I did though now sometimes I wondered. I appreciated his many virtues.

But he'd never hurt me because I didn't care enough. And that was exactly what I wanted. I wasn't going through exciting again.

And so, in my emails, I was happily engaged, I had no intention of changing that status, I was very happy with my life. And I was sure he wouldn't like me in person anyway, because I was very stand-offish and actually not sexy in the slightest, which I euphemistically phrased as not being very touchy, certainly did not possess the beauty he proclaimed absolutely screamed from the picture I'd sent him, and really didn't take to people very well or very often.

He responded in kind, alternating teasing with sarcasm, never backing down an inch from his contentions that I was sexy as hell, that with the right man (implication himself) I'd be touchy as hell, that for somebody who didn't take to people very well or very often, I certainly seemed to have a large circle from which to draw descriptive entertainment. However, when broken down and analyzed, he didn't really tell me anything about himself. Well, he did, but he didn't, though I don't know if that makes any sense. I resolved to rectify that situation.

You know so much about me because I talk a lot, but that's what you get when you start corresponding with a writer. You get some long-ass emails, and talking to you in my little missives has become the high spot of my day. But I know so little about you. Let's start telling each other some little known fact or tidbit about ourselves that not many, if any, people know. As in, don't tell me you're a crack shot, I can figure that out by myself. Tell me you tear up over Disney movies or you're a great cook. I'll go first. I'm a classical pianist, formal lessons third through twelfth grade and some in college, though I don't play much anymore and would have to practice for several hours in private before I'd ever consider playing in front of anybody now. Which makes me sad at Christmas, like now, when I hear the Hallelujah

Chorus because I used to be able to play that and I know I'll never be able to again. And while you're at it, I have three questions that you don't have to answer but I'd really like to know. (1) Did you remember me from that complaint you served for Mark, really? (2) You pursued relentlessly through the course of one whole day and then you completely disappeared for two and a half weeks. Why'd you go away? And why'd you come back? And would you have come back if I hadn't emailed you about that bug your system had caught? (3) And have you ever done this with anybody else? You're a natural flirt, you know you are.

I hit the send and wondered what the response was going to reveal.

Chapter Seven

I didn't expect an answer that day and I didn't get one. I knew he was out in the field. He'd told me that via an earlier email and besides, it was a bad weather day which translated into good hunting weather for any process server/bounty hunter as outdoor workers such as construction and roofing men stayed home, another secret of the trade he'd shared. The problem was I had an unsettling feeling that I'd have known where he was even if he hadn't told me and that was just crazy.

I like long-ass emails. AND receiving yours has become the high spot of my day. We've both wondered what this connection is that you like to deny, and music could be a major part of it. I'm was actually a brass player in grammar and high school, actually played in the brass section for a couple of local symphonies when I was a teenager. And no, I haven't played in years. I'm a sucker for the chick-flicks on Oxygen and Lifetime and I'll tear up in a heartbeat. Tears don't make weakness. Yes, I'm a crack shot, with several trophies for first place in some competitions back in the days on the force when we drank till twelve and pissed till dawn. But they never knew about my musical past. And now it's time and probably past time to tell you something I hope doesn't sound pure stalker. I think about you far more than you can guess, so much so that I'm throwing caution to the wind and telling you that my Christmas wish is to meet at a restaurant of your choosing so we can actually see each other while we talk. And by the way, that was five questions, not two, and I'm a little hurt that you don't know how special this is and could even think I've done this before. No, never.

I closed my eyes. I was in so much trouble. And I needed to talk about it with the only person on God's green earth that would even halfway understand. I hit Stacy's intercom button. "Break," I said, when she answered. "Now."

"Cal's on a roll, trying to get him out the door. I need to get him out of here first."

"How long?"

"Ten minutes?"

"Hurry. Please."

There must have been something in my voice bordering on desperation. She appeared at my desk in seven minutes flat. I knew the effort it took to get Cal Spencer out the door with the minimum of seven or eight boxes of notebooks and files that accompanied him to any deposition or hearing.

"Damn, you're better than I am, little sister, fast work!"

"Yeah, whatever! Let's go!"

The parking garage on the floor below the offices was the staff go-to for times when we had to get away from attorneys and computers for ten minutes to maintain sanity. A few laps around the perimeters usually kept us going. It was a bit cold today though, so we settled into the front seat of my car.

"Well?!?" Stacy turned to face me. "So—give!!"

"Oh, Antsypants," I said, reverting to my big sister's pet name for baby sister. "I am in so much freakin' trouble!"

I pulled out the last emails between us that I'd printed. "See, it's like this—"

I talked at what probably approached the speed of light and I'm not sure anybody but a sister would have understood me. Then I mutely handed her the printed sheets.

Her eyes moved rapidly down, her expression changing, softening.

"Ohhhh..." she breathed. "Ohh, my Lord! He writes just like you do, this is almost prose poetry in places." Her expression hardened. "Dump him."

I started. "Excuse me? You just said..."

"Not the prose poet, Ari, get real. Scott. Dump Scott. Yesterday. Now. Last week. Last year."

"I know you've never really liked him, Antsypants, but he's what I need."

"Like hell! This—" she shook the paper emphatically. "This is what you need!"

"I've never even met him!"

"Yeah, but you're going to. You can lie to yourself if you want to, but you can't lie to me. Or him either, apparently. Now, go get him! I know you better than you think, and it's time to wake up! You've been sleepwalking for years, get over it! And for God's sakes, go get laid by somebody that knows how to do it!"

"I'm not getting laid, I don't know where that thing's been! And just wait till we go back in and I show you his picture! With his career! He's ex-Fort Lauderdale PD and ex-Florida Bureau of Investigation! Can you say chick magnet?"

"And you're so sure of where Scott's thing's been for the last year?"

"Well, actually, pretty sure, yeah."

"Oh, hell, so am I. I was just being pissy 'cause he's so damn boring! But Ari, where it's been ain't been doing you a lot of good."

"Excuse me?"

"I said don't try to lie to me. I know better. And I've seen you BGR and AGR, don't forget. And I know what you looked like during GR!!" That was private slang between myself and Antsypants for "before" a certain individual whose name I did not permit to be spoken and "after" a certain individual whose name I did not permit to be spoken.

I sighed and Stacy pounced.

"So, you'll go back in and tell him where and when?"

"Yeah," I breathed. And then more strongly, I re-affirmed. "Yeah. I think I'm going to do just that."

"Praise God and Hallelujah!!"

I sat back down at my computer and stared at the screen.

Okay. But here's the deal. This Thursday would work for me. There's a little funky Mexican restaurant called Rosita's, pure Mexican Georgia Redneck, between Warner Robins and Macon. It's a dive but I love it. If you let me know when you're close, I'll leave to meet you. My cell is 555-7777. Text or call when you're outside Macon. And I'll take the rest of the day off to finish Christmas shopping and you can trail around after me if you still feel so inclined after lunch. You might not even like me, you know. My voice might grate on your nerves. I'm a bitch from hell when I get mad. I'm really not very touchy. Whichever one of us gets there first, just stay in the car and wait till the other arrives. And we can get the first hug you keep harping on out of the way, and if you want, even a first (probably last) kiss out of the way, 'cause I'm not stupid enough to think that's not going to happen, instead of sitting there wondering about it all through lunch. And in case you don't know, this makes me extremely nervous and more than a little scared.

I hit the send before I could change my mind, something I'd become quite familiar with over the last few weeks. Five minutes later my cell phone announced the arrival of a text. *Please don't be scared of me, baby girl.* There wasn't a name, but not much question about the source.

I'm not afraid of you...I'm afraid of me. I sent back. And programmed his number into my cell. And that afternoon, with the exchange of a few Emails, it was so arranged that sometime between 11:30 and 12:00 on Thursday next, two days away, my life as I knew it would be over.

Chapter Eight

He caught a batch of rain on I-75 coming up, so I got there first. I sat, chewing gum furiously, watching the traffic for a slowing Chevy Equinox. I'd known he'd drive either a small SUV or a pickup—what else would be logical for a bounty hunter—but I'd forgotten to ask the color when we exchanged vehicle information. Probably silver, a good color for the shadows. And there it was, a silver Equinox, slowing for the turn. I closed my eyes, spit my gum into the dregs of my coffee cup. I got out and stood waiting, leaning against the door as he walked towards me.

Six-three, he'd told me early on, thirty-nine, old enough to know better but to do it anyway. There was more silver in the dark hair than there'd been in the picture. He smiled and opened his arms and for just a moment, I actually gave in and hugged back. Then he lowered his head and found my mouth and for just a moment, I kissed back. He pulled away.

"God, you taste good. With or without the gum." His mouth returned to mine and I gave in again, but not for long. It seemed to satisfy him, though, at least for the moment.

When the waitress asked if we wanted booth or table, I automatically said booth. I needed that table between us. That didn't work out so well, though, as he slid in right next to me.

"Too close?" he asked.

"No," I lied. Worlds too close. To the waitress, I said "Small guacamole salad and a chili rellano, please. And tea."

He perused the menu briefly and flipped it shut. "Two chicken burritos, please. Unsweetened tea." And under the table, he rested his hand on my knee. An electric bolt of heat shot through me. I knew I should pull my thigh back over. Instead I felt it lean towards him.

I turned to the bowls of salsa and chips as though seeking sanctuary from a church altar. The first bite reminded me with a jolt that even though I loved Rosita's food, her salsa wasn't my favorite as it was made thin and, to my tastes, exceedingly hot. And our tea wasn't even on the table yet. And today, I wasn't even going to love the food because I was going to have a hell of a hard time eating anything. I glanced around. Nobody here that knew me. The attorneys ate at Rosita's occasionally, but almost always on a Friday when they made it a tradition to eat what they termed "funky". And nobody from Scott's accounting firm ever came in here, which had figured highly in the choice of meeting spot.

"Safe?" he asked, amusement in his voice. "Nobody here to run tattling back to the fiancé?" I'd forgotten that he had a Floridian no-accent rather than a southern accent.

"So it appears," I said, leaning back. "Good drive up?"

"After I ran out of the rain. Wanta loosen up a little bit before you break?"

"I don't know if I can. And I don't even know what to say or talk about or—"

"Well, you've been just overflowing with questions in the emails lately."

The waitress deposited the plates with the usual warning they were hot, and I picked up my fork, promptly burning the hell out of my mouth on the first bite. To hell with this. Yes, I'd been overflowing with questions. Questions mostly unanswered.

"Yes, I have, haven't I, and you've studiously avoided answering most of them, too." I turned to face him, and asked the most pressing. "Why me?"

He laughed. "You truly don't know, do you?"

"Know what?"

"I thought you had to have at least have some glimmer of an idea as to what you are."

Well, that didn't sound good. Not at all. What the hell did he think I was? "And what do I think I am?"

"Ariel. Honey, you're a witch. One of the most powerful ones I've ever run across. And I figured nobody with that much power could possibly not know. At least a little bit. Guess I was wrong on that one."

Okay, I was in the Twilight Zone. "And you know this how?"

"Because I'm a warlock. War-N-Wit, remember? Inc."

"Inc. Of course." I sat and stared, not believing I was sitting here listening to this. "And you know I'm powerful because—"

"Because you're basically a telepath. You read people. And right now you're thinking that I'm a lunatic, but you just can't make yourself quite believe it. Right?"

"I don't read people, I—"

"The hell you don't. Those thumbnail sketches you do of people all the time? Way beyond descriptions of eye and hair color. You read their souls."

"And you're—you don't know what I'm thinking right now!"

"Yes, I do. You're broadcasting. Got to work on those shields, baby girl."

"Even if I'm broadcasting, you couldn't—"

"Yes, I can."

I stared. "Because you're a telepath, too?"

"Mostly. A few other abilities thrown in, but mostly that, yeah. Let me tell you something, any good profiler is basically a psychic. Any good law enforcement man is a profiler. And I've lost one guy in my entire career and he went to Mexico and died to get away from me. I called the attorney looking for him and told him to get an exhumation order and I'd bring in the coffin, I was so damn mad at ruining my record."

I was *not* still sitting here listening to this. Was I? Why the hell wasn't I already out the door and back in my car?

"It's not what you're thinking. Witchcraft is the old religion, the old truth, the truth that everybody used to know but has forgotten. It's the magic running underneath, through everything, through everyone, the good, the power, the music of the universe. And everybody has the capability if they want to reach for it. Witches and warlocks are those of us who, consciously or unconsciously, know how to tap into it. Remember telling me about being a really good cook when you don't even like cooking? What's cooking but the most essential form of making potions? Listening to nature and what it tells you to combine with what? When you actually reach for that power instead of just subconsciously using it—" He shrugged. "You have no idea what you'll be able to do."

I sat back, knowing that my eyes were wider than saucers.

"You have the most beautiful eyes," he said. "That blue rim around the dark green that runs into the brown around the pupil."

"I don't have a blue rim around my eyes," I protested, which was an absolute lie. I'd noticed it before, but it was so slight I'd thought I must be imagining it.

"Sure you do. Puts out a blue aura around you. You really should talk to your sister, you know."

"My sister? Antsypants?"

He laughed. "Yeah, Antsypants. Don't know if your parents had any power or knew they did, but they sure named the two of you perfectly. Ariel and Anastasia. Perfect names for a beautiful pair of witches. Antsypants knows a lot more than you do about what the two of you actually are, not nearly as closed to it. Why do you think she seems so—well, bright—and you seem so mysterious?"

"Nobody thinks I'm mysterious except you. The words usually used are boring and steady."

He shrugged. "Yeah, well, like I said. Most people don't have a clue what they're actually looking at. Knocked you out enough on that, I think. Want to move on to other unanswered questions?"

Please. Immediately. Anything else.

"Okay. Did you really remember me from the first time I talked to you? On Mark's case?"

"Absolutely. I recognized you as soon as you answered the phone."

"Recognized me?"

"Don't get ahead of yourself, baby girl."

"Okay. So—you pursued so relentlessly that day because you recognized me?"

"Uh-huh. You were back, you see. Well, not back, exactly, just found. I knew that if I was right, if you were really who I thought you were, you'd come back. And you did. Within a month."

"But then you vanished. For two and a half weeks."

"That was for you. I was sure, but I still didn't have a clue if you knew."

"You've already said I didn't have any idea I'm a witch, which I'm not—"

"Yes, you are, but that's not what I meant. I meant, I didn't know if you knew who I was. And I knew if you did, even if you didn't know you did, you'd contact me. Which you did."

I shook my head but it didn't clear a thing up. "I still don't know who you are!" I exclaimed. "You're—you're—talking like a crazy person and I'm sitting here listening, which I still don't believe—"

"You're listening because you know I'm right. So let's cut to the bare essentials. We've been here before, you and I, many times, we are one, Ariel, we are each other's eternal soul mates, each other's other half, and

I know it and you know it. And if nothing else, I intended to establish enough contact so I can find you easier next time. And if you refuse to believe it and believe in us and I have to wait till next time, then I will. But I will find you again. Because you can run but you can't hide. I just want as much of you as I can get this time so it won't take so long next time." He shrugged again. "Last time I didn't find you till we were both so much older it almost wasn't worth it. That one was a bitch. And I don't intend for it to happen again."

Chapter Nine

The world stood still, closed in, retreated, kaleidoscoped back out into swirls of scenes of places and times I'd never been, never seen. Hot, bright sun beat down on an arena covered in sand and blood, my heart ripping apart as I looked at the bodies lying so still amidst the roars of the approving, raucous crowd. I felt the biting cold, so cold it burned, coming from the snow stretching out across what I knew, knew with absolute certainty, to be the Russian steppes. I cringed from the visions of the shadowed chambers filled with monstrous man-made instruments of pain and the screams rolling out of them. I stood on the mountains in the mists and heard the faint echo of bagpipes. I saw blue water and shining white sand and smelled the salt air.

I swayed and felt the blood drain out of my face. He stretched his arm out and encircled me quickly, pulling me close. I didn't pull away.

"Oh, God! Too much too quick, huh? I'm sorry, I didn't think you'd go into total flashback."

I was beginning to get my bearings back a bit. "I'm fine. And it wasn't a flashback, it was—it was—it was a whole lot of whatever it was. Which was nothing. I'm crazy, you're crazy. This is a—shared delusion." I sat up straight. Time to put the conversation back on a normal frame of reference. "Are you through? I have a lot of shopping to do, are you coming or are you a typical man who doesn't like to shop?"

He raised his eyebrow. "I'm not a typical anything."

You're telling me. But for the rest of the afternoon, he was charmingly normal as he walked beside me in the mall, offering opinions when I asked, carrying bags without protest. I looked at Kay's Jewelers and remembered that I was almost past due to get my ring cleaned and setting checked. Scott was insistent about that as it kept the warranties in place. He'd be really hacked off it I let that warranty lapse.

"Do you mind if I pop in here a minute? You don't have to come."

"Need your ring cleaned and don't think it's tactful to wave your engagement ring in my face?"

I knew my eyes widened. He laughed.

"I'm not reading your mind, you looked at the store, you looked at your ring, you looked at me. Not very forthcoming with the big bucks, though, is he? Kay's?"

My ring was not, in fact, particularly large, but it was elegant. I didn't really like flashy and being a typist, actually didn't like large rings on my hands, and jewelry had never meant anything to me anyway except insofar as who had given it to me or who it had belonged to.

"I like it," I said.

"Honey, any man putting a ring on your finger ought to put one on big enough to blind folks passing your desk while you type. A stone from the Miami or Houston market. Special setting. One of a kind ring for a one of a kind witch. While you're giving your two week notice, that is."

"You have something against wives working?"

"'Course not. But you'll have a hell of a time commuting from Quitman. And besides, you'll be working with me. You're a natural, I'm thinking you might even be better than me at the prelims. Who do you think the 'Wit' is in War-N-Wit?"

"Suppose Wit never shows up?"

"Oh, but she's standing right beside me. I know you don't ever plan to see me again after today, but that ain't happenin'. Going to be fighting you hard on that one. But I won't be back up till you're ready, either.

That deer-caught-in-the headlights, waiting for me to pounce look is getting to me. Go get your ring cleaned. Ice cream cone when you finish, maybe?"

This was beyond disconcerting, this ability he had to know exactly what I was thinking. And the hell of it was, it could be explained either by his line of work, or by the fantasy that he was a telepathic warlock.

I opened my mouth, but nothing came out. "Vanilla," I finally said, conceding defeat.

"I knew that."

He didn't try to hug me or kiss me goodbye. He cheerfully deposited my bags in my truck and shut my car door. "Drive careful," he said. "And remember—"

"I can run but I can't hide," I finished. "Rain's moving back in, you drive careful too."

"Yes, ma'am."

I drove off, fully resolved not to ever, ever see the man again. Or talk to him. And because I was feeling considerably more like the cowardly lion than a powerful reincarnated witch, I'd email him that tomorrow. That resolve lasted for a whole twenty minutes before I picked up my cell phone.

"The weather report just said there's some really heavy rain moving up from I-75."

"Yeah, I got a radio too, baby girl."

"So be careful."

"I will," he assured me.

Chapter Ten

I wasn't such a fool I'd even thought I could fix supper for Scott after spending the afternoon with another man and I'd made it clear that I needed the evening alone to finish up Christmas details, wrappings, etc. I was not a happy camper when I heard the key in the door. I wasn't even ready to talk to Stacy after this afternoon, and I sure as hell didn't want to talk to Scott.

"Did I just walk into Santa's workshop?" he asked, glancing at the boxes and rolls of wrapping paper and sheets of tissue. When agitated, I habitually swirled like a tornado between multiple mindless tasks that required no concentration, and was wrapping presents and running back and forth to the kitchen where Christmas sugar cookies were baking.

"I told you I was going to be busy," I said. "Hand me that roll of tape over there, this one's out."

He complied. "Did you get a chance to get your ring checked while you were out? You really shouldn't let deadlines get so close, you know."

Considering my profession, that sent sparks of crimson rage flying out of my head. I felt them.

"Excuse me? I coordinate deadlines for three freakin' attorneys! Do you have any idea what that involves? And anyway, my ring costs 800 bucks. Or would have if it hadn't been on sale for 500, so it's not like we're talking about the Kohinoor diamond here, you shouldn't worry about details so much."

That hit a nerve. "You picked it out, you don't like big jewelry on your hands, remember? And you don't know what juggling numbers for a bunch of different companies means either, do you?"

"Or in other words, I'm just a secretary and you're a CPA?"

"Well, that's what we are, aren't we?" He frowned as he surveyed my mass of confused paper and boxes. "Did you maybe go over your budget a little bit here?"

"And is it any damn business of yours if I did?" I snapped.

"Honey, you don't stop to think of after effects sometimes, I'm just pointing out—"

"Don't. Point. Out."

His face registered the pained patience utilized in dealing with a toddler I absolutely detested. You want to pull out our college transcripts and compare 'em? Take a bet which one of us had the 2.1 average and which one had the 3.9. Which was only because I hated the PE courses, by the way. If you want an athlete, you got the wrong gal.

"You have been ill as a hornet's nest for the last month, you know that?"

Yeah, actually I did, but in fact Scott thought I was ill as a hornet's nest anytime I didn't immediately stop what I was doing and come running whenever he called my name. He had no idea how ill I actually was.

"You are under no obligation to stay and suffer the effects," I said, glaring over the box I was attacking. "I believe I told you I was going to be busy and needed an evening to—"

That was when it hit. The muscles in the back of my neck tightened into a vice grip, my arms went numb. I was dizzy to the point of ceasing to breathe, my heart pounding. I gasped and grabbed the back of my neck, panting. I'd hyperventilated a few times in the days AGR which had scared the living shit out of me as I'd thought I was having a heart attack in my twenties, and that's exactly what this felt like. As unsettled as I was, though, I didn't think I was anywhere near stressed enough to hyperventilate. And I didn't think my brain was the source of the echo ricocheting around my skull either. *Not now, damn it!!!!*

"Ariel? What the hell? You've been doing too much, you're white as a sheet—"

Good thing I was sitting down. Otherwise, I'd have certainly fallen. It was getting better, though the after effects were making my muscles feel like jelly. I had to get rid of Scott. As soon as possible. Time to play the delicate Southern flower.

"I'm sorry," I said, looking up with my best waif-like expression plastered on my face. "I ran around the mall all afternoon and started on all this as soon as I got home, and I just realized I haven't eaten and—"

"Good Lord! No wonder you're ill! Well, I tell you what, I'm going to heat some soup in the microwave for you and then you're going to turn that damn oven off and go to bed, how's that sound?"

Sounds like you're a controlling asshole. But whatever got him out of here the quickest.

"Sounds good," I affirmed, in a fever to whip out my cell phone and hit a certain number even as I derived a bit of satisfaction from the thought of Scott actually fixing something for me to eat for a change. And I was getting shaky, I hadn't eaten a lot at lunch and really hadn't stopped since I'd gotten home, because then I might have to think.

He was back in five minutes with a mug of tomato soup. I took it, wondering how in the hell he'd been engaged to me for six months and didn't know that though I loved tomatoes, I didn't like tomato soup and used it for cooking purposes only.

"The oven timer dinged while I was in there, I took those cookies out and turned it off."

"Great. Thanks. I'm fine now, you go on. I'm just goin' drink this and collapse."

"You're sure you're really all right? I mean, you're not sick or anything, are you?"

The expression on his face begged me to confirm I wasn't sick. And I knew I shouldn't take that personally; I'd never known a man who wouldn't rather do almost anything else other than take care of a sick wife or girlfriend. Well, except clean a toilet.

"No, I'm fine. Go on. I'll call you tomorrow."

"When you get up, remember to lock the deadbolt."

"I will."

The minute the door clicked I clunked the mug of soup down on the coffee table so hard it sloshed and pulled my cell out of my pocket.

"Hello, baby girl."

Well, at least he was alive. And he didn't sound shook up, but there was something different about his voice.

"What in the hell was that?" I demanded.

"What was what?"

"Don't get cute with me! Something just happened, I know it did, there was this—this blast—that hit me out of nowhere—"

"I'm fine. Real gully-washer coming down, wasn't paying enough attention. I hydroplaned a little, that's all. Got my attention, though."

"It got a hell of a lot more than your attention! The muscles in the back of your neck went rigid and you damn near hyperventilated, so don't tell me it was nothing!" I shouted furiously. "Not to mention that echo shouting 'Not now!'"

"I believe it was "Not now, damn it," he said calmly. "Made me mad as hell, I can't get killed now, of all times. I just found you."

"And why the hell weren't you paying attention if it's raining all that hard? And why the hell are you talking on the damn phone if it's raining that hard?!"

"Because you called me. And I was—well, really, I'm about wiped out, precious. Didn't tell you because I figured Miss Responsible would insist we reschedule today, but I was up most of last night running down a military man who thought he was immune because he was on base, like I don't have passes to all the military bases."

"You what? You trailed after me around a mall for four freakin' hours in Christmas crowds which exhausted me when you've been up for how many straight hours?!"

"For a hell of a long time now, but it took me a lifetime to find you and almost a month to get you to commit to a definite day and there was no way in hell you were getting out of it."

"You—you—man, you! You're a stupid asshole!"

"Hah! See? You do care. And you're coming along really fast, too, picking all that up. Don't worry, nothing's going to happen me. I'm a warlock guarded by an angel. Who's a witch."

I didn't say anything for a moment. "Asshole," I repeated. And hung up.

Chapter Eleven

I don't remember much of the next few days. I think I was in automated, self-defense shut down mode. Stacy didn't ask any questions and I knew she wouldn't until I indicated I was ready to talk. We were sisters. We knew each other inside and out, even with the five years age difference. I'd always taken it for granted all sisters did and for the first time, courtesy of Mr. Self-Proclaimed Warlock, I wondered if she and I might take the sisterhood thing to a level past that of other sisters.

But it wasn't fair to keep her in total suspense and I wasn't ready to explore any possibilities that we communicated on a deeper level than most sisters. So on our first break of the next morning post Chad Garrett a/k/a warlock, I merely volunteered the information that I was still monogamous. Her reply was succinct and to the point.

"Shit. Not for too much longer, I hope."

"I'm—processing some things," I said.

He pretty much left me alone to process on that Friday, last work day before Christmas on the following Monday, other than a few humorous emails. I sent a few humorous emails in return, but that was all, until I forwarded him my personal email address right before leaving. Saturday and Sunday passed in the blur of holiday visits and family and friend get-togethers that preceded Christmas Day itself.

And during the course of Saturday's pre-holiday revelry, I became aware that I was beginning to become aware of—what? I wasn't sure. A subliminal hum running through the air and under the ground? An increasingly bright luminescence that began to glow around everything and everyone I saw? Not exactly. Not yet. But it was—forming. Wasn't it?

I sent a text Saturday night, hoping that he was engaged in Christmas business rather than stake-out business, but there was no reply. I reminded myself again that he had family and friends and holiday events too, and Saturday became Sunday.

The subliminal hum seemed louder that day, the luminescence shone more brightly and nowhere did it shine more brightly than in my baby sister's face as she sat by our parents' fireplace on Christmas Eve during my family's traditional festivities. Unless she was looking at Scott, that is. How, I wondered, had I missed that? The intensity of her dislike for him. I sent another innocuous text that night, but again, there was no reply.

Monday, Christmas Day, I stared out the car window as it ate up the interstate miles on the way up to Scott's parents, that ever-present hum and luminescence still haunting me. About half-way there, the quality of sound and light changed. A giant POP sounded in my brain and all at once, I wasn't just hearing the subliminal hum or just seeing the underlying luminescence.

I was part of it and it was part of me and I knew, knew with absolute certainty that there was an underlying power, a grand magic and music of the universe. Everything and everyone was connected, intertwined. And in that connection was the ancient, universal truth, lost and twisted and forgotten through the ages. Before there had ever been a "Bless you, my child", there had been a "Blessed be." The religion of the old ones. And I knew why modern conventional religion had never been enough to fulfill me and bring me, for lack of a better description, inner peace though I had no doubt it did for others and though I'd always been more than slightly envious of those for whom it did. I was a witch. I was one of the ancients.

In the next breath I backslid. *Oh, my God! I was going to die and go to Hell!*

It only took a moment for the serenity to return. No, I wasn't. I wasn't abandoning anything, I was expanding it. God was the power and the music and the magic of the universe. I'd just found It. Or Him. Or Her. I was pretty sure the power was gender neutral. Life itself was magic. All you had to do was open your mind and let it find you.

I looked over at Scott. It was Christmas. I owed him a normal Christmas Day with his parents. In one sense, I hated this happening at Christmas, though it was undoubtedly the best Christmas present I'd ever had in my life. I didn't want to leave him a bad memory associated with the Christmas season, though I had no illusions that this was going to scar him for life. He wanted to marry me because I was suitable, sensible by his standards, at least most of the time anyway, and low maintenance. The world was full of suitable, sensible girls. I supposed from here on out, I wasn't going to be considered sensible by anybody's standards, other than the standards of a certain private investigator by the name of Chad Garrett. And Stacy.

I pulled out my phone and slid the keyboard free.

"Who you texting, honey?"

Why had I never noticed that he always wanted to know who I was calling, who I was texting, who I was emailing? And in that moment of oneness with the world, I knew it wasn't his fault and that it wasn't fair to expect him to be something he wasn't and never would be.

"A friend," I said and a text reading "Merry Christmas! Love u." went flying out over the cell towers of Georgia.

The response took all of two minutes. "Thank God! Merry Christmas to u baby girl...should I come? Love u more than u know."

I smiled. I'd known that 'Love u' was going to get his attention. "Not yet" I sent back. "Still processing... but soon."

I didn't bother to close the screen.

"Glory Hallelujah!"

I gave Scott his normal Christmas Day with his parents. It was easier than I'd thought it'd be; I seemed to have a new gentleness, a new understanding that didn't carry with it resentment of what people weren't, just acceptance of what they'd never be. And on the ride home, I gazed up out of the window and watched the stars dance in an intricate ballet of shimmering light against the black canopy. I'd never fully appreciated that dance before.

I didn't intend to return his ring that night but he forced the issue when it became apparent that he didn't intend to leave.

He stared at my outstretched hand extending it back to him.

"You're joking, right? Not funny, Ariel, not today."

"No joke. I'm sorry, but this just isn't going to work, Scott. And I wouldn't have done it today if it hadn't been obvious you didn't intend to go home."

"Just who doesn't it work for? Works for me."

"Not for me."

"And you don't care about anybody or anything but yourself, is that it?"

I closed my eyes. The question used by every individual I'd ever known my entire life any time responsible, intelligent, sensible, self-sacrificing Ariel didn't do exactly what was expected of her. But this time it wasn't going to work.

"Oh, I care," I said. "Just not enough."

Chapter Twelve

The next work morning I sent my sister our private signal of the need to visit the parking garage as early as it was reasonable to need a break. "Right now, right now?" went speeding through the BLAH email system. The level of urgency in any such request was indicated by the number of question marks and exclamation points that followed the last "right now". Sometimes, depending on the level of stress being experienced at the moment by one or the other of us, they stretched out for a whole line. This one indicated an ordinary break. I didn't want her to think I was having a panic attack.

"On my way," she responded, and I got up and headed for the parking garage.

She was already in the front seat and turned to face me as I got in.

"Ready to tell me about it?" she asked.

"I am, but not on a break. Whatcha' doin' tonight? How 'bout pizza? My place or yours?"

"Mine. Yours has Scott vibes. Homemade?"

"Joint sister homemade pizza."

"What're you going to do with Scott?"

I held out my left hand for inspection.

"Glory Hallelujah!" she almost shouted.

"Yeah, I got that reaction from somebody else recently, too."

"Wonder who? You're really going to make me wait till tonight?"

"For that? Oh, yeah. But I do want to ask you something now."

"Okay. What?"

"What if—" I hesitated.

"What if what?"

I took a deep breath. "What if I told you I'd recently discovered I might be a half-ass, half-practicing witch and that I've been one my whole life?"

"I'd tell you I believe you, of course. That's what sisters do."

"Yeah, but what if I told you I was deadly serious? Would you try to get me in the nearest psychiatric ward as soon as possible?"

She smiled. "No. I'd just tell you that I can talk to dead people and I don't even have to be related to them."

What was that he'd said? *You should talk to your sister*. And he'd known that from a picture.

"For—for real?" I asked.

"Yeah. You want to haul me off to the nearest psychiatric ward? Mom almost did."

"Mom what?"

"Oh, yeah. You don't remember? 'Course, you were fourteen and all intent on being a teenager and I was only nine and a pain in the ass. But you don't remember when she hauled me off to a child psychiatrist for six months?"

"Of course I do," I said slowly. "But that was because of school, because you were having problems fitting in with the other kids—" I broke off abruptly. Stacy had never had a problem fitting in anywhere in her life, that had been a lousy excuse.

Stacy laughed. "Yeah. She wishes. First she took me to one who told her it was a lot more common than most people thought, and then she took me to one who told her I was schizophrenic. So I smartened up and shut up and told everybody I was just making it up and they decided I just had the ordinary imaginary friends. And I never told anybody else. Anything."

I sat and stared at her, my heart breaking at the thought of a nine year old walking around with that.

And carrying it alone all this time. "And you never told me? You didn't think I'd believe you?"

She shrugged. "I told Mom, Ari. Who loudly proclaims to love us more than anybody else in the world ever will. As long as I'm normal. As long as you're normal. Don't tell me you don't know that and it's not one of the reasons you never opened up. You always knew that. I almost did tell you a few times, I've always wondered—did you see anything? But you don't, do you? You just—you just know things. Well, that's not right, either, it's not like you know what's going to happen or anything, not like a fortune teller. You know people. You know who and what they really are and sometimes you know what they're thinking. I think that depends on how hard they're thinking it and how much you like them."

"I've never told you I know what people are thinking sometimes."

"Oh, no, you've always been real careful about that. Without even knowing or meaning to, I think. You're real good at passing it off as ordinary observation and educated guess."

I sat in stunned silence and let it soak in. "And all these years we've never told each other?"

She smiled. "But we knew. We always knew. You know we did."

"Sister hug!" I proclaimed. We reached for each other over the console and squeezed each other breathless.

"So. What earth-shattering revelation by the name of bounty hunter Chad Garrett brought this on?"

"Am I broadcasting? What else do you do besides talk to dead people?"

"Is that what he calls it? Broadcasting?"

"Yeah."

"Well, yeah, you are, but you're the only live person I can read. Visitations and funerals are a bitch, though, I tell you what. And sometimes I know what's wrong with people. Like when Amy Buford was trying to get pregnant last year? And finally went to the doctor and she's a diabetic and that was the problem? Well, I didn't know what the problem was, but I knew there was something wrong with her. Back to Chad Garrett—"

"No," I said firmly and opening the car door. "Tonight. Still want your place? Scott's no longer a factor at mine."

"Yeah, but his vibes still are. That's gonna take a while to clear out. You need to burn some sage."

Chapter Thirteen

I told her all about it that night over the pizza recipe that we'd created when I was eighteen and she was thirteen, the one that had our friends who lived five miles away calling in on Sunday afternoons asking if we were making pizza.

"So, again I ask," I said, licking the remnants of pizza sauce off my fingers. "Do I need a psychiatrist?"

"I believe every word," she declared emphatically. "Every word. Why wouldn't I? So, now I ask—with all that, why am I sitting here eating pizza with you instead of him sitting here eating pizza with you? Not that I think the two of you would be sitting here eating pizza."

"Well, damn, get graphic, why don't you?" I laughed. "Because—I'm not ready. This is all so new, and so old at the same time, like when I hear—" I broke off. "Do you have any trace memories? Of ever being here before? Like *déjà vu* only not?"

"Such as?"

"Such as hearing a foreign language and feeling like you know it, you just can't remember it? I do that. With Italian and Russian. Russian, for God's sakes! Most people can't even pronounce a Russian name."

"Never noticed, but I'll definitely start paying attention. He could help, you know. Sounds like he's already come to terms with all this magical stuff that's so new-old to you."

"So have you. And I didn't even know it."

"Not like he has, apparently. It's always been almost completely unconscious for you and actually, mostly for me. For him, it sounds like it's really super conscious."

I shook my head. "No. I mean yes. I mean, I just need to sort it out on my own some more before I'm ready to see him again."

"Well, don't take too damn long. Wit. War—N are waitin' on you, you know."

* * *

Just because I wasn't ready to see the master warlock yet didn't mean I was out of contact with him. Through the next two weeks the emails and texts flew and we burned up the cell towers between Macon, Georgia and wherever the hell he was at the time which ranged from various back roads in the Alabama boondocks to Tallahassee to Savannah. And God knows where else. And minute by minute, day by day, and phone call by phone call, I felt myself draw closer and closer to the time we'd call each other home.

The end of the second week brought with it that announcement so dear to all working girls' hearts—we weren't going to make deadlines on a massively complicated, mind-boggling, drawers of filing cabinets full corporate litigation case unless we worked on Saturday and probably Sunday. "We" in this case included me, Mark McCray, the senior partner whose case it actually was, Jon Tennille, his secretary Amanda, one of the younger attorneys by the name of Nathan Armstrong, and the litigation paralegal Dana Marlow.

It didn't happen that often, not to me, anyway, though Dana and Amanda pulled Saturdays fairly frequently and I wasn't really upset about it. Actually, I took it as sort of a confirming sign that I wasn't ready to text the words, "Come now," down to Quitman, Georgia—or wherever the roving PI was located at the moment. I was disappointed about that, too, but I was in the process of coming to believe that nothing that ever happens is accidental, and that when the time came—and it was drawing ever closer—I would know.

It was about 12:15 that Saturday when I realized that I hadn't eaten anything that morning. I was bad about that and I was getting past peckish and was just about in danger of getting shaky. I wasn't the only hungry one, either. Nathan came down the hall and hollered into Mark's office.

"Hey! I'm goin' down to Frick & Fries, you wanna come?"

Frick & Fries was a Macon institution. It'd been in business since the 1920's on a diagonal stretch of Cotton Avenue and was always crowded. It was the spot where lawyers rubbed elbows at the counter with janitors. And it still looked exactly the same as when it had opened. The menu remained eternal. Fried chicken to make Colonel Sanders weep, hot dogs with a secret sauce kept in a vault, and hamburgers with meat patties that ran way past the margins of the buns. The fries we won't even go into. Frick & Fries knew the secrets of seasonings long before anybody thought to put anything other than salt on a fried potato.

I started salivating.

"Yeah, I'll go with you," Mark said, coming out of his office. "But let's bring it back. What about Jon?" He went down the hall past me. "Jon! Me and Nathan going to Fricks, you want anything?"

Jon Tennille walked down the hall towards them. "Oh, yeah. I'll take two hotdogs."

Okay, I was hungry. I was working on Saturday, a Saturday when I'd been seriously considering summoning my own personal warlock back to Macon. And at this exchange between the attorneys who apparently didn't even notice me sitting there, or Amanda down at her desk, or Dana over in her little cubbyhole, let alone consider us anything but an extension of our computers, or even stop to think that we might be hungry too, I was pissed.

I gave way to the only vent for such a high state of piss-off available to working girls. I mentally chewed their asses off. "I do not *believe* y'all are that freakin' rude and insensitive!" I shouted at them in my mind. "You've got three girls you've hauled down here on their Saturdays, and you don't even have the manners to ask them if they're hungry, let alone offer to buy their lunch?!?!"

That was when Jon Tennille did a sort of double-take. "Oh!" he said, something of a puzzled note in his voice. "Oh, guys, wait a minute! Amanda, you want something from Fricks? Ariel, what about you? And where's Dana?"

Holy hell! Like Steve Erkle from the old sit-com, I asked myself, "Did I do that?" And you know, I believed I had. I smiled sweetly. "Two slaw dogs, please. With fries."

When the food arrived via the attorney delivery boys—and wasn't that a novelty to savor—I decided to try one more push when they started parceling out orders at our desks.

"Be nice to eat at the break room table in a group," I projected out to Jon Tennille. "Hall's goin' to smell like chili dogs and fried chicken if we don't."

"No, wait, Mark, don't do that," said one of the most senior partners in the firm. "Take it to the break room. We'll all eat in there."

They headed down the hall. Dana came up beside me and leaned close. "You know," she whispered in my ear, "that's the first time in all the times I've been down here working on Saturday with any of 'em that they've ever bought my lunch." I smiled. Oh, yeah. I was coming right along. It was time.

Around 4:00, the discussion began as to whether to push on until later or to come in on Sunday. I'd never been hesitant to voice my opinion and I wasn't now.

"Mark, whatever it takes. Let's get through it tonight. I don't want to come in tomorrow. I have plans," I said.

"Well, it might be 6:00 or 7:00—"

"I don't care. I don't want to come in tomorrow."

"Okay."

I realized as I sat back down in my chair and inserted the earphones that I hadn't even said please. My hands were already curled over the keyboard when I glanced at my phone. Then I picked it up. *Late notice but can u come tomorrow? Figure the PI doesn't need my address.*

I got home at 8:00. I was exhausted, but I didn't have to go in tomorrow. Hadn't had a text back from Chad yet though, and pulled out my phone to double check just as it rang.

"Am I dreamin' or is that text to come for real?"

"It's for real. Sorry for the late notice, but something happened today. Chad, I think I did something." I explained my little lunchtime drama. "But it couldn't have been me, could it?"

"Oh, of course not," he guffawed. "Since your friend Dana told you they'd never bought anybody's lunch before when they were working Saturday, I'm sure it was nothing but total coincidence, them developing manners with you shouting at 'em like that."

"But—but is that bad? I mean, we're not supposed to do things to people, are we?" Oh, my. How far I'd come in the space of a few weeks, crediting myself with the actual power to do things to other people.

"Baby girl. We are never supposed to use any power for anything negative. That risks losing it. And you didn't need me to tell you that. You know that, the same way you know how to breathe, without even thinking about it. But I don't see as how making a group of lawyers sprout manners could ever be bad. So don't worry about it."

That's what I'd figured but I was still relieved. "So—can you come tomorrow? Did you already look up my address or do I need to give it to you?" I teased.

"Why don't you open your door?"

"No!" I said, clicking the phone shut, and racing to the front door. He was pocketing his phone just as I threw the door open. I grabbed his arm, pulled him in, wrapped my arms around his neck, and kissed him as though I were starving. Which I was.

He pulled me as tightly up against him with one arm as was humanly possible as he pulled the door to with his other.

"Glory Hallelujah!" he said.

Chapter Fourteen

I hadn't managed to turn the lights on when I got home before stopping to check my phone for a reply text, and the only light came from the small lamp I habitually left on that sat on the counter dividing the kitchen from the living space. It was perfect.

He felt so good, even through our clothes, but not as good as he'd feel without them. I slid my hands inside his shirt and from that point forward I have no memory of how any of our clothes divested themselves of our bodies, or how we actually made it through the bedroom door and found the bed. We found the memories, too.

Because one thing I knew with absolute certainty. This wasn't the first, or even the thousandth, time we'd made love. First times are awkward, no matter how hot for each other a new couple is. First times are self-conscious, full of hesitations—should I do this? Should I do that?

This was a melding, a merging, a becoming, a renewal. Of tongues, of hands, of bodies, and far beyond that, of souls. Mutual exploration of flesh that was already well-known, remembered pleasure points targeted, exploited, exploded, before moving on to the next one. He burned so cool, something I found I remembered, that coolness, so at odds with the heat most males threw off, that heat that had always made me feel as though I were being burned alive during intimacy, but not in any pleasurable way; rather, as though I were being consumed.

I didn't feel in the least consumed as his mouth and hands ran down my body, just complete. Of course.

Because my mouth and hands were running down his body with equal fervor. I exploded within seconds but not in any fashion I'd ever experienced before; rather than the sudden burst that dissolved quickly, an electrical current engaged and coursed throughout every nerve in my body, intensifying until I didn't know if it was pleasure or pain. I only knew I'd explode into fire if it didn't ease off.

"Stop," I begged, not sure if I wanted him to and not sure he'd even heard me. He had, though, and shifted on the bed, moving with a combined precision and tenderness that I'd never thought any flesh and blood man could possess, a rhythm I matched as though I'd known it forever, moving until we both melted like a candle whose light is temporarily extinguished by the wax turned liquid by its flame.

He lay against me, his mouth gently kissing my eyes, his fingers running slowly through my hair. I opened my eyes and smiled.

"No man outside the pages of a romance novel knows how to do things like that," I said.

He smiled back at me. "You taught me. Through many years."

Through the rest of the night we dozed, we roused, we merged again. During one sweet episode I felt something slide onto my finger, but I was way past the point of caring what or being capable of ascertaining such if I had cared and finally, before dawn broke fully through, we slept.

I woke with my head cradled on his shoulder, my arm thrown over his chest, and filtered light beams streaming in through the bedroom curtains. I stretched, lazy as any cat, and caught a glint of brilliant light. Coming from—my hand? Surely not. I stretched my hand out in front of me and shrieked.

"OH! MY! GOD!" I furiously punched his shoulder. "Chad! This—this—"

He stretched and yawned. "It's called an engagement ring, baby girl."

"Oh, hell no, it's not! This is—this would buy a freakin' car!"

I gazed in mingled horror and admiration at the marquis solitaire sparkling in its circlet of white gold, smaller diamonds running down the band on either side.

"No, it wouldn't."

"Yes! Yes, it would! Mostly anyway."

"I told you. Man puts a ring on your finger, it needs to be big enough to blind folks while you type. While you give your two-weeks' notice. Stones are from the Miami market. One of a kind ring for a one-of-a-kind witch. You don't like it?"

"I'm too scared of it to know if I like it! This is— what if a stone comes loose? The solitaire gets chipped? It gets lost for heaven's sake?"

"It's called insurance, darlin'. Just enjoy it. And, uh, small request, please? Don't take it off without warning me?"

"I can't wear a ring like this all the time! It has to come off when I'm cleaning, or—or—making biscuits! My God, what that would do to it!"

"Which is why the wedding band is plain, so it doesn't have to come off. But until it goes on, just warn me if you're taking this off, okay?"

"Because?"

"I'd feel it," he said simply. "And you'd scare me."

"You wouldn't—" I broke off, remembering the night of his hydroplane incident when my own neck muscles had knotted into ropes and I'd almost hyperventilated. "Okay. But if you feel it go off and you're out of calling or texting range, just know it's going right back on as soon as I finish doing whatever it is I don't want to do with it on."

"Deal."

I looked up and ran my fingers through his hair. "You're more silver than you were at Christmas."

"Bother you?"

"Nothing about you bothers me. And damn, I never thought I'd say that when we were sitting in Rosita's and you announced you were a warlock. And we were long-lost lovers But you really are goin' to be completely silver at a very young age."

"Yeah, I've used a lot of power since—when did this start? Let's see. October 5, I think."

I laughed in delight. "You remember the exact date? First time you talked to me?"

"Hell, yeah."

"And using power—that—oh shit! I'm starting to use power! Aren't I?"

"Hell, yeah."

"So am I going to start going silver?! I mean, it looks great on guys, but on me—"

He laughed. "Damn. You looked at yourself lately?"

"Sure. Every time I brush my hair."

"And you haven't noticed anything?"

"Like what?"

"Damn. Goin' to make me get up," he threw back the covers. "Oh, well, we won't be gone long enough for it to get cold."

"What are you—" He took my hand and pulled us over to my dresser, putting me in front of him.

"Look."

"Look at—oh. Oh." I breathed, staring at my eyes. The blue rim, which had heretofore been only a tiny rim, visible only to me, or so I'd thought, until he'd made it clear it was noticeable to him, was at least a sixteenth of an inch wide, edging out towards an eighth.

"Welcome, precious. To the world of magic."

Chapter Fifteen

He tried to cajole me into taking the day off Monday, but I knew I had too much going on at the office. I kissed him good-by and watched him drive off. First order of business when I entered the office would be the infamous two-week notice. According to the chain of command, that should first be given to the Office Manager, but I'd never paid much attention to the chain of command even in my most conservative days and anything about me remotely resembling conservative had irretrievably waved bye-bye.

The first order of business actually turned out to be surviving the ecstatic hugs of my sister, waiting for me by her car, and her oohs and aahs over the Marquis solitaire that still scared the living shit out of me.

"I told you to come over yesterday afternoon," I scolded. "It would have been fine, he wants to meet you as much as you want to meet him."

"Yeah, well, not y'all's first weekend, three would have still been a crowd."

We parted at the lobby and went down our separate halls, my hand self-consciously turned inward. I couldn't shake the feeling there was a glaring headlight announcing my imminent arrival, but nobody noticed.

First stop was Anderson's office.

"Well, is that you?" came the usual jovial greeting. "I had the greatest weekend, we ate at the Oyster Bar and walked on the beach, and it's just fun to have fun! A little work, a little play, not that I could do this without you here keeping the office—"

"Sure you could, Anderson. You will. I quit."

Dead silence.

"You what?"

"I quit. Two weeks' notice. You're the first to know, couldn't not tell you first, could I?"

"You're going to another firm?"

"No. I'm getting married. And changing careers, too."

"You and Scott got back together? But what's that got to do with your quitting? You weren't going to quit—"

"Am now. Too long a commute, sorry. And I would have gotten back together with Scott when hell froze over, no, he's out of the equation."

"But—but—you only broke up with him two weeks ago! You can't go and marry somebody you just met, Ariel, be sensible!"

"Now Anderson. What's that you're always saying? 'It's so much fun to have fun!' Along with, 'life's too short not to enjoy it', as I recall. Anyway, I didn't just meet him, met him last October."

He was beginning to get his bearings, and his gaze sharpened.

"Too long a commute? From where?"

"Quitman. Remember your PI who located and corralled your witness in something under three hours?"

"You're joking."

"Nope."

"You don't know a thing about him! PIs are shady characters, always out at all hours, no steady income, good one week and bad the next—"

He broke off as I held my hand out.

"His business stays pretty good. That happens a lot when you're the best there is at what you do, don't you think? Now, don't worry about a thing, all the cases are in good shape and I'll be sure nothing's hanging when I leave. Everything's going to be fine, Anderson."

I walked out of his office and over to Ash's to repeat my performance and by the time I left his and headed to Mark's, I knew damn well the tsunami was all over the office and I wouldn't need to make any further explanations. Corrections, yes, there'd be plenty of room for them by the time the storytelling was done, were I inclined to offer any corrections, but actually, I didn't really care what anybody thought about any of it. I hadn't known there was that kind of freedom in the world. Or that it felt so good. I looked down at the sparkling diamond. "Love you!" I whispered, and rubbed a finger lightly over its surface. A warm glow settled in my stomach and moved a tad lower. And the diamond winked at me. I swear.

* * *

By ten o'clock I was automatically throwing my hand out from the keyboard for ease of viewing as the girls approached my desk. Even some of the attorneys cast surreptitious glances. Of course, they tried to maintain a neutral expression but a few of 'em just couldn't pull it off. It'd be a cold day in hell when some of those guys parted with sufficient funds to put a ring like mine on their wives' hands and an even colder day when the thought of doing so occurred to them in the first place. Professional men tend to be tightwads, a tidbit of knowledge I'd picked up over the years of association with lawyers and, through Scott, with accountants.

It wasn't a cold day from my perspective, though. I'd talked to Chad a couple of times, he was back in his office and setting up his agenda of new locates, services, general investigation for the next few days. And the warm glow that had started in my stomach and moved a tad lower kept moving lower still and it wasn't just warm anymore. It was the full-blown heat and full sensation of lazy, sensual love-making.

I picked up my phone and pulled up text mode.
Quit it!
Response was immediate.
U quit it u started it!

73

Did not! I texted furiously.

Did too quit rubbing damn diamond or polishing or whatever the hell ur doing.

I looked down at my finger and the diamond winked back again. Oh, hell. I was. I was rubbing the surface of the stone every time it was inspected, polishing off any possible imaginary smudge.

I sighed. It was going to be a long day. *Sorry.*

Im not but u play u pay.

You're telling me, I thought, and concentrated on my organizational lists for each of my lawyers so as to leave them in tip-top shape. Doing so involved frequent ups and downs as I grabbed files to check on their pleadings indexes and general location.

An incoming email from Stacy called out, *Right now right now?!?!??!?!?!* Okay, it was really time for her stress-relief break. And none too soon for me, either, though from the number of ?! in the string, little sister was having a typical Cal Spencer morning. He was detailing a case to death but he wasn't spinning completely out of control. Had that been the case, the string of ?! in the signal would have stretched for the rest of the line.

Right now right now, I sent back, and grabbed my phone and coffee cup. I beat her to the garage and took the opportunity to check in with my personal private investigator.

"You are driving me insane!" I hissed.

"Well, right back atcha', baby girl," he advised. "And could you stop pin-balling around the office like a steel ball in a pin-ball machine? You're making me tired!"

"Good! Then maybe you'll be too tired to—to—whatever the hell it is you're doing that's making me feel like we're still in bed!"

"I'm not doing anything on purpose, I can't freakin' help it! You're driving me just as crazy as I'm drivin' you, trust me! You sure you got to give two whole weeks?"

"Of course I do! You don't just walk off a job and leave folks hangin'! Besides, you never know when you'll need a good reference!"

"You're about to become an apprentice PI, you won't ever be in a law office again!"

"Yeah, well, promises, promises. You never know, and besides, the firm's a good contact, and we still haven't talked about what we're doing about my apartment—"

"Oh, to hell with your apartment! Just break the damn lease, I don't care about losing the freakin' deposit!"

The opening of the door signaled my sister's arrival, and her first words indicated that she was following the conversation very nicely.

"I'll take your apartment, Ari, don't be silly. I don't have a lease, I'm month to month."

"See?" The voice over the phone evidenced a keen sense of hearing.

"Really? You don't like my apartment!"

"I didn't like your apartment because of the Scott vibes. I'll have it fumigated and then I'll clean with lemon Lysol and burn a lot of sage."

"Anastasia Anson!" I exclaimed over the laughter in my ear. "That is just mean!"

"Oh, God, I love that girl already! Let me talk to her!"

"This three-way conversation is getting complicated," I observed to the car roof and hit speaker.

"Hey, Magic Man!" I grinned. Leave it to Stacy. Magic Man was perfect.

"Hey, Antsypants! Can you possibly keep your sister on track and make sure she doesn't find any more things to worry over? Because two weeks is killin' me as it is, don't need any delays."

"I can try, but she's a worry-wart. You know that."

"Yeah, just like I know you're not. Are you?"

"Nope. And neither are you."

I looked at Stacy's face and listened to Chad's voice coming from the phone and I could feel them reading each other. I wondered again how in the hell I'd lived this long not hearing, not seeing, the magic that was everywhere for anyone who wanted it.

"No. But she has to authenticate everything, you know that. She has trouble just accepting things the way you and I can, she's got to analyze everything first. It's the writer in her."

"Yeah, I know. Gotta love her."

"Don't we though? You do have just as much power as she does. Different, but just as strong. I wondered about that."

"Not nearly as much as you do, though."

"Yes, you do. Both of you."

"As much as we'll ever have?"

"Not even close."

Stacy laughed and handed the phone back.

"So, Magic Man. What's on your schedule?"

"I'm going through Macon tomorrow. Need to check on a drug runner I been after for a while, pops in and out of Cobb County a lot. Not gonna find him this time, though. Damn bounty hunters and deputies been beating the bushes, got him spooked. He's not staying anywhere for long. That's how it works though, they muddy the waters all up and then call me. I'm for the impossible."

"Damn bounty hunters? Like you're not one?"

"Among other things. But what I am that the amateurs aren't is smart."

"And so modest, too. Not to mention psychic," I pointed out.

"That too, of course," he conceded. "So, early lunch while I'm going through? And late supper coming back? Don't know how late."

I laughed. An opportunity to show him some local color. "Frick & Fries," I said. "Call me when you're getting off the interstate and I'll meet you over there.

And then you can come back to the office—oh. You probably don't have time."

"Not this time, baby girl. I'd love to but I need to get on up there."

"That's okay. And then just come home. I'll have supper waiting, doesn't matter how late."

"Don't want but one thing."

"Well, that can be the main course. Actual food can come between that and dessert."

"Oh. My. God. I love you."

"I love you. Later."

"Later."

I hung up, realizing I'd had a conversation that could be rightly classed as "intimate" right in front of my little sister. She burst into laughter at my expression.

"I'm all grown up now," she advised. "Even had sex myself a time or two. Did Scott already get all of his things out of your apartment?"

"Oh, hell yeah. And the few things he left I collected and personally delivered to his office. Why?"

"'Cause I would pay money for him to show up while Chad's there. Especially if he had an extra key made he didn't give back to you."

My first reaction was sheer horror. My second was a mental picture of that face-off should such ever come to pass. And I had to admit it. I'd pay money to see that myself.

"Antsypants, that is so far beyond just mean I wonder sometimes if you've crossed over to the dark side."

"Be funny, though. Admit it."

"Hysterical."

Chapter Sixteen

Around 4:00 o'clock it occurred to me that I hadn't told my parents that my wedding was still on. Sort of. I mean, the only changes were the groom. And the venue. And the size. And the time. All positive changes, at least in my mind, especially the groom. I'd never wanted a big wedding but between my mother and Scott's mother, things had rapidly escalated out of my control. The whole damn thing, while still nothing on the scale of what most people considered a "big" wedding, was much bigger and much more formal than I'd ever wanted. The only up-side to the whole thing was that with the actual projected ceremony still four months into the future at the time the whole possibility became dust in the wind, the invitations hadn't been ordered, let alone sent, and no deposits for anything had been made.

Nothing was getting out of my control this time. When I thought about it though, all I really knew was we were getting married in two weeks' time because neither one of could stand it for any longer than that. And that was absolutely all I cared about. A courthouse wedding worked for me. I hadn't even asked Chad about his family and any preferences he had. Well, I could ask him tomorrow night when he came back through from Cobb County. Of course, we'd be otherwise occupied but sometime during the night—because I knew full well he wasn't leaving till the next morning—we'd have a chance to talk about it. Maybe. No, definitely. I'd definitely take a few minutes to discuss it. If I even remembered it, of course. But I'd better remember it. I had to be able to tell my mother something.

And on that thought, my cell phone signaled a call from, of all people, my mother, who didn't even give me time to say hello.

"What on Earth do you think you're doing?!?"

"Excuse me?" I ran for Anderson's office and closed the door. This was obviously not going to be a discussion for the hall.

"You! What are you doing?!? I ran into your boss in the grocery store! And of course he assumed I knew all about it, I'm your mother, which you have obviously forgotten! And you're actually planning to marry some stranger you just met and you haven't even told your family!?"

Shit. Anderson shopped in Kroger—the same one my mother used, of course—on his way home frequently, he enjoyed food. He was prone to sudden cravings and always satisfied his cravings as soon as possible.

"Stacy knows all about it," I defended myself.

"Oh, how nice to know how far Dad and I rank on your list of people who might be interested! You absolutely cannot go off half-cocked and get married! When is this supposed to happen, because I insist you have a long engagement! And if you don't come to your senses, then we have to have time to plan—"

Oh, hell no, not going there, no way! And besides, if there was one thing Chad Garrett, and therefore myself, as the one who reaped the benefits wasn't, it was half-cocked, though I figured I might not ought to share that.

"Mom, that's enough! I'm grown up now, remember?"

"So I thought but obviously—"

"Mom, you have absolutely no control over what I do."

"Excuse me? What did you just say to me?"

"I'm sorry you heard it in the grocery store, I didn't intend for that to happen. But I met him three months ago and—"

"When you were still engaged to Scott?"

"Don't go there either, Mom. I was never in love with Scott, I never even loved him. Hell, I never even liked him! Now I'm in love. Capital L, Capital O, Capital V, Capital E. His name's Chad Garrett. I'm getting married. In two weeks. No fancy wedding. End of discussion."

"But—"

"End of discussion. And you don't have to worry about any plans because—" I broke off as an idea flew into my brain from out of the blue. "Because we're getting married in Vegas."

It was the first time in my life I'd ever seen—well, heard—my mother completely speechless.

The office phone rang as soon I hung up. Anderson.

"Ariel, I think I may have—"

"Don't worry about it, Anderson. It was my fault. I should have remembered just how small a town this really is in some ways and I just didn't."

"So is your mother okay?"

"No. But she will be."

And this time when I hung up, I hit Magic Man's speed dial. Which was two and would have been one had that not been pre-programmed as voice mail.

"Did you have any plans as to exactly where we're going to get married?"

"Funny you should ask. It's going to take me a few days to confirm this, especially since I'm going to Cobb County tomorrow, but I got a parole skip I'm getting surer and surer is in Vegas. If it turns out she is—"

"She?"

"Crime's gender neutral, you know. So I was thinking, by Thursday I ought to be able to fly out and collect her. And that—"

"And that Vegas would be an absolutely perfect place for a telepathic witch and warlock to get married."

"You don't like it?"

"I just told my mother I was getting married in Vegas. It just flew into my head."

"But is Miss Definition of Conscientiousness going to take Thursday and Friday off in the midst of her two week notice?"

"Oh, yeah. What are they going to do, fire me? Is Mr. Definition of Impatience—"

"Hey, that's not fair. I waited my whole life for you. And then another two months for you to agree to meet me. Though not particularly patiently, you got me there."

"Okay. Is Mr. Definition of Semi-Patience going to be willing for me to finish up here when we get back?"

"I'll work off my laptop and phone and anything I can't handle from that, I'll run back and forth to do. Already decided that anyway, this is killing me."

"Well, that oughta get the Scott vibes out of the place for Stacy."

Okay. That was handled. Anything else I hadn't thought of that I should think of? I groaned. Of course there was. Anderson ran into my mother in the damn grocery store. Half of professional Macon was in and out of Frick's all the time. Including Scott.

I told myself to toughen up. There were worse things than talking to Scott. Being burned at the stake, for example. Or hung. Or tortured. Which I probably had been at some time in the past. Christ, I didn't even remember his phone number, I'd just punched in his speed dial, now several weeks deleted. Which had been eight, incidentally, Stacy being two, Mom being three, Dad being four, Anderson being five, Ash being six, and Mark being seven. It hadn't even occurred to me to reassign the numbers to make Scott top dog. No help for it; I'd have to look up the office number and call him there.

"And may I tell him who's calling?" asked the switchboard operator. I detested that and no receptionist at any Macon law firm would ever ask it. One of the judges, now retired, used to blast the ears off any lawyer whose office asked him that should he happen to call, his theory being that it didn't matter two hoots in hell who was calling, which it certainly shouldn't.

For the first time in my life, I answered that question exactly the way I wanted to.

"No, you may not. If he's not in, I'll take his voice mail, please."

Dead silence. Then Scott's voice.

"Scott, I felt I should let you know before you heard it through the grapevine. I'm—"

"Engaged. And sporting a diamond big enough to choke a horse."

"I'm sorry the grapevine moved faster than I did."

"So it's true."

"Yes. On both counts actually."

Short, ugly laugh. "You actually pulled that 'money doesn't matter to me' line off real good, Ariel. Never knew you were such a good actress."

"I'm not. And money doesn't matter to me. Nor the size of a diamond. He picked it, I didn't."

"Are you kidding? You deserve the Oscar. How many months were you cheating on me?"

Okay, he was entitled to be hurt. And pissed. And I knew he'd never really known the first thing about me. But he wasn't entitled to be vicious. What surprised me, however, was the realization that I'd always known he could be; that in fact, the viciousness lurked only slightly underneath the pleasant, dull surface.

"I never cheated on you. I handed you back your ring the same day I realized for sure I wasn't going to marry you."

"Was that the same day you realized you were going to marry him?"

"Yes, it was."

"Before or after you saw the damn ring?"

"I'm not talking to you anymore, Scott. I never meant to hurt you. And I called because I didn't want to blindside you if you saw me—or us—around town before I had a chance to tell you. I don't have any control over what you think of me or what you think I did to you. That's your baggage, not mine. But I'll tell you this and whether you admit it's true or not, you know deep down it is. We really, truly, don't even like each other. We both just figured it was time to get married. And things would have been very bad, probably very quickly."

I hung up before the waves of black rolled out over me from the receiver of the phone, more shaken than I cared to admit. He'd have slapped the shit out of me if he'd been in front of me. And it wouldn't have taken two weeks of marriage for him to have slapped the shit out of me over something.

God, Stacy! I thought. *You did everything to make me see that but come right out and say it. And you'd have said it, first and last, before I actually married him, wouldn't you, even knowing I wouldn't have believed you!*

I wasn't surprised at the response that resounded in my brain.

Damn straight! That's what sisters do!

Chapter Seventeen

He called to alert me to his imminent arrival at about 11:15.

"Too early for you?"

"No, I'm starvin'. Didn't eat breakfast 'cause I knew you'd be here around now. Too early for you?"

"Hell, no. Been up and on the computer since 5:00."

He was telling me? I knew exactly when he'd woken up and I knew exactly the state he'd woken up in, a state that seemed to be a condition precedent to waking up for all males past puberty.

"Good. Take the Second Street exit and—"

"Baby girl, it's called a GPS. Is Stacy coming, I hope? Not still trying to give us privacy in the middle of a lunch crowd in the local diner hangout, is she?"

I laughed. "No, she's coming. We'll go ahead and start walking over. Parking might be tight, that's our building garage on the corner of Second and Cherry. You could whip into the second floor if you need to. Love you."

"Oddly enough, I have very little trouble finding parking spaces. Usually. Love you."

I looked up as I shut my phone to see Anderson looking at me thoughtfully over my desktop credenza.

"I never heard you say that to Scott, I don't think."

"Doubt I ever did."

I collected my sister and we went out the back door of the building to cut through the alley over to the little diagonal formed by Cotton Avenue cutting into Cherry Street.

"Note to self," observed Stacy. "It's a little less crowded in here at 11:30 than at 12:00 but not enough to shout about."

"Hey! Booth in back being vacated! Go grab, I'll go ahead and order."

Stacy and I liked the slaw dogs, I'd get Chad a chili dog and a slaw dog and fries for everybody, of course—that was when somebody behind me grabbed my left hand and pulled it up and back. Not just somebody. Scott. Of course.

"Well, well, for once the scuttlebutt didn't exaggerate."

"Hello to you too, Scott."

He didn't release my hand and pulled back harder, ostensibly to convey to anybody paying attention that he was getting a better view. In actuality, he was squeezing hard enough to hurt.

"Oh, yeah, that'd be enough to make anybody trade cars. Or men."

"You don't want to do that, Scott," Stacy said from behind.

"Ah, the cheerleader cheering from the back," Scott said. "And why don't I want to do that?"

I caught the vibration in the air and glanced back over my shoulder at the door just as Chad walked through it, just as Stacy said, "I mean, you really don't want to do that."

Chad moved so fast I didn't actually see the progression from door to counter and then his hand was squeezing Scott's wrist.

"You should learn to listen to the ladies, Scott. You really don't want to do that."

He'd caught a few pressure points, obviously. Scott's hand spasmed as he dropped mine. I turned and caught the glare in his eyes as he looked at me, which didn't sustain itself but a second as it moved to Chad. He turned and walked out the door.

"Well," said Stacy, as she moved to put her arm around my waist. "That was some lunch time drama. You sure know how to make an entrance, Magic Man."

"Natural talent," he said modestly, and hugged us both simultaneously. "You okay, baby girl?"

"Tip-top," I affirmed, and turned back to the counter to collect our tray. Actually, I was more shaken than I wanted to let on, but not because of Scott. Because I had more than a sneaking suspicion that if Scott hadn't let go, Chad wouldn't have just kicked some ass. He might have deleted some ass. Further, it was a bit unsettling to realize that my only concern with that was that it would have been way too inconvenient to start out married life with such a legal tangle over our heads, which was a glimpse into a part of my personality I hadn't known was there. I supposed it would be a handy trait to carry into my new profession.

We settled in the booth I'd sent Stacy to stake out and I distributed the food. Chad picked up my hand, sporting red splotches from Scott's grip.

"What a charmer," he observed. "That hasn't happened before, I'm assuming?"

"No," I confirmed. "Though I'm pretty sure it would have started happening if we'd actually gotten married. If Mark hadn't needed a complaint served down in Tifton. Don't know how I missed it. Stacy didn't. Thought you couldn't read anybody but me, Antsypants, how'd you know if I didn't?"

"I don't read anybody but you. I mean, not really read 'em, not the way you and Chad read people. I read you. You knew, you just kept pushing it out."

I shuddered mildly. "Don't remind me."

"So, Vegas wedding?" Stacy asked. "You two owe me. I was on the phone with Mom for two hours last night. You've completely ruined my wedding, whenever that happens, 'cause she'll stake it out like a gold mine."

"Sorry, honey. Guess you'll just have to run away to Vegas too." My bounce-back abilities were improving.

Last month, I wouldn't have let anyone see it but a scene like the one with Scott would have had me in internal shakes for the rest of the day if not longer. Now, I was attacking my slaw dog with gusto.

"Lots of options in Vegas. Just because it's Vegas doesn't mean you can't have a pretty wedding. Got any ideas?"

"Well," I said, glancing over slyly for the reaction. "I searched around some last night. And the Excalibur offers medieval weddings where you can rent your costumes, and the guys' stuff has all sorts of outfits, from King Arthur to knights in armor—" I broke off as Chad choked on some of Frick & Fries famous flaky ice. "I'm joking!" I laughed while pounding his back. "What really grabbed me was this really neat package for a Gothic wedding where the couples can be anything from vampires to werewolves to—"

"Witches and warlocks!" Stacy chimed in in delight. "Now that's just about perfect!"

Chad choked harder.

"All right, all right!" I sighed in defeat. "Since it's Vegas of course you can be Elvis! Why didn't you just say so in the first place?"

"Yeah, that'd work!" Stacy, reading me as perfectly as always, played it to the hilt. "But first we have to make sure we get some of that Grecian formula, turn the silver back to dark, Elvis can't be silver!"

Chad took a deep breath. "I don't know why it never occurred to me the two of you together would be deadly and dangerous. You're—joking? Really?"

"And here I thought that'd be right up your alley. Yes, I'm joking. Feel better? I really had you going there?"

"Well, I didn't think you were totally serious, but there's always that margin of error. I was thinking more in lines of booking the Venetian for a couple of days and just something simple and pretty at the —"

"White Wedding Chapel?"

"Yeah. You too?"

"Oh, yeah. I'm not quite unconventional enough to marry King Arthur. Or Elvis. Though he could walk me down the aisle."

"Baby girl."

"Okay, okay. I don't know anything about Vegas hotels, though."

"The Venetian's good."

"Okay, you know more about it than I do, obviously. But I thought this was a working trip?"

"Now a double job for the same amount of trouble. Prostitution charge. Turns out her pimp skipped too. And that they hooked up in Vegas. Won't take long, pimps and their girls don't tend to be all that bright. And do tend to be pretty predictable. Thought we'd have a few days to ourselves and I can grab the skips on the way back. Which is another ulterior motive, I don't transport female skips without a female operative."

"Wise move," I affirmed. "Legally speaking."

"Knew you'd approve. And I don't particularly want another female operative."

"Another wise move. I sure as hell don't want you operating with another female."

"Which would have been completely business, and you know it. And if we do run a day or two over—"

I shrugged. "What are they goin' to do? Fire me?"

We walked back to his SUV and as he hugged me goodbye he whispered in my ear. "I'm not that stupid, honey. I'd never delete anybody's ass in front of witnesses."

"Good to know," I said. "You sure the skips on the way back aren't a problem?"

"Piece of wedding cake," he said.

Chapter Eighteen

He was there by eleven that night and only went back to Quitman Wednesday morning to pack and coordinate. He actually beat me home that day, and my end-of-the day tension flew out the car window as soon as I saw the silver Equinox in the extra space in front of my unit. I hadn't been looking forward to the evening alone, even though he was with me all the time now, just as I was with him, even when we weren't together. I'd gotten used to the ever-present presence. Now I reached down on purpose to rub the big central stone of the ring periodically. It intensified the presence. How the world can change in the space of five days, this interweaving that was so complete I couldn't actually remember why I'd fought so hard for so long, pushing it away while pulling it closer.

Thursday morning we headed to Hartsfield International Airport, one of the busiest in the world even before the new security measures of the post 9-11 world. I don't know why it hadn't occurred to me sooner, but it didn't trigger until we were actually on the road that Chad would sure as hell be taking firepower.

"What are you doing about your gun?" I asked. "We're not going to get arrested, are we? Or detained?"

"Baby girl."

"Give me a break, I'm new to the world of bounty hunters and PIs and law enforcement."

"Don't worry, I could actually carry it on the plane, but it'd be a lot of trouble, checking in with all the right people, bigger pain in the ass than it's worth. It's in the baggage."

"You can do that?"

"Anybody with a license to carry concealed can do that. You just have to tell 'em and show 'em your license. And if a terrorist tries to hi-jack us, I'll just sic' you on 'em."

"Excuse me?"

"Your mental push thing that got you girls lunch last Saturday, remember? I'm thinking one of your latents might be a tad bit of mind control."

"Get serious."

"I am serious, you've got a lot more—"

He broke off as his phone rang. "Damn, these people never give up." His thumb hit the steering wheel control to accept the call. "War-N-Wit, Inc. Chad Garrett." He listened a minute or two and frowned. "Look, I already told you. I'm not the man for this job. I look for live bodies. Usually pretty bad ones. I've got a full plate for the next several weeks and I wouldn't be able to put any time in this." He frowned again. "Yes, you can check back. But the answer will still be the same. War-N-Wit, Inc. deals with the living. The modern American justice system. So I don't want to give you any ideas that my answer will change in the next few weeks. Have a good day."

His thumb hit the hang-up button and he glanced over at me. I raised my eyebrows, saying nothing, in the universal female sign language that needed no telepathic ability to translate.

He sighed. "Okay, here's the thing. There's magic in the universe. And there are those of us who understand it, at least a little, and to a certain extent, more than most people, anyway, we can use it. And there are those who don't understand a damn thing but pretend they understand everything. And try to use it. Pretenders. And they're who give magic and witchcraft a bad name. Because those of us with real power, we don't talk about it to anybody but others we know to have power."

"You announced within five minutes of meeting me that you were a warlock and I was a witch and we were reincarnated lovers, an eternal couple."

He laughed. "That's because you're a witch and I'm a warlock and we're reincarnated, eternal lovers. And I knew it. And I knew you knew it way down deep and I didn't think anything less would bring it to the surface. But believe me, I don't tell anybody anything personal unless I'm damn sure who I'm talking to. None of us do. You didn't even talk about it with your sister. For years."

"So, that call?" Time to get to the point here.

He sighed and glanced over before changing lanes. "There's a group called Resurrection. Membership is contingent upon being reincarnated. Status is contingent on how many times."

"Say what?"

"To be a member you have to be reincarnated. And how high up you go in the membership depends on how many times you claim you've been reincarnated. The more times, the higher the status."

I sat and digested this. "You mean—like being a Daughter of the American Revolution or something? You have to show your bloodline? Only in this case, your past lives?"

"Exactly."

"But—but—how in the hell would you prove—"

"Exactly. You wouldn't. You couldn't. I mean, my trace memories are stronger than most. But that's because of you. I remember you, not a particular past life. And I don't have any idea how many times, except I know for sure it's been a least a few for the connection to be this strong. Probably more than a few. And I'm sure it goes back a very long way. One of the strongest trace memories I have is Rome, and don't you dare laugh. Another really strong trace is something about Russia. And one from the tropics somewhere, the Caribbean maybe or Mexico or South America."

His words sent a chill down my spine. I flashed back to our first meeting at Rosita's, the sudden kaleidoscope of rushing scenes, the heat and sand and blood of a Roman arena, the bone-chilling, mind-numbing cold of the Russian steppes, shining white sand and the smell of salt air. I shook my head to clear it as he continued.

"But I'm not about to get up and claim I was Caesar or Alexander the Great or King Arthur, or one of the Borgia popes, for God's sake!"

"And these people do?"

"Oh, my God! You have no idea! And worse, they've got my name! How the hell they think anybody's gonna investigate any past life?"

"I guess they figure a reincarnated warlock ought to be pretty good at it?"

"Yeah, and just how in the hell would they know I'm a reincarnated warlock? If in fact they do or think they do. That's the part that bothers me, this is my professional life, completely aside from what I believe personally. I don't need a reputation as a crackpot, I'm damn good at what I do and I've worked hard as hell at it. Nobody else's business if a psychic twinge now and then's been a really big help. And I sure don't have the words 'reincarnated warlock' listed in my resume, believe me!"

"No, you certainly don't. Background listed includes Fort Lauderdale PD and Florida Bureau of Investigation but no Warlock University or Reincarnation College."

"You looked?"

"First serious flirtation day. Absolutely."

We were beginning to run into the first streams of Atlanta traffic and the subject of Resurrection fell by the wayside in negotiating lanes and airport traffic and security checks, which went a lot smoother than I'd thought they would. Which called forth a question.

I leaned close and raised up on my toes to target his ear. "Do you by any chance have any of that mind control push thing you were talking about?" I whispered.

"Not a speck. And no, even if I did, I wouldn't have tried to use it on you, for two reasons. One, it's not love if one party's in control of the other and two, you're way too powerful, there's no way any mental push from anybody else'd have any effect on you other than to piss you off. Okay?"

"Okay."

And things stayed okay right up until we landed at McCarran in Las Vegas and Chad began glancing around, obviously looking for someone.

"What?" I asked.

"Not what. Who. Oh! Good, right on time." He moved forward, heading to one of the biggest, roughest, toughest-looking bikers I had ever seen. "Spike! Thanks, man, I really appreciate this." He handed over our luggage tickets. What? I was entrusting my underwear to a six foot six gorilla in a black leather jacket and black chaps? "Baby girl, this is my buddy Spike. Spike, this is my lady, Ariel."

I held out my hand cautiously. "Nice to meet you, Spike."

He lifted my hand in a courtly gesture and kissed it. "*Enchanté*, mademoiselle," he proclaimed, in a voice as smooth and soft as melted butter.

For real? I looked over at Chad. "Can it, Spike. She's taken. And she's about to be a madam, not a mademoiselle, though I suppose that's the wrong thing to say in Vegas."

Spike laughed. "Better get that license quick, man, she'll get snapped up. Your ride's right out front, buddy. I'll check in with you later. Your bags'll be waiting for you at the Venetian."

Spike headed to the baggage pick-up area and we headed to the front of the terminal.

"Who on earth and how did you meet him?"

"Long story. Impressive, huh?"

"Scary, huh? Until he talks. My God, that voice!"

"He's a doctor."

"You're kidding, right? Not a gynecologist I hope, not with those hands." I shuddered mildly. "And he doesn't scare his patients to death?"

"Pediatrician. Kids love him. And he cleans up pretty good, doesn't usually look that rough. And where—oh! That's my man, he brought me his Roadster!"

Chad stopped in front of a massive black motorcycle, two helmets strapped to the back. I froze.

"You're kidding, right?" I felt the blood draining out of my face.

"This is a Harley-Davidson Road King, show some respect."

"And we're riding it?"

It began to filter through to Chad that I wasn't thrilled at the prospect. I was petrified. One of Scott's few unexpected ventures away from the conventional involved motorcycles, though nothing this big. He'd started out with one of the smaller Hondas, a Shadow something or other, I think, which he'd retained when he bought the next-size up Shadow something. And he'd been determined that I was going to learn how to ride the smaller one, notwithstanding the fact I had absolutely no desire to do so.

"Oh, com'on, honey! You already drive a stick-shift so the gears shouldn't give you any trouble, there's nothing to it! If I'd known you were going to be stubborn about it, I'd have traded it in and gotten some benefit from it instead of wasting the money. I just thought it'd be a fun thing for us to do together, don't want it to sit and go to waste."

And of course, as I always did, I'd given in. Because it was much easier to give in to Scott than to listen to him when you didn't, which of course was the magic secret of how he usually got his own way. Everybody gave in to him just to shut him up because he never shut up for anything less. I had one lesson on the thing. One. Because while cruising up and down the country road curves of the outermost Macon subdivisions, I practiced the oft-repeated instruction that you didn't turn the wheel, you leaned into the curve. I leaned the whole time it flew off the road, depositing me squarely into a ditch on top of a concrete pipe covered with blackberry thorns, the damn cycle on top of me, still running, while gas leaked out of the tank and sent clouds of vapor into the air. I'd been certain the whole thing was going to explode into flames all around me in the three or four minutes it had taken Scott to realize I wasn't behind him and come back to check. He said it was three or four. I didn't know. It felt like an eternity. To his credit, even he shut up about me becoming a lady biker after that.

I looked at the Harley and back at Chad.

"Oh, shit," he said. "I'm sorry, it didn't occur to me you were scared of motorcycles. I'll see if I can catch Spike, and if I can't, we'll go rent a car, no big."

"I didn't know you rode motorcycles," I said.

"I don't have to, not with you."

"But you really like 'em, don't you? I mean, this is some serious bike, isn't it?"

"Oh, yeah."

"Like a real biker's bike?"

"Oh, yeah."

"Like a Bikers' Week in Daytona bike?"

"Bikers' Week is great, but not one of the things I can't live without. You're the only thing in that category. Well, along with air and water and food, I guess."

I laughed and moved to the back of the Harley, unsnapping the bungie cord holding the helmet.

"And it would never upset you if all I want to do is ride with you and I never, ever, want to learn to ride one alone?"

"Nothing you want to do will ever upset me as long as it's with me. I think we've both had enough of doing things alone."

"Then let's go!" I said, fastening the helmet strap under my chin.

"You sure?"

"I'm sure."

"Then here, you'll need this, too." He unlocked the back compartment and pulled out leather jackets. Black, of course. We climbed on and maneuvered out of the parking lot. We hit the open road and he opened the Harley up. I wasn't fool enough to think he was letting it do anything near its top speed, and not fool enough to think he wouldn't be close to top speed if I wasn't on it, but it was fast enough. And it was wonderful. I laughed into the wind and tightened my arms around his waist, and that felt wonderful, too. And the last vestiges of the old Ariel blew away in the wind.

Chapter Nineteen

We blew by the "Welcome to Las Vegas" sign and into Las Vegas proper. At the first light, I leaned forward and shouted in his ear. "Let's go ahead and get the marriage license first thing."

"Right now?" he shouted back.

"Right now," I affirmed. "Marriage License Bureau's on Clark Street. You know Vegas?"

"Pretty good, yeah, but why right now?"

"Don't know. Just do it."

He shrugged and started off when the light changed, weaving through traffic towards the requested destination. Gotta love Vegas. The Marriage License Bureau stayed open 8:00 a.m. to midnight, seven days a week, and all you needed was $60.00 cash and a valid ID. Gotta love the internet too.

Our mission accomplished with the speed of an assembly line, we walked back out with the license tucked safely in my jean pocket. I couldn't pin why I'd become intent on the immediate acquisition of that license but one thing I'd become increasingly convinced of over the last few weeks. When an inner voice started talking, I'd best start listening.

"Shit!" Chad exclaimed suddenly.

"What?"

"My skip. Right there. On the corner. Getting into the car with—double shit! My other skip!"

"Well, what are we waiting for?" I ran towards the Harley and grabbed for the helmet.

"I didn't want to do this now! I didn't want to do this first!" Chad grabbed for his helmet.

"Stop complaining and follow that car!" I'd always wanted to say that but never thought I'd have the actual opportunity.

"I can track 'em later and—"

"Later you might not find 'em! There they are, now go!"

"This isn't going at all the way I planned." He revved the motor and took off.

I noted the car—an older model Camry, rather the worse for wear, black with the fading color spots that older black cars not taken care of properly seemed to acquire. Plate number UL something—ULV! I got the last letter as it rounded a corner, and leaned forward to concentrate as we followed. ULV0609.

The car took what appeared to be a loop or a bypass and got onto something called the Las Vegas Expressway. They were leaving Vegas. Chad shouted back at me.

"Next real town's Indian Springs!"

I pounded his back. "Pull over!" Time for a conference and we couldn't shout loud enough and long enough to have it on the Harley. He complied and ran onto the shoulder, slightly above what I hoped was the last exit that turned back into Vegas but not far enough behind us that the Harley wouldn't be able to backtrack without getting us killed. Maybe there were advantages to bikes I'd never fully appreciated. He didn't turn the engine off, though, and combined with the road noise and the passing cars, we were still shouting.

"Are there many places on this highway they can turn off?"

"Not a lot they'd want to. Like I said, next real town's Indian Springs, which is logical for a hooker and a pimp."

"Why?"

"Military town."

"Can the Harley catch 'em if we take a short side trip and come back?"

"Side trip where?"

"White Wedding Chapel. Then we'll hop right back on the expressway—"

His eyes widened. "Oh, hell no! No way. We're booked for tomorrow morning, the actual White Wedding Chapel, and you are going to have a normal, pretty wedding! If we don't get 'em this afternoon, the hell with it, we'll go back out Saturday and—"

"We might lose them!"

"So we'll lose them! So what?"

"So you've lost one man in your whole career and he went to Mexico and died to get away from you, remember? You are not losing these skips!"

"The Chapel's probably booked!"

"They have four Chapels, plus an option that's never booked!"

"What?"

"The Tunnel of Love Drive-Thru. Not much point in a drive-thru if you have to book it, now is it?"

I'd never thought to see Chad Garrett shocked at anything, but he was shocked close to speechless. But only close.

"You're shittin' me, right?"

"No, I'm not! I knew there was a reason to go ahead and get the license! Now we're wasting time, get off at the next exit and we'll get this done and get back on the road after them! I made sure I got the license number, too. "

"The rings are in the bags. At the Venetian! With our clothes!"

"The guy doesn't always have to have a ring at the wedding, I'll give you a private ceremony later! Just use my engagement ring! And what's better than leather jackets and motorcycles for Vegas anyway? Now get this thing on the road and freakin' move it, will you?!"

He stared at me a few seconds. "This is not going at all the way I planned," he said for the second time, placing his feet back on the cycle and revving the motor.

We backtracked to the exit and wove our way over to Las Vegas Boulevard which turned out to be only about 10 minutes away from the Las Vegas Expressway. Now I ask you, what better sign that this was meant to be could a witch and warlock want?

We entered the white columned drive, covered by its deep blue canopy adorned with celestial cherubs playing harps and lettering overhead proclaiming "I can't live without you." Not one other wedding was in process and I took that as another sign. We rolled up to the window.

"I do not believe you're making me do this!"

"You don't want to marry me?"

"Don't even go there, you know what I mean!"

"Welcome to the Tunnel of Love at the Little White Wedding Chapel!" sounded over the speaker. "License, please?"

I pulled it out of my pocket.

"Will you be requiring witnesses?"

"Yes," I said firmly.

"And as you're by yourselves, a commemorative photo –"

"Yes, please, and can you mail it?" I gave my address. I wasn't going to be there much longer but Stacy was moving in so no problem.

"And do you have your own vows—"

"Standard and can you do the express version? We're kind of in a hurry here."

I pulled my phone surreptitiously out of my other jeans pocket and hit the camera button on the side. Chad's expressions through this exchange were priceless and I intended to get at least a few of them.

The window's voice changed to one of alarm and a head emerged through the glass.

"You're not in labor and on the way to the hospital, are you?"

"On a motorcycle? Of course not!" Okay, that expression I had to have. I raised my arm and snapped a quick one of my almost husband.

"We've seen stranger things, honey, trust me! Okay, let's do this—"

I pulled the diamond off and thrust it into Chad's hand so he'd be ready at the appropriate point, snapping another expression of his horror when the transfer was safely completed.

"...and by the power vested in me by the State of Nevada, I now pronounce you husband and wife! Okay, you can kiss the bride."

"Not for long you can't!" I modified, giving him a quick peck. "Okay, where's your guy, camera, action, let's go!"

The cameraman rushed out for our commemorative photo.

"You got the address, right? Thanks! It was a great wedding!" I punched Chad's back. "What are you waiting for? Let's go!"

This time it was almost a moan. "This isn't going at all the way I planned."

We roared away from the Tunnel of Love Drive-Thru and headed back to the Las Vegas Expressway.

I kept my eyes in motion once we passed the last Vegas exit, trying to keep a view of both sides of the road to see if anything might have occasioned them pulling off. Chad had to look ahead anyway, he was driving. About fifteen miles out of Vegas, there was a ramshackle motel over on the right, set back a little from the highway. And was that?—I couldn't tell, it was too far back, but too similar to take a chance that it wasn't. I punched his back again and pointed over to the right. We'd passed the exit, but there was that great thing about bikes again, much more maneuverable than cars.

We pulled into the parking lot and Eureka! Yes, ULV0609.

"That's it," I said, pulling off my helmet and swinging my leg over to dismount. "I love the 69 for the hooker and the pimp, sort of personalized, don't you think?"

"Baby girl, that's more than likely a stolen car, ULV is the personalized plate for University of Nevada at Las Vegas. That plus the car plus the 69 just screams that some college kid's going to walk out of his dorm and yell." Chad kicked the kickstand out and got off,

"So we're doing some 69'er a good turn, too. Go register."

"Excuse me?"

"Go. Register. We just got married, remember?"

In fact, the speed of the cycle, the vibrations of the big motor, the miles pressed against Chad's back like a second skin—well, okay. You figure it out. I was hotter'n a pepper sprout.

"Here?"

"Don't you think they'll stay put an hour or two? And you also have to figure out some way to get 'em back to Vegas, don't you?"

"This is a flop-house, Ariel, have you lost your mind?"

"So I figured. It's Nevada, prostitution's legal, isn't it?"

"Only in licensed brothels—which I promise you this is not—and under strict regulation and regular medical screenings—which I promise you ain't happened for the girls who work this crib! You're crazier than a loon if you think I'm going to touch you—"

I moved close, threw my arms around his neck, and delivered a kiss that threatened his tonsils.

I pulled back. "I have never in my life," I whispered, "done anything wild, anything crazy, anything spontaneous. Until you. You reap what you sow, Magic Man. Give me this wild, crazy moment as the first wild, crazy moment of the rest of our lives."

He stared down at me, his mouth trying desperately not to turn up into a grin I might take as encouragement.

"This is not going at all the way I planned." He turned and walked toward what passed for the flophouse office.

Chapter Twenty

"You're crazy, you know," he said, as he came out and headed down to Unit 6.

"Totally bonkers," I confirmed as I followed. "You bring out the best in me. You're not carrying me over the threshold?"

"I'll save that for home, if you don't mind." He inserted the key—no modern update such as a pass card here—and turned the lock. It squeaked. "Home in Quitman. Holy. Shit."

The door opened on a room probably originally beige but now aged to just plain dirty. It was carpeted with thin, industrial grade indoor-outdoor carpet, worn thin and stained from untold pairs of shoes. Double beds sported mismatched spreads, one in an orange and brown wave pattern, the other a red and yellow floral pattern. Both screamed "Dollar Tree". I was pretty sure the brown plaid curtains had been in place since their original debut into the room, long before the Dollar Tree spreads took up residency. Two mismatched, scarred occasional tables topped with mismatched lamps wearing ragged shades and a few cheap western prints scattered on the walls completed the décor.

Chad stood frozen in his tracks. I stepped on in and grabbed his hand to pull him inside.

"Okay, lock it," I ordered.

He tried to comply but the actual lock on the doorknob didn't cooperate. There was, however, a chain latch. He put it in place and tried to actually lock the real lock again. It still didn't work. He pulled on the door and it swung open in the confines of the chain latch probably an inch and a half.

"Okay, that's it!" he exclaimed, taking the chain off and attempting a hasty retreat.

"Oh, hell no!" I stopped his hand and pulled the mismatched table closest to the door flush up against it so at least there'd be some noise should any inquiring soul open the door. "This is the greatest adventure I've ever had in my life! It's a good girl's dream fantasy! A chance to be a hooker in a cheap motel! You're telling me any normal, hot-blooded man hasn't fantasized about hookers in cheap motels? Give me a break! I don't think so! Now you sit down over there and wait for me!" I specified the bed on the far side of the room, so that at least it wouldn't be in full view of the inch and a half immediate view afforded by the chain latch. When he made no move forward, I pushed him toward the target area. He shook his head and pulled back the Dollar Store spread to inspect the sheets. They looked clean and smelled of detergent and fabric softener.

"See?" I said triumphantly. "Not so bad. Now wait for me!"

I crossed over to the bathroom door and went into the bare-essentials bathroom. I didn't bother to inspect the shower stall—there was no tub—but the toilet and sink and tile actually appeared spotless and of course, being tile and porcelain, would have been much easier to keep clean than the cloth and fabric of the main room. And the towels were clean, too. I started stripping and laying my clothes over the towel racks.

"What the hell are you doing?"

"Necessary prep work," I called back, sitting down on the toilet. I took off my high-heeled black boots and removed my jeans and panties, pulled back on my boots, threw my previously discarded black long-sleeved blouse over my shoulders, and walked out of the bathroom towards him, working the blouse in an impromptu strip tease. His eyes widened.

"Told you, darlin', it's fantasy time. You telling me men don't fantasize about naked women in high-heeled boots walking towards 'em?"

"*Merrrrcccccyyyy,*" he ground out, Roy Orbison style.

"Not in this lifetime," I said, landing on top of him. "Not from this witch."

And I didn't give any. If that was a problem for him, he didn't complain much, except when I tried to turn and flip underneath him.

"Hell, no, your skin's not touching these sheets any more than I can help!" he growled. I laughed.

"Paranoid much?"

"Protective," he clarified, devising a few ways to get me in position to accomplish his purposes—without touching the sheets any more than he could help—with astounding creativeness.

"What about your skin?"

"Lots tougher than yours, honey, I'll risk it. And bathe in surgical soap when we get back to the hotel. The real one."

Lack of available positioning curtailed the length of my hooker fantasy somewhat. I'd have liked for it to have continued a bit longer, but then we did have two skips to get back to Vegas. And then to Georgia. I finally conceded and granted a small amount of mercy,

"What possessed you with the boots?" he asked, watching me walk towards the bathroom to retrieve the rest of my clothes.

"Are you kiddin'? Like I'm walking barefoot on that floor! So—how we gonna do this? Take the car and leave the bike?"

"I leave that bike, I'm a dead man and you're a widow. Spike'll kill me."

"So I drive the car back?"

"When hell freezes over. You're a fledging bounty hunter! We'll leave the damn car here, let the local guys come get it. Besides, all my gear's in the bags. At the Venetian. Don't have a gun on me, not that these guy's gonna need one, but I don't even have a pair of handcuffs. I'm calling Spike."

"What's he gonna do, go back to the Venetian and ask to look in our luggage? And I'm sure he'll love getting hauled into a bust, local pediatrician brings in pimp and hooker!"

"Actually," Chad grinned as he stood in the door of the bathroom zooming down his phone's contact list as I put myself back together. "Actually, he's got his own. And he'll love this. Be just like ole' times."

"He was a bounty hunter?"

Chad shrugged. "One of the things we have in common. Gotta eat while you're in med school."

Well, he knew his bounty hunter pediatrician, all right. As the phone was on speaker, it didn't take much to figure out Spike thought the request was the best thing since white bread.

"Oh, man! For real?! Where exactly are you?"

"Bout fifteen miles up the Vegas Expressway headed to Indian Springs. Name of the place is—oh, hell, baby girl, what is the name of this place?"

"Look at the damn sign! Aren't you out front?"

"Not exactly."

"Then where the hell are you?"

"Don't ask. Ariel—"

I slipped the chain lock and looked out.

"Western Courtyard," I supplied.

"Could be a lot worse," Spike commented.

"Could be a lot better."

"You got 'em corralled yet?"

"Nope. Sort of thought handcuffs would be good first. Seein' as how my wife's in the mix and all."

"Your wife? Not till tomorrow, remember, I picked which tux I'm wearing and everything. My white one."

"Yeah, well, put it back in the closet. And don't ask."

"If you say so. Fifteen, twenty minutes, tops."

Chapter Twenty-One

"Twenty-two minutes," Chad proclaimed as Spike opened the door of his shiny black Beemer, "but who's counting? You losing your edge, bro?"

"Don't take as many chances with a Beemer as you do with a rusted-out Chevy."

Chad shook his head sadly. "The things money does. Makes slaves of us all, steals spontaneity, curbs that wild, free spirit...."

"Oh, bite me," Spike said mildly, opening the trunk and pulling out two sets of handcuffs. He handed them to Chad and then pulled out two wicked looking guns. I took a wild guess they were Glocks. Then they passed off to each other so that each was armed with one pair of handcuffs and one gun.

Chad raised an eyebrow. "You ready?"

"Let's do this thing," Spike confirmed.

"Baby girl, you stay over there," Chad pointed to the far side of the Beemer. "You got it?"

"Some partnership," I said.

"Your time'll come. Just not this time. You got it?"

"I got it." I did, of course. I wasn't stupid.

The assumed stolen, spotty black Camry was parked in front of Unit 4 and there wasn't exactly a dearth of parking spaces, so logically our skips were in Unit 4, right? So why the heck was Chad walking down to Unit 9? I almost called out but caught myself. This was Magic Man, and if he was going to Unit 9, he must know what he was doing.

Just when they approached the door, it flew open.

"He's crazy!" the bond-jumping ho shouted, running straight for the pediatrician moonlighting bounty hunter. And based on size, if I was running to strangers for protection, he'd be my first choice, too.

"I'll kill you, you cunt!" The bond-skipping pimp, wild-eyed, shirt flapping open over a wife-beater T that had waved bye-bye to white some time ago, came charging out the door. He was brandishing a hunting knife that looked as though it'd be at home in the hands of Jim Bowie. "Think I wouldn't notice you snortin' my stash?"

Apparently, he noticed Chad and Spike for the first time.

"What you starin' at, ya assholes? Stare at me, will ya? I'll give you something to stare at!" And he charged at Chad, knife straight out in his right hand.

Chad pivoted and swung his left leg up and wide, a sideways kick, aiming for the hand brandishing the knife. I'd seen the move on the TV and movie screen of course, and it always worked. It simply disarmed the assailant with the least amount of physical harm to said assailant.

I was proud of Chad's quick-thinking and restraint. Sure, he could have just shot him, but do you have any idea of the legal problems we'd have to get through, even for a justified shooting? In a split-second, that feeling changed to pain. And oh, shit, did it hurt!

Guess what? That move doesn't always work the same way it does on TV and in the movies. If the angle's wrong, guess where the knife goes? Three guesses and the first two don't count.

Chad's face went white. He brought the leg doing the kicking down at an unnatural angle, standing on the side of his left foot, rather than the ball of it. Didn't slow his speed down any, though. His arm reached out and grabbed the offending wrist that was no longer wielding the knife, seeing as how it was now protruding straight through his foot, twisting said wrist up and back as he slapped a handcuff on it.

"Fucker!" screamed the pimp. "That hurts!"

"Good! Keep screamin' and I'll break it for you! Son-of-a-bitch!!" exclaimed my new husband, as his foot turned downward and the knife made a bit of contact with the ground. Didn't seem to bother Chad that much, other than the involuntary 'son-of-a-bitch!' but my stomach cramped and fell out of my body.

Spike, during this rousing melee, had already cuffed the ho's hands behind her back, despite her outraged screams.

"You asshole! You 'sposed to be protecting women come runnin' atcha gots a knife-holdin' maniac coming after 'em! And you cuffin' me?! For real?!?!"

"Oh, yeah, sweetheart, for really real!" Spike confirmed, moving her—okay, maybe not so gently—towards the Beemer. He opened the back door and shoved her inside.

"Ariel! Can you—"

"Yeah, I got it," I confirmed, moving to the other side of the Beemer, on guard against any door flying open and any ho hauling ass out of it.

No longer encumbered by the ho, Spike sprinted over to Chad and the pimp and finished the handcuff job. He'd just about gotten back to the Beemer when the back door flew open and the ho flew out. I've never been athletic, don't get the wrong idea. But my husband had a knife in his foot, which I just incidentally felt as though it were sticking in my own, and this was my wedding day, for God's sake! My wedding night!

"Oh, hell no!" I shouted, and took a flying leap straight at her, my arms around her middle. I lay there holding on through the shouts and flailing arms until Spike scooped her off me.

"Some damn," he said mildly, putting her back in the backseat. Both his hands finally being free, he pulled his keys out of his pocket and clicked the locks. He held his hand out for me, and I pulled myself up, limping as I headed towards Chad.

"Oh, shit, that flying tackle mess up an ankle or a leg, hon?" Spike asked as he followed.

"No, that's fine."

"Then what—oh, shit! You're not, are you?"

"Am I what?"

"Never mind. Of course you are." We'd reached Chad by that time, and with me on one side and Spike on the other, hobbled him over to the car.

"Okay." Chad was pale, but obviously in full control. "So, here's the deal. You take the bike back, I'll glare at 'em over the front seat and dare 'em to move and Ariel can drive the Beemer—"

"Sorry, son, that won't work," Spike interrupted. "We'll have to leave the bike. I'll call in, get a patrol car to come out and grab it, got a few favors I can call in. One of the guys'll ride it back."

"No point in all that, easier just to—"

"Magic Man," said Spike. I started. You mean that wasn't just mine and Stacy's nickname for him? "You taken a good look at your wife yet?"

"What—" Chad turned to me, his hand reaching out to turn my chin towards him. I could feel the beads of sweat running along my hairline, and knew they had nothing to do with heat. I couldn't see my reflection but I was sure I was paler than he was. I knew my eyes were wide as saucers. "Shit!!"

"Oh, yeah," said Spike mildly. "You are in so much trouble now, Magic Man. You got two fronts to guard. 'Cause what happens to you—she feels. Be nice if you could shield a little there, I'd hate for her to pass out before I get your ass to the ER."

"No ER. You still got your own ER, know you do. How else would you still have favors to call in?"

"First things first. Get in the damn car, I'm calling ahead to have a welcoming committee out front at the LEC. And then I'll take a look in the private ER. No promises, though. Depends on where that knife is exactly, whether we stay there or head to the Medical Center. You're in my territory now, son."

We all piled in the car. I was feeling a little better. Chad must be—what had Spike called it? Shielding.

We were pulling away from the Western Courtyard when I heard the low whisper under his breath.

"This did not go at all the way I planned."

Chapter Twenty-Two

Spike was in process on Chad's foot in the private ER when I started at the sound. Chad's cell phone. Ringing in his jacket pocket from the chair across the room. A ringtone I'd never heard before.

"Shit! Get that, baby girl!"

"Man, I am stitching a foot here! To hell with the damn phone!"

"I need that call!"

I scrambled for the phone while Spike threw up his hands and stopped work momentarily.

"Far be it from me to interfere with a man and his informant!"

Informant? I raised my brow and frowned as I handed Chad his phone. Of course it was. Why else a special ringtone?

"Whatcha' got for me?" Short, sharp, to the point. "No. Keep an eye out the next day or two. Pay attention to any pattern, any movement. I'll be there soon as I can. You give this to anybody else, I'll—"

A loud squawk of protest came sounded from the earpiece.

"Good. Long as you remember that."

Chad clicked the phone shut and looked at me. "Baby girl—"

"We're doing Vegas some other time, right?"

"I'm sorry but—"

"But that call was from somebody who shall be nameless but whose function is spelled i-n-f-o-r-m-a-n-t. Who just told you where somebody was you been looking for. For a while. And you trust his information because you own his ass. How'm I doin' so far?"

"Pretty damn good, I'd say," said Spike. "All right if I continue this repair job while you two fight?"

"We're not going to fight," I said. "It's our job. We're going to go get him. Whoever it is."

"No, we are not. You're a fledgling bounty hunter. In training. You can go on the preliminary run to verify. You are not going in for the take-down."

"We'll see about that," I declared.

Spike started whistling the tune to "Hot Time in the Old Town Tonight".

* * *

We sat in the silver Equinox, shrouded in night shadows, across the street from the dilapidated house in the decrepit neighborhood of one of the worst sections of Marietta, watching for movement.

"At least it was convenient," I said.

"Convenient?"

"Close to the airport. Picking up the car and all. At least it was handy."

"True."

"How long you been after this dude?"

"Zander Stevens. Not your average bad-ass. Lots more going on with him than drug-dealing, that's just what he got caught at. Been after him a long time. Other folks been after him a lot longer than I have, spooked him and he went to ground. Nothing worse than a bad bounty hunter. Once you get the scent, you got to run 'em till you get 'em. You let up, they get away, takes 'em awhile to get comfortable, start moving enough for you to find the trail again. Figured he'd come back here eventually. Seems to be his abode of choice. Comfort zone or something. Why I had some eyes looking in the neighborhood."

I stared at the house. Something in the air. The whole neighborhood screamed despair, poverty, hopelessness. But there was something else, too. Something I couldn't peg. But it wasn't coming from the neighborhood as a whole. No, it was specific. Located squarely in that house.

And it wasn't just me, I thought. Chad felt it, too. I could feel him feeling it, just as I knew he could feel me.

"Baby girl."

"What, Magic Man?"

"Whatcha' think?"

"Don't know. There's something different about that house. I know there is, but I don't know what. Can't read it. Can you?"

"Nope. Always known it was there, felt it when I first started tracking him. But I think I know what we need to translate it."

"Yeah? What?"

"A ghost whisperer. We know any good ones?"

I laughed softly. "Well, now that you mention it, I might just be able to hook us up with one."

Chad hit the ignition switch and the Equinox hummed softly into life. He pulled away from the curb, just another shadow amidst other shadows.

"We're going back to civilization, get us a hotel room, get some rest." He grinned. "Among other activities. And we'll call Stacy early in the morning and ask her to drive up here and translate for us."

Chapter Twenty-Three

I called Stacy from the warm comfort of Chad's arms in an Alpharetta Best Western king size bed at 7:00 a.m. the next morning.

"Hey, Antsypants! You got any plans this weekend?"

"Whassss—what time isss it? Jezzzzzzzzz, Ari, it's 7:00 o'clock! In the mornin'! And it's Saturday!!!!!"

I grinned at the progression of degree of wakefulness in her voice.

"Yeah, well, just be glad I didn't call you last night. At 2:00 a.m."

"Where the hell are y'all?"

"Alpharetta."

"Nevada's got an Alpharetta?"

"Alpharetta, Georgia."

"What are you doing back already?"

"Long story. We were kinda hoping you'd drive up."

"Because?"

"Because we need a ghost whisperer."

* * *

The house looked worse this time than it had in the wee hours of the night before. Rain'll do that. It sat in darkness, and that something that neither Chad nor I could peg was even more palpable tonight. I turned in my seat to keep a constant view of my little sister's face as she sat in the back. I'd never seen her while she was in the grip of her own special power and I didn't intend for anything to happen to her, no matter what she sensed.

Her face drained of color.

"So many," she whispered.

"Stacy?"

"So many. He's used it. Many times. Over years. Death house."

"Stacy!"

She was almost in a trance. And I was almost climbing over the seat to get to her. Chad's hands held me back.

"Leave her alone, Ariel! Don't interfere!"

"He takes them. The lost ones. Inside that house. And they never come out."

"Stacy!"

"Who are you?" Stacy asked.

"Stacy, you know who we are!"

"She's not talking to us, baby."

"Leanne. Such a pretty name. Such a pretty girl. You had no business out on the streets at fourteen, Leanne."

"Oh, shit!" Chad exclaimed. A tall man in a heavy nylon coat and a knit skull cap was walking up the street, his head and shoulders hunched against the drizzle. He headed to the door of the house.

Stacy came back to us in a rush.

"Chad! That's him! Don't let him go in! We have to get him. Now!"

"Not so loud, honey! We need back-up, we'll stay and watch while I call this in—"

"*No!!* He has a girl in there! Still alive! Leanne told me! If he goes in—by the time anybody gets here—we have to stop him now!"

Chad looked between us and closed his eyes briefly. I could feel his frustration. A serial-killing drug dealer to take down and two novices to worry about.

"Lord help," he said. "'Cause somebody sure needs to." He leaned over and kissed me hard and quick and opened the door. "Ariel, get your ass over in this seat and get the hell out of here while Stacy calls 911. We're at 1191 State Street. Do you hear me?"

He didn't wait for an answer. Probably because he knew the one he'd hear. I was glad the windows were cracked so I could hear them. I hoped. Stacy was already on her cell.

"We're at 1191 State Street in Marietta. We have—"
Oh, God, don't tell 'em, honey, they'll never believe us! I thought, but I underestimated my little sister.

"...we have a break-in attempt, somebody's trying to break in our house, he's got a gun, please hurry!"

She clicked the phone shut. The man stopped, head up, all senses alert as Chad approached, a predator sensing danger.

Chad's hand moved inside his jacket. I knew it was on the Glock in his shoulder holster.

"Hey, buddy, I'm lookin' for Zander. Somebody told me he's the man to see if you want the best. Can you help me out here?" I strained forward. I could barely hear.

"You not lookin' to score, man. You get yo' ass on gone, do you know what's good for you."

"Hey!" Chad threw up a hand. Not the one on the Glock. He kept walking towards Zander. "Chill, man! All I want is a little piece of action." He was closer. Zander, high-alert mode activated, debated whether to run, hold, or attack. I could feel his indecision vibrating in the air.

"No, man. You lookin' for me." I saw the material of Zander's coat change shape under the street light. It poked out in a straight line. The line of a gun barrel. I heard the retort of the gunfire at the same moment I saw a blackish-red flower bloom on Chad's shoulder. Almost simultaneously, I heard two more gunshots. Much louder gunshots. Two blackish-red flowers bloomed in Zander's chest. A look of amazement crossed his face. And then he fell.

I was out of the car and running, Stacy hot behind me, as Chad staggered. He fell forward just as I reached him, the blood pumping furiously. Arterial blood. Had to be. He looked at me and said, "Twice, baby girl. You always shoot twice. Once to take 'em down, once to finish it."

I caught his arms just as he fell, and we went down together. Not because I wasn't strong enough to hold him up. At that moment, the adrenaline was pumping so furiously I could have held him up had he weighed much more than he did. We went down together because he was passing out from the sudden massive blood loss. And so was I. Without losing a drop.

Chapter Twenty-Four

Somewhere off in the shadow lands where Chad and I floated, I heard sirens. My sister's urgent voice. The shouted orders of the responding officers. Not everything. Bits and pieces of running, jumbled voices.

"Miss, calm down. ...what went down...yes, an ambulance is on the way..."

"...my sister and brother-in-law...private investigator, you'll find his ID at the hospital...that man...check the house! You have to check the house....where's the fuckin' ambulance?!" Oh, yeah, Stacy was getting hot.

"Miss, it's on the way...house...swat team...."

"...don't need a swat team...need a forensic team...check under the house...ambulance...Don't you dare try and separate them, you don't understand...." I felt her kneeling beside us, her arms around us.

Another somebody was beside us too, one of the officers, I assumed. "I need more padding! Pull all you got from both cars...move your asses!"

More sirens. A different tone. Ambulances.

"No! You do not separate them!"

Tell 'em, Stacy. You go, girl!

"Where the hell's she hit?"

"That's the thing. She's not!"

"Vitals are as bad as his, she's gotta be hit somewhere!"

"She's not! You work on him!"

"Get the plasma going! Gotta replace the blood!"

"Move your ass out of the way! I go with them! Don't you dare try and stop me!"

And through it all, I felt Chad slipping, fighting back, slipping, fighting back. I latched on with a psychic vice grip and pulled with everything I had. And entered total blackness.

* * *

I was floating somewhere. I didn't know where. Somewhere black. Somewhere soundless. I didn't know how long I'd been there. And out of the darkness came light. A pinprick at first. I felt a hand grabbing mine, and though I couldn't know it or actually feel it, I knew it. And felt it. Another hand was grabbing Chad's hand. And tugging. Then a buzzing noise. A voice. Furious. Intense. Insistent.

"You listen to me, Mister! You get your ass back here and you bring my sister with you! Do you hear me?!?!"

I opened my eyes. An ER trauma unit. I was on a stretcher, Chad on a stretcher beside me.

"Stacy? Chad?"

"Oh, my God! Thank you, thank you!"

"You can stop shouting now, darlin', I hear you."

Chad's voice.

"Okay, Miss, we've gotten some blood back in him, he's stabilized. And I don't know what the devil that's got to do with your sister's condition but since she's back, and he's back, we got to knock him out again, take care of that shoulder. Can you let us do that now, you think?"

I laughed. My little sister had apparently raised some holy hell in our absence.

"Baby girl, you okay?" His voice was stronger already.

"I'm fine, Magic Man." I was, in fact, sitting up on the stretcher, hampered by the IV, though why the heck they'd thought I needed one or what it was, I didn't know. "Can y'all get this thing outta me?"

The doctor stepped over and ripped off the tape. "Stay still." I felt the foreign object leave my skin with a stinging sensation. I stood and moved to the head of Chad's stretcher, stumbling a bit. Stacy steadied me as I leaned over and kissed him.

"Hell of a honeymoon, Magic Man. You behave and let them take care of you. We'll be here when you come back."

"'Kay. Love you."

"Love you."

I watched as they wheeled him on to the ER. Another doctor spoke.

"Your husband's a lucky man, Ms. Garrett. He's alive because the officers kept pressure on that shoulder long enough for the paramedics to start replacing some of the blood loss. Close to bleeding out there."

"You're telling me," I said.

"Damnedest thing I ever saw. You, I mean. You wouldn't care to explain that, now would you?"

"Oh, I wouldn't mind. But you wouldn't believe me."

"Probably not." He nodded. "Well, let's get you two settled in the right waiting room. You sure you're okay?"

"As long as he is."

"You're not gonna pass out when they start the anesthesia, are you?"

"I don't think so, I know it's coming. Seems to make a difference."

The doctor shook his head. "Nope, I probably really don't want to know anyway."

Stacy picked up the bag furnished by the hospital to hold our personal things and we settled down in a waiting room outside the right surgical unit.

"Did they get the girl out all right?"

"Yes. They're going through the house now. I suggested—strongly—that they go underneath."

"How many are they gonna find?"

"Fifteen. Maybe more. Maybe as many as twenty."

"Dear God."

"They'll be wanting to talk to us, of course."

"Of course."

"I just told 'em Chad was a PI bounty hunter and we'd stumbled on this Zander guy unexpectedly during routine surveillance, that Chad hadn't actually thought he'd be there. Figured he could field the rest."

"Good figuring."

Chad's phone rang. It took me a minute to pin the location. The bag of our personal items.

I pulled it out. New career calling.

"War-N-Wit, Inc. Ariel Garrett. How can we help you?"

Chapter Twenty-Five

I glared down at my husband. The honeymoon was over. Probably a good thing, since as honeymoons go, this one had been a killer. Almost for real.

"The doctor said you needed to stay at least three days! So if you think you're walking out of this hospital within thirty-six hours of almost bleedin' to death, you got another think coming, Magic Man!"

He flung the white hospital bedcovers back with his right arm, sat up and swung his legs off the bed. He was good, I'll give him that. I doubt anybody but me would've noticed the white tinge around his lips or the faint grimace when his left arm and shoulder moved. Then again, nobody but me could feel the sting from the torn flesh around the bullet hole in his shoulder. Neither of us had ever expected such a fringe benefit but apparently, we took the phrase "flesh of my flesh" to new levels.

The soreness wasn't so bad. I knew it was there and I could keep it at a distance. My foot still twinged from the healing knife wound through his foot from last week, too. I grinned. All in all, an extremely memorable trip even without getting married. And not too many folks could say they'd gotten married on a motorcycle in the White Chapel's Tunnel of Love Drive-Thru.

"Doctors always tell me I need to stay in the hospital. I haven't listened to one yet, not starting now." He started across the floor towards the bathroom, hospital gown flashing glimpses of bare butt. Great butt, but then I'm prejudiced.

"Hell!" He reached around to grab the flapping sides of the gown. "Besides, I hate having my ass hanging out in the wind."

"Nobody here to see it but me," I advised. "Besides, your ass is always hanging out in the wind. Occupational hazard."

"Yeah, but man, what a rush!" He left the door open and I heard the top of the toilet lid lift.

He was incorrigible. I shook my head. No changing the unchangeable. Chad's cell phone sounded his business ringtone from the nightstand. I picked it up.

"War-N-Wit, Inc. Ariel Garrett. How can we help you?"

No answer.

"Hello?"

"I was under the impression that War-N-Wit, Inc. was Chad Garrett. Who are you and what are you doing answering his phone?"

Excuse me? It was a man's voice, but prissy and rude as hell. However, War-N-Wit was my husband's—and now my—baby. He'd bled for this company many times in the past and he'd undoubtedly bleed for it again in the future.

The sound of a shower caught my attention. I hoped he'd keep his shoulder dry. And his foot reasonably out of the water, though those stiches were doing nicely. I hadn't even asked a nurse whether it was all right for him to shower. And I knew he hadn't asked because he didn't care if it was all right or not. If he wanted a shower, he'd take one.

"Ariel Garrett, sir." I turned my attention back to our caller, probably the caller who'd hung up last night when I answered the phone. "Chad Garrett's wife and partner. How can we help you?"

"I do not want Chad Garrett's wife. I want Chad Garrett. I want the War of War-N-Wit."

For real? Well, we've all got our own little bag of rocks to tote around. I didn't much like that emphasis on the "War", though. Like he knew what War-N-Wit really meant. Only special people with special talents should catch the meaning behind the name. But if he did know what it meant, it was time to let him know who he was talking to.

"Well, sir, I'm sorry, but you've got the Wit of War-N-Wit, and my husband is not available at the moment. So I'm afraid you either talk to me or you don't talk."

For a minute I thought he'd hung up. But no. Don't know why I thought I'd be that lucky.

"I am Mr. Oliver Hedgepath. I have been endeavoring for some time now to engage the services of Mr. Garrett but he always seems to have a full schedule. However, things are rapidly shifting to the point wherein I need his immediate assistance. I'm afraid I'm going to have to become insistent about it."

And lots of luck with that, buddy, I thought. Anybody who thought they'd get Chad Garrett's attention because they insisted on it must not live in the real world. Either that or they didn't know him very well.

"Well, sir, in fact, we've had a very full schedule these last few days. And at the moment Mr. Garrett is recuperating from the aftereffects of our last engagement. But I would be delighted to relay a message, providing of course you give me one." I'd always had the knack of parroting the tone of a person I was conversing with by phone. An invaluable talent for a paralegal. I could be as country or as redneck or as official as I needed to be. Or, as in this instance, as prissy. I wouldn't be at all delighted to relay a message though, that was a bald-faced lie. I absolutely didn't like Mr. Oliver Hedgepath. And from his pained tone, he absolutely didn't like me, either.

He sighed. Apparently he'd decided I was an obstacle that must be overcome. Well, at least he wasn't completely stupid.

"I am the major domo of a very important organization. That organization is under attack. I believe Chad Garrett is the only man who can help me.

I have already explained this to him, but I don't feel he's given it the import it demands."

Faint alarm bells juggled my memory. That phone call Chad had taken on the way to the Atlanta Airport en route to our wild Vegas run.

"Mr. Hedgepath, would you be referring to the Resurrection Society?"

Shocked silence on the other end of the line.

"Mr. Garrett discusses his confidential phone calls? Perhaps I misjudged him."

"Mr. Garrett discusses his business calls with his business partner—who is also his wife. Perhaps I should remind you that my husband specifically advised you not to expect his answer —which was no— to be any different should you check back with him at a later date. Something on the order of 'War-N-Wit, Inc. deals with the living. The modern American justice system.'"

Chad walked out of the bathroom, towel wrapped casually around his hips. Dry bandage, so at least he'd been careful.

"Baby girl, I sorta hoped you'd join me."

I waved the phone in the air and motioned for him to *sssssshhhh*. He raised his eyebrow and I hit the speaker button just as Mr. Hedgepath recovered from the latest shock to his system; namely, that I have almost total recall. That shocks a lot of folks, actually. Very handy talent to have.

"Young lady, you are impertinent and a detriment to your husband's business. You are female and therefore cannot possibly have any expertise in this field. Now, I demand to speak with Mr. Garrett."

I winced. But he'd asked for it. Chad's face darkened as he grabbed the phone, not bothering to take it off speaker.

"Hedgepath."

"Oh, so the young lady has a modicum of sense, she's finally given you—"

"Hedgepath, I will not work for you. I would never have worked for you. You have no idea how lucky you are you're not in the same room with me. Because no one talks to my wife like that. Do not ever call this number again." He hit the "end" button and turned to me.

"And don't you ever just stand there and let anyone talk to you like—"

"Whoa, darlin'. I wasn't goin' to. But you came out of the shower and took over."

He blew a *whoooo* through his lips. "Yeah, I guess I did. But you're not working at any law office and you're not hired help. You don't have to take insults and I don't want you to ever take any. Understand?"

"Magic Man. I wasn't goin' to, trust me."

"Okay. Just don't." He walked over to the carry-all Stacy'd delivered from the hotel before she left for home. He pulled out fresh jeans and a fresh tee and started dressing.

The surgeon chose that moment to check on his patient.

"And what do you think you're doing, Mr. Garrett?"

"Checking out."

"Oh, no, you're not, you need another full day minimum—"

"Watch me. Get me the release form, I'll sign it."

"What release form?"

"The 'against medical advice thing'. I'll sign it."

"You're real familiar with those forms, I'm guessing?"

"Yes. I am. Now get it."

"Mr. Garrett—"

Mr. Garrett, still enraged courtesy of Mr. Oliver Hedgepath, turned to the doctor. His eyes turned from blue to silver. He glared. That was all. He didn't speak.

The doctor sighed.

"One 'against medical advice form'. Coming up."

While Chad completed all medical forms and insurance documents with a speed that confirmed this wasn't the first time he'd checked himself out of a hospital, I called my office. My old office. Officially I still worked there, after all, at least for a few more days. The story'd been all over the news, and some of the other girls would be worried about me. Possibly even a few of the attorneys. It wasn't everyday twenty-one bodies—the total count—were dug out of a basement. With apologies not nearly as heartfelt as I hoped they sounded, I advised that what with my new husband getting himself shot during the take-down and all, I wouldn't be coming back for the rest of my two weeks' notice. I sorta left out the part about him checking himself out of the hospital this morning. I didn't even feel guilty about it. When you got right down to it, pretty much all any attorney wanted was a live body at the desk answering the phone, anyway.

I brought the Equinox around to pick him up. I parked in the "Pick-Up" Circle and opened the passenger door.

He looked at me. "You're kidding, right?"

I'd expected that. "Which means you want to drive?"

"It's my left shoulder, nothing wrong with my right arm."

I sighed. "Yeah, well, it's a long drive from Atlanta to south Georgia. How 'bout I take it at least to Macon? Or are you that scared of my driving?"

"I guess that'd be okay." He grumbled as he maneuvered himself into the passenger seat and pulled the door shut with his right hand.

Finally. We were headed home. Home was Quitman, Georgia. I'd never seen it and it didn't matter. I'd never even asked for any descriptions or pictures. Home was wherever Chad was. Nor did I ask any questions about it on the trip there. Sight unseen, it was part of me. Because he was. And I'd love it. Because I loved him. I knew he couldn't wait to show it to me. The miles rolled by, the conversation accompanied by Sirius radio on whatever music decade hit our fancy.

About mid-way between Atlanta and Macon, he broached the subject of Hedgepath and the Resurrection Society. Lord knows I wasn't going to.

"Baby girl."

"Um?"

"I never told you. Probably should have, but I didn't want to scare you off, what with you just realizing you're a witch and all." He paused.

"With a lead-in like that, Magic Man, this ain't the time to stop talkin'."

"Mostly what I do is strictly ordinary run-of-the-mill legal support. Investigations, background checks, skip traces, service of process, bring in a bounty every now and then."

He stopped, apparently not sure how to proceed. I rather enjoyed the novelty of that, but after a few seconds, I decided I'd help out a bit.

"The word mostly implies not always."

He sighed. "Yeah. It does." He sighed again. "Magic's very old. It comes in many shapes and sizes. And strengths. And it's dangerous if it's misused. Because it can turn dark. And dark magic poses a problem not just for those of us who have magic and respect it, but because —"

"It's a danger to everyone, magical or not."

"Exactly. So over the years, a sort of—well—Guardianship's been set up."

"But it's not listed in the Yellow Pages."

He laughed. "No, it surely is not."

"Are you a Guardian?"

"No. But they call me occasionally. When they feel something might need to be checked out."

"Does that work in reverse, too? Any of us ever call them? When we think something might ought to be checked out?"

"Yeah."

"You think Hedgepath and Resurrection oughta be checked out?"

He sighed. "Much as I dislike that whole set-up and much as I disliked it from the start, I'm beginning to think something new has entered the picture. There's always been something about Hedgepath that didn't strike the right chord with me, but today, I don't know, it wasn't just 'cause he pissed me off so bad, it was something else. How'd he strike you?"

"I detested him instantly. Just on his voice and attitude."

"Yeah. Something dark and getting darker. So I'm thinking when we get settled in at home, I ought to make a call."

"And possibly do some investigating. Not for Hedgepath and Resurrection. But about them."

"'Fraid so."

"Your area of expertise. Your call."

We hit the 247 Bypass around Macon and kept heading south. I could feel his anticipation growing with every mile, and I didn't argue when he tapped my shoulder and signaled for me to pull over so he could claim the wheel. We made the switch and a few miles outside of Quitman, he reached over and turned off the radio.

"Almost there?"

He pointed to what looked to be a farm road off to the right.

"Is that an actual road?"

"It's your new driveway."

"Really?" I glanced around in delight at the fields of pines on either side. It was moving on into February but that didn't make any difference in an evergreen forest that was perpetually green. It didn't make all that much difference in south Georgia, anyway, where the winters were so mild they wouldn't be classed as real winter by most of the country. A few hundred yards in, he stopped at a closed gate, let down the window and punched a code into the code box on the post. Overhead a sign proclaimed *Pine Whisper Plantation.*

The driveway seemed endless.

"How long is it?"

"Bout a mile. We have about 300 acres, some in pines, some in pasture. We keep a few horses, a few cows. I hope you're not disappointed with the house. It's not big, it's just been me, but I wanted to wait till I found you. So we can build whatever you want when we're ready."

"Disappointed? You're kiddin', right? You didn't tell me we had a farm."

He laughed. "What's the matter, you don't read? It's a plantation. But just a baby one."

The road dipped over a hill and I exhaled in whistling delight. "*Ohhhhh!* It's a tree house!"

"Well, it's called an island house. It's made mostly out of old wood from a couple of barns we tore down. And I scavenged for more old wood so the deck'd match. You like?"

I stared in wonder. It was a jewel. Old, old board. It sat high off the ground on a stilt foundation under a thick stand of oak trees. Unless you looked closely, you'd swear it was floating in the branches. A deck completely encircled it, with long steps running from either end of the deck down to the ground. He'd put in large sheets of clear and open glass rather than conventional windows on all sides. The view out across the fields must be stunning.

"I never imagined. I can't wait to see inside!"

"Yeah, well, looks like you might have to for a minute." He pointed to the left. An older gentleman walked across the open pasture towards us. He wasn't alone. A large dog walked beside him. He wasn't on a leash, but he heeled perfectly.

The dog stopped, His ears perked and his head raised.

"Thor!" Chad called.

The dog leaped into action, racing towards Chad's voice. As he neared I wondered at his breed. A shepherd, I first thought, but there was something—well, I'd know in a few seconds. Thor skidded to a stop in front of Chad, lifted onto two legs and placed both feet on Chad's chest. Laughing, Chad held out his right arm to prevent contact with his left shoulder.

"Manners, boy, manners! Yeah, I missed you, too. Down now." Thor obeyed instantly.

I looked down—though not very far—into ice-blue eyes. No, not ice-blue. Somewhere between ice-blue and silver. Wolf eyes.

I vaguely heard Chad's voice, even registered the words. "This is Thor. He's a Canadian Timberwolf-husky blend."

I didn't need to register the words to recognize Thor. I felt it instantly, that connection, like spiritual bonding. As powerful as last Christmas, when I'd given in and faced myself, accepted my gift and known once and for all I wasn't like most people. I was a witch. Now, looking deep into those ice-blue, silver eyes, the spirit of the wolf flew into me. I understood the thing I hadn't yet pegged about Chad's eyes in an instant. The spirit of one wolf awakened the spirit of another. The wolf was Magic Man's spirit animal. Mine, too. I broke my stare with Thor and looked up at Chad.

"Holy. Shit."

"What?"

"Your eyes. They've turned almost silver."

"You're surprised?"

He gave a grin and shook his head. "Well, no, I'm not. Not in the slightest."

The older man was approaching now.

"And this is Buddy. Jim McAfee, officially, but known and loved by all as Buddy. He looks after the place—and Thor—for me when I'm gone. Got a little modular home over back of that grove over there. Buddy, this is my wife, Ariel."

"Ma'am." Buddy gave me a courtly nod and an appraising glance. He seemed satisfied because he smiled and said, "I'm guessing things just gonna get stranger and stranger 'round here now."

I laughed. "And why would you guess that, Buddy?"

"Peas in a pod. Two peas in a pod. Took him awhile to find you. The wit to his war. Oh, yeah. Hate to see the young'uns. And I ain't plannin' on doing no babysittin', neither, warnin' both of you right now. Kid'll probably be levitating in his playpen with the two of you for parents."

Oh, Lord! I hadn't thought of that. He might be right. But I'd worry about it later. For right now, I was on an adventure.

"How many folks call you Magic Man?" I asked.

"Just you and Stacy. And Spike. And Buddy. And a few others."

I laughed. I'd take a wild guess the "few others" might refer to those he called "the Guardians".

"So just the folks who know you well, huh?"

"Guess you could say that. Ready for the tour?"

"You feel like walkin'?"

"Baby girl."

"Sorry. I forgot. Admit no weakness."

Buddy laughed. "Yeah, and we can always take the golf cart."

"It's not a golf cart, Buddy, it's a —"

"I know, I know! Call it what you want, Magic Man, it's a fancy golf cart. I'll go collect it, Miss Ariel needs to get settled. Go show her the house."

* * *

I raced ahead of Chad up the steps, though Thor beat me in. I knew what I'd see before I saw it. Walls of old board stained in glowing, golden oak, protected by coats of clear polyurethane and highlighted with dream catchers and oils of wolves roaming a great forest.

Floors stained to match the walls, spotlighted with rich, deep pools of oriental rugs. A leather couch, with matching loveseat and recliners in chocolate brown. Warm fleece throws draped across the backs of the furniture created spots of color. The main room was a great room with a cathedral ceiling. A fireplace insert was set into one corner, with built in desk work-stations set into the middle of each adjoining wall creating an office-study. Each unit was surrounded by built-in shelves, each complete with comfortable chairs.

"*Oooohhh*," I breathed softly.

"Like it?" He came to stand beside me as I inspected the vacant work station. A writer's heaven, perfect height, shelf space, drawers.

"Did you do this before you found me?"

"Yes. Didn't know you'd be a writer, but I always knew you'd be my business partner. Partners have to have desks. Will it work for your writing, though? 'Cause I'll modify it however you need."

"Oh, yes! My laptop will think it's died and gone to heaven!"

A kitchen alcove sat in the back, small but set up as a cook's dream with appliances any chef would kill for.

"And here's our bedroom," he said, moving toward an open door. The same décor dominated the bedroom. Country comfortable furniture, a king-size bed with built in drawers in the base, rich colors against warm neutrals. "Our bath's through here, and there's another small extra room with a little bath. And that's it."

"It's so far beyond perfect it oughta be illegal." The big dream catcher over the head of the bed, intricate as a spider web, radiated peace and protection. "The dream catchers are unbelievable. So are the wolf oils in the Great Room."

"The dream catchers are from the Cherokee Reservation in North Carolina. Got kinda an affinity for 'em, my great-great and maybe another great, I never remember—was on the Trail of Tears. His name's recorded and everything."

"That doesn't surprise me, somehow," I said.

A horn honked from outside.

"Buddy's got the Ranger," Chad said. "Wanta quick tour around before dark?"

"Sure. That would be the golf cart?"

Chad laughed. "A glorified golf cart, yeah. It's a Ranger. Mini-jeep, more or less, hunters use 'em for the woods and lots of farms have 'em."

"You don't use it for huntin', I'm guessin'." This man, so much a part of the rhythm of the universe, didn't hunt. Well, he did. Just not animals.

"No, baby girl," he laughed in confirmation. "I only hunt the bad guys." The horn beeped again. "And your chariot awaits."

* * *

We piled into the bright red Ranger, Thor pressed close against my side. We toured the ponds stocked with catfish and bream, the pastures with the small herd of cattle, the stands of fruit trees and groves of pecan trees. I met the pygmy goats and the barn cats. I exchanged blown breaths with Stalwart, the roan stallion, and Lady, the golden brown mare, and Sweetpea, their little daughter not a year old yet.

"You ride?" Chad asked.

"Never in my life," I said. "I've never even touched a horse before."

"Really?" Buddy grinned. "Now that I wouldn't believe, quick as they took to you. But then again, seein' as how it's you, I guess I do. Never petted a goat either, I'm assumin'?"

"You'd assume right," I confirmed.

"Well. Some damn."

We headed back. Dark came early in February. Out of the corner of my eye, I saw a fleeting image of a big black cat. I hadn't met that cat. He must not care for the company of the other cats. But I'd seen him moving in the bushes off and on through the whole tour.

"Where does that black cat stay?" I asked. "He must be a loner, he's never with the others."

"We don't have a black cat," Chad said.

"We do now," said Buddy. "Been seein' him around the last month or so. Just here and there. Out of the corner of my eye. And then he hightails it outta here like he don't much want anybody to see him."

Chad sighed. "Well, there's always room for one more. Hope he's not completely wild."

"Don't think so," Buddy said. "Haven't seen anything makes me worried 'bout him causin' a problem. And the way Miss Ariel's takin' over all the animals, she'll have him on the deck drinkin' outta a saucer in a week."

"Got other things to do on the deck tonight," Chad said. "Like soak in the hot tub. Let's go home."

"The deck's got a hot tub?" I could feel my ears perk like Thor's. "I didn't see it."

"Around on the back. Oh, yeah. Buddy, home if you please."

"You got it, Magic Man."

Chapter Twenty-Six

The chill in the air made it perfect for a hot tub dip on a February evening while twilight merged into full dark. I hadn't seen the back of the house on the quick tour, but the hot tub nestled under a little roofed alcove, patio furniture placed invitingly along its long length. Risers of steam spouted like geysers above the surface. Thor settled down beside the tub. I slipped into the end facing out onto the deck, submerging slowly so my naked body could adjust to the heat. Finally, I leaned my head back and sighed. Magic Man thought of everything. Soft lighting glowed from small spotlights placed around the little enclosure and a skylight in the alcove roof streamed mingled moonbeams and starlight down onto the surface of the water.

The water rose higher as Chad settled against the other side of the tub. He smiled and entwined his legs with mine. I smiled back and closed my eyes for a moment, savoring the heat of the water and the feel of his skin, creating another type of heat. Touch wasn't enough. I needed to look at him looking at me.

I opened my eyes. And screamed.

Chad's head whipped around and my shoulder protested the sudden movement in echo of his. The healing bullet wound was still very tender. It didn't slow him down any, though. He turned completely in the tub at the speed of light, backing up against me and covering me from sight. Thor, issuing continuous low growls, moved threateningly forward.

A short man in a gray three piece suit stood in the alcove opening. There was even a watch chain attached to the vest button from its pocket.

"Could you call your dog off, if you please?"

"Who the hell are you?"

"Hedgepath. Oliver Hedgepath."

"Thor. Guard."

Thor moved closer, the growls still rolling from deep in his chest.

"I believe I asked you to call your dog off, not—"

"There's another word that'll have him going straight for your throat. Want me to say that one?"

"No, I don't believe I'd care for that."

"How the hell did you get in here?"

"The gate was open."

"Bullshit. How'd you get this far without Thor knowing it?"

"I suppose the wind was right."

"Bullshit. Why are you here?"

"You told me never to call your number again."

"Exactly. So why are you here?"

"I have to speak with you. Which would be easier were you not both cavorting in a state of undress in—" The disapproval in his voice was palpable.

Chad half-rose. "Man, I am in my own hot tub with my own wife on my own deck in the middle of 300 fucking acres!"

I shrieked and grabbed him around the waist with both arms to pull him back down and against me. He was the only cover I had.

Even Hedgepath could see his time was running out.

"Allow me two seconds. Please," he said, and reached inside his vest. He pulled out a photograph. "Look. Just look."

It was a picture of a necklace of some sort. A large, tear shaped crystal. In the picture, I could see glints of greenish—no, bluish—no, indigo light. I shook my head. It was changing colors. In the picture.

Chad's face was totally blank. "Turn around. Stare straight ahead. Don't shift your eyes a millimeter." To be sure that was clear, he added, "Thor. Guard front."

Hedgepath turned slowly and Thor walked with him. When Hedgepath was completely turned, Thor sat in front of him.

Chad reached over to the side table beside the tub and grabbed the white terry cloth robes we'd left there, handing me one. "Com'on, honey, he's not looking. He knows better."

I got out rapidly and wrapped myself quickly. Chad belted his robe and released Thor from guard duty. He walked up to Hedgepath and took the photograph.

"So. The foundation of the Resurrection Society. I wondered. If you were completely full of shit or only half full."

"You see this picture and you dare to ask?"

"It could be a fake. In which case you'd be half full of shit instead of completely full because I guess at least you're putting some sort of test on your members. Even if it's a faked one."

"I assure you it is not a fake."

"And you know this because, of course, you're this Tear's Seer."

"I know this because I was this Tear's Seer, yes."

"Was?"

"Was."

"There's only one at a time for each—"

"Exactly."

"So a new Seer's in town. Guess you gotta deal with it. Move over."

"What's the crystal?" I asked. "What does it do?"

"The fact that you have to ask, young lady, shows you have no business—"

"Hedgepath." Ice water wouldn't have been as cold as Chad's voice. "You don't remember what I told you about how you talk to my wife?"

"My apologies."

"Not sincere ones, I'm sure. Move it, Hedgepath. Move back and sit down."

"I'd rather not sit, if you don't mind."

"Didn't think you would. So. You have one of the Tears of Isis. And at one time, you could use it. When did you lose it, by the way? The power?"

"It started fading a few months ago. October, November. It was gone by the end of December."

"So. Like I said. There's a new Seer in town. Some town. Somewhere."

I wanted to say I didn't understand, but I didn't because that would elicit another insult from Hedgepath and I didn't want Chad to hurt him. I'd just have to wait for a full explanation and piece together what I could now.

"Yes."

"You know who?"

"I'm rather hoping it's you."

"Me?"

"I've been following you for a long time. And your power is growing. I think it's grown tremendously just this year. And you'd be the least of all possible evils because you have a deep and abiding respect for magic. An innate understanding of how dangerous it can be in the wrong hands. And if it's not you, I need you to find him. The new Seer. So that I can monitor him, be certain—"

"Don't even go there, Hedgepath. You'd be lying in your teeth. You don't give a damn if the new Seer's good or dark. You only want to make sure he's not a threat to you and that major domo thing you got going on at your elite society. Notice you've never mentioned the membership dues. Are the coffers getting a little empty over there? Let any new members in lately?"

Hedgepath fidgeted. "There haven't been many applications in the last few months, fortunately. So I've—delayed—any initiations."

"Convenient. But you can't delay much longer."

"No."

"So what do you want me to do about it?"

"I told you. I think the new Seer might be you. When you look at the picture, do you feel anything, see anything?"

"It's a picture, Hedgepath."

"Yes, but still. If it's you, there might be some twinge, some sign—"

"No twinge, no sign."

"Then you must see the Tear itself. Keep the photograph to remind yourself of the importance of what we're dealing with. When can you come?"

"I didn't say I'd come."

"You'll come. There's no reason to insult my intelligence by implying you won't. No person of power would dare deny this. The implications of a rogue Seer getting his hands on one of the Tears of Isis—"

"Would mean nothing to the world in general because believe it or not, most folks don't think they're reincarnated and don't want to prove they are."

"And you wouldn't like to view your past lives?"

"Everything I need from any past life I already got. Her name's Ariel Garrett."

"Seeing the past isn't the only power a Seer has. Suppose this new Seer does lean to the Dark Side? Chad Garrett—Magic Man, I believe, is the moniker you have in the world of magic—doesn't want to keep an eye on anyone as powerful as a Seer? And if your power has grown that much, you need to know it. And I'd hope you would be responsible enough to—"

"Drop in at the Resurrection Society every now and then."

"Well, yes."

"Then you'd better hope I'm not the Seer."

"But you'll come?"

"Once."

"Friday night?"

"Where?"

"Savannah. The Society renovated one of the old houses on Bull Street."

"Ah. How fitting. A renovated house on Bull Street. In Savannah. Yeah, those coffers are probably getting pretty low."

"Renovating an historic home is a service to society."

"On that street? Yes, a very expensive one."

My brain was still processing Chad's remark as to "how fitting" Resurrection's location was, and then I had it. *Midnight in the Garden of Good and Evil.* Savannah. Bull Street. The Mercer House, pivotal location of the true event that triggered both the book and the movie was located on Bull Street. Any house located on Bull Street screamed money.

Hedgepath ignored the jibe. He reached inside his vest again and produced a business card which he handed to Chad. "I trust you don't need directions."

"My GPS works just fine. And I'm very familiar with Savannah."

"Friday evening, then. Seven o'clock. I'll see you then."

"You'll see us then."

Hedgepath sighed. "Bring her if you must. Is it safe for me to move? Your animal won't attack me?"

"Not if I don't tell him to. I'm still thinking about that."

Hedgepath nodded. He turned and walked toward the deck stairs.

"Hedgepath!"

He turned back.

"Don't ever show up here like this again."

Out of the corner of my eye, the black cat I'd noticed earlier walked delicately along the deck railing. He stopped about two feet away from Hedgepath and hissed. Then he leaped from the railing into the tree branches.

Hedgepath nodded again. And walked down the steps. He disappeared into darkness.

* * *

Chad looked at Thor.

"Boy, how in the hell you let him get by you? That ever happens again, I'm shipping your ass back to Canada."

Thor whined apologetically.

Chad walked quickly to the kitchen door and reached inside. Floodlights lit the yard. No one was there.

He grabbed his cell and hit a number.

"Buddy. Check the power circuits for the gates." Long pause. "All of them are working? No glitches, no down time?" Longer pause. "Shit. Didn't think so."

He turned back to me. "Nobody came through that gate in a car. And nobody disappeared that quick from the yard, either." He raced down the steps, me trailing in his wake, and stopped a few feet away from the bottom.

"Thought so," he said. A crumbled gray suit billowed out over a pile of sand. A gold fob watch rested on top. "A man to watch, our Mr. Oliver Hedgepath."

"Sand?" I asked, reaching into the storehouse of useless information that seemed to file itself away in my brain. "A—a—golem? That was a golem? But I thought golems were big and clumsy and didn't talk. Or talk well. Like—like—Frankenstein!"

Chad reached down and touched the fine grains. "Not your ordinary golem, no. You know about golems, baby girl?" He picked up the pocket watch.

"I read a lot," I said absently, bending down myself. Like I'd know what I was looking for. "Golems are creatures of Jewish mythology. Creatures made of sand that act on the command of their makers. 'Bout all I know about 'em. Except I didn't think they'd be quite that articulate. Or that they actually existed, in fact."

"Well," said Chad, standing straight. "That wasn't your ordinary golem, no. Very sophisticated. Sort of a cross between a golem and an—"

144

"Astral projection," I said. "Of course."

"Damn. You know about them, too?"

"Just about as much as I do about golems. Sort of— a person projects out his spirit, like a 3-D image, it lets 'em be places they aren't. But I didn't think anything like that actually existed, either."

Chad laughed. "I think I've said this to you before, honey. Welcome to the world of magic. But damn few people can do either one of 'em, and I've never seen a mixture of the two before. The man's good. Or more likely, not good. He parked down from the gate and just sent the golem around it. There's no fencing right there, just thick woods. And by now he's hauling ass back to Savannah."

I shivered. Bare feet in the yard in February'll do that to you. "Can we go back in?"

"Sure. Com'on. Sorry, you've gotten cold." He put his arm around me and we walked back up the stairs and into the house. Chad went over and turned on the gas fireplace, adding the dance of flickering flames to the low lighting of two lamps. He laid the picture down on one of the scattered occasional tables.

We sat down on the big leather couch and wrapped ourselves up with each other. Thor claimed the rug between the couch and the fireplace.

"So what the hell's this Tear of Isis?"

"Most people who've even heard of it think it's a legend."

"And you?"

"Always had my doubts. Still do. All we have is a picture. Produced, via golem, by a man who just radiates confusion. Because magical or not, Thor should've known he was there. However he was there. Which means a little cloaking was thrown into that mix, too."

"Cat didn't like him, either. Did you see that black cat?"

"Yeah. Buddy's right. You'll have him drinking milk out of a saucer in a week."

"Well, I'm gonna try. Always had a thing for black cats. This Tear of Isis thing. Say it's real. What does it do?"

"They. What do they do. There're three of them. If they still exist or ever existed. So what's one of 'em doing in the possession of Hedgepath in a renovated house on Bull Street in Savannah, Georgia?"

"What's Magic Man doing in the middle of a 300 acre farm outside a crossroad like Quitman, Georgia?"

"Point taken. The Tears of Isis are supposed to be just that, of course. Crystalized tears of the Goddess Isis. Discovered in the Temple of Isis during the excavation of Pompeii in 1764."

"Pompeii? Not Egypt?"

"Nope. Pompeii. Anyway, what they do is, they allow anyone with any trace memories of a past life to view them. Their past lives."

"Seems sorta iffy to me. If the viewer is the only one viewing them, they could claim they were anything—anybody."

"Enter the Seers. One Seer for each Tear. And they don't see just their own past lives. When they gaze into the Tear while another person's holding it, they see the lives of the other person, not their own."

"For real?"

"That's the story. Whether it's real, your guess is as good as mine. I'm too much of a skeptic. I've seen too many things having nothing to do with magic, just with people, to ever blindly believe anything without having the proof in front of my eyes. Of anything, magic or otherwise."

His voice had darkened. It matched the shadows in the room thrown by the flickering flames from the fireplace. That law enforcement background. I took it as further confirmation of my suspicion all of his experience wasn't listed on the Bio page of his website. I knew he'd seen things, done things, the ordinary person couldn't imagine and wouldn't want to. And I'd never ask about any of it unless he wanted to share. He continued, "So I don't believe every magic fairy tale I hear unless I experience it myself, or know somebody I trust did."

I stretched my hand out and picked up the picture again. "Interesting, though. Very pretty. The real thing must be absolutely beautiful, full of changing colors. It even shows some of the colors in the picture."

Chad reached over and took it from my hand. "Does it? I don't see anything."

I looked again. "Hints here and there. Must be the lighting. And I'm pretty sure you'll be calling the—what did you call them? The Guardians?"

"First thing in the morning."

"I'm tired. You ready to go to bed?"

"Depends. How tired is tired?"

"Not that tired."

"Then let's go to bed."

* * *

We went to bed, but not to sleep. Until a bit later. And I dreamed. Dreaming's nothing unusual, of course. But these dreams were different. Reality superimposed on a fantasy backdrop. Or maybe they were fantasy superimposed on a backdrop of reality. Technicolor visions of a woman, me but not me. Of a man who was Chad, but not Chad. Of a place that was Rome, but not Rome.

In my dream, the woman swam naked in an outside pool, moving away from the man. But not in fright. She raised up on her arms and lifted herself out of the pool, laughing down at the man who swam after her. He grabbed her waist and pulled her back down into the water, into his arms. And then the scene shifted to a banquet hall full of people and someone was talking to the man, someone of authority, giving commands. The woman stood to the side, ears straining to hear. I felt sharp spikes of fear, buzzing like bees, flying at light speed inside her. The vision moved

147

into a big arena, full of sand, a crowd screaming, full of anticipation. Like an American crowd at the Super Bowl. Charioteers surged out into the big track. I felt panic gathering in my chest, a scream building in my lungs. And then I woke up. Shaking violently, pouring sweat, and gasping for breath.

"Ariel!" Chad had me, gathered up against his chest, stroking my hair. I was still shaking. "What? What is it?"

"Dream." I shuddered against him, beginning to quieten. "Just a dream. But it was so—and nothing really happened, it wasn't like a nightmare, I didn't see anything to make me panic, it's more like something was coming."

"You're awake. And you're here. And you're with me. Nothing's ever going to hurt you when you're with me. You know that, right?"

I nodded my head against him. I knew that. Nothing was going to hurt me. But what would stop something from hurting him? Nope, not going to bring that up. Not tonight. I settled against his side and went back to sleep.

Chapter Twenty-Seven

The next morning I woke to winter sunlight streaming through the big plate-glass windows of the bedroom. I heard Chad's voice from the Great Room. What time was it, anyway? I glanced over at the clock. Nine-thirty. Nine-thirty?! I hadn't slept that late in I couldn't remember when. I got up, grabbed my robe, and followed the smell of coffee out the door.

Chad was over at his desk unit, on the land line. I waved as I followed the coffee trail and he waved back.

"...love the way you always wait till the Statute's bout to run, Jimmy. You ever gonna learn?"

Ah. The life of a process server. He had an SOS call from an attorney who needed to get a complaint served yesterday because the two-year Statute of Limitations was about to catch him. Who'd driven his secretary nuts getting the complaint and service package pulled together when he'd probably had the case sitting in his office for at least a year. Either that, or he'd filed the complaint and depended on the county Sheriff's Department to serve it, which was fine if the person being served was an ordinary citizen with a real address where they actually lived. Not so much if the person being served wasn't a particularly upstanding citizen and moved around a lot.

I poured my coffee. I knew this story, even if I was hearing only one side of it.

"Jimmy. One more time. If you got two addresses and both of 'em are six months old, and I go out there and neither one of 'em's any good, you get charged for both addresses and then I have to come back here and do a skip trace anyway. If you let me do the skip trace, then I run 'em till I find 'em and you don't pay anything if I don't find them." Okay, that meant the attorney on the other end of the phone didn't even know where the dude he needed served actually was.

"But if the skip trace shows 'em five hundred miles from either address you got, you've saved a lot of money by just letting me find 'em in the first place...Jimmy! Those damn locator programs you have access to run six months behind and you know it! Mine don't. That's why people call me." And that meant the attorney on the other end of the phone didn't want an irate client when he had to tell them *ooopps*, guess what, folks? You uh, sorta, kinda, can't sue 'em now 'cause we waited too late to file the complaint. No way was he going to admit he'd waited too long. Probably he'd say his secretary calendared it wrong. But he sure as heck didn't want to spend any money on it because clients whose claims had lapsed under the Statute of Limitations due to an attorney's error weren't too keen on paying that attorney's expenses.

I laughed. I couldn't help it. Attorneys were the same everywhere. They all wanted the job done before they even knew they needed it but they never believed anybody else's expertise in getting that job done was worth paying for.

"Okay, I'm waiting on it. Send me what you got...No, Jimmy. I don't think I can serve the damn complaint. I know I can. So do you, or you wouldn't have called me."

He hung up and held his arms out to me. I laughed and came and sat in his lap, holding my cup carefully.

"Watch it! This coffee's hot, we don't need to scald ourselves."

"Not as hot as you are, baby girl."

"Beginnin' to wonder if you still thought so. You didn't wake me up. Why'd you let me keep sleeping?"

"You needed it. Been an eventful week, what with Vegas and weddings in the Tunnel of Love Drive-Thru, and bringing in bounties, and bringing down serial killers. And besides, you were real restless last night after that dream of yours woke you up. Wanta tell me about it?"

"Wouldn't know what to tell. Just dreams of people who were us. But not us. In places I knew but didn't know. So. An attorney with a deadline. Depending on somebody else to beat it for him."

"You know, I'd have loved you just as much no matter what you did for a living. But it is real handy, you being able to follow conversations like that and know exactly what's going on on the other end of it."

"He gonna let you skip trace the guy?"

"Oh, yeah. He can't afford the time for me to backtrack if those two addresses he's got from six months ago aren't right. I'd make more money if I just took their addresses and ran with 'em, but then whoever I'm looking for would be really hard to find. 'Cause every friend and relative I hit trying to get to 'em would be dialing their cell number before we got out of the driveway. You going to settle in today, unpack? Set up your desk?"

"That'll take me two minutes. All I've got is what's with me. We didn't exactly plan on all this excitement, I'd sorta thought I'd have a chance to get some more of my things." Not that that was a problem, since Stacy was taking over my apartment lease. "And I hate to mention this, but we really do need to see about getting my car down here."

"Like hell. Your car's a twelve year old Civic, honey. Tell Antsypants to sell it. We'll go car shopping in a day or two."

My frugal nature, honed by years on a secretary's salary, screamed in protest. "There's nothing wrong with my car!"

"So let's get you a new one while there's nothing wrong with the old one and you can get some money out of it."

"I'm still goin' to need my clothes, you know."

"We can go clothes shopping, too, whatever you need till we run back to Macon."

"You don't like my clothes either?"

"I love your clothes. But you're not in a law office anymore. I'm thinking you're going to be mostly in blue jeans. Like me, you didn't notice? You've always bought mostly for the office. All secretaries do. Now you need to buy for comfort and a different type of style. For the house, for the road. Part of this job is blending in with everybody else. Unless we've got a job where we need to look like deadbeats. Or sometimes, high-rollers. Depends on the job. "

I eyed him cautiously.

"Or drug-dealers. Or bikers."

"Well—yeah."

What absolute freedom I had now! I could live every fantasy I ever thought about.

"You gonna let me be bait? Like in a bar?"

"If you want to and the occasion arises. And if I'm sure it's a situation I can handle. 'Cause actually, that'd be pretty damn handy on occasions. These tough-guy types, they'll sure cozy up to you a lot better'n they'll cozy up to me. You could slap a service on one of 'em before I could even strike up a conversation to verify the name. But don't worry, they sure as hell won't be getting cozy enough to scare you or hurt you. "

I laughed. "You mean there're actually situations you don't think you can handle?"

"When it comes to you, all bets are off. I'll keep pushing buttons on a smart-ass trying to refuse service if I'm sure the worst thing'll happen is me and the other guy'll both end up in the Emergency Room. Not if you're in the mix, though."

I moved to get up. "Well, let me go get dressed and I'll set up my laptop. That other desk looks mighty lonely. Tell me when you want some breakfast." One thing we'd discovered early on. Neither of us were big breakfast eaters until we'd been up a while. Breakfast tasted best about two hours after being fully mobile.

"Been getting breakfast by myself for a while now, don't expect you to turn into a cook-on-demand, you know. Or maid on-demand."

I kissed his cheek. "I know. That's why it's so much fun to spoil you a little. Because you don't expect it."

The little yellow envelope on the computer screen signaled the arrival of a new email. "Bet that's the info for today's skip trace. You're going to teach me how it's done, aren't you?"

"Yes ma'am, I surely am."

* * *

I went to dress, which in my case translated into washing my hair and blowing it dry. I wasn't functional till I washed my hair in the morning, it was my re-set button. My make-up routine was fine-tuned from years of office life and accomplished in five minutes. And I dressed in blue jeans and a cotton sweater, reveling in the novelty of blue jeans on a week day. Oh, yeah, I could get used to this real quick.

Chad was in front of the computer, staring at the screen.

"Want breakfast yet?"

No answer. I walked up behind him and looked at the screen. It was full of variations of the same names with different social security numbers and addresses.

"Chad?"

No answer. He didn't hear me. He wasn't, in fact, even here, I didn't think. He'd told me once that every good profiler was a psychic and every good lawman was a profiler. I knew exactly what he was doing. He wasn't thinking, exactly, he was absorbing. And when he'd finished absorbing, he'd process it and then he'd either know where this skip was or where to start looking for him. Right now, I was superfluous.

I started back towards the kitchen and paused, looking at my laptop. I'd set it down next to the desk and it was still in its carry case. I refilled my coffee cup

153

and then came back to the desk. Two minutes later, my laptop was plugged in and up and running. I hadn't written in a good while. I'd just finished a novel when Chad popped into my world and turned it upside down, and I hadn't started another one. Ideas had to "brew" in my brain for a while. And when they'd brewed enough, one character or another got up and started walking and talking. When that happened, it was time to start writing. And I was living with a walking, talking character.

I sat down and started typing.

"No lightning bolt streaked from the sky the day my life as I knew it began to end..."

* * *

I didn't come out of the world I was creating—well, in this instance, re-creating might be a better description—until a cup of fresh coffee passed under my nose. I started and looked at the time in the corner of my computer screen. Almost one o'clock. Little late for breakfast or even brunch, but there was a tantalizing aroma of bacon in the air.

I took the cup from Chad's hand, pushed the chair back and stood to stretch.

"So how long did you stay in your trance?" I asked. "'Cause you were certainly in one when I came out from washing my hair. Is that bacon I smell?"

"Couple of hours, maybe. I thought BLTs for lunch would be good and you'd probably be hungry. I always am when I've been concentrating that hard, and you could give me lessons on the trance thing."

"You've never seen me in the writing zone before. So, you know where your guy is?"

"Not exactly, but I know where to start looking. Wanta go on the hunt tonight?"

"Sure. Did you check on our Mr. Oliver Hedgepath while you were in that trance, too?"

"With the Guardians, you mean?"

154

"Uh-huh."

"I called, they haven't called back yet."

"You mean you leave the Guardians a voice mail and they just—get back with you? By phone?"

"They got day jobs, darlin'. Everybody's got to eat. How'd you think anybody talked to 'em if not on the phone?"

"Oh, I don't know. Telepathically, maybe."

"I'm good, baby girl, I ain't that good."

I laughed. "I'm actually glad to hear that. And I'm starving. Lunch and then skips? And the Guardians? Whenever they call back?"

"My perfect day."

* * *

After our bacon, lettuce and tomato sandwich lunch, we hit the road. Chad didn't have a definite address on today's subject to be served, but he had the family network. A big one. And leaving at three would get us over to the general area of a little crossroad called Wixford, near the southwestern border of Georgia, between five and six o'clock. Chad considered that prime hunting time. He even had a phrase for it. "After the school buses run."

It seems Mr. Darrell Killman, detained while trying to leave the scene of an accident, hadn't seen fit to keep his insurance company—or anyone else, for that matter—advised of his whereabouts after that accident. Further, he'd managed to keep his location to himself for almost two full years, thus avoiding service of any lawsuit. Today, though, his luck was about to run out.

We ran though the Georgia backcountry, pasture land dotted with lakes and circled by trees. The phone rang about halfway there. The dashboard screen identified the caller as simply "G". No great intellect needed there. The conversation came in loud and clear over Sync.

"Yo, Magic Man! Whut up?"

155

I wasn't sure what I'd expected but that wasn't it. Then again, I'd never expected Spike, the big, black-bearded bear dressed in black leather I'd met in Vegas, to be a pediatrician either.

"Got a persistent little gnat by the name of Oliver Hedgepath all up in the air with some story of there being some new Seer for one of the Tears of Isis. He's head hauncho at some society calls itself—"

"Resurrection. Ollie's harmless enough. So's Resurrection. Unless something's changed. Why's he's calling you? A new Seer?"

"You know about him then?"

"Yeah, been around about ten years or so. Got an old house outside some little town in your neck of the woods, Rebecca, Georgia, I think that's the place."

"Gone uptown and upscale since then, G. Address he gave me is Bull Street. Savannah, Georgia. You know what real estate costs on Bull Street in Savannah, Georgia?"

"Not off-hand, sorta out of my territory but from that tone I'm guessing a lot?"

"Multiplied by several times. For the average Joe, fixer-uppers on Bull Street aren't really in the budget. When's the last time you looked at Resurrection? Did it have a big membership fee attached to it?"

"Haven't looked in years." G's voice, whoever G really was, sharpened. "And you think we'd ignore something like a membership fee, big or little, attached to a something on the fringes of magic? Way to insult somebody, Magic Man. Of course there's not. There wasn't any fee at all. You mean there is now?"

"Don't have a figure but I threw out some bait while I was fishing last night and from the reaction, yeah, there is. You mean Ollie never set off any vibes with any of you when you checked him out?"

"Not a one. But that was a long time ago. Too much going on to keep up with everybody. And he's damn sure set something off with you, huh?"

"Appearing on my deck in the form of a golem powered by astral projection while I'm in the hot tub with my wife is not the way to endear oneself to me, no. Especially when Thor didn't have a clue he was there until he was like—already there. Know what I mean?"

"The Oliver Hedgepath I know doesn't have that kind of power. You don't have that kind of power. Hell, nobody should have that kind of power! It's too close to the edge. And I heard you'd found your Wit for War-N-Wit, congratulations."

"Thank you. And exactly. This Oliver Hedgepath's short, prissy, precise. Well-dressed in a fussy sort of way. Well, the golem was. That sound like him?"

"Yeah, but anybody who can power a golem like that could probably sustain a glamour without any trouble. At least when he needed to. So looking like the Ollie of record wouldn't be that big a problem. What's he want from you?"

"Thinks I might be the new Seer. Or so he says. And if I'm not, then he wants me to find him. The new Seer. Allegedly so he can be sure the new Seer's not on the dark side."

"He's using a golem powered by astral projection and he's worried about somebody else being on the dark side?"

"My point exactly. I'm thinking he might be thinking if he can find the new Seer and eliminate him, the Seer's power might revert back to him. If, in fact, he ever had it."

"He had it. Or at least, the Oliver Hedgepath I knew did. You definitely need to check this out. When are you supposed to meet him?"

"Friday night. At Resurrection Headquarters on Bull Street. Which is okay, I'm always up for a trip to Savannah. I want to walk River Street and Bay Street with my wife. Vegas got cut kinda short."

G laughed. "So I heard. Definitely check this out thoroughly. Consider yourself on assignment with all fringe benefits."

"There are no fringe benefits. Not even expenses. And how the hell you know about Vegas?"

"Exactly. So why the hell you think we'd turn a blind eye to a big membership fee in a paranormal based society, I don't know. Didn't hear about Vegas so much as Atlanta. You don't think taking down a serial killer with 21 bodies in his basement makes the headlines? And tell Wit hello for me. Sitting right there, isn't she?"

"She is."

"Well, hello, Mrs. Magic Man. Welcome. To the world of magic!"

"Thank you," I said. "I think."

* * *

We rolled into Wixford and on through it, turning onto a State Highway. The skip-trace had shown a good portion of the Killman family lived off that state highway, on a few side roads. I hoped the last name wasn't prophetic. Killman wasn't all that reassuring.

"First stop," Chad said, pulling into a driveway. It was pretty typical of rural Georgia. An older house of red brick, fifties' style. It could use some paint on the trim. And some work in the yard. Some maintenance on the concrete driveway wouldn't be amiss, either. It sported a network of cracks. An outbuilding boasted several sets of mounted deer skulls. "They always run home to Mama, general vicinity, anyway, but sometimes brothers and sisters don't like each other all that much. Sibling rivalry, you know." His eyes moved around the yard. Assessment mode. "So sometimes you'll get more out of them. Or, more likely, out of their sibling-in-laws. This is his brother's house. Sister-in-laws don't usually like family moochers. Stay here for right now." He opened the door and started to get out. A loud slam sounded from the side of the outbuilding and a woman started walked towards us. Chad paused. "And maybe I'll stay right here, too."

158

The woman stopped about five feet away from the Equinox.

"Hep ya?" she asked.

"Hope so," Chad responded. "Mrs. Killman?"

"That's me."

"Nice to meet you, ma'am. Chad Garrett. This is my wife, Ariel."

The woman nodded at us.

"We're trying to get in touch with a Darrell Killman. Understand he's your brother-in-law?"

Mrs. Killman's mouth puckered as though she'd bitten into a sour apple. "Well, some things we got no control over."

"Yes, ma'am, I understand."

"What's he done now?"

"Well, I don't know that he's done anything, ma'am, it's just that he was involved in an accident a few years back and seems nobody can locate him. Insurance companies kinda like to keep tabs on the folks involved until everything's settled, you know?"

I couldn't decide if Mrs. Killman actually chewed tobacco and needed to spit, or if there was a wad of chewing gum in her mouth and talking about her brother-in-law just made her want to spit.

"Oh, hell, yeah, I remember that. Jerk tried to run 'fore the cops got there, like he's always run from everything. Almost ended up in jail. Glad somebody stopped him, he's caused the family enough trouble without making us bail him out of jail. My mother-in-law, she'd do anything for that boy. Most of his problem."

"Yes, ma'am. So do you have any idea where we could find him now?"

Mrs. Killman narrowed her eyes. "Well, he's been running in and out of his mama's house for the past few months, but you go there, she's gonna try to tell you she don't know where he is. And if he's really not there right when you are, she's gonna tell him somebody's lookin' for him." Oh, yeah. Mama would. This Mrs. Killman was a smart lady. "But she's been braggin' he's turned a new leaf and got a job he's actually workin', but I don't know where at. They don't live real close, the family's scattered through four or five counties. Tell you what, though. You need to talk to Grandpa. My husband's granddaddy. Tough ole' bird, love him to death. Don't like freeloaders, pissed as shit Darrell is takin' such advantage of his mama, pissed as shit at Arlene for lettin' him do it. I mean, Arlene's 50, but she's still that man's little girl, you know?"

"Yes, ma'am, I'm sure. How do we get to Grandpa's?"

"Well, thing is, he's up at his lake house with Grandma on a fishing trip. And it's a couple of hours from here on some real back country roads."

I didn't laugh but it was a near thing. We were on what was about as back a country road as I'd ever seen. But apparently there were back country roads and then there were "real" back country roads.

"Is there any way you might consider giving me Grandpa's phone number? Or getting him on the phone for me so I could just talk to him?"

"Don't mind a bit giving you his phone number. Or callin' him for you. But honey, he ain't gonna answer it. Won't even know it's ringin'. Don't have a land phone at the lake place, they both got cells, but neither one of 'em ever answer it. Leave 'em turned off unless they want to use 'em. They don't even know how to work voice mail, wouldn't call you back if they could. Worries us all to death, but what can you do? Can't hogtie 'em."

"Ok. Next request. Can you give us directions?"

"Honey, I'll do better'n that. I'll draw you a map. 'Cause you'll need it. When you get there, tell him Betsy sent you."

* * *

160

We needed it. I'd never realized there were so many unmarked and unnamed roads in the state. The last three roads had been dirt.

"You know, the pisser is we're probably gonna end up twenty miles from where we started," I said.

"Or not. She said Arlene didn't live real near, family was scattered over four or five counties. In Georgia, that could mean a hundred miles, you know how big these rural counties are."

"True." I squinted at the hand-drawn map. "Okay! Last turn should be coming up on your right."

Sure enough, the last one on the right turned out to be the actual driveway. I could see lake water sparkling under the moon.

"This time you get out with me. A couple walking up to a door won't look as threatening as a man alone to two old people in an isolated cabin. Don't wanta give 'em heart failure."

"No problem. Other than walkin'. My legs are numb."

We parked and walked up to the door. Grandpa, in blue jeans and a red flannel shirt, flung it open before we could knock.

"Who the hell are you and what you doin' up here at this hour?"

"Betsy gave us directions, sir. Said you'd be the best man to talk to."

"Betsy? Well, hell! Best granddaughter of the bunch, by blood or marriage! Get on in here, get that little lady out of the cold!"

It was, in fact, pretty damn cold, but I knew Chad made it a point never to enter a house if he didn't have to.

"I'm fine, sir, thank you, we don't want to intrude."

"Roy?" That must be Grandma. Baby blue fleece robe, tight silver blue curls, the kind that came from a once a week beauty shop wash and set and frequent perms. "Roy, it's twenty-eight degrees out there! You get that child into this house right now! Betsy sent 'em?"

"That's what they say," he yelled back to Grandma, then shook his head at Magic Man. "Don't argue with Mae when she's on a roll—you'll just make the rest of my night miserable! Get on in here!"

A roaring fire crackled from the interior. Chad pulled me gently. "Come on, honey, they're worried about you. They're good folks."

Yes, they were. I could feel it.

"So why'd Betsy send you way up here?" Grandpa asked, waving his arms to shoo us inside. "Go on, go on, sit down!"

"How you take your coffee, folks?" Grandma called over the kitchen bar.

"Black, please!" This was my third "field-trip" with Chad, but my first serve. I wasn't sure if it was proper protocol to take that coffee, but I didn't care. The opportunity hadn't come up during my bounty-hunting training in Vegas when I tackled the runaway ho. It hadn't come up during the stake-out for the serial killer in Marietta, either. But I was taking it anyway. We hadn't seen a convenience store in the last hour. I needed that coffee.

Chad explained our mission. Grandpa wasn't upset at us, but he was pretty steamed at grandson Darrell. And not too happy with daughter Arlene.

"That little asshole! Arlene's spoiled that boy all his life, she's flat-out ruint him! Whole problem with America, spoiled brats never made to act like men! Hell, she didn't do a lot better with Donnie, Betsy's twice the man that boy is!"

I hoped Betsy never heard that compliment. She'd been really helpful to us.

"Yeah, he's been laying out at Arlene's past few months off and on. Right now, though, he's workin' at the Burger Palace over in Arnett, Arlene said he had an apartment over there, means he's at some flophouse, mor'n likely. Don't got the flophouse address, but ain't but one Burger Palace in Arnett, it's on the main drag when you run through town. What there is of it."

"So I go back to the main highway and—"

"Oh, hell no, son! Go back out my driveway, turn right, not left headin' back the way you come, just turn right and keep on going. Five miles down the dirt, runs right into Grover Mill Road. Turn right, stay straight 'bout ten miles, runs right into the State Highway to Arnett. Turn left, Arnett's 'bout fifteen miles down that road. Save you an hour and a half, easy. It's damn near as straight as the crow flies."

I stood and we made to leave. Chad turned back to the old couple.

"We really appreciate this," he said. "And we appreciate the hospitality. But sir, I got to tell you—I wish you wouldn't invite strangers into your home like this. It's really not safe, we could have been serial killers for all you knew."

Grandpa snorted. "Boy. This old man didn't fall off the turnip truck yesterday and I ain't lived this long without knowin' who to trust. Ain't just any strangers gettin' invited in. But even without tellin' me Betsy sent you, I'da known. Known you two were righteous folks."

Chad smiled. Grandpa had a spark of magic. It wasn't terribly strong, but it was strengthened by the common sense gleaned in what had to be almost eighty years of living. Grandpa and Grandma were all right. On impulse, I leaned over and gave Grandma a hug.

"Miss Mae, I do believe that coffee saved my life tonight. Thank you so much."

She hugged back. "Wait, child. Let me get you a Dixie cup. Some to go, don't you know?"

* * *

We pulled out of the driveway and turned right, armed with coffee to go in Dixie cups. Grandpa's directions got us into Arnett in forty-five minutes.

Damn good thing, too. Arnett looked to be rolling up its sidewalks.

The Burger Palace was on the left, about half-way down the State Highway. The parking lot was empty, but the lights were on inside. Two broom-wielding teenagers were silhouetted through the windows.

"It's probably locked," I said.

"That's what drive-thru windows are for, baby girl."

"Yeah, we've got a real affinity for drive-thru windows, all right."

He grinned. "Well, this time we're already married and we're not in Vegas, so what say we just get us a deadbeat. Or a hamburger. Or both. I'm kinda hungry."

"Business before pleasure."

"Absolute."

He pulled around the building and up to the window. Already closed, of course. He let the window all the way down and honked the horn. Nobody paid any attention. He honked again. Nobody paid any attention. He slammed his hand down on the horn and kept it there.

Finally, a heavy-lidded kid with scraggly blonde hair falling out of its tied back ponytail came to the window and hit the intercom button.

"We're closed!" He started to turn away and Chad laid on the horn again.

"What's your problem, mister?" His eyes were open now, but his voice squeaked.

Magic Man let the window down and asked, "Is Darrell Killman working tonight?"

"Yeah. He's the manager."

Gee. I wouldn't have thought from Betsy and Grandpa's descriptions little ole' Darrell'd be capable of managing the Burger Palace.

"I need to talk to him. Get him out here, please."

"He's counting the registers, he ain't gonna come." The kid started to turn away again.

"Hold it!" Chad produced a small bright pink piece of paper that he held up to the window for the kid to read. With his other hand he held up his PI badge.

"Son, you need to open that window, take this piece of paper and read it and then you need to get Darrell over here to talk to me."

"Done tole you! We're counting money, we ain't opening that window! You want me to call the cops?"

"If you don't listen to what I'm saying, I'll be the one calling the cops. Let me give you the gist of what this paper says. It says you're about to commit a third degree felony. Federal law prohibits interference with service of process pursuant to Title 18 U.S.C. 1501. And that anybody—in this case, you—who knowingly and willingly obstructs, resists, or opposes any officer of the United States or other person—that would be me—duly authorized in serving or attempting to serve or execute any legal or judicial writ of process of any court of the United States is subject to fine or imprisonment or both." He dropped the pink sheet and held up his phone so the kid could see it. "So one more time. I need Darrell Killman at this window. Now. And my finger's on the 9 of the 911 call. They respond real fast to fellow officers of the Court."

"Hold it! Just a damn minute! I'll get him!"

"Better be to this window son."

The kid disappeared, and Chad eased the SUV back down the side of the building, into the darkness of the back parking lot and cut the engine and the lights. He opened his door and swung his legs out.

"What're you doin'?" I asked.

"Baby girl. He's gonna come flying out the back door."

Two seconds later a spill of light hit the blackness. There was a soft click as a door closed.

"Bingo!" Chad said softly, and then he was gone. It always amazed me, how fast he could move. I doubted I'd ever get used to it.

Killman, who was short for a man and pudgy by anybody's standards, didn't stand a chance. Chad ran right past him and blocked his path.

"It's not polite to leave without saying goodby."

"Okay, mister, what the hell you want?"

"I want you to sign this," Chad handed him a pen and the service copy of the complaint.

"What is it?"

"It's a return of service on an official lawsuit, now properly served by a duly authorized individual. Me. You need to get a lawyer for any more information than that. Sometimes I'll explain better to folks but not when they try to skip out on me."

"I ain't gotta take this!" The service copy hit the ground.

"You don't have to take it, buddy, I just have to leave it. And when you don't take it—and sign for it, 'cause I don't like any doubt I've done my job and the right person's served—I just add in to my report to the Court that the subject was uncooperative, belligerent and tried to avoid service. Judges don't like that much when they get a case in front of 'em and start looking at it."

Killman glared. "Okay, I'll sign for it."

Chad shrugged. "Up to you. But you're the one threw it down on the ground, I'm not picking it up."

Killman glared harder. He bent and picked up the papers and the pen. "Where do I sign?"

"Right here." Chad pointed. Killman scribbled. Chad took his part of the paperwork and left Killman his. "You have a good night now," he said, and walked back up to the Equinox.

"You never asked them if they had any burgers left," I said while he buckled his seat belt. "We're both hungry."

"Yeah, but if they had any left, they'd spit in them before they handed them over. We're only about 15 miles from I-75. Something'll be open on the way home."

Chapter Twenty-Eight

It was nearing dark when we hit the outskirts of Savannah for our Friday night appointment with Resurrection and Oliver Hedgepath. I was sorry to be away from my new home this early, even for a few days. I loved Pine Whisper Plantation. Everything about it. Thor, the farm animals, the cats. That black cat, especially. There was something about that cat, though I couldn't exactly peg it. Buddy said he wasn't social, but over the last few days, I'd seen him constantly out of the corner of my eye. Like he was checking me out. Watching me. Weighing me. Oh, well. Buddy was in charge of the animals when we were gone and he'd promised to keep a special eye on him. It went without saying Thor'd be sleeping on his bed with him.

Chad navigated smoothly through the Savannah streets. The huge live oaks sporting their beards of Spanish Moss curtained the sidewalks, shadowy tendrils elongated in the winter dusk.

"How well do you know Savannah?" I asked.

"Pretty well."

"You knew Vegas pretty well, too."

"Yeah."

"And Atlanta. You know every major city in the country pretty well?"

"Nope. But I know a lot of 'em." He stared out into the dark. "Be glad to get this over with. Then we can do Savannah tomorrow and tomorrow night. How well do you know Savannah, baby girl?"

"Not at all. Been through it, read a lot about it, but I've never actually been in it."

"You're kidding, right? Not even for St. Patrick's Day?"

I knew Savannah was famous for its St. Patrick Day celebrations, just as I knew River Street was supposed to be the heart of Savannah, but I didn't know it from personal experience.

"Nope."

"You've sure led a sheltered life, darlin'. But that's kinda nice, actually, that you're seeing it for the first time with me. We'll play tourist tomorrow on the trolley car bus tours and then hit River Street and Bay Street tomorrow night. I know this steak house on Bay Street where the steak melts in your mouth. We might even hit River Street for a while tonight, too. Depends on Hedgepath and Resurrection, I guess."

He turned smoothly onto Bull Street. I stared gap-mouthed at the house on the corner as we passed it.

"Mercer House!"

"Yes, ma'am."

I'd seen it in pictures. Hell, I'd seen it on the movie screen, this house once owned by Savannah's own song writer Johnny Mercer but thrown into national prominence by *Midnight in the Garden of Good and Evil*. The movie screen didn't do it justice. Even in twilight—maybe especially in twilight—the house dominated the corner. Alive, almost. I actually heard Moon River wafting out onto the street. Chad drove on past and parked in front of a house near the end of the next block.

The house sat on the front of the lot. All the town houses did. City lots were narrow in any city. Savannah's houses stood proud, testaments to the hospitality of a more gracious time. The amount of iron work visible on each announced to the world the wealth of the original builders. The more ironwork, the richer the family. Historical fact. This house was different. It seemed to be folding in on itself, hugging darkness, holding it close.

As if to emphasize its affinity for the dark, the last vestiges of day left the sky as we walked up the steps.

"We're early," I said.

"By almost an hour."

"On purpose?"

"Yes, ma'am."

Out of the corner of my eye, a black cat streaked under the bushes. I started.

"What?" he asked.

I pointed. "A black cat. Just like ours. It went under the bushes."

"World's full of black cats, baby girl. Ours is two hours away, back at Pine Whisper. And anyway, cats aren't anybody's. They just are." He rang the bell. We stood, waiting, for at least three or four minutes. He rang it again. "And this is why we're early. Always good to keep somebody you're not real sure of off his guard."

"He could not even be here."

"He's here. He's just not staged as well as he'd like to be yet."

Chad was right. Hedgepath answered the door in another few minutes, but not like he was happy about it. His prissy preciseness was—off—somehow. Flustered.

"I believe I specified seven o'clock as our appointment time."

"Don't believe I specified that's when we'd be here."

"Common courtesy would dictate—"

"We can leave."

Hedgepath swallowed. Hard. He held the door wide. "Come in."

We entered the foyer. It was much as I'd expected in this style and era of house. Very spacious, squared, with arched openings into the rooms leading off its three walls. Black and white square marble tiling gleamed on the floor like an illuminated chessboard. A crystal chandelier hung from the domed ceiling. Twin tables with graceful curving legs in the Regency style flanked the largest arch in the longest wall, straight across from the front door. They were topped with matching Oriental urns filled with fresh flowers. It opened into what I supposed would be called the drawing room. Matching larger, heavier Oriental urns stood under both the tables. I supposed the rooms opening from the shorter walls would be called the sitting room, or the parlor. Or maybe the receiving room or the study. My ancestors hadn't moved in the social circles that made use of those rooms and I for damn sure didn't move in the society that still did.

Hedgepath gestured us towards the larger room. "I keep the Tear in its own special cabinet. In the drawing room."

Damn. I was right. A drawing room.

He walked up to a glass display case, museum quality, clear glass walls. The Tear of Isis lay against a bed of blood-red velvet, carefully presented like a shining diamond pendant in a jewelry store. It was absolutely stunning. I'd never seen anything like it. Fully an inch and a half long, it was a perfect crystal tear, elongated and shimmering with undercurrents of color that never quite materialized. Hedgepath opened the case and lifted it by its silver chain.

"So. Let's see what the Magic Man sees," he said, handing the chain over to Chad. "First you, by yourself. What do you see?"

Chad took it and held it in up so that it hung suspended in front of his eyes. His pupils narrowed and then expanded. I felt surprise ripple out. So. The Tear was real. And its power was real. I knew he hadn't been too sure of either. As to what he saw—now, that I didn't have a guess at. He lowered the Tear's chain.

"Nothing I didn't already know, actually," he said. "But yes, now I believe this is really one of the Tears of Isis. And that the legend is real. Which is more than I was sure of before."

Hedgepath laughed shortly. "Oh, ye of little faith! So. Now let's test the rest of it. We'll look together."

"Okay, let's get this over with. Though I don't really care to know what your past lives hold. I'll look with my wife."

"No! The two of you are so entwined that's no test at all! You're much more powerful than she is, you've probably tapped all her memories without even having to use the tear!"

"Well, damn," I said. "Insulting much?"

"Not to mention inaccurate," said my husband. "But just to satisfy you, Ollie, let's go ahead and do this."

"My name is Oliver."

"I can think of names much more appropriate. You want to test this or not?"

Ollie knew not to push any buttons. He moved over to stand beside Chad and Chad handed him the Tear. Hedgepath raised the chain of the Tear again, so that both of them gazed into it. This time, no surprises rippled out of Chad's mind and into mine. He didn't see anything. And he hadn't expected to. He'd never thought he was the Seer.

"Well?" Hedgepath asked impatiently.

"Well, I think it's pretty obvious," Chad said. "I don't see anything at all when I'm not holding it. Don't see a bit about any of your lives, Ollie. And I'm actually pretty pleased about that."

"That's impossible! I was a Knight! I rode under the banner of the Black Prince! I was with him at Crecy and Poitiers! I was one of the first Knights of the Garter!" In his agitation, he swung the Tear in an arc and it caught the light. And all at once I was floating in ether, looking down on a scene I didn't want to see. A fat, balding man in a red dressing gown, moving on top of a young girl half-dressed in the classic maid's uniform of England in the 1800's. He slobbered on her breasts while tears ran down her cheeks.

"Why, you liar!" I exclaimed. "You were a miserable fat slug of a man who raped the maid whenever your wife wasn't looking!"

Hedgepath stared at me in horror. Chad just grinned.

"I wondered about that." Magic Man laughed. "When old Ollie told us his power'd started fading in October. When did we first make contact, baby girl? October 5, if I'm not mistaken."

"That'd be it," I confirmed.

"See, Ollie, Ariel finding me—or me finding her—sort of triggered her powers. She was pretty powerful, even then, but she had no idea she was a witch. She didn't really believe it until December. That's when you lost the power completely, I believe you said."

"Impossible! No Seer has ever been a witch! The Seer is always a warlock! No witch has that kind of power!"

"Guess there's a new breed of witch in town," I said over Chad's laughter. "Better get used to it, Ollie. Anyway," I continued, while Hedgepath half-choked on his own ire, "Isis herself was female, what the hell makes you think she wouldn't pick a witch over a warlock any day of the week and twice on Sunday, you miserable little turdsniffer!"

I hadn't even thought of that particular epithet since fourth grade, but somehow, still furious at my vision of the fat, bald pig and the weeping girl, it seemed utterly perfect.

Chad laughed harder.

"This is a mistake! Whoever you saw was not me!"

"Like hell it wasn't! And we're leaving!"

"Works for me." Chad took my arm and we headed towards the door.

"No! Wait! We have to come to an understanding! Resurrection needs the services of the Seer! Whoever the Seer is! Please! I've readied a room for you—"

"When hell freezes over will we stay in a room in this house." I held tight to Chad's arm and spat back at Hedgepath. "We're leaving!"

"You're a witch, you don't give orders to warlocks!"

Chad held the door open for me, while I turned back for one last volley. I didn't spit in his face, but it was a near thing. "Like I said, Ollie. Oh, wait! Neville, wasn't it? Neville Thornsbury. Pig par excellence. There's a new breed of witch in town! Get used to it!"

* * *

I stormed out the front door, slightly ahead of Chad, and paused at the top of the walk. He threw his arms around me from behind and kissed the top of my head.

"That—was—awesome!"

I turned in his arms and he kissed my lips. "Absolutely awesome!" he said again.

"Can we get out of here, please?"

"Yes, ma'am!" He opened the door of the SUV and held out his hand, a courtly gentleman helping his lady into a carriage. I laughed. He liked to open the car door for me and help me in, but I frequently forgot and did it before he had the chance.

He came around and got in. As we pulled back into the street, a black streak shot out from under the bushes in Resurrection Headquarters' yard and through the bars of the wrought iron fence into the next yard.

"There's that black cat again," I said.

"Honey, he's not your black cat. I promise."

"Our black cat."

"Nope. Not even. He's yours. He's decided. You really oughta name him."

"Micah," I said, not even thinking about it.

"Okay, that was quick. Why?"

"Don't know. You don't like it?"

"Your cat, baby girl. His name's whatever you want it to be. I was just curious, you came out with it so fast. So. 'Fess up. You can be honest. You really don't like Hedgepath, do you?"

"Oh, I love him to death, you couldn't tell?"

"Not so's you'd notice, no."

I looked over at my husband's profile as he drove. There was a secret smugness in the lift of one corner of his mouth.

"You asshole!"

"Excuse me?"

"You knew the whole time. Didn't you?"

"Oh, hell, no, I didn't know. Remember, just because I knew the stories of the Tears of Isis didn't mean I believed them. I didn't disbelieve them, I was just—reserving judgment. But for him to latch onto me like that, considering the connection between us, it occurred to me he might actually be feeling your power, not mine. And then the timeframe, when he said his power started fading in October and was gone by the end of December. I believe it was actually Christmas Day you had your own private epiphany?"

Yes, it had been. Last Christmas Day had given me a gift I'd never thought any mortal could possess. The day I'd known with absolute certainty I was a witch.

"Don't know why that'd make you suspect it was me, though."

"I didn't right off. Not until we were back inside and you picked up the picture and looked at it. You said it had hints of color and I figured then—because to me it was clear as glass. Nothing special."

"And tonight when you saw the real thing?"

"More impressive, I'll admit. But I doubt I see it in its full glory like you do. To me, it just looks like a chandelier drop or something similar. I bet to you, it's brighter than a diamond."

"And you'd be right," I said. "I've never seen anything like it. And that pig shouldn't have the right to touch it!"

"Nope. So the question is—what're we gonna do about it?"

"And the answer is?"

"Time to check in with G."

"Who is G, anyway? Sounds like a James Bond character."

Chad laughed. "His name's Gabriel. Gabriel Smith. But the G's for Guardian."

"As in the Archangel?"

"Yeah, as in the Archangel."

I'd never thought I'd say such a thing in anything but jest, but all things considered, I wasn't completely joking when I asked, "Not really the Archangel, though. Right?"

"Lots of guys named Gabriel. But in all honesty, baby girl—sometimes I'm not real sure. And there's sure as hell a lot of guys named Smith, if you know what I mean."

"Welcome," I said. "To the world of magic."

* * *

We placed a call to G and left a message. Then we checked into the hotel on Bay Street where Chad had made reservations. I'd never spent any time in Savannah, but the Historic District, by all reports, rocked and Chad had been emphatic about staying there for the convenience of walking distance. And even in February, the temperature wasn't bad, though the night wind coming off the Savannah River made the forty-five degree temperature feel a lot colder. Our leather biker jackets and jeans and boots took care of that with no problem. We walked along Bay Street.

"Okay, baby girl. First things first. Food. Right up here. Steaks to die for."

Maybe so, but a quick glance at the menu told me the ribs weren't slouches, either. "I don't know if I want ribs or steaks."

"There's always tomorrow night, baby girl. You don't see another restaurant rings your bell, we'll come back here. But I bet you see plenty of places you'll want to try. Savannah's not short on restaurants. We'll try 'em all, one trip or another. I come back to Savannah as often as I can."

We both ordered steaks and munched on the fresh bread and ate our salads. And yes, the steaks melted in your mouth. The only problem was, I kept feeling a tingle. The kind you feel when there's a target painted on your back. A target someone's shooting daggers at. I glanced around, hampered by the high backs of the booths. The tables in view were occupied by older couples with younger couples. Probably parents and kids. Several held just younger couples. Others were young parents, out with the kids. A few were students. Savannah had a big college population since it had a very prominent art-technology college. Everybody seemed upwardly mobile or already well-established in life. A general cross-section of life in a good restaurant with mostly upper middle class patrons. I couldn't peg any source for the daggers.

"I hope G doesn't call us back right now. Be sorta hard to talk."

"Sure would. I turned the phone off. I'm having a night out on the town with my wife. But don't worry, he won't call till we're back in the room."

"You didn't give him a time."

"Didn't need to."

Our waitress came back to check on us. Diana, according to her name tag. Lovely girl, excellent at her job. I was pretty sure she was a student at that art-techno college. She seemed a bit more flustered with this table check than she had initially.

"Dessert?" she asked.

"Oh, I couldn't!" I declined.

"No, me either, thank you, Diana." It didn't surprise me he'd noted her name. Chad noticed everything. "Gotta save room for the candy shops."

"Headed down to River Street, huh?"

"Of course. Those hot pralines calling."

"Sweet Toots has homemade ice-cream in the back, too."

"We'll keep that in mind, thanks."

We crossed Bay Street and Chad headed to a set of steep, uneven stone steps. Savannah was a port city. Naturally, its first two streets had paralleled the shoreline. River Street itself was a product of the seafaring history. The incoming ships coming into the river from the deep channel corridor out of the Atlantic needed ballast in their cargo holds to sail to Savannah. That ballast usually consisted of New England rock. And that rock had to be removed from the cargo holds before the ships were re-loaded with the cotton they'd come to fetch in the first place. So what to do with the New England rock? Build Savannah streets, of course. Like River Street. Laid with rock from far away places. Lined with walls of the same material. Now it served cars and tour buses rather than horses and wagons. And the rails on which the cotton carts had run back and forth from the warehouses to the ships' bellies were still embedded in the street.

River Street was a low-lying street. So naturally part of that rock was used to build walls up against the land, a bulwark against the floods of the Savannah River. And atop that wall was born Bay Street, connected within every block to River Street by a series of steep, off-kilter steps.

How far off-kilter wasn't readily apparent until you were actually going down them. Each step was much higher than a normal step but no step was equidistant from the step above or below. I made use of the railings running with them with the hand not holding Chad's. Otherwise, I'da busted my ass.

Lights and noise spilled up into the hollows of the stair alcove.

"Here it is," Chad said. "Georgia's Bourbon Street."

Having led the sheltered life Chad had so rightly observed I'd led, I'd never been on Bourbon Street either, but the very words conveyed exactly the proper atmosphere. The sidewalks were so crowded the pedestrians spilled out into the cobbled street. And not a horn honked when they did. Cars moved slow on River Street. They were intruders, allowed only on sufferance. This was a street for people and everybody knew it.

We'd come down the stairs on the upper end of River Street. I looked down the sidewalk. And entered another world of sights and sounds and noises. Stores and shops ran along one side, occasionally cut by one of the alleys holding yet another set of connecting stairs to Bay Street. The other side of the street fronted the river and proliferated with sitting areas and benches and memorials for folks to sit by the water and view the docked ships. One of the riverboat tours night tours passed by as I watched, and the shuttle boat from one of the hotels across the bay unloaded its bevy of folks to walk along River Street.

Every other shop seemed to be a restaurant or a bar. Music blared out the open doors—standing room only inside. We moved down the sidewalk, holding hands. I was a newlywed, of course we held hands, but my grip was tighter than usual. I wasn't about to lose him in this crowd. Besides, I could still feel an occasional dagger hitting that target on my back.

One bar had a country rock band. A few shops down, another had blues. Further down, another featured karaoke. Between the bars stood clothing shops, souvenir shops, jewelry shops. And then, oh, wonder of wonders! The first of the many candy shops. Standing in front of the doors, you could smell the sugar. You could taste the sugar. The taste actually floated on the air, flavored with caramel and vanilla and the scent of hot, roasting nuts, mingled with honey and maple. Nobody could resist going in.

Conveyor belts and mechanical pulleys pulled and cut and wrapped the current batch of taffy, dumping the different flavors directly into each respective basket. There were lollipops and bubble gum and caramel apples and candy apples. Sample plates of pralines just out of the oven, cut into small pieces, sat out for the taking. I wasn't shy. I took one. Then I took another. Oh. My. Lord. It melted in your mouth. I'd never tasted anything like it. I was the proverbial kid in a candy shop.

We bought two pounds of hot pralines and moved back into the flowing crowds, down to a little jewelry shop displaying imported earrings. Okay, so they were the cheap kind. But they were gorgeous. Long, intricate swirls of filigree, dangling curlicues and patterns woven within the delicate strands of silver, stamped into the gold and bronze colored metals. I never actually wore this type of earring much. Suitable Ariel wore suitable jewelry. Tasteful hoops and studs, mid-size squares and buttons. These earrings? Not so much. Exotic. Suitable for clubbing. Like I'd ever clubbed. I bought three pairs. And I was gonna wear 'em whenever the fancy took me. Like every day, even.

Back on the sidewalk, street musicians started up two stores down, Motown style. The crowd gathered quickly, street dancing under the moon. Another dagger hit my back. I glanced around again. Out in the street, walking with a crowd that had shifted off the sidewalk, I saw our little waitress, Diana. Ah. That explained the extra tension I'd felt at her last check. She was ready to end her shift. Then I gasped, losing my balance, and grabbed Chad harder. A black cat shot out from under my feet, across the street, and over to one of the riverfront parks.

"Damn!" I exclaimed, regaining my balance. "Did you see that?"

"Yep. Black cats are after you tonight, baby girl. And no, it's not yours—Micah, you said? And no, it's not the same one we saw on Bull Street, either."

"I know. But still—coincidence much?"

"Witch much?" he retorted. "And now Seer of the Tear of Isis, too?"

'Don't remind me. Let's go get some of that homemade ice cream at Sweet Toots and sit by the river."

We got our ice cream cones and crossed the street to find a bench. We watched moonbeams dance on the waves and ripples of the river. I sighed and leaned against him. His arms tightened.

"You do know somebody's been watching us? Besides black cats, I mean," he whispered in my ear.

"Oh, yeah," I confirmed. "Since the restaurant. Shoulda known you'd know, too."

"Can't catch the same face anywhere, though. Passed some of the same faces a couple of times in the shops, but that wasn't it. Not the same twinge."

"I saw our little waitress right when that cat tripped me up. Out in the street crowd. But that's nothing strange, I'm sure a lot of the college kids work in the restaurants and I'm sure when they get off work, they hit River Street."

"Did you? I missed that, too busy making sure you didn't fall. But no, that's nothing strange. Hell, a lot of them live in the apartments over the stores down here."

"That'd be some college experience. Wonder how they manage to pass the first course."

"Well, at least they have a hell of a good time."

"True. I'm gettin' sorta tired."

"Then let's stop in at one of the places that sell the tour bus tickets so we'll have them in the morning. G oughta be checking in pretty soon, too."

"Tour bus?"

"You'll love it. Easiest way to see Savannah."

* * *

Chad turned his phone back on when we got to our room. Voice mail showed one message.

"And I'm sure we know from who," he said.

"Whom."

"Baby girl."

"Sorry, couldn't resist. Hedgepath?"

"Of course. Can't stay on the Seer's bad side."

I groaned. "Get it over with."

181

Chad laughed and sat down on the bed, patting the cover invitingly. I joined him and he played the voice mail.

Hedgepath's voice grated every nerve I had. "I apologize for any misunderstandings or miscommunications we may have had. However, the importance of this matter demands that we all put our personal differences aside—"

"*Yewwwwwwww,*" I said, over the message. "I can feel the slime from here!"

"—and handle this as befits adults for the good of mankind. The Seer has a responsibility to the Tear of Isis and I have a responsibility to make sure she realizes it. Please return this call so we can arrange a meeting to discuss the situation. Goodbye."

Chad burst out laughing. "Okay, way to win friends and influence people."

"Ain't it though? I'm the Seer even though I don't deserve it and he doesn't understand why in the hell I've been chosen, but he's going to make sure I do it right because I certainly don't have enough sense to handle it on my own. But—and this is the real question—Chad, what's he really after? Okay, so the Seer can see somebody's past lives. Great parlor trick. Good conversation piece. That won't buy you a cup of coffee. There's something else, there's got to be."

"Got to be. The Tear hasn't been the subject of a lot of research, but it's been speculated it's got other powers and properties. You feel any different? Notice anything different?"

"Let's see. In the last three months, I met a warlock soul-mate I've reincarnated with over quite a few centuries. I found out my baby sister's a ghost-whisperer. And oh yeah! I found out I'm a witch. And now I've found out I'm the Seer of the Tear of Isis. Different? Oh, no. My life's completely normal, what could be different?"

"You're beautiful when you're sarcastic."

"I know. Any ideas on what this other power or powers of the Tear could be? That I don't even know I have?"

"Not a clue. Other than whatever it is, it's got to be something that's generating Hedgepath money. And a lot of it. You wanta even guess a price tag on that house? On the furnishings?"

"No, I'd be scared to."

"Exactly."

"You think G's got a clue?"

"I hope so."

G must have radar. He picked that exact minute to call.

"Yo, Magic Man! Whut up?" Must be his standard greeting.

"There's a new Seer in town, all right," Chad said.

"But not you."

"And of course you knew that already. Just like you already know who the new Seer is."

"Kinda thought maybe, and so did you, don't lie about it. Her power's been growing so fast she's sending ripples into the mystic mix even up here. She's probably a damn tidal wave up close. Hello, new Seer. We got to get you a handle, Ariel. Something befitting. Snazzy but classy. I'll think on it. Lady Seer? Lady Tear? I'll think on it. So. What's the assessment on Hedgepath?"

"He's a pig. A slug. A megalomaniac. A miserable excuse for a man. An embarrassment to magic." Was that me? Taking over the conversation like I'd moved in the inner councils of high magic all my life?

G laughed. "You got to learn to be a little clearer there, we need more definite statements. Okay. Then he's not the original Oliver Hedgepath. Not the one I knew. Which I didn't think he was from your first phone call. Damn. I hate that. Ollie was a gentle man. That's two words, gentle man, not just gentleman. Though he was that, too. I hope he's all right, but I sure wouldn't lay any bets on it."

"Bottom line here, G," said Chad. "This past lives thing just isn't enough for all this. It has nothing of value insofar as any shyster or con artist could use for the type of money Hedgepath—or whoever the hell he is—has been pulling in, not even with whopping membership fees into Resurrection. Legend has it the Tear gives its Seer other powers. What are they? Anybody know? And by legend, the Tear picks its own Seer. It picked the original Hedgepath. It picked Ariel. You say the real Hedgepath was one of the good guys, a gentle man. Ariel picks up bugs and puts 'em back outside, I kid you not."

"Not all bugs," I said. "Just bugs like Daddy Long-Legs and Lady Bugs and stuff. I wouldn't put a cockroach back outside."

G laughed, and Chad continued. "So the Tear only entrusts its powers to white magic. How did this Hedgepath ever become the Seer in the first place? It would never have picked him, not for any length of time, no matter how short."

"Don't know," said G. "But I'm going to put some research people on it. Get back with you as soon as I get any answers. Or don't get any answers, as the case may be."

"Hedgepath left us a message he wanted a meet."

"Of course he does."

"Be nice to know a little something before we see him again."

"Set it for tomorrow night. I'll try to have something for you before then. And I wouldn't call him back until morning, either. Let him sweat. Because whatever the reason is, he's damn sure sweating."

"My thoughts exactly." Chad agreed and said goodbye. Then he tossed the phone on the the nightstand and grabbed me, falling back onto the pillows. "Savannah's such a romantic city," he said. "Such a great place to finish an interrupted honeymoon." He reached over and clicked off the lamp.

Tossed clothes. Tangled sheets. Entwined limbs. Moving mouths. The magical melding and merging, every time a first time. Electrical current building in intensity to circuit overload. Always, amazement at the coolness of his body against mine, never overpowering, never oppressive.

"No man outside out the pages of a romance novel knows how to make love like that," I whispered, my mouth against his neck.

"You always say that," he whispered back.

"Always true."

"Because you taught me. Over many years."

"And you always say that."

"Always true."

We slipped into slumber together and I chased dreams throughout the night. Or maybe they chased me. Through prisms of light, ever shifting, scenes in flash mode, bright as daylight. The man and woman I'd dreamed of our first night back at Pine Whisper Plantation. Me and not me. Chad and not Chad. In a grand epic thrown against a panoramic screen. Rome. White togas. Rich purple. Deep crimson.

White columns of marble stretched out against the brilliant blue of the Mediterranean sky. Always, floating in the fringes of every scene, the profile of a warrior, a screaming eagle emblazoned on the sides of his helmet, the distinctive crest of a Roman soldier proud at the crown. The image solidified. Caeso Gellius Acilianus. The name so clear it could have been a credit at the end of the panoramic epic that filled my dreams.

The woman stood beside him. Livia Rufinus. At a state dinner. And then in their home, the privacy of their own baths. Then in the stables, spirited horseflesh surrounding them. I could smell the stable smells. In the markets, fresh fruit, the smell of citrus tangy in the air. Jewelry, pottery. Furs. The known universe, consolidated into one open-air market.

Gellius Acilianus. Chad Garrett. Roman soldier. Bounty hunter. His personality hadn't changed much from that life to this, and probably not in any intervening ones. He didn't give a damn about the rules now, and he hadn't then. Which is why I sat in the Roman Coliseum, heart pounding, holding screams within. Furious with Gellius. Enraged at the Roman Powers that be. Waiting. Waiting for the charioteers to emerge from the doors and enter the track. He, a patrician of Rome, didn't have to do this. Or he wouldn't have had to, had he been able to play the game, keep his mouth shut and his opinions private. Though there was something else, too, something just out of the range of my dream.

I chased the dream for it, that something else, but the cacophony of noise distracted me. Roaring crowds, pounding horse hooves, clash of metal on metal, hideous sounds of wheel spokes cut by the wicked razor-sharp blades of the other chariots as they jockeyed for position. In my dreams, one chariot flipped, end over end. My private movie screen moved in slow motion, the body falling beneath the hooves and wheels of the other chariot, tangled in reins. Gellius Acilianus. Broken. The sand absorbed the rivers of blood pouring from his body. In the stands, I started screaming. And didn't stop.

* * *

"Ariel! Ariel, wake up! Wake up, damn it!"

Chad leaned over me, shaking my shoulders. I gasped, and he grabbed me and pulled me to his chest.

"What in the hell happened? You wouldn't wake up, you scared the shit out of me! I hope the police don't knock on the door. Anybody who heard that's gonna think somebody's getting murdered!"

I sorted myself back into the present. Chad Garrett. Ariel Garrett. Savannah. Not Rome. Not Livia Rufinus.

Not Gellius Acilianus. Maybe not now, but he used to be. Gellius, I mean. And Livia owed him one.

I did something I'd never done in my life to any living human being, something I'd never believed I'd do. I pulled away from him, reared back, and slapped him. Hard.

"*Owwwww!!!* What the hell was that for?"

I glared, though I'm sure that wasn't noticeable in the dark.

"That was for Livia, Gellius! Since she never got a chance to do it! 'Cause you were dead! 'Cause you couldn't play well with the big boys! Just couldn't keep your mouth shut!"

"Oh, shit. You didn't see that in the Tear, though, I made sure I was turned away from you. Just in case."

"I don't think the Seer always needs the Tear. Especially for themselves."

"Now if you could just figure out what else the Seer can do."

I lay back down and turned on my left side, my back snuggled close to his chest. "I'll sleep on it. You seriously think anybody heard me screamin'? How loud was I?"

"To me, pretty damn loud, but I think that was just 'cause you scared me to death when I couldn't wake you up. But these rooms are supposed to be sound-proofed, so I doubt the cops'll show up."

"Hope not," I said. Must be something about the flashbacks. Exhaustion hit me. I closed my eyes and went out like a light.

Chapter Twenty-Nine

Another voice mail from Hedgepath greeted us when we got up, his usual nauseating blend of superiority trying to be conciliatory.

"I fail to see why you two are not treating this with the importance it deserves. But whatever I can do to impress on you how absolutely necessary your cooperation is in this transfer of power from one Seer to the next, I will do. The courtesy of a return call would be greatly appreciated."

"Bite me," I said to the voice mail. "I'm hungry," I said to Chad. "Breakfast?"

"Your wish is my command and all that jazz," said Chad. "We'll grab some hotel breakfast and catch the tour bus at the Bay Street stop. But we need to call Hedgepath back now, can't talk on the tour bus and you know we got to play nice with him, don't you? Especially since you just happen to be the new Seer. I don't want him to get desperate and do something stupid."

"Like what?"

"Oh, I don't know. Make a threat. Lay a finger on you. Hate to have to kill him. Especially before we figure out what the hell he's been doing he so desperately wants to keep doing."

I sighed. "Yeah, I know. Damn it."

We didn't have to call Hedgepath back, though. Chad's phone announced an incoming call before we got the chance.

"Three guesses and the first two don't count," he said.

"Let me take it," I said, knowing how irate it made the man to talk to me, a mere woman. A mere witch. "War-N-Wit, Inc. Ariel Garrett," I said, hitting speaker.

"And exactly the lady I need to speak with," Hedgepath said. It was costing him a lot to sound halfway jovial. I heard the strain in his voice.

"Why, good morning, Mr. Hedgepath."

"Did you get my voice mails?"

"Yes, sir, we did, and were just about to call you back when you called us again. I have you on speaker. So we can all discuss whatever arrangements might be necessary for—oh, what did you call this? The transfer of power?"

A surge of black and crimson color rolled out of the phone. I could see it. Frustrated rage. He kept his voice steady, though, I'd give him that.

"I believe I might have called it that, yes. I thought we could discuss this over dinner tonight, like civilized people. Seven o'clock back at Bull Street?"

"You're inviting us to dinner?"

"Yes, I am."

"Well, that's very hospitable of you, Mr. Hedgepath—"

"Call me Oliver. We're practically family, Ariel."

My eyes widened at that one, and Chad threw out a cautionary hand. "Don't!" he mouthed at me.

"How nice of you to say so," I said, choking back my initial reaction to being classed as any part of Hedgepath's family. "But thank you, we won't impose for dinner. We're making this trip a bit of a substitute honeymoon, our first one got cut unexpectedly short. We'll drop by at six, if that's all right."

"Does that mean I should plan on five?" A trace of venom got through on that reference to our early arrival Friday night. I'd better get off the phone before we both lost our polite facades.

"No, sir, I told you. This is a bit of a replacement honeymoon, we have plans for the day. And the rest of the evening."

"Seeing a bit of Savannah, I hope? You should consider one of the tours. Well worth it for an introduction to the city."

Chad cut in quickly. "I know Savannah well, Ollie. I think we'll forego playing tourist on the trolley bus."

"You know best, of course. Six o'clock, then?"

"Six o'clock."

I hit "End" and turned to Chad. "Let me guess," I said. "You don't want him to know what we're doing today."

"No, ma'am, I surely don't. Though I'm more interested in him not knowing where we are than what we're doing. Not that knowing we're on a tour bus would give him a clue where we were unless he watched us get on and off at the stops."

We ate our hotel continental breakfast and walked to the Bay Street stop for Old Town Trolley Tours. A ticket for one of their tours brought with it the privilege of getting on and off the tour buses at any stop. The buses were scheduled so that a bus stopped at all the scheduled stops about every twenty minutes. No parking problems, no navigation problems, no way to get lost. Though I didn't think I had any reason to worry about getting lost. I was beginning to think Magic Man knew just about every street and probably every alley in every major city in America.

We grabbed a prime seat on the next tour bus, not too close to the front, not too far back. Chad settled comfortably with his arm across my shoulders. "What I thought was we'd go around on the whole tour once so you could sort of get your bearings, see where you want to get off and do some exploring. Then go around again back to St. John's Cathedrdal. Because I always go in St. John's and light a few candles. And whatever other stops you wanta get off at."

"Do you? Light candles? For who?"

He smiled, not a particularly happy smile. "Shouldn't that be for whom? For a few folks. And by then, we'll want lunch. Clary's is just up the street from it. Local spot. It gets some tourist trade but it's still a neighborhood hang-out. And you get to split an éclair with me after lunch, or I'll eat the whole thing by myself."

The tour bus finished loading the passengers at this stop. The driver closed the door and started the smooth spiel of humor and information honed to a fine art that belonged to the professional tour guide.

"Ladies and gents, a little background info to get you started here. For those of you just joining us, remember we'll be making fifteen stops during this tour and you're welcome to get off and back on one of our tour buses at any point, but please remember, we can only stop at the actual designated stops. So please don't try flaggin' us down in-between stops and then get mad when you think we're ignoring you. Big fines for that, and the company don't pay 'em, that'd come out of our pockets! Now, from this point in our tour, we'll be coming up on City Market, built over the original center market of the city..."

We'd actually gotten on at one of the last stops on the tour which meant we reached the company's home base at West Boundary Street and Oglethorpe rather quickly. Like many older cities, the old train depot had been turned into a Welcome Center with several museums and served as a central point for several tours. We changed buses to start the tour from the beginning.

This driver resumed the professional spiel of tidbits of city history. "Welcome folks, we'll be coming up on Telfair Square in just a few minutes, the first of 'The Jewels of the City'..."

The Savannah Squares were indeed little jewels scattered throughout the city, twenty-two of them, framed with huge live oaks bearded with Spanish Moss.

"Love that Spanish Moss, don't you?" asked the driver. "The early settlers stuffed mattresses and pillows with it. That was before they figured out lots of bugs live in Spanish Moss. Once they figured that out, it kinda put the quietus on that use!"

The passengers all laughed.

"Georgia's one of the original thirteen colonies, you know," the driver continued. "Had some specific rules in its charter. One of them was no lawyers, y'all know that?"

"Damn," I said to Chad. "They shoulda stood firm on that one."

We went around the entire tour once, just so I could see where everything was. Savannah was full of museums. Full of old houses with lots of history, like the Sorrell-Weed House, famous for its exorcism and wall topped with broken glass cemented into the stone. Full of squares, those city delights. Squares that used to have the actual park bench where Tom Hanks once sat as Forrest Gump, where the statute made famous by Midnight in the Garden once stood. Both those artifacts had been moved for their own protection. Savannah had lots of local "characters" and the driver wasn't shy about sharing their stories. Restaurants and eateries abounded, many of them also used as movie sets. Savannah was a popular movie locale, and the tour drivers referred to those movies frequently.

"If y'all look over on the left there," said our driver at the corner of Bay Street and Jefferson, "you'll see one of our local night spots by the name of Club One. Famous for its alternate lifestyle, if y'all get my drift. Now, if y'all saw *Midnight in the Garden of Good and Evil*, y'all might remember somebody in that movie who's one of the headliners at Club One. Not on a regular basis anymore, she's moved to Charleston, but she comes back home once a month. As a matter of fact, she's here tonight. Savannah's own—"

"Lady Chablis!" I exclaimed with the driver. "Chad! What are the odds we're here on one of the weekends Lady Chablis's back in Savannah!"

He jerked his head around to stare at me.

"We're not. Are we?"

I smiled back. I didn't say a word.

"We are," he said in resignation. "Aren't we?"

"Yes, we are."

"Okay. After Hedgepath, we'll walk up to the Club and get tickets for the late show before we eat. Just in case it's a full house." He sighed. "The things I do for you."

I leaned over and kissed his cheek. "Only truly secure men would go to a drag queen show, darlin'. And you are definitely one of the securest men I know."

We changed buses one last time back at the main terminal, so we could go around again to the Cathedral of St. John. We exited and went inside. The entire structure, inside and out, was a true work of art, the Stations of the Cross detailed and perfect and achingly sad. Chad lit his candles. I hung in the background. This was personal. I left him alone a few minutes.

When he was ready to go, we walked down the street to Clary's on the corner of Abercorn and Jones, its stained glass sign with the Irish green lettering throwing bright color out to the street. Something was different though. Had been since we'd changed buses for this final tour loop. Like daggers in my back again.

We went in and picked a table. "They've got to have some of the best hamburgers in the world," said Chad. "But I feel the corned beef calling."

I couldn't get past the menu's description of the hamburger. I ordered an original with cheddar cheese. It was so good I ignored the daggers. Which were now hitting me from the front.

I leaned forward. "How close are we to Bull Street?"

"Real close. A couple of streets over from us. You feel it, too, of course. Shoulda known."

"Yeah, but it started with the last bus, it didn't just happen."

"I know. But it's not stopping me from having my chocolate éclair."

After the chocolate éclair, we walked back up to Lafayette Square and sat on one of its benches to wait for the next bus. When we saw it coming, we walked over to the boarding point and resumed our second round trip tour, getting off at River Street to explore in the daylight. We wandered in and out of shops. I was getting tired and the afternoon was getting on, so we headed back to our hotel. From nowhere, a black cat ran under my feet. I gasped and stumbled, barely managing to avoid a fall by grabbing onto Chad's arm. As I straightened, I found myself eye level with a newspaper box. The headline hit me hard in the stomach, but it was the picture that stabbed my heart.

"Chad!" I pointed to the newspaper. "That was our little waitress last night!"

"Savannah Student's Body Found in Alley", screamed the headlines. Our little waitress Diana smiled at us from the front page.

"Damn it!" Chad reached in his pocket and inserted quarters into the slot. I grabbed a copy as soon as the latch lifted.

"The body of college student Diana Tolbert was discovered in the early morning hours in an alley near the restaurant where she worked..."

"Chad, that's not right! I saw her last night walking right down River Street! Why would she be back up by the restaurant?"

"Com'on." Chad took my arm. "Let's cross the street and sit down over in the park. Time to check in with G."

I held back. It had been such a great afternoon I hadn't even thought about or needed a trip to a ladies' room until the last half-hour or so, and then I'd figured we were heading back to our room to change before dinner and hadn't looked for one. It seemed the game plan was changing. I had a feeling we weren't going to be back in our room anytime soon and this personal problem wasn't going to do anything but get more pressing.

I glanced at the shops behind us. A restaurant. Good. "Let me make a side trip to the ladies' room first. Why don't you go in and get us two coffees to go while I do. Be out in just a minute."

"Sounds like a plan."

He walked to the bar area while I headed for the door with the feminine silhouette. I heard the door open and close while I was in one of the two stalls. I nodded to the woman waiting by the sink as I walked over to wash my hands, though I was surprised to see her just standing there. The other stall had been empty when she'd come in. And she still didn't seem in a hurry to take either of the stalls now that I was out.

I turned from the mirror to the paper towel dispenser. From nowhere, a hand flashed out, smothering my nose and mouth with a cloth reeking with the sickeningly sweet smell of chloroform. The hand was attached to an arm wearing the pinstriped black sleeve of a man's coat. The cuff of the dress shirt glowed blindingly white as I followed it down into darkness.

* * *

I came abruptly out of total black but not into full light. Candlelight, that was it. And firelight. I was upright and could pass as a duct-tape dispenser, my arms secured at wrist and elbow bend to the arms of a chair. For good measure, another swatch of duct-tape ran on top of and across my fingers, rendering them immobile too. From the curve of the arms and what I could see, I was in a straight-backed chair of the Empire style. And just in case that didn't hold me, another few turns of duct tape ran under my breasts and around the back. My ankles were crossed and looped with the damn stuff, too. Well, standing up and taking the chair with me was out. At least for now.

Taped as they were, I couldn't stand flat and didn't think I could balance on the sides of my feet.

I looked around the room. I knew I was in the Bull Street house. The Empire style chair itself was a dead give-away and so was the room. It was wallpapered in dark red that seemed almost black in the muted candle-fire glow. It had been almost five o'clock when I'd seen the newspaper. It had to be full dark by now though the heavy velvet drapes, also dark red and trimmed with gold edging, wouldn't have let much light in in any event.

It was a bedroom. Against the far wall stood a heavy canopied bed matching the décor of the last century that dominated the whole house. There was an antique washbasin, complete with a water pitcher in Wedgewood blue and white. The knick-knacks on the fireplace mantel looked like somebody'd robbed the British Museum. Not to mention the andirons holding the burning logs looked to be the original cast iron ones placed there when it was built.

But the kicker was the man sitting in a matching chair across from me. He was dressed in a three piece suit, complete with watch fob and chain. He wasn't stuck to his chair with duct-tape. I didn't think he needed to be. He was a lot more immobile than me. He stared straight ahead, but I was pretty sure he wasn't seeing anything. I'd never seen anybody in a catatonic state. Until now, that is.

"Hello, Mr. Hedgepath," I said. "We haven't met before, have we? 'Cause I'm pretty sure you haven't left this room in a while, have you?"

No response. And no surprise.

The door opened. It creaked. Surprising, really, in a house this recently restored and so well-maintained.

I wasn't surprised to see Oliver Hedgepath walking in. Or at least, the Oliver Hedgepath we'd been seeing.

"Well," he said. "Ariel Garrett. The new Seer of the Tear of Isis. You've led me a merry chase."

I didn't respond.

"Cat got your tongue? Oh, dear, where's that caustic repartee I've come to know and hate? Can't think of any new names to call me?"

"I know exactly what to call you. Dead man walkin'." I deliberately spaced out my next sentence, punctuating each word. "My. Husband. Is. Going. To. Kill. You. You know that, don't you? Whoever you are?"

"Well, he's done it before. Several times, as a matter of fact. But I've done it to him a few times, too." He dropped the glamour cloaking him as Oliver Hedgepath. The man now standing before me was tall. Not fat, not thin. Soft-looking, though. Longish dark hair threaded with gray. Surprisingly smooth face, no character lines. Obsidian eyes. The eyes gave him a reptilian air.

He moved closer and held the Tear of Isis in front of me. I saw the man I'd seen last night, rutting like a pig over the helpless maid. Neville. That time around, he'd been Neville Thornsberry. Now he was fully clothed, in a room straight out of Regency England, a man's private study. A young girl stood in front of him, shaking with rage, but she wasn't any maid. And she wasn't helpless.

"No daughter of mine's marrying any damned tenant. You're Lady Anne Thornsberry and you're marrying Edward Davenport! He's a Baron, girl, you're not throwing your life away on a farmer!"

The girl, Lady Anne. She was me. This pig had been my father?

"I'll marry who I please! And who I please is not some fat pig willing to replenish your coffers so he can wallow on top of me like you wallow on the maids when you think no one's looking!"

The slap delivered two hundred years ago stung just as much now as when he'd delivered it.

"You shut your mouth, girl! My coffers need no replenishing!"

Her hand—my hand—covered her cheek. "Your coffers are empty! Tradesmen are pounding on your doors! You've gambled almost everything away and I will not be the sacrificial sheep to save your miserable skin! I'm in love with Jamie Daniels! I'm marrying him. Yes, a farmer! A tenant on your lands! Until the merchants take them from you!"

Pounding on the doors. "Sir Neville! Sir Neville! The Sheriff's here! There's been a terrible thing happen! Jamie Daniels, he were set upon on the road on the way back from market last e'en. He's dead, Sir Neville!"

Lady Anne—me—stared at Thornsberry. Her—my—hiss carried the venom of a cobra. "You! You did this!"

"I told you, girl. No daughter of mine's marrying a farmer."

The vision in the Tear faded. I looked at the man I still only knew as Hedgepath.

"You know, the first thing I'm doing when we finish all our business this time is calling my daddy and tellin' him how very grateful I am he's my father."

He laughed shortly. "Yeah, well, lot of good all that did me. Seein' as how you ran away to London and became a governess. You owe me a debt of thanks on that one, after all, girl, the Duke you were working for was fool enough to fall in love with you after his wife died and married you. Ended up a Duchess in that life. You always have landed on your feet."

"He was a good man," I said, knowing absolutely that was true. "But he wasn't Jamie. And I never loved him. Not that way."

"Love! Useless emotion. Clouds the brain. Been Magic Man's downfall before, the times I've taken him down. Day-dreaming on the way back from market, undoubtedly, any fool knew you had to watch for highwaymen that day and time."

"Especially when a Lord's hired them to take down the nuisance interrupting his plans." I said. "Avarice. Greed. Egomania. That's been your downfall, hasn't it? The times he's taken you down."

"Yeah, well. You win some, you lose some. I'm not going to lose this one."

Hedgepath's cell phone sounded. He laughed. "Wonder who that is? But we won't answer it right now. Let him stew a while longer." The ringing stopped, signaling the arrival of a voice mail. He retrieved it and held the phone so I could hear.

"Hedgepath. I'll be seeing you."

The glamour throwing imposter laughed again. "Oh, I'm counting on it, Magic Man," he said. He turned and left the room.

Chapter Thirty

"Well, Ollie," I said to the real—and very catatonic—Oliver Hedgepath. "This is another fine mess you've gotten us into. Any suggestions? Thoughts? Ideas? How the hell did you hook up with that turdsniffer anyway?"

I didn't expect any response, which is good, since I certainly wasn't getting one. Okay. First things first. Chad knew who had me. The Hedgepath we'd come to know and so not love. So Bull Street was the first place he'd check. Except he'd need to talk to G first and see if the Guardians had come up with anything that might shed some light on what hidden secret the Tear of Isis held that was so damn valuable. And who in the world of magic was powerful enough and dark enough to use it. And I hoped he was rational enough at the moment to know that and not just storm blindly in.

And damn it, I needed to know what information G'd been able to come up with, too. After all, I was the one sitting here. And whatever power the Tear had that the fake Hedgepath had been using, accessing it clearly hadn't done Ollie over there any good and probably wasn't going to increase my IQ much, either.

I heard a rustling sound under the bed. Oh, lovely! Too much noise for a roach. Or even for a bunch of roaches. A rat? A snake? A bat? None of the above would have surprised me much. It was an old house renovated by a practitioner of dark magic.

A dark head emerged from the bottom of the antique coverlet. This wasn't the best light in the world, but still—too big for either a rat or a snake. A bat I didn't know about and it was dark under that bed, though I didn't know if a bat would actually care to nest under a bed. Then shoulders emerged. Not big enough for wings, but maybe its wings were folded. And then the bundle of dark fur stood and stretched.

"Micah?" Now that was a silly question. First, my black cat wasn't even technically mine. He was a stray who'd just decided he liked Pine Whisper Plantation. Which was over a hundred miles away. And since I'd just decided his name was Micah, for whatever reason I'd decided it, he certainly wasn't privy to it. Probably wouldn't answer to it if he was. He was a cat, after all. I'd seen a black cat at least four or five times on this trip, twice outside this house.

He walked across the floor toward me, precise as a ballet dancer, a cat with a purpose. No languid feline stroll for this cat. He bounded up into my lap and started purring. I found the sound and vibration soothing. Calming, in fact. And in calming down, I could think with a greater degree of clarity.

Chad and I had a connection. By now, I accepted it so naturally I didn't even consciously think about it anymore, even though I'd spent several months fighting it before I admitted it. We could feel each other. Even on the day I'd first physically met him, as opposed to the two months prior to that when we'd first embarked on our email courtship, I'd felt his sudden panic when he'd hydroplaned on the interstate on the way home the night of our first meeting, felt it so intensely that I'd damn near hyperventilated. Any sudden, unexpected trauma affected me as much as it did him. I mean, I'd never actually had a knife stuck through my foot, but I knew what it felt like because he did. I'd never almost bled out either, but thanks to our serial killer take-down, I knew what that felt like, too.

I'd never asked—because up until now nothing traumatic had happened to me—if he felt my pain as intensely as I felt his. But I was sure he did. Had he actually passed out while collecting our coffee to go when Hedgepath chloroformed me? Maybe not, but I'd bet he'd been knocked to hell and back and probably out of commission for all practical purposes. Otherwise, he'd have called Hedgepath before now. Probably scared the hell out of the restaurant staff. I hoped they hadn't called an ambulance because trying to explain to medical personnel would be a bitch.

I'd gotten that far in my thought process when the cat raised his paw and started swatting my left hand. At least, I thought he was swatting my left hand. After a few swipes, I realized he was swatting at a target. A target barely outside the duct tape, now that I noticed and I was sure glad of that. My engagement ring. The engagement ring with the diamond big enough to buy a car. And I'd have been pissed if Hedgepath had taped over it with duct-tape and gotten sticky adhesive on it, too. That was the feminine side of me talking. The masculine side of me reminded me the diamond had other properties. As in, when rubbed, it intensified our mental connection.

I hadn't rubbed that stone over the last few weeks, I'd had no need, as we'd been together pretty much twenty-four-seven. But I needed every bit of mental and physical connection I could get right now. Because if I got enough, it was possible I could hitch-hike enough energy to actually somehow see-hear what he was doing and saying. And if he was talking to G, I needed that information just as much as he did. Only problem was, I didn't have any way to rub the diamond, my hands being taped as they were.

The cat wasn't just swatting aimlessly. He was actually pushing the ring with his paw. Making it turn sideways on my hand. He was trying to push the diamond between my fingers, whereupon I'd be able to rub the stone merely by wiggling my fingers even the little bit that the tape allowed me to move them. I tried to spread my fingers as much as possible under the sticky mess of the tape, which wasn't much. It was enough, though, and the diamond moved smoothly between my ring finger and third finger. I started wriggling my fingers, rubbing that stone like my life depended on it. Because I figured it did.

"Micah, you did that on purpose, didn't you?" I asked.

No answer.

"Cat got your tongue, huh?"

Low growly purr. Almost as though in disapproval.

"Okay, it was a bad pun," I conceded. "But very apropos, don't you think? And even though you won't admit it, you did it on purpose, we both know you did. So thanks. More than I can tell you. If we ever get back to Pine Whisper Plantation, you got a quart of cream in the 'fridge waitin' on you whenever you want it. To hell with milk. How's that?"

Low purr. Of pleasure, this time, I'd swear it. This cat had a great vocabulary. Understood every word I was saying. And it was my cat. It was Micah. I didn't care if we were a hundred miles from home. It was Micah.

There it was. The warmth in the pit of my stomach, moving lower. And higher. And expanding. And enveloping me in the strength of Chad's arms. I felt his body pressed against mine. I reached out with everything I had and the room around me dissolved. I was back on River Street, or at least my consciousness was, floating above Chad. He was striding down the sidewalk, charging toward the nearest steps up to Bay Street. He was almost running, his cell phone to his ear, intent on getting back to the hotel and retrieving the SUV.

His lips were moving, but I couldn't actually hear him. I pushed harder, reached further, stretching my senses. There was a bright flash behind my eyes. And then I had it. The connection.

* * *

"G, we're out of time! I can't wait for confirmation, didn't you hear me? That bastard's got my wife!

Chloroform, I can still taste it. Even second-hand it knocked me out long enough for him to be completely gone! And then I was still too damn dizzy to stand up straight for at least ten minutes! Lost enough time."

"You won't do her any good dead. Which you might be if you go charging in when you don't know what you're charging into!"

"I'm better than that, G!"

"You'd damn well better be."

He'd reached the steps leading to Bay Street and charged up. The sounds of passing traffic made it harder to hear as my consciousness floated above Chad's in whatever ether it was floating in. But at least I could hear him. And more importantly, I could hear what he was hearing on the other end of the phone.

"The Tear. Anything on what it does to make it worth all this to the fake Hedgepath? He murdered that girl last night, G. Our waitress. For nothing but the use of her image and the chance to tail us for an hour. Surely the Guardians have some idea of anybody powerful enough and dark enough to do that!"

He'd reached the parking deck at our hotel now, punching the up button at the outside elevator.

"About the Tear itself, all we've found are rumors over the centuries that the Tear intensifies whatever other powers the Seer has."

"And that's it? What the hell good does that do anybody but the Seer? Unless they can somehow use the Seer's powers."

"Exactly. Hit me over the head with a two by four, I'll finally figure it out. This Ollie impersonator. He has to be able to use another's powers. Otherwise, how would he have harvested the Seer's ability in the first place? So whoever this dude is, he's a—"

"Psychic vampire, a bottom-feeder. You got a possible name? 'Cause if you don't have anybody like that blipping the radar screen, G, the Guardians are falling down on the job."

"Give the man a cigar. Now. As to who he is—we know he's got some sort of vampiric power whether or not he actually guzzles anybody's blood which wouldn't surprise me. But he at least guzzles power. Since whatever he's doing revolves around Resurrection, he actually is—was, excuse me—able to use the Tear to confirm the past lives things. So he's got something else that makes that profitable to him. Especially when combined with the possibility the Tear intensifies whatever other powers the Seer has. So, based on all the foregoing—"

"G. Who the hell is he?"

"His name is Legion."

"Very funny. What's his name?"

"Legion. That's the name he's using."

"Damn. He thinks he's that good?"

"Or that bad. And that's all we got right now, we're still working on the original name. Kind of in a bind here, if we knew the real name, it'd help discover what other power he has he needs to intensify. And if we knew his other powers, it'd probably be a lot easier to come up with his real name. Whatever it is, it's something that really helps if you're running a scam. Old Ollie was a garden variety medium with a touch of pre-cog. Both of which could be useful scams to run. What powers does Ariel actually have?"

The elevator arrived and Chad charged through before the doors completely opened, stabbing the button for the third level viciously.

"I'm not altogether sure yet and neither is she. She didn't even know she was a witch until last Christmas, she just always explained everything away as being a logical, educated guess."

"So she's in the 'knows things' category. Pre-cog? Clairvoyant? Telepath?"

"Telepath, mostly."

The elevator stopped and Chad charged the doors, again without waiting for them to fully open.

"Like to see you two in action. You're one of the strongest telepaths I've ever met."

"Even not knowing what it was, she was already as strong as me, G. And the Tear's intensified that already, I think. She dreamed last night. One of our past lives. Woke up and slapped the shit out of me for something happened two thousand years ago. Without the Tear. Apparently, she didn't need it."

"I'm sure you deserved it. Any other powers you suspect might be lurking down underneath just waiting to break through?"

"Nothing definitive yet. Probably several, though. She's complicated."

"All women are complicated, Magic Man, and witches more than most."

"She takes it to a new level, trust me."

He reached the SUV and unlocked the door, wasting no time in cranking up. He threw it into reverse. Then he braked quickly.

"Wait a minute! Savannah's full of rich eccentrics. It's famous for it. So the reincarnation thing's the original hook, it'd grab 'em big time. Proves they're special. For them, it'd be better than being a Son or Daughter of the American Revolution or the Confederacy. Marks their pedigree, they'd love it. But just a big membership fee wouldn't net the type of money that restored that house. Somebody with a big dose of mind-control capability, though, somebody who could psychically push another person to do what they were told—"

"Especially if the Tear, through the Seer, intensified it. Oh yeah, they'd—"

"Stand in line to empty their bank accounts into his."

"Cookin' with gas, Magic Man. So he's taken Ariel to drain her. He needs the Seer's ability to intensify power to make his mind control power strong enough to have that big an effect."

The SUV gained speed and started moving. The connection started to fade as it cleared the parking ramps. I'd have to work on this physic eavesdropping thing. I wiggled my fingers again and rubbed the diamond faster. That was a little better but not much. They were still fading in and out, like a cell phone conversation running through a bad spot of cell reception. Then I had it. I couldn't hover. I had to keep up with the car. I concentrated hard and falling back on legend, imagined I was riding a broom. I felt a rush of wind around me. I actually felt it blowing my hair. And suddenly I was flying. Which was a good thing, because Chad sure as hell wasn't standing still.

"Then he's bitten off a hell of lot more than he'll be able to chew this time," Chad said, and actually laughed. Well, I was glad I could provide some amusement. He stopped for a traffic light and I overshot the car and had to backtrack a bit, so I missed the first part of his next comment. I got back in time for "... I just didn't remember it 'cause I only know of one time I'm sure she did it, she's got to be pissed as hell first. And come to think of it, hungry."

"A pissed, hungry witch is not a good combination, no."

It would have been nice to know what Chad remembered resulting from some past incident wherein I'd been both pissed and hungry since I didn't remember anything notable at the moment, but I'd have to worry about that later. Because two things happened simultaneously on both planes I was inhabiting at the moment.

Chad's line of traffic got the green light and began to move again. At least, it moved until the tremendously loud blast of a big rig's horn screamed in my psychic ear as the lead car on the left hand side of the Whitaker and York intersection decided to ignore its red light and play chicken with an eighteen wheeler. It lost.

"Shit, damn, hell, fuck!" said my husband, looking at the blocked intersection.

I'd have loved to stay and chat, but the sound of the doorknob turning broke my concentration. The cat—Micah, whether anybody but me ever believed it, jumped out of my lap and tore back under the bed, disappearing from sight a second before the door opened.

At least I didn't have to insult Ollie over there any longer by addressing the turdsniffer as Hedgepath.

I smiled brightly at him.

"I believe your name is Legion?"

* * *

Legion did a good job of dead-panning it, but his eyes gave him away. I'd surprised the hell out of him.

"It's possible I owe you an apology," he said.

"Do tell?"

"I might have underestimated you slightly." He walked toward me carrying a glass of ice water, a long straw already in place. "Here. I'm sure the lingering taste of the chloroform isn't pleasant." He bent and held the straw to my lips. I closed them firmly and shook my head.

"No?" He straightened. "Sure? I realize you're embarrassed by your eminent defeat but wounded pride's no reason to be uncomfortable."

I laughed. "Embarrassed? No. Cautious. God only knows what's in that water. Eye of newt and tongue of toad. Or knock-out drops. I'd rather keep the cotton mouth, thank you."

He shrugged. "Suit yourself. I'll go continue my preparations for Magic Man's arrival then. Wouldn't want him to feel unwelcome."

He turned back toward the door. As he walked a kaleidoscope of shifting scenes and places flashed through my brain at high speed, flying backward in time. I caught glimpses of different times, different names. And then I was back. Back at the beginning. Back with Caeso Gellius Acilianus and Livia Rufinus.

Livia stood, out of sight, straining to hear the conversation between Gellius and Tiberius Antius Magnus. Odd, how easily the Latin words clarified in my English-speaking brain.

"You're a fool, Gellius. One night. One night with your wife relieves you of this duty. I'll send another out against Gaius' driver in this bet. Yes, you're very good, but I can send a professional charioteer, not one of my soldiers who cannot refuse my orders. One night with Livia."

"Rome will fall before you touch my wife."

"Then you will die. And I will have her every night."

"We will see."

Rage two thousand years old flew over me, burning even hotter now than it had then. Rage at Tiberius, whose lust and arrogance killed Gellius. Rage at Gellius, whose pride and honor allowed Tiberius to kill him. Leaving, just incidentally, Livia to deal with Tiberius on her own. She had, too, but the fact she'd had to enraged me even further. Honor be damned. No woman gave a damn about honor if it meant harm to those she loved. And here he was. Back again. This bastard had haunted us through all our lives. Every damn one of them. Starting with that one.

"Legion!"

He stopped and faced me. "Yes?"

"You've always underestimated me, you know. Haven't you? Neville. Diego. Koro. Boris. Tiberius." That name I almost spat. "Legion. Oh, yeah. Legion's just perfect. When one knows all the facts, of course."

"I will truly enjoy dealing with you. After I've evened the score with Magic Man, of course. I believe after this we'll be three and three." He moved for the door again.

"We will see," I said, deliberately quoting Gellius. The phrase didn't register with him. Obviously, he didn't remember his score with me. Good. I wanted to see the look on his face when he did. When he remembered. His score with me.

* * *

Micah emerged from under the bed. He walked back to me and rubbed against my ankles. Then he sat on his haunches and looked at me. And jerked his head toward Ollie.

"Excuse me?" I said. "Did you just try and tell me something?"

He rolled his eyes, as though exasperated with my failure to speak fluent cat. He jerked his head back toward Ollie again.

"Okay. You want me to do something with Ollie. Well, what? I'm open to suggestions. 'Cause hate to tell you, darlin', but he's a few shovels short of a full load right now. You hadn't noticed?"

"*Hsssssssssssssssssssssssssssss!*" Micah said, clearly expressing his disgust with my limited human intelligence. He stood up, took a few steps towards Ollie and bounded up in his lap. And proceeded to wash Ollie's hands for him. His unbound hands.

"Look," I said. "I'm not quite that dense. I know Ollie's hands aren't taped. I just don't know what use you expect me to make of it right now. Present circumstances being what they are and all."

Micah glared at me.

"Don't look at me in that tone of voice!" I said. "It's not like he can hear me, you know. I mean, I can't just make him wake up!"

"*Meeeeeooooowwwwwwwwww!*" he purred approvingly. That's when it hit me. I knew what I'd missed when I'd overshot the SUV and had to backtrack. What Chad had been telling G.

"...I only know of one time I'm sure she did it, she's got to be pissed as hell first. And come to think of it, hungry."

Mind control. Mind dominance. Power of suggestion. That sounded better. Less power trippy. The Saturday I'd been working at the office on the case from Hell and the attorneys seemed to have sorta kinda forgotten about us girls as they issued their lunch orders to the designated pickup person. It had been the first time I'd ever shouted that loudly at anybody. Not out loud, of course. In my mind.

I still wasn't sure if it was me or their mamas' raising kicking in that had made them remember to feed us, too. Chad'd been certain it was me, though. And oh, yeah, at the time, I'd been pissed. And hungry, too. I wasn't currently hungry. Somewhat nauseated, in fact, there was a reason chloroform hadn't ever made it to the top ten recreational drugs of choice. But I was damn sure pissed.

I took a deep breath and stared straight at the catatonic Oliver Hedgepath, locking in on his eyes.

"Mr. Hedgepath! Can you hear me?"

Nothing. Micah leaped up on Ollie's shoulders and curled around his neck. He started humming like a little generator, attempting to up the amperage of my mental shout.

"Oliver! Oliver Hedgepath! Snap out of it! You're better than he is! Don't let him beat you! I need some help here!"

Nothing. Micah's purring leaped into highest gear. My eyes narrowed into slits, gathering every shard of the concentration I was rolling into one big ball. I tilted my head back slightly and then threw it forward. I felt the power streaming like laser blasts from my eyes. And I saw it enter his.

* * *

Ollie gave an all-body jerk, shook his head, and looked at me. And sneezed.

"Excuse me," he said. "I'm allergic to cats."

"Hssssssssssssssssssssssssssssssssss!" Micah exclaimed and jumped down from Hedgepath's shoulders.

"He didn't mean to insult you," I said soothingly. "I'm sure he's very grateful. Or will be when I explain the situation to him."

"Excuse me?" Ollie asked again. "I'm sorry, I don't understand what you're saying to me."

"That's because I wasn't talking to you," I said, completely in sympathy with Alice when she went through the looking glass. "Hello, Mr. Hedgepath, I'm Ariel Garrett. Welcome back. Now, you think you might possibly walk over here and get this duct tape off of me?"

"Oh, dear, you are in a fine mess, aren't you?"

"That's actually my line, but yeah. I really am."

Ollie attempted to stand up, but didn't quite make it.

"That's okay," I said. "You've been sitting still for quite a while. Bound to be a little woozy at first. Try it slow and a little at a time."

It was a slow process, but he made it all the way to his feet this time. He started towards me, taking a few steps at a time. He grabbed onto the arms of my chair when he got there.

"It's okay," I said again. "Take a minute and breathe."

"No, no, I'm fine. Been out of it too long. Where are we? This isn't my house. I have a lovely house, but this isn't it." He reached down under the chair arm, attempting to find the start of the tape.

"Savannah. I doubt we'll get this lucky, but you might wanta check the dresser drawers for scissors, something to cut with. Duct tape ain't the easiest thing in the world to get off. And not trying to put any pressure on you or anything, I'm not sure how long we have before he comes back. Whoever the hell he really is this time around."

"Robert?"

"That's his name?"

"Robert Robertson is how he introduced himself."

"And that didn't strike you as kinda weird right there? Who names a kid that?"

"*Hsssssssssssssssssssssssssssssssss!*" Micah interjected, reminding me we had more serious matters to deal with. Then he leaped up on top of the dresser and gave it an inspection.

"*Meeoowww!*" he said approvingly. He swiped his paw across the left back side of the dresser and something clunked on the floor. I only caught a glimpse but if I was right—

"Mr. Hedgepath, I do believe if you go look, Micah just knocked a carpet cutter down on the floor. Been a lot of renovation goin' on in this house, very nice of the carpet people to leave it."

"Quite," he said, standing straight and making his way over to look. "And do call me Oliver. Or even Ollie if you like. " He reached his goal and bent down. He leaned heavily on the dresser, both to get down and back up. "And yes, indeed. Carpet cutter. How did you get here? Robert's fine hand obviously, but why'd he bring your cat?"

"He didn't. Bring my cat, I mean. Long story. What I can't figure out is why you're still alive."

"He needed me alive. You can sustain the glamour of a dead person for only so long. You need a living body to sustain it for any length of time." Ollie began his shuffling gait back to the chair, though he was moving a bit faster now.

"I'll file that away for future use," I said. "Now, get my hands loose, please."

"We'll have you out of this is in two shakes, my dear. I'm very glad to see you, you know," he said, cutting smoothing through the tape at elbow, wrists and fingers near the edge of the chair arm, the spot affording the least exposure to my skin. Good thinking, that thing was sharp.

Ollie was sweet but too slow. "Thanks!" I said, and grabbed the cutter as soon as he ripped enough tape off. I cut through the tape around my body on both sides and was just bending down to get my feet when Micah hissed again. I heard the sounds of footsteps in the hall and slashed the tape around my boots without much consideration for finesse. Damn. Cut the leather on my favorite pair of boots. Expensive ones, too.

"Get to the door!" I hissed at Ollie. "Move it! Be ready!"

"Magic Man's taking longer than I expected," Legion said as the door opened. "I thought we might proceed with some of the preliminaries—"

Micah leaped straight for his face, spitting and clawing. And drawing blood.

Chapter Thirty-One

Legion literally fell into the room, fisted hands flailing desperately at the black fury of fur. I pushed Ollie out in front of me, rushing him through the door.

"Get out of the house!" I said, shoving him hard towards the stairs. "Just get out of the house! Hide in the side yard, my husband's on his way, watch for him!" In the nick of time, I remembered to add, "But don't let him see you! He'll think you're the bad Hedgepath!"

"But what about you?"

"Takin' this bastard down. Don't worry 'bout me, just get out!"

Good thing Ollie'd had a chance to navigate a little before Legion'd come back, he was actually moving pretty good at this point. He charged down the steps.

Micah gave a meow I hadn't heard before, one of pain. Some of Legion's hits were connecting. *Hurt my cat, will you? Okay, another nail in your coffin, bub.*

"Micah! Enough! Retreat, retreat!"

Was that me? Why did I suddenly sound like a commander in a guerilla raid? Micah flew out of the room.

"Follow!" I ordered, heading for the stairs. I needed to get down to the lower floor, get all the lights off. And stalk him while he thought he was stalking me.

Low moans mingled with curses came from the room. Cat claws hurt, that was a fact. Too much to hope Micah'd gotten an eye, I supposed, but he'd been doing some damage, for sure.

I flew down the steps, Micah in front of me. Now, where was that damn foyer light switch? Ah. Got it. And the front door was wide open. Ollie'd made it out. On to the drawing room. Light switch. Got it. Damn. Lamps. I flew around the room, clicking switches furiously. I could hear Legion, so enraged the steps shook, coming after me. Then I heard a loud bam, followed by a series of successive bams, very close together. I didn't laugh out loud, but it was a near thing. Bastard had fallen down the steps. Good. Door to another room. Already dark, so I didn't have to worry about finding the light switches. Parlor, receiving room, study, whatever, I didn't particularly care what it was called.

I heard a slam and then a click. He'd closed the door and locked it.

"Not smart, witch! You should have run while you had the chance! I know you're here, you couldn't have gotten all the lights and still made it out! I'm coming for you! Again! I know this house, witch! You don't! The dark serves me, not you!"

I didn't think he really believed that or he wouldn't have turned the foyer lights back on. But I had no problem with the dark. I'd taken the dark and made it mine, made it mine the first night Gellius lay dead in Rome, when I'd fled to the stables, no thought for anything but getting home—wait a minute. I'd been in Rome, that hadn't been home?

The memory crowded in, and I gave it my full attention. Because if it was pushing in, it was trying to show me something I needed to remember.

* * *

No, Rome wasn't home. Home was an outpost of the frontier. Lower Gaul. Gallia Cisalpina. Gaul this side of the Alps. In modern parlance, northern Italy. That's where we'd lived, where we'd been stationed. Gellius had made our province so secure and so wealthy we'd caught the eyes of Rome. Who'd called us back to take it from us and give it as a reward to one of their cronies. They'd send us to another province, one not so well-run and well-maintained, so we could do it all over again. A never-ending cycle, and our successors would run the countryside back into the ground, of course, without a thought to the people of that province, the laborers who produced the spoils. But it was the way of Rome and we were Romans. Back to Rome we'd gone. Where I'd caught Tiberius' eye.

But I wasn't staying here. I was going home. No matter if I couldn't claim our villa, if I had no authority over the Roman troops still there. I had better. The people loved me. And they'd loved Gellius. He'd trained them well, which wouldn't have pleased Rome at all had it been known. But it hadn't been known. He'd trained me well, too. Our people hated Rome. So did I. It was time Rome knew it.

* * *

"Witch!" Was there a tinge of uncertainty in Legion's voice? Why, yes. I believed there was. "You can't fight me, I'm stronger than you."

Like I was going to answer and tell him exactly where I was? I didn't think so. He was trying to pinpoint my location so he could concentrate the energy of the mind messages I felt creeping through the air towards me. And apparently he didn't even remember these first-floor rooms all connected into each other. I started to move across the room, looking for the doors that would put me behind him.

"Witch! Come out and show yourself...show yourself...show yourself...there is no you, you are only a vessel for my commands...my commands...my commands..." That I heard, but not with my ears. *"You must obey me...obey me...obey me..."*

Fat chance. Not even close. I smiled into the darkness. And two could play that game. I could drive him crazy without giving him a clue where I was.

"Legion! Is that all you've got...all you've got...all you've got...."

Sharp intake of breath.

"Come and get me. If you dare...if you dare...if you dare..." I concentrated and imagined my unspoken words swooping like a flock of birds around his head, assaulting him from every angle.

"Witch!"

Oh, so I'd shaken his concentration there. Enough so he'd gone to actual speech. But not as much as I was going to shake him. Because Livia was still trying to tell me something. She had some memories she wanted to share. So I could share them with Legion. And in so sharing, make them live again.

* * *

Heat. Cold. Rain. Hunger. Thirst. Facts of life for guerilla warriors. Livia stood outside her tent in the early dawn, wrapped in her cloak against the rain. The people had taken her in. And she'd taken them away from the villas where they'd labored for Rome, deep into the forests. In three years, she'd made Rome pay. Quick strikes against every trade convey crossing the province. Murderous night raids against every Roman invasion sent to re-take control of the province. Rome didn't know who the guerilla leader was but they knew what that leader was. The Scourge of Rome.

And today, the final fruition of those three years. Tiberius himself was here, sworn to secure the province and bring the Scourge of Rome back for public execution. Livia looked over at her guerilla fighters, readying the fine horseflesh stolen from the Roman villas. She threw the hood back from her hair and strode to her own horse. Gellius' horse. The horse she'd

218

ridden out of that Roman stable three years ago. One of the best-trained battle horses in the Empire.

Mounting, she raised her hand in signal.

"We ride! Remember! We take the leader alive!"

* * *

"Witch! I'm not afraid of you!"

"Yes, you are…you are…you are…just not as much as you're goin' to be…goin' to be…goin' to be…"

Fast forward. I didn't need the battle. I needed the end. Legion's end. Tiberius' end. It floated, just out of my reach. I narrowed my eyes. And grabbed it.

* * *

Livia stood, the cloak of her hood shadowing her face. Tiberius, pouring sweat and blood, was on his knees in front of her, head bowed under the extra weight of the helmet. She leaned forward and jerked it off.

She raised her hand and gestured to one of her warriors. He grabbed the reins of the horses still in the traces of Tiberius' own Roman war chariot and brought it over to her. Then he stepped to the back of the chariot, grabbing the braided leather rope already attached to it and tied it securely around Tiberius' already bound hands.

"Show yourself!" Tiberius demanded. "What coward strikes from the night like a thief without honor and destroys the countryside? What leader keeps their face covered when they judge a man? What barbarian executes a soldier in such a way?"

She stepped forward and threw back the folds of the masking cloak.

"I do," she said.

Sharp intake of breath. "Livia Rufinus?"

"No. Livia. The Scourge of Rome."

* * *

"Enough, Witch! Time to end this! And I'll drink your powers like fine wine!"

I smiled. He could try. He could try now. He was right. Time to end this. Now that I knew how.

I stepped out of the doorway connecting to the foyer.

"Legion, you are so damn stupid you didn't even realize I've been behind you the whole time? Gotta watch these old houses, the rooms all interconnect with each other, you know."

Enraged beyond words, he hissed as he lunged at me. Not like Micah's hiss. The evil, almost subliminal hiss of a large snake.

But I was ready. I had the memory, coiled and intertwined securely with the power. I could feel it, invisible, pulsating in my hand.

I pulled my arm back and threw it like a fastball. Straight into his brain. I concentrated and felt it as it spread out, enveloping every thread of consciousness he held, replacing every memory he'd ever had. Permanently. The memory of Livia stepping up into his war chariot. Taking the reins and urging the horses into a gallop down the northern Italian hills, Tiberius tied behind it.

* * *

I walked over and looked down at Legion, sprawled on the gleaming black and white chessboard marble tile of the foyer. Little mewling sounds came out of his mouth as the one loop of memory I'd planted in his brain played on, over and over and over again.

"Livia six," I said. "Tiberius zero."

I walked into the drawing room, over to the case holding the Tear, and lifted it out. I held it up and it twinkled back at me.

"You don't belong here," I told it. "Time for you to return to the good guys."

I walked outside to check on Ollie. And it was about time for Chad to show up, too.

"My dear!" Ollie rushed up the walkway toward me. "I'm so relieved you're safe! Hurry, over here in the side bushes! Robert—he'll be after us!"

"No, he won't," I said. "He's had a stroke."

"A stroke?"

"Seemed that way to me," I said. I looked down the street and saw headlights, coming at too fast a clip to be a casual driver. "And you need to move over behind those bushes till I can tell my husband you aren't that Hedgepath."

Tires screamed as they braked. Our SUV cut to the curb. Chad left the rear-end sticking out in the street and the driver's door standing wide open. I rushed out and into his arms. I was fine, of course, but he didn't know that. He was scared to death.

"Hey, ease up! You're goin' to break my ribs!"

He whooshed out a long expelled breath.

"You're okay? You're sure you're okay? Hedgepath, whatever the fuck name he's using—he didn't hurt you?"

"I'm fine."

"He's not gonna be fine much longer, I promise you that!" He turned me loose and headed for the house.

I grabbed his arm and pulled him back.

"Down, boy! Taken care of. Complicated. Right now, though, I need you to meet the real Oliver Hedgepath. He's fine, and he's the good guy. Okay, Ollie, you can come out now!"

Ollie emerged from the shadows and I did the honors. "Chad, this is the real one. Ollie, this is my husband, Chad Garrett."

Ollie offered his hand. "Oh, my. Your husband's the legendary Magic Man? So pleased to meet you."

"Don't give him the big head, Ollie," I said as they shook.

"Well, I'm happy to meet you, sir," said Chad. "And glad you're alive, though I've got to say that surprises me."

"Oh, but Robert needed me alive to keep using the glamour. I was quite safe as long as he needed the identity."

"Robert?"

"Robert Robertson," I said. "You believe that's the best he could come up with?"

"So where is he now?"

"Com'on. I'll show you."

We walked back in. Legion, sprawled on the floor, was still making those mewling sounds that would have broken my heart had they been coming from anyone else.

"He's had a stroke," I said.

"But not really," Chad said.

"Nope. He's caught in a memory loop. He's Tiberius Maximus. Tied behind his own war chariot. For the rest of this lifetime."

Chad smiled. He reached out and took my face between his hands and kissed me.

"Waited two thousand years to tell you how proud I was of you. Of Livia. The Scourge of Rome."

"I always hoped you'd seen that."

"I saw."

"Well, I don't fully comprehend the reference," Ollie said, "but that's all right since you two do. And wherever he is, he deserves it."

"Absolutely."

"So what now?" I asked.

"Find a house phone," Chad said. "Preferably a portable. He knew he was in trouble and just managed to dial 911 before he collapsed. And then we're outta here."

"Oh, dear, but I don't have my wallet or checkbook or car—"

"Ollie," I said. "Don't be silly. You're coming with us."

"Don't you want to find your cat?"

"What cat?" asked Chad.

"Micah," I said. "We won't find him, Ollie. He's already gone back home."

* * *

We dropped Ollie off the next afternoon at his home in Rebecca. I think I was almost as relieved as he was to find it still intact, still un-sold, and the utilities still in working order. It was pretty dusty though, and he'd been heading for the furniture polish and Mr. Clean when we'd left him. We assumed Legion kept it as a fallback, just in case he needed a hidey-hole. I'd become very fond of Ollie and knew we'd found a new member of our rapidly growing extended magical family. We were almost to the turn-in to Pine Whisper Planation when Chad laughed suddenly.

"Whatcha' laughin' at?"

"Myself. Just remembered what I told you on the way to the airport when we were flying out to Vegas."

"And what was that?"

"That I thought you might have a 'tad bit of mind control.' Understatement much?"

"Just a little, maybe. I never did get to see the show at Club One, either."

"We'll be back in Savannah, baby girl. On a first Saturday in the month and I'll take you to see Lady Chablis. I love Savannah. In spite of Legion."

"Yeah, I do, too. Glad G didn't think that memory loop thing was a misuse of power. Sorta worried me after I thought about it. Not at the time, of course, but afterwards."

In fact, G had been delighted when we reported in and said he couldn't have done it better himself. That was a relief. Didn't wanta start out on the wrong foot with the Guardians. On our way to Ollie's house, he'd called and reported the Savannah-Chatham Metropolitan Police Department was delighted with the excuse to assume control of Robert Robertson and the Bull Street House. Seemed he'd been under investigation due to a large number of complaints. Apparently, some of Savannah's richer denizens were discovering large transfers of money from their accounts to his and had no recollection at all of how that might have happened.

We turned into our driveway that qualified in length as a country road. "I'm glad to be home," I said.

"Me, too."

Chad pulled up in the yard and parked. As I got out, I spotted Micah. He was sitting on top of the deck rail, keeping watch. When he saw me, he nodded his head and leaped over into the tree branches.

"That's okay," I called after him. "We'll be talkin', darlin'! 'Cause you can run—but you can't hide!"

Chapter Thirty-Two

I guess the powers of the universe felt we'd earned at least a little bit of time off patrol duty because nothing much out of the ordinary happened during the next few weeks except routine PI cases. This was more than fine with me since I was still learning the business and didn't really consider any of it to be "routine". All good things come to an end, though, and my husband signaled the end of our "routine" streak when he came through the door a month to the day since we'd rescued the real Ollie from his enforced captivity in Savannah.

"Okay, time to get you outfitted." Bags looped over both his arms.

"Outfitted? For what?" I eyed the bags with suspicion. When Chad Garrett announced I was getting outfitted, it didn't necessarily mean he'd seen an outfit he thought I'd like. Though it could. No, when a private investigator-process server-bounty hunter said it was time to get outfitted, the possibilities were endless. Last week I'd been a waitress at a truck stop. Quite successfully. That was one bail-jumping long-distance trucker who wouldn't be trucking for a while. And I netted twenty bucks in tips, too.

"Don't sound so suspicious," he said, disengaging himself from the bags and piling them on the couch. "Maybe I just saw a few things I knew you needed. Take a look."

I shot him a disapproving glance but it didn't work well with the grin I couldn't stop. Chad Garrett knew women. He'd made major inroads on completely re-working my formerly office casual closet. Now I wore jeans that fit. Really well. Plush sweaters in rich colors. Leggings that molded my calves and thighs and just smoked with boots and long tunics. Lord knows what he'd be bringing in when spring and summer hit.

I opened the first bag and pulled out the contents, holding it up in front of me.

"It's perfect!" I exclaimed. "Just the thing every well-dressed nun wears in the convent. Complete with wimple! And Rosary!"

"Oh, hell! I forgot that was in there. I'll explain later. Lay it over there and get to the rest of it."

"Can't wait to hear." I sat on the couch and dug in to the "real" bags. Thor tried to help by nosing the bags towards me. Ten minutes later, I'd unearthed a black leather biker's jacket, black square-toed biker's boots, three pairs of black leather biker's pants, black leather biker's chaps, and a varied assortment of black t-shirts with various biker logos and lots of lightning bolts.

I sat back and surveyed the bounty spilling off the sofa onto the floor, excitement mixed with dread. The only thing Chad loved more than his motorcycle was me. I knew that. I'd known that ever since Vegas. Problem was, though I'd sorta, kinda begun to enjoy riding with him on the back of his bike, motorcycles had always scared the hell out of me and deep down, they still did. And in another week or so, I was going to be on one for a pretty long trip. Bike Week in Daytona. A biker's heaven on earth.

"Baby girl, don't worry so much. You'll be hearing the Eagle call before you know it."

I laughed. Daytona Bike Week was a big deal. Any Bike Week anywhere was a big deal. And Chad loved them all. A true biker made plans for next year's Bike Week before the current Bike Week was over. Chad's Daytona Bike Week plans passed being plans. They were traditions. Vegas buddy Spike always trailered his bike out so they could ride down together. They had standing room reservations, the next year paid in advance, from one year to the next. All hotels within a three hundred mile radius, from South Georgia down to Orlando, were booked solid.

"You need to eat. I've got your headache," I said. "Supper's ready."

I cleared my lap of the black t-shirt emblazoned in crimson *Ride the Wind* and headed for the kitchen of our little house. We sat down to green salads, spaghetti and garlic bread. My cell phone rang, my sister Stacy a/k/a Antsypants' ringtone. We'd asked her to come to Bike Week with us but she'd declined.

"Hey, Ari!"

"Hey, Antsypants!"

"Listen, I've been thinkin'. Did Chad ask me to go to Daytona with y'all because it was the polite thing to do or would y'all really not mind?"

I laughed. "I thought you knew him better than that, girl! Of course we'd love for you to come! I'd beg you to come if I thought it'd do any good. I don't want to be the only first-timer in shock all by myself. I need moral support."

"Yeah, but the room thing—"

"Darlin'! We told you. He booked one of the suite things with a little adjoining bedroom, always does, 'cause he's always running into an old buddy from somewhere without a room. Not that he'd invite one of 'em back this year, of course, but it's perfect for you. If you want it."

"But y'all have his friend from Vegas comin'—"

"Spike's got his own room booked with the same set-up, for the same reason. Besides, Chad can't fit two of us on the back of his bike while we're tootlin' around Daytona!"

"The Intimidator doesn't tootle!" Chad interjected.

"Sorry. My apologies to the Intimidator. While we cruise around Daytona Beach."

"That's better." Chad grinned.

"Well, I've been thinkin' and—"

"And in the meantime you broke up with whoever it was you didn't want me to know you were sorta, kinda seein', right?"

"Don't know why I bother even trying, it never works. Yeah, I did."

"Who was it?"

"Use your crystal ball."

"Not one of the attorneys?" My stomach knotted. Sometimes outside the pages of fairy tales, secretaries/paralegals did actually marry one of the bosses and live happily ever after but in real life, romantic involvement with folks you worked for tended to be professional suicide. And besides, I couldn't think of one available attorney at BLAH at the moment even remotely worth it.

"Oh, hell no! Cameron Stallings, the Calhoun Hasty firm."

"Ah. Well, he's eye candy for sure, but—"

"But that's about all. Well, the view was good for a while. But if I go, you're not goin' to try to hook me up with Chad's buddy, are you?"

"Antsypants! He lives in Vegas! Why would I ever try to set you up with somebody you'd move almost clear across country for?"

"Because I'm your pesky little sister you can't wait to get rid of?"

"Not since you were six, honey. And not even then really, I just had to sound like a big sister. So you'll go?"

"It really sounds good, gettin' away a few days," she said, a wistful note in her voice indicating she'd really hoped Cam Stallings had more to him than looks.

"Then it's settled. We'll have a blast! And you'll love Spike, he's a big biker teddy-bear. But you don't have to love him, of course," I backtracked quickly. "I just meant we'll all have a great time."

"If you say so," Stacy said. "I need to be there by when?"

"Friday. Before lunch but the earlier the better."

"Okay. See y'all then. Love."

"Love."

I turned my attention back to Chad. "Now. About that nun's habit in with my biker gear?"

"Well, I've got a handle on a skip."

"Gee. That's a surprise. And I'm assumin' since there's a nun's habit on our couch, it wouldn't be the first time you've had a handle on this particular skip? Or maybe even a hand?"

"You'd assume right. I wouldn't get within fifty yards of him. But you can. Tomorrow."

"Lovely. So tell me all about it."

Chapter Thirty-Three

I peered around the corner of the Tallahassee alley where we'd parked the SUV. Yep, there he was. The skip. Danny Delvecchio, a/k/a Ferret a/k/a Dapper Dandy Dan. At the moment, operating as Father Daniel right in front of the Teen Rescue Center run by St. Benedict's and soliciting donations with practiced ease. I shoved the wimple completing my nun's ensemble above my eyebrows. Damn thing kept slipping down.

"One more time, from the top," Chad said.

"Magic Man! It's not rocket science! He's just a sleazy con man parading around as a priest. Which is really low, even for a bail-jumping con man."

"Sure is. So from the top. You're going to—"

"I'm going to rush up, grab him and babble about a poor boy doubled over in the alley who's probably overdosed and come with me now, I need help. That about it?"

"That's about it."

"Okay. I'm on it!"

I peered around the corner again. Good a time as any. I hitched my habit up a bit and headed toward him in a sprinting semi-jog.

"Father! Father, I need help—"

Before I could grab his arm, I heard an echo. Not in my voice though.

"Father! Father, I need help!" And a hand, not mine, grabbed Dapper Dandy Dan's arm from behind.

"Oh! Thank you, sweet Jesus!" The hand dropped Dandy Dan's arm and grabbed mine. "You're even better! The Lord provides!"

An older nun hauled me through the door of the Rescue Center, her habit flying out around her legs.

"One of the girls—she's in labor and I'm all by myself right now, even all our kids are gone this morning! We didn't know she was pregnant. She's been hiding it under big sweatshirts. I've called for an ambulance but I don't know if they'll make it, she's been in labor for a while, I think, she's in denial! She refuses to believe she's having a baby!"

She pulled me through a curtain separating the front room from a back room used as a dormitory. The girl lay on a cot under a sheet she clutched close, refusing to let go. And she was all of fourteen. Maybe.

"Sister Marie! Please! It's just a stomachache! You've got to let me up, I'm not—" She broke off and writhed in pain. Sister Marie dropped to her knees besides the cot.

"Sandra, you've got to listen to me! I've called for help but it might not get here in time. You've got to let us help you, child. You are having a baby and if you don't listen to me and open your legs, you can hurt it. Badly. You don't want that, do you?"

Wisps of gray hair peeked from Sister Marie's wimple, and a harsh ray of sunlight highlighted every wrinkle on her face. Her hand, visibly work-worn and roughened, smoothed the girl's hair back from her forehead. Sitting there in a halo of harsh sunlight, face lined with compassion and concern, she was the most beautiful woman I'd ever seen. I felt like a fraud. Until I remembered. I could help. There was no such thing as coincidence. I was here for a reason.

I dropped down on my knees on the other side of the cot and took her hands away from Sister Marie.

"Sandra! Look at me!" Her eyes rolled, a wild colt caught in a maelstrom of pain she didn't understand. "Look at me!" Beautiful dark eyes focused on mine. I concentrated and gathered strength. My streak of mind control scared me shitless, because to abuse a power is to lose it, but certainly it was time to use it now.

I concentrated and threw power through my eyes into hers. Just a bit. "Sandra! You *are* having a baby, honey. It hurts, I know it does, but it won't hurt as much if you relax and listen to Sister Marie. Open your legs, honey, the baby's head doesn't have much room and you can hurt it if you keep clamping down. Open your legs and relax! And breathe! Breathe with me! It doesn't hurt as much now, does it? No, it doesn't. It doesn't hurt. It doesn't hurt."

Under the covers her thighs spread apart. Sister Marie threw the sheet back and parted the girl's legs wider.

"Whatever you're doing, Sister, keep doing it! Please!"

Sandra tried to raise her head to look down at Sister Marie, panic rising again.

"No! No, don't look at Sister Marie. Look at me. Look at me. It doesn't hurt. It doesn't hurt."

"It doesn't hurt!" Sandra's voice was full of wonder. "It doesn't hurt!"

The baby's cry sounded with the wail of the ambulance pulling up outside.

"Thank you, God!" exclaimed Sister Marie, wrapping the baby in the cot's coverlet. "Thank you for this new life and for sending us Sister—what's your name, child?"

"Ari—Agrippa. Sister Mary Agrippa," I said. Was Agrippa even a feminine name? Was it even Christian? I had a vague memory connecting it to Rome. Too late now, though.

The paramedics barreled into the room and took over, sending Sandra into a fresh panic.

"No! I don't want to go! Not by myself!"

"Sister Agrippa, you should go with her. I've never seen anything like the way you calmed her down."

"No! I mean, no, Sister Marie, you should go. You know at least some of her history, they'll have questions. You go."

I bent over Sandra and send a bit more power into her eyes. "You need to go with them and you need to do what they say. I'll come check on you later at the hospital, I promise. You have to start a new life now, honey, because you've got a new life to take care of. You've got people to help you. And you've got a baby to think of." I knew some runaways ran because their parents were nightmares. But I also knew most parents of runaways lived a walking death, wondering every moment if their child was dead or alive. I added a little push to my next words. "If you know in your heart your parents love you and want you and are worried to death, you call them, you hear?"

"Okay. You promise you'll come to the hospital?"

"I promise."

The stretcher rolled out the door with Sandra, baby and Sister Marie. I sat down on one of the empty cots and went limp for a minute. Then I straightened back up. I'd just helped birth a baby. Dapper Dandy Dan a/k/a Father Daniel didn't have a prayer's chance in hell. I whipped my phone out of the pocket of the jeans I was wearing under the habit and called Chad.

"How much of that did you get?"

"I knew there was an emergency of some sort as soon as the real Sister grabbed you and pulled you in. And I knew you could help, that it was the real reason we were here in the first place. Heard the ambulance coming blocks away, knew right away it was headed to the Mission. But I don't know what kind of emergency."

I filled him in.

"So what about our ol' Dapper Dandy Dan?"

"Can you see if there's a back door?"

* * *

Talk about brass balls. Dandy Dan must have them. Through all that pandemonium with the ambulance, he was still out front manning the donations desk. I glanced back towards the dormitory room, making sure the curtains didn't show any shadow behind them. All clear. I went out the door to Father Dan.

"Father, can you please come help with me something? It won't take a minute."

He looked at the donations box.

"I really shouldn't leave—"

"No problem. We'll just take it inside with us." Jerk. That box might have twenty bucks in it but he couldn't leave it for a minute to help a nun? Even if I wasn't really a nun? This was one skip I really wanted to take in. I picked the box up and he followed the money like a dog following a bone.

"Okay, let's get this done. What do you need?"

I motioned him ahead of me towards the dormitory.

"I need help getting the cot mattress changed. The one that just had a baby delivered on it isn't reusable, now is it?"

He turned around with a pained expression on his face, slightly green around the gills, and started back toward the door, moving fast.

"Oh, no, not my department, that's not my—"

I stuck my foot out and he sprawled on the floor. Chad, moving with his usual cat-like speed in such situations, appeared from behind the curtains and jerked Dan's left hand up. He slapped a handcuff on it, grabbed his right hand and repeated the process.

"You mean it's honest birth blood, not blood money, huh? Well, you're right about one thing. Your hands really shouldn't touch it. They're too dirty."

"Not you again?"

"Oh, yeah, Danny Boy. It's me."

He hauled Dandy Dan up and we started out the door just as two more Sisters started in.

"What in Heaven's name is going on here? Why are you manhandling Father Dan?"

I figured I was the best person to defuse this situation. After all, we shopped at the same clothes store.

"Sisters, I'm Sister Mary Agrippa. Did Sister Marie by any chance call in for reinforcements?"

"Why yes, she did, Sister! And she said you were amazing! So why is Father Dan—"

"Sisters, I'm so sorry to tell you this, but Father Dan's been using the Mission as his front. He's not even a priest. He's just a bail-jumping con man who's been using you as cover while he stole money intended to help the kids."

"Oh, no!" The stricken looks on their faces hurt. But then, their lives truly were based on faith. And it infuriated me all over again that Dandy Dan could do this and not even care.

"I'm sorry, Sisters." One look at Chad told me it hit him the same way. "But he won't be bothering anyone for quite some time. I don't know how much is in his donations box over there, but whatever it is, at least your work'll get some of his collection efforts."

"No!" Dandy Dan didn't look slightly green around the gills now. He looked really green.

"Oh?" Chad's eyebrow raised. "Maybe you'd better check that box, Sisters."

"Oh, but should we? Take tainted money?"

I moved to the box and grabbed the lid. "Best way under Heaven to untaint it, Sister." I looked down and my eyes widened. "Oh. My. God."

Dandy Dan groaned. Chad shuffled him over and looked down. He laughed.

"So, Father Dan. You laundering drug money or you running bets?" The box held five big bundles of hundred dollar bills. Not a fortune, but enough for the Mission not to worry over the food bill for a while. Or any other bill.

"But we can't take that! It's not ours! And it's— it's—"

"If not the Mission's, then whose is it?" I asked.

"And who would you give it back to?" Chad added.

"They'll kill me over that money!" yelled Dan.

"Oh dear, we can't put anyone in danger—"

"He exaggerates, Sister. He'll be in a nice, safe jail. Who'll hurt him?" asked Chad.

"Well, the roof is in very bad shape, but—"

"Fix the roof, Sister. And feed the kids well."

* * *

"I dread telling Sister Marie I was a fake," I said, walking down the hall of the maternity ward of the South Central Medical Center.

"You're lots of things, baby girl, but fake ain't one of 'em. Here it is." He stopped in front of Room 577. We knocked on the semi-open door and were hailed in.

"Yes?" Sister Marie came toward us. "I'm sorry, do I know—" She broke off and looked at my eyes. "Sister Mary Agrippa."

"Not exactly. I mean, not only. I mean—"

"Child. Hush. Today you were Sister Mary Agrippa. And you did a great thing. Sister Grace and Sister Therese called and filled me in this afternoon about Father Dan. We do carry cell phones, you know." She pulled hers out of the pocket of her habit. "Impossible to stay in touch and coordinate all our work in today's world without them. It crossed my mind that as you left with the gentleman escorting Father Dan to the authorities, you might be with him."

"Yes. I'm Ariel Garrett, Sister. This is my husband, Chad."

She smiled and stuck out her beautiful, work-worn hand. "Very pleased to meet you, young man. You do this sort of thing often?"

"Fairly often, yes ma'am."

"Did you get a chance to kick him in the balls on the way to turn him in?"

I didn't choke but it was a near thing.

"No ma'am, I didn't."

236

"Pity. I'd have done it for you had I been there. Oh, well. Come in, dear. Sandra, here's the wonderful lady who helped us have that beautiful baby this afternoon. And Ariel, these are Sandra's parents, Ed and Beverly Jamison. Sandra gave me their names and permission to call them while the doctors finished all the childbirth repairs."

"You came!" Sandra exclaimed. "You promised you would, but I wasn't sure."

"Of course she did!" Sister Marie frowned at her. "She promised and she's a woman of her word. It's in her eyes."

I smiled. "I'm so glad you called your parents, Sandra." I turned to the Jamisons.

"And so happy to meet you."

Both the Jamisons stood and shook my hand. "Thank you. For sending our daughter back."

"I didn't do anything," I protested. "I'm sure she'd have called you this afternoon."

"Maybe."

We admired the baby for a few minutes and took our leave. Sister Marie took hers a few seconds later and called out behind us as we hit the elevator button.

"Garretts!"

We turned.

"I don't know exactly what you did but that baby would have been in trouble if you hadn't calmed Sandra down. And I don't believe for a minute she'd have called her parents without that parting salvo from you, I've been trying to get their names out of her for three months. And you, young man—" She turned to Chad. "You've done us a great service, getting that slime wad off the streets. Even if you didn't kick him in the balls. You have great gifts, both of you. Gifts from God. You know that, don't you?"

"Yes, ma'am," Chad said. "We do."

And we did. Because in the final analysis, all persons of power, every witch and warlock, knew there was an underlying power, a Grand Conductor, of the magic and music and majesty of the universe.

"And you'll never abuse those gifts."

"No, ma'am."

"You'll be in our prayers."

"Thank you, Sister. We take any help we get."

The elevator door opened and we stepped on. As the door closed, Sister Marie smiled and waved.

"Blessed be, Garretts!"

My eyes widened and the elevator slid downwards.

"Do you think Sister Marie's—"

"One of us? Not necessarily. But I wouldn't rule it out."

"You know what?"

"What?"

"I think I hear the Eagle calling. I'm ready for Daytona."

"Me too, baby girl. Me, too."

Chapter Thirty-Four

Spike pulled in just before dark Thursday afternoon behind the wheel of a shiny black F-350 pickup towing a shiny black and stainless steel motorcycle trailer. I glanced over at Chad, lost in cyberspace as he gazed into his computer screen. The Great Room of our island house wasn't big but economically designed to serve as both general living and office space. Right now he didn't even know where he was. I knew that look. He was tracing a skip and for Chad Garrett, that didn't mean just finding the cyberspace trail of past addresses. He was out there himself, in cyberspace, mental eyes following the path of the person he was looking for. Watching him. Seeing him. Becoming him. Just as profilers followed the criminals they looked for.

"Chad! Spike's here!"

Thor chimed in, too.

Chad shook his head slightly and returned.

"Damn good time, he only left yesterday morning."

We piled out to greet him, Thor in the lead. Raised a gentleman, he didn't jump the guest's bones but he sure wanted to. Spike laughed and patted his chest and Thor gave him a doggy hug, jumping off the ground a bit to include a face-wash.

"Boy! I promise I washed my face this morning, you don't need to worry about it!"

Chad and Spike did the male thing good buddies do that starts with a handshake and ends up in a half-hug with lots of back pounding. Spike hugged me, grabbed a small bag and we headed in.

"Is that all you brought?" I asked.

"The Dark Angel's already all packed up, honey."

Silly me. Of course it was. Our things were already packed in the Intimidator, too. One thing I'd learned about these bikers. Their bikes had names. Though I hadn't known Spike's Road King was the Dark Angel when I'd made its acquaintance back in Vegas. It was a monster, the epitome of biker luxury. The Intimidator wasn't as big but it was sleeker, meaner-looking somehow. And it was a Honda, not a Harley-Davidson. Chad thought Hondas attracted less attention than Harleys. We frequently found ourselves in situations wherein the less attention attracted, the better.

Spike didn't have to worry about that and couldn't not attract attention if he tried. On first impression, at least in biker gear, Spike was a black-haired six foot six gorilla. He'd grown a beard for Bike Week, as had Chad. Gotta have a beard for Bike Week. I liked Chad's so much I planned to campaign for permanent retention. On Spike, it was the crowning touch of gorilladom. Until you heard him talk, that is. His voice could still melt butter.

I glanced up at the porch as we climbed the steps, checking for Micah, the puzzle wrapped in an enigma. No way was he an ordinary barn cat. After his participation in our recent escapade with the Resurrection Society, I wasn't sure he was even a cat at all, though what else he could be I didn't know. He liked to inspect all visitors as they passed, including prospective clients. Most were approved with a purr when they passed by. Occasionally, they'd rate a hiss. I didn't doubt he'd approve of Spike and sure enough, he purred like the Dark Angel's motor in high gear.

"Hey, guy!" Spike paused and put his hand out to stroke Micah's fur. True to form, Micah leapt nimbly off the porch railing into the tree branches.

"Shy?" Spike asked.

"Unique," I said. "Long story."

"Your sister's not here yet?"

"She's coming in tomorrow morning."

"What's she do?"

"She's a paralegal. Like me."

"No, I mean is she—well, like you. Does she do anything—special?"

"Sure, she's special, she's my little sister!"

"You know what I meant."

Magic made Spike uncomfortable. He simultaneously believed and didn't. He believed Chad and I had power but he didn't understand how or why. Chad said he was in denial. He firmly believed Spike was a magical cauldron waiting to explode. I didn't want to create any tension by telling him exactly where Stacy's primary power lay.

"Yes, honey, I'm sorry, but she's special. We're just a growing little private Coven here, sorry."

"Makes life exciting. Makes me feel needed, too. This group needs somebody to balance it out as the poor, ordinary human."

We'd just settled at the table with nachos and tall beers when Chad's phone sounded. A ring-tone I'd never heard before. A ring-tone I didn't like a bit. Because Chad tailored his ring-tones. Business calls arrived to the beat of "This Gun's For Hire". Informants were announced by "Down in the Boondocks". Calls from G and the Guardians came in with the theme from "The Twilight Zone". So it was a no-brainer to surmise a call coming in to the strains of "Secret Agent Man" couldn't be good. Especially since I'd never heard it before. And especially when coupled with the look on Chad's face when he looked at me, which didn't even take into account the blank poker face Spike sported as he concentrated fiercely on the tortilla chips.

I could hear the gears in Chad's brain clicking. If he answered it, I'd hear the conversation. If he got up and went outside to answer it, I'd know he didn't want me to hear the conversation. A lose-lose situation.

He yanked the phone up to his ear, thumb hitting the button.

"Yeah?" I could hear the voice on the other end but not well enough to make out any words. "When and where?" More indistinguishable noise. "I'll look into it." He ended the call and put the phone back in his pocket.

"So," I said lightly, scooping up the cheesy, meaty nacho sauce on a chip. I held it in front of my mouth for a minute. "Is your phone goin' to self-destruct in sixty seconds or what?"

I popped the chip into my mouth and chewed.

He laughed. "Don't suppose it'd help any to claim it was a wrong number?"

"Not a bit."

"Didn't think so."

Spike decided it was safe to relax his facial muscles. "Thought you didn't, um, I mean, hadn't, um—"

"I don't and I haven't. Meant to change that damn ringtone, too."

"But not delete the number?" I raised my eyebrow slightly.

"It's not a number you can ever delete."

"Slavery's been abolished in this country since 1863. No indentured servitude anymore, either."

"Sometimes you might need to know something only the caller from that number can tell you."

"Like somebody's gotten out of the pen and is comin' for you?"

Spike laughed. "Damn, she's good. You know she knows, Magic Man, why don't you just spill it?"

"Okay, it's like this. All my work experience doesn't show up on my resume."

I didn't just laugh. In southern parlance, I hollered. I laughed so hard my sides hurt.

"Oh!" I gasped for breath and tried to stop laughing. "Oh, that's hysterical! So can you tell me something I don't already know?"

"Like I said, Magic Man, she's damn good. Even if she couldn't read your mind in the first place."

"I don't read his mind, exactly, I just—"

"Whatever the two of you do, you both do it damn good, darlin'. Close enough description for me."

"Okay, okay," Chad said. "I did some work a few years back for an agency that doesn't advertise for employees. To mingle in groups where most people don't fit in real well. That agency's misplaced one of their guys and they want me to keep an eye open for him, that's all."

"You rode undercover with an outlaw biker gang," I said.

"I didn't say that."

"Yes, you did. The timing did. We're leaving for Bike Week. If they know you, they know that. So that's where they want you to look for the operative they've misplaced. So he's a biker. I know most bikers and most motorcycle clubs are like you and Spike. They love motorcycles, riding, and the road. I also know there're such things as outlaw gangs. And I don't think there'd be any reason to have an operative go undercover in a regular bike club. Either you or the guy who's gone MIA. Which operative would, by necessity, have to be a hell of a biker to begin with. How'm I doin' so far?"

"Pretty good."

"Spike, that number ever ring on your phone?"

"Oh, hell no!"

"But you know about it."

"My connection's through Chad. I just helped him out once, I never actually worked for 'em."

"You don't think it's risky, runnin' around Daytona during Bike Week? Like maybe somebody might recognize you?"

"Baby girl, nobody's going to recognize me."

"Because you had spiral curls down to your shoulders?"

Spike laughed.

"I'll take that as a yes."

"Half-way down my back, matter of fact. Red ones."

"Still the voice thing."

"Ain't nobody goan connect Chad Garrett's voice wid'a Alabama Sno'man, darlin', ya know whut I mean, c'mon back?"

My mouth dropped open. Chad's voice was usually accentless, especially for Georgia where the southern lilt varied region to region, sometimes county to county. A stranger'd just spoken at my table, in a deep, backwoods country drawl that bore almost as little resemblance to Chad's normal voice as it did to mine.

"You got any more of those?" I demanded.

"More of what?"

"Accents."

"Yeah."

"Like what?"

"Like whatever I need at the time and place I need it. Cajun. Hillbilly. The Bronx. Brooklyn. Texas. The Dakotas." His accent kept changing. "Now can we finish eating? It's not a big deal, I just said I'd keep my eyes open while we were there."

"Sure," I said. No point in beating the subject to death. Or letting him know I knew damn well he'd be doing a lot more than keeping an eye open. Members of law enforcement, no matter the branch, were a brotherhood. Bikers were a brotherhood. And that cut both ways. Because what would happen to an undercover agent who'd infiltrated an outlaw gang, taken their oaths, eaten with them, ridden with them, sworn brotherhood with them—and then betrayed them—I didn't even want to think about. Chad knew that a hell of a lot better than I did. This missing operative was a brother in all categories. A biker. A biker agent who'd infiltrated an outlaw gang. No, this Bike Week wasn't a social event anymore. Not for Chad Garrett. And I knew it.

Chapter Thirty-Five

Stacey beeped her car horn at precisely ten a.m. the next morning. Amazing. Neither she nor I were noted for timely appearances. Thor tore out the door in front of me and Micah assumed his perch position on the porch railings, though where he'd come from, I had no idea. I'd tried to turn him into a house cat with no luck, but wherever he stayed, he never missed a visitor.

She bounced out of the driver's door, already road-ready in black leather pants and black leather jacket, and ran toward me. With her glorious swirl of reddish blonde hair and bright blue eyes, she looked fabulous.

"Sister hugs!" she shouted.

"Sister hugs!" I shouted back. We met in the middle and did the sister thing. Chad and Spike came out of the side garage where they'd been fine-tuning the bikes. Stacy and Spike didn't just see each. They *saw* each other. A faint surge of delicate pink like the shading on a blush rose filled the air between them. Umm. Something new, I'd never seen anything quite like it. I made the introductions.

"Spike, Stacy. Otherwise known as Antsypants. Stacy, Spike. Also known as Dr. Forrester, but I don't have a clue as to any other name." And I didn't. It'd never occurred to me before but I didn't know Spike's real name.

"Spike works just fine," he assured me. "Even the kids call me Dr. Spike. Hi, Stacy, nice to meet you."

"You, too."

There was that surge again. That faint path of pink in the air between them. This time a darker pink. Definitely.

"How'd they get Antsypants out of Stacy?"

"It's not from Stacy. It's from my whole name. Anastasia. Anastasia and Ariel. Our folks swear they didn't smoke a lot of pot in college but what with our names, we've never believed 'em. How'd you get Spike?"

"Long story."

"You don't have a hug for your favorite brother-in-law?" Chad asked. "And where's your bag? You pack like we told you?"

"You know I do!" Stacy delivered the hug. "And I packed what you told me. Don't know about the how you told me."

I'd be real surprised if she had. It was something that had to be seen, not explained, manipulating clothes into the tight rolls that fit a bike's saddlebags.

"Well, let's go fine-tune," Chad said, grabbing her bag out of the backseat of her car.

Stacy's brows raised.

"Chad! Give me the bag and let me go pack the saddlebag!"

"Not meaning to be insulting here, babe, but you just watched me do it one time."

"Yeah, I know," I said, deftly transferring the case from his hand to mine. I'd already stashed Stacy's saddlebag in our bedroom. "But women got this thing. We just don't like men handlin' our underwear. Unless we want 'em to. I can do it good enough."

Stacy laughed. "Oh, my God! You've really come out of your shell, haven't you?" I'd always been the reserved one. Borderline prim and prissy on occasion. Stacy'd always been the spontaneous one. Until Chad.

Stacy and I excused ourselves from masculine eyes, adjourned to my bedroom and I rolled her clothes, including undies, into some semblance of the neat, tight rolls packed in my own saddlebag. It was close enough for horseshoes anyway. Everything fit.

Ten minutes later we were on the road, leaving Buddy in charge of Thor and the rest of the menagerie.

I made a special point of checking Micah's whereabouts. Sure enough, he held vigil on the porch railings. The question was—would he stay there? Or even at Pine Whisper. Sometimes Micah showed up in the damndest places. I glanced over at the Dark Angel. Stacy rode with her arms around Spike's waist, foregoing the sissy bar on the back of the seat. Stacy'd never met a stranger in her life, and while she wasn't as relaxed as she'd be a hundred miles down the road, she clearly didn't feel self-conscious. Considering their proximity to each other on the back of that bike, I wasn't surprised to see the path of pink surrounded them like a halo. Getting darker every minute.

I shook my head, deliberately clearing it of the spider-webs of alarm that always shrouded me when I climbed aboard the Intimidator. I tightened my arms around Chad's waist, threw my head back, and let the road and wind take me.

* * *

A faint wail sounded behind us right before the county line, growing steadily louder. I glanced over at the rear view mirror, expecting the Sheriff's Department's Crown Victoria to whip on around us and pass. Instead, the lights flashed the unmistakable signal to pull over. Spike and Chad maneuvered up to the entrance to a handy farm road and cut both bikes' engines, standing straight-legged to hold them up.

The Crown Vic's door slammed. Chad turned his head to watch the deputy's approach.

"Hey, Dave!" Chad knew all the deputies, no surprise there. I'd met a few of the county deputies but I hadn't met this one yet. "What's shaking?"

"Right now, Chad, you are."

"How so?"

"Well," Deputy Dave scratched his head. "It's like this. You're under arrest."

"Say what?"

"I know, I know, and I'm sorry as hell, and if you say I said that I'll call you a liar, but I got a warrant from Magistrate Court to arrest you and instructions not to fart around about it. Buddy said y'all had just left for Daytona and I'da been up the creek without a paddle if I hadn't caught up to you."

"Arrest me for what?"

"You have the right to remain silent. If you give up—"

"Dave! I know the damned Miranda Rights as good as you do!"

"—the right to remain silent anything you say can and will be used against you in a Court of law you have the right to have an attorney—"

"Dave!"

"—if you cannot afford an attorney one will be appointed for you now do you understand these rights?" He finished in a mad rush. "Chad, I'm sorry, you know you gotta let me say it!"

"I know this is a bunch of bullshit and so do you. Question is, you gonna tell me what type of bullshit it is or let me get sucker-punched? Any more sucker-punched than I am right now, that is? I didn't leave your ass hanging in the wind last year when you were getting jumped by those four thugs at the Texaco when I pulled in to gas up!"

Deputy Dave took a deep breath. "I know, I know. And yeah, I know I'da been in the hospital instead of the ER if you hadn't pulled in when you did. I know that, okay? But you didn't hear this from me. Right?"

"Dave, you're deaf and mute. Okay?"

"Richard Quisenberry. Trespassing and harassment."

"Quisenberry? Why that—"

"Quisenberry's that serve you did Tuesday. The federal complaint." I'd typed it up and put it in the system. Disguised in pretty language, it alleged the local stock broker was engaged in fraudulent activity. In legal shorthand, he was in violation of the RICO Act.

In layman's terms, racketeering. "Anything unusual happen you didn't tell me about?" I hadn't gone with him on that serve. It'd come in suddenly and I'd been in the middle of baking. Not a good idea to leave pound cakes unattended in the oven.

"Not a damn thing. I got to his office, door was open, nobody up front. I shouted out, no answer. But somebody was there, I knew that. Just not anybody willing to show. So I drove to his house, knocked on the door. Wife answered, said he wasn't home, he'd be there about six. I parked across the street from his house, waited for him, served him. That's it."

"You didn't have any reason to do any of that 'cause it was an illegal serve 'cause you didn't have an Order to serve him in the first place," Dave said. "Chad, what were you thinkin'? And because you didn't have an Order to serve him, you had no business being in his office after hours, 'specially since he says you walked in while he was in the Men's Room, stompin' and stormin' around opening doors and hollerin' for him to come out if he knew what was good for him."

"I what?"

"And after that, you terrorized his wife and scared her to death when you parked across the street. Like you were stakin' the house out and stalkin' her, don't you know? The Judge and the Sheriff were eatin' it up with a spoon, Chad, you know they jump on a chance to take you down a peg, way you're always showin' em up!"

"That is the biggest bunch of bullshit—"

"And now you know everything I know and I am so fired if anybody finds that out!" Dave finished. "Chad, why the hell would you try to serve him without an Order of Service? You know how they are about that in this Circuit! I shouldn't have to tell you!"

"Dave. It was a Federal complaint!"

"So?"

"So you're a deputy! A law enforcement professional! Don't you know the difference?"

I jumped in before Chad could hurt Dave's feelings. He hadn't had to tell us all this, and the more we knew and the earlier we knew it, the better.

"You don't need an Order of Service to serve a Federal complaint, Dave. Anybody over eighteen can do it. I could've done it. You couldn't do it, I guess, not officially, seein' as how you're State. But that's the difference, Federal doesn't need an Order. So this whole thing is based on the Magistrate Judge gettin' pissy about there not being an Order of Service?"

"You sure about that?" Dave asked, like I'd spouted heresy.

Lots of counties in Georgia gave private process servers permanent Orders of Appointment and Chad had them. Everywhere they were offered. But the Southern Judicial Circuit was one of the few circuits where permanent appointments weren't available, and either the attorney or the process server himself did have to run a Judge to ground and get an Order signed allowing him to serve a paper. It was part of the good ol' boy system that wasn't going to change. It gave the Courts and the Sheriff's Departments a little extra clout. In the State Court system, that is. It didn't give them shit when it came to Federal procedure. And the Federal boys weren't going to be happy a Magistrate Judge thought it did.

"Yes, Dave. She's sure. I'm sure. You ought to be sure."

"So," Stacy said. "First things first. This is a town big-wig, I'm thinkin'?"

"Oh, yeah."

"And you served him and he didn't like it. In a nutshell."

"Tight nutshell," Spike said.

"But he's a really big big-wig or he couldn't have gotten this warrant issued on this."

"Right. Big checkbook when it comes to the local elections."

"Bottom-line," I said, "the basis of all this is the no Order of Service thing. Because you were certainly authorized to go inside his public, unlocked business and wait for him at his house since you were trying to serve process. Though it's stupid to try and charge trespass at the office anyway. Because it's a business open to the public. Even after hours, if the door wasn't locked, of course it's reasonable to go in. I mean, hell, technically, even vampires don't need to be invited into a business. The public's invited."

"Ma'am?" Dave's eyes widened.

"I'm just sayin' how ridiculous this is, Dave, I don't mean it literally."

"Yes, ma'am." He didn't look convinced. I wondered if Chad's local reputation was more colorful than we'd supposed.

"Now, the house—"

"The house is even more ridiculous," said Stacy. "Where else are you goin' to try serve somebody first, other than their business or house?"

"But it still all boils down to a pissin' contest about the Order of Service thing." I said.

"Which I don't get. Any lawyer, let alone any Judge, knows Federal Complaints don't need—ah! Magistrate Court. How silly of me."

"Why?" Spike asked.

"Because in lots of rural counties like this, most Magistrate Judges aren't lawyers, just elected officials," explained Stacy. "Here, I'm assuming?"

"Oh, yeah" I confirmed. "That good ol' boy system. And throw Judge in front of a grocer's name, he automatically thinks he graduated from Harvard and sits on the Supreme Court. Their three-week crash course after election mostly just teaches 'em enough to be dangerous. Though come to think of it, down here I think the Mag Judge was an insurance salesman."

"But I still got a warrant and I got to take Chad in," said Dave.

"Well," I said, "there's that, yeah."

"So Chad, can you please just get in the squad car—"

"Hell, no, I'm not getting in the squad car! We're on cycles, didn't you notice? Neither my wife nor my sister-in-law can operate a motorcycle and if you think I'm leaving the Intimidator—or my wife—by the side of the road, you're crazy! We'll follow you in. Ariel, you got a plan?"

"Damn straight I do. That complaint was out of the Middle District."

Stacy laughed. "Thank God for small mercies!"

"Sorry, I don't quite get why that's so good," said Spike.

"I do. The girls are paralegal eagles, remember? They know people. And the Middle District's their home stomping ground."

* * *

Back at the station, they hauled Chad off to the proverbial "back room". They didn't invite me. No surprise there.

"Y'all can wait out in the waitin' area, honey," the secretary offered.

"Thanks, but we'll be outside. Call us when we can talk to him, please?"

"Will do."

I had calls to make and people to talk to and I didn't have any intention of doing it in the waiting area.

We trooped out and stood in the parking lot by the bikes. I looked at Stacy and raised my eyebrow.

"Pete Donavan," she said, without hesitation. "If he's not there, try for Rick Ingles."

"Not Troy Shannahan?"

"Not an ADA anymore. Left and went into private practice two weeks ago."

Spike looked awestruck. And the private pink highway between them darkened a bit more.

"Damn, you two know your stuff, don't you? What's an ADA?"

"Assistant District Attorney," Stacy explained.

"With the added advantage that all three of 'em left our old firm to go Federal," I added. "So they know us."

We lucked out. Pete Donavan was in. And when I explained the situation, he wasn't happy about it.

"Damn small town hicks think they freakin' write the law! Okay, get me the Magistrate Judge's name—never mind, that was stupid, I'll look it up. Give me five minutes—"

"Not that quick, Pete, the deputy wasn't supposed to tell us all this, I have to wait till I'm supposed to know—" My phone signaled an incoming. Chad. "Hold on for me, Chad's calling. Must be his one phone call."

I clicked over.

"My one phone call. Trespass and harassment based on illegal serve on Quisenberry," he confirmed. "Go get 'em."

"Will do," I confirmed, and clicked back over to Pete. "Okay, now I officially know. I just hope the Judge is in. It's Friday afternoon."

"Well, if he isn't, the Sheriff has to be," Pete said. "And after I read him the riot act, I'll throw in some hints that incidents like this are the stuff civil complaints for false arrest are made from, too, if you want to throw that around yourself. Stand by for fireworks."

* * *

Twenty minutes later a 90's model pink Cadillac careened into the parking lot. It came to a screeching halt and parked at the wrong angle in a diagonal parking space marked "Reserved for Staff".

A short, pudgy man with a very red face and thinning hair threw the door open and stormed inside.

"Whatcha' bet that's the Mag Judge?" Stacy laughed.

"Pink Cadillac?" Spike looked slightly nauseous.

"I've never met him but Chad did tell me his wife was a real Mary Kay success story. Let's mosey on in, why don't we? Maybe throw in the names of the attorneys we're considering for the false arrest complaint."

Chad was walking out the door by the time we got back in, the short, pudgy red-faced man at his side.

"Now, Chad, I'm real sorry 'bout this misunderstandin', don't quite know how it happened. You're a professional, you know mistakes happen—"

I walked up to Chad and hooked my arm through his.

"So! Everything straightened out? Judge Ogles, I take it. Never met you, sir. Ariel Garrett."

He almost tripped over his feet in his haste to take my offered hand.

"Delighted, Miz Garrett, delighted to meet you. And sorry for the inconvenience, like I was tellin' Chad, just don't understand how the mix-up happened. Sure hope there's no hard feelin's, we're all in the same business, just want to keep the legal system movin', you know."

"Oh, I understand completely, Judge. I've spent years in a law office as a paralegal. One of the big ones, up in Macon. Know a lot of the attorneys, too. So I know all about the inner workings of the legal system. State, Superior, Federal. Stressful field, very stressful. 'Course the advantage is I always have an attorney when I need one. And I always know which one I need."

I smiled brightly and Judge Ogles turned slightly green.

"*Erphm*, yeah, well, I hope you don't need one anytime soon."

"I hope she doesn't need another one anytime soon, too," said Chad, throwing the slightest emphasis on 'another'. "Baby girl, I'm ready to blow this joint. Let's get back on the road, the Eagle's not just calling, he's screaming."

Chapter Thirty-Six

We hit I-95 and rolled into Daytona right at sunset, heading straight for N. Atlantic Avenue and the hotel. Traffic was horrendous and slow and Chad's brush with the jail cell had cost us two hours. Masses of bikes and bike trailers and pickups and cars moved bumper to bumper on the roads and jammed into parking lots, so it seemed like a good idea to make sure we had a place to lay our heads when it was time to lay them, reservations or not.

The desk clerk's eyes widened as he looked at the computer screen. Not a good sign. He looked up at Spike and Chad and blinked nervously. Nope, not a good sign.

"Uh, sir, I'm sorry, but it appears those rooms were—they're not—they've already been taken."

"Excuse me?"

"They, uh, they—those rooms aren't available, sir."

"The hell you say!"

The clerk backed up behind the desk. I would have, too. I'd never heard Spike's voice sound like anything but melted butter—damn, that man had a great voice—but he could growl like a grizzly, too.

"Get the manager up here. Now." Chad didn't make a move toward him but the poor guy backed up some more anyway, just to be safe. He reached out a cautious hand and grabbed the phone. Even more cautiously, he reached out and punched a button.

"Mr. Harris? Can you come up front, please?" He hung up and backed away some more. "He'll be right up."

He was. And very flustered to boot. The first day of Bike Week's enough to make any manager of any hotel run screaming through the streets. He was a consummate professional, though. I could see the memory chips churning in his brain. He forced a smile and offered his hand.

"Mr. Garrett! Mr. Forrester! Nothing finer than returning guests!"

I made a mental note Spike didn't advertise the M.D. after his name when in biker mode.

"Not when they're as pissed off as we are."

"I'm sorry, I don't—"

"Both of us have had standing reservations with you booked a year in advance for at least five years. And your clerk here tells us our rooms have already been taken?" Chad pointed back at the desk clerk, standing a good distance back from the desk. "The year I bring my wife and sister-in-law with us?"

"I'm sure there's been some mix-up." The manager went behind the desk and commandeered the computer. "Just let me—" He broke off and frowned. Then he turned to the desk clerk and frowned harder.

"Tyler? What's going on here?"

"I just took the desk an hour ago, Mr. Harris! Jeff was on duty!" Tyler grabbed a ringing phone and turned aside.

"And Jeff took some money under the counter to do some room-switching, I'm thinking," said Chad.

"In which case Jeff's ass better be grass," Spike added.

Mr. Harris abandoned any pretense of professionalism. "His ass is grass whether he took money for it or not! He's completely fucked up—ah, excuse me, ladies, my apologies—he's completely screwed up the reservations!"

"So what are you going to do fix it?"

"I don't have any idea in hell! Too many rooms I know were reserved by returning guests—"

Spike's spine stiffened to showcase every inch of his impressive six foot six and wide shoulder span. He put the mellow back in his voice, which made his looming bulk even scarier. I'd have been scared if I didn't know him, for sure.

"We really aren't worried about how you fix it for anybody else. We're only worried about how you're going to fix it for us. Because these ladies aren't going to be sleeping in the streets. I'm sure you understand that?"

Mr. Harris blanched. "I don't have anything—"

"Sure you do," Chad assured him. "You just haven't seen it yet."

He turned back to the screen and chewed the inside of his cheek as Tyler hung up.

"Mr. Harris! That was a cancellation!"

"Tyler, don't joke with me about something like—"

"No! For really real, Mr. Harris! And what with all this, I told the guy we wouldn't even charge his card!" Tyler's wide smile turned to a worried frown. "I didn't figure you'd mind."

"Mind! Hell, boy, you're up for the next promotion! What room is it?"

"Let's see." Tyler took over the computer. "Looks like—it's a double! Two queens!"

"We had suites."

"But I don't—I can't—"

"Let it go, guys. We'll work it out," I said. Besides, I needed the ladies. And pretty damn quick, too. "Take it and get the room cards."

* * *

We parked the bikes as near our room number as possible and I snatched one of the cards away from Chad. Racing ahead, I swiped the card and hit the bathroom. When I came out, the three other members of our merry quartet were dropping saddle bags on the bed and taking stock of the situation.

"They have bathrooms in the lobby, you know," Chad said.

"Yeah, real crowded, real small ones, didn't you notice? There was a line in front of the Ladies."

I looked around at the room. It held two queen beds with a nightstand between them, a nightstand on each of the other sides, and nothing else. There wasn't room for anything else. This room hadn't started life as a "double".

"Well, so much for sleeping on the couch," said Spike. "Or asking for a cot. Nowhere to put one. Okay, I'll take the floor."

"You can't sleep on the floor!" Stacy and I exclaimed in unison. "Look, guys, it's not what we planned but it's what we got," I continued. "And damn lucky to get it. No point in anybody sleeping on the floor. Besides, we'd step on you if we had to go to the bathroom! It's very simple. Chad?" I gave him a look demanding back-up. He sighed.

"Yeah, it is. The girls take one bed, we'll take the other and we can pile a bunch of pillows in the middle so Spike and I won't accidently touch each other." He shuddered. Guys. You had to love 'em.

I laughed. "You two would guard each other's backs to the death in a fight but you're afraid you might accidently touch each other? Boys don't have nearly as much fun at sleep-overs as girls, do they? Too worried about the macho thing."

"That's why boys have twin beds or bunk beds in their rooms and girls have canopied double beds."

"Guess so. So—are we doin' Daytona or what? 'Cause I'm getting hungry."

* * *

We roared off into the night, headed back to Daytona's Main Street. It was already dark but the streets were full of light. And bikes. A steady parade of them, from the smallest and simplest to the biggest and most elaborate. Bikers of all shapes and sizes. Dress code ranged from "classic" biker solid black to "gothic" biker—solid black with lots of chains and tattoos, complete with white face paint and brilliant red lips, painted to drip blood. Dogs of all sizes rode with their biker humans. The smaller ones peeked out from saddle bags and carriers, or even their owner's jackets. Bigger ones perched between the rider's legs. Lots of women rode their own bikes and lots of others rode "bitch" like me and Stacy. The one constant among them all were the jackets with the identifying insignia. The "colors". The club identity. Even I knew the respect rendered by the clubs to a biker's colors.

Parked bikes lined the streets. The names flashed by. Gilly's Pub 44, Boot Hill Saloon, Main Street Station, a big Harley-Davidson dealer, Dog House Bar, Full Moon Saloon, Bank & Blues, Dirty Harry's. We cruised slowly up the street, the guys' heads turning side to side. Looking for a place to park I assumed. I figured I was right when Spike turned into a spot that looked barely large enough to hold the Dark Angel. There was another spot a few bikes up for the Intimidator.

We all unstrapped our helmets and I waited for Chad to get off so I could swing my leg over.

"Wait," he said. "Now listen. With bikes, it's look, don't touch. Don't touch anybody's bike."

Stacy and I looked at each other and back at Chad. "Oddly enough, darlin', that's not a problem. Believe it or not, neither of us feel any compelling need to caress a Harley-Davidson."

"And besides, we were raised to be polite and it's not polite to touch other folks' things," Stacy added.

Spike laughed. "Told you, didn't they? You forget Chad, they're ladies. They're not club mamas."

"Sorry. It's just—you get in trouble touching bikes down here. Because of that." He pointed to a slow-moving trailer-truck driving by.

"And that is?"

"An outlaw gang cruising for bikes. They grab 'em to strip for parts. Toss 'em in those, they're called crash vans. Big business for 'em, very profitable. Bikers like us, individuals, we never leave the bikes out of our sight. Pick a restaurant. And that one," he pointed, "has some damn good barbecue. With a great bar and live entertainment, so we won't have to try and find another parking spot."

"Sounds good to me," I said.

Hungry as I was, I pulled Chad back as Stacy and Spike went on in.

"Wanta show me the picture?"

"What picture?"

"The picture you got last night or this morning from those folks who want you to keep an eye open for the missing person. You can't look for somebody if you don't know what they look like. So I know they emailed you his file. Last night or this morning. And I'm pretty sure Spike's on the lookout, too. I'm another pair of eyes."

Chad rolled his own eyes but didn't argue. He pulled out his phone, maneuvered to the right spot and turned the screen toward me. I studied it closely. Typical biker. Not anyone who'd stand out in this crowd. Naturally not. Wouldn't be much of an undercover man if he did. I concentrated on the mouth and eyes. A voice clip would've been better, I'm good with voices, but we take what we can get.

"Thank you," I said. "Now let's eat."

Yep, great barbecue. Though of course I was so hungry pretty much any food would've tasted great.

"Do we need to be?" Stacy asked through a mouthful of pickle.

"Need to be what?"

"Club mamas," she said. "Spike said we weren't club mamas."

Chad choked. "No!"

"You sure?" I asked. "I mean, this biker thing the two of you have—"

Spike took over, seeing as how Chad was still choking. "Honey, club mamas are strictly one percent clubs. They have club mamas, the other ninety-nine percent of bikers most certainly don't. And to be a club mama, a woman has to sleep with the club. The whole club. Every member. So there won't be any jealousy. No, the two of you don't have club mama in your futures."

"Damn sure don't," Stacy affirmed. "What's a one percent club?"

"An outlaw club," Chad clarified. "Also known as an OMG. One-percent Motorcycle Gang. Roughly one percent of bikers ride outside the law. They're one percenters. Look around. You see a 1% patch on a jacket as part of the colors—that's an outlaw biker."

Stacy glanced around. "And they just advertise it? Oh! Over there. There's a couple. And there's a few more."

"It's Bike Week. Daytona's neutral ground. It's for everybody. But you still don't let your bike get out of your sight. Why we're sitting at this table and Spike and I have a full view of the bikes." And in fact, we were at a table near a window and Chad and Spike were both positioned for a full view of the outside.

"Then what are you gonna do about them at night? At the hotel?"

"We know some guys in a big club stay at our hotel every year, too. The big clubs always park together and keep a sentry on duty all night. They let us park with them."

"*Ewwwwwwwwwwwwhhhhhhhh!*"

A shriek sounded from the loud and raucous table next to us. A chair banged back and high-pitched feminine laughter exploded as a gyrating body danced in the floor space between tables.

"Okay, honey, you been waiting to do that all night! Get your eye-full!"

Stacy's eyes widened as the long-haired blonde thrust out her considerable chest, now showcased by the white t-shirt dripping beer. I'd already noticed bras weren't considered a necessary part of the wardrobe for Bikers Week. Certainly not by this blonde."

One of the guys at the blonde's table clapped madly and shouted "Too many dry t-shirts in this place! Let's fix that!"

A deluge of beer exploded over my chest. Stacy gasped with me and I knew she'd been baptized too.

"Aw man! No fair! These chicks wearin' bras!"

"You gotta be kiddin'!"

"C'mon, lil' darlin's, you gotta get with the program here!"

"You want a program, buddy? How's this for a program? How's this feel?" Stacy surged out of her chair and drew the arm holding her beer mug back in a modified version of her fast pitch that had terrorized every neighborhood ball game we'd ever played. She got two of the cat-callers with one shot. Full in the face. I wasn't sure she'd gotten the one calling attention to our under-apparel wardrobe and besides, I didn't want her having all the fun, so I stood up and tossed mine. I got two of them too, not as forcefully as Stacy's toss, but I'd never been an athlete.

The tossed bikers sputtered. The blonde with the impressive chest screamed "Bitch!" She grabbed her mug and tossed the contents in our direction. She'd never played neighborhood ball though. It went way wide and caught a biker sitting at a table next to ours.

"Son-of-a-bitch!" Everybody at that table picked up their mugs. Beer exploded over Chad and Spike and quite a few innocent by-standers.

"Ass-hole!"

"Fucker!"

Within minutes, the whole place joined the action. Clouds of beer rained down over the whole room.

Chad grabbed my hand, Spike grabbed Stacy's, and pulled us, non-too gently, toward the door, ducking under arms and weaving through bodies. As we passed the register, Chad tossed our bill and a hundred onto the counter.

"Keep the change!" We barreled out onto the street and stood. We all looked at each other.

Chad shook his head.

"Damn, can't take you two anywhere."

Chapter Thirty-Seven

We found a t-shirt shop, not hard on Main Street, and changed in the back. I handed a plastic bag to Chad.

"Stash this on the bike."

"Didn't you just chuck those? No point hauling around wet t-shirts."

"No point at all. These are our bras. Both of 'em are Vicky's Secret bras. We're not tossin' fifty dollar bras, boy, you crazy or something? Besides, mine's the red and black one you like so much."

"And mine's my best black lace."

"Thanks for sharing," Spike said. That pink highway running between him and my little sister darkened even more. Now it was hot pink.

"*Okaaaay*, then let's stop and stash this on the Intimidator. Then how 'bout that place over there? Live jazz, the action's a little less—overt—in there. Bikes'll still be in sight, too."

"Works for us."

We started off toward the live jazz club. Spike stumbled and almost fell.

"What the—"

A black cat shot out from under his feet and wove his way through the stands of bikes.

"Oh, shit," I said.

"C'mon, Ari! You've never been superstitious about black cats," Stacy said.

"I'm still not. But that wasn't just any black cat."

"Then what was it?"

"Honey, that's not your cat. I promise. That's not Micah."

"Yeah, that's what you said in Savannah," I reminded him.

Spike raised his eyebrows.

"Wait a minute! You think that's your black cat? From Pine Whisper?"

"I don't think. I know."

"No offense, sweetheart, but that's just nuts!"

"No, it's not. It's trouble. Big time."

"One little cat can't cause that much trouble. Even if it is yours, which it can't be."

"He doesn't cause trouble. He gets me out of trouble. Which means it's coming. Big time."

* * *

I didn't really notice the action was any less overt over at the jazz club. What I did notice was a group of bikers and their female companions at a far table. Bikers wearing 1% patches. Staring at Chad. The colors identified them as the "Dark Rulers". I pulled his arm and maneuvered us toward the edge of the body-to-body dance floor.

"What's the matter, baby girl? Getting tired?"

"Don't look, but see that group over there at the table under the crystal light thingy?"

"Well, since I'm not supposed to look, not really."

"Smart-ass. Edge around and look. But not like you're lookin'. You're the damn professional, not me."

He laughed. "I knew what you meant, just couldn't resist. Okay, let me turn you around here. Okay, got 'em."

"They're staring at you. Hard. Especially one of the women."

"Jealous? I don't get upset when guys stare at you hard. Unless they try to touch, of course."

"Will you be serious? It's like they recognize you. Especially her. You told me nobody'd recognize you."

"You mean from my checkered past?" He shrugged. "Nobody ever has."

265

"Which doesn't mean nobody ever will. Do you recognize them? Especially her? And don't you dare ask me if I'm jealous!"

"No, I don't recognize 'em. You're getting tired, aren't you, and don't lie about it."

"A little, sure, but I'm all right." And for damn sure I wasn't so tired I didn't notice the psychic shield he'd just thrown up.

"Nope. Main Street'll be here tomorrow. Let's collect the crew and head back. Think they're getting along with each other?"

Which meant he sure as hell had recognized the woman staring at him and wanted to get the hell out of there. Without it seeming like he did.

I glanced around, trying to spot Spike and Stacy on the crowded floor. There they were. Surrounded by their private halo of color, now edging past hot pink over to red.

"Oh, yeah."

* * *

The hotel room wasn't a bit bigger when we got back, but all Stacy and I really cared about was the shower. We'd stopped smelling beer hours ago, but the residue was sticky.

"You go first," I said. Big sisters looked after little sisters. Big sister habits died hard.

"You go first. You got a lot more directly on you than I did."

"Okay, we'll do it the fair way. Paper, rock, scissors. Ready?"

"Ready."

"One, two, three—" I looked down at our hands.

"Rock breaks scissors," Stacy said. "You go."

"And to avoid tying up the bathroom, we'll make it a double." Chad slipped neatly through the door and pulled me in after him.

"Excuse me?" I hissed furiously.

He leaned close and whispered in my ear. "Baby girl, we're in a double room with two other people. For several more days. Got to grab opportunity when we get it."

I turned and started the water.

"Only thing you're grabbin' with somebody right outside that door is a shower. And with two other people out there who'd also like to feel clean, you're doin' it damn quick."

"You're a fascinating blend of pure lady and wild child, I ever tell you that?"

"Yeah, frequently. Now move it."

* * *

We all showered the beer residue off and hit our respective assigned beds—which meant extra pillows piled in the middle of the guys' bed to their complete satisfaction so as to assure no accidental touching. Unfortunately, showers usually revived me somewhat no matter how tired I was. They also had the same effect on Stacy. From the changed rhythm of the guys' breathing, hot water didn't have the same effect on them. They were passed out. I stared at the ceiling and tried to wind down. Wasn't working. Wasn't working for Stacy, either.

"Ari?"

"Yeah?" I braced myself and grabbed the edge of my pillow. From years of slumber parties, I knew what was coming.

"Gottcha!"

"Gottcha first!" I rolled and snatched my pillow from under my head, slamming it into Stacy's pillow before it connected with my face. Both of us perched on our knees and plummeted our pillows against the other.

"What the hell—" The two large bodies from the next bed sat up at the same time.

"Pillow fight! You snooze, you lose!" As one, we bounded across the twelve inch space between the beds onto theirs and started pelting. Besides, all the fresh ammunition was on their bed. That male "don't touch each other" thing. They sputtered, grabbed for pillows, and came out swinging. Pillows flew everywhere, in every direction.

Calling up memories of too many pillow fights to count, both of us swerved and twisted Ninja-style. The guys didn't have a chance. Then I lost my balance and fell full forward onto Chad. On the way down, I knocked Stacy off balance and she smashed into Spike, knocking him flat onto the bed and landing full on top of him. The aura of color surrounding them pulsed and turned crimson. So did Stacy's cheeks. Spike's Las Vegas desert tan was too dark to turn crimson, but there was some extra color there, for sure. Stacy sprang back up, grabbed a pillow and started swinging again.

Since we were making so much noise ourselves, the vibrations filtered through first. Pounding feet shook the walkway in front of our second floor room.

Then we heard the outside screams.

"Coward! Why'd you want it, you ain't man enough to handle it?"

"Help! Get her off me!" Strangled coughs and gasps for breath. "Crazy bitch tryin' to fuckin' kill me!!"

"You wanted it, honey, you got it! Too much for you? Come back here and take it like a man!"

"What the hell—" Stacy bounded to the edge of the bed and fumbled at the lamp, bringing the room out of shadow.

More voices chimed in from outside.

"*Whoo-whoo!!* You go, girl! Show him who's boss!"

"Man up, dude! You're embarrassing all of us! You're actin' like a sissy girl!"

Chad and Spike groaned simultaneously and threw the covers off their respective sides.

"Shit!" Spike, impressive biceps highlighted by the tight white t-shirt and sleep pants, navigated towards the chair by the door where I'd seen him stash his medical bag. "Owww!" His bare foot smashed into the corner of the bed.

"What the hell is going on out there?"

"First case of attempted death by boobs of the night, probably," Chad said, throwing the door open.

"Death by boobs?"

A naked biker was on his knees in front of our door. His equally naked lady friend stood in front of him, bent over slightly. She clasped his head tightly between her impressive chest equipment. The gasps for breath reached new heights of desperation.

"Are those real?" Stacy whispered in awe.

"Not in a million years," I whispered back.

"Okay, honey, okay!" Chad grabbed her hands and pried the laced fingers apart. "You've proved your point, let him loose!" The biker slumped onto the walkway, gulping and wheezing. Spike knelt beside him on the concrete and opened his bag.

"Steady, guy, c'mon, you'll live. Probably." He pulled out his stethoscope and started checking the man's heartbeat.

One of the bystanders catcalled. "Oh, man, check this out! The doctor from the Cartoon Channel! Dude's got Spongebob Squarepants on his stethoscope!"

Spike ignored him and kept listening.

"Got Mickey Mouse in there, too, Doc?"

Satisfied, Spike whipped the stethoscope out of his ears with the practiced ease of all doctors. "Okay, guy, your heart rate's settling on down. Don't think you're about to have a heart attack. This time." He reached into his bag and pulled out his penlight. The penlight had Mickey Mouse perched on the top.

"Shit! He does have Mickey Mouse! What's next, Doc, Donald Duck?"

Spike steadied the top of the man's head with one hand and flicked the light quickly back and forth between his eyes.

"And if you don't throw any more booze or speed into your system tonight, you might not die of an overdose, either, but I don't guarantee it."

"Doc! C'mon, I said you got Donald Duck in that bag, too? What kind of doctor are you, anyway?"

Spike replaced his stethoscope and penlight and closed his bag. Then he stood up. Slowly. Taking his time, he straightened to his full six foot, six inch height. His wide shoulder span seemed to increase. He walked over to the catcaller. The five foot, ten inch catcaller.

"Pediatrician. You got a problem with that?"

"Nope. Not a one."

"Didn't think so."

Chad and Spike came back in the room, clicked the lock, and flipped the inside safety bolt firmly.

"Death by boobs?" I asked again.

"Yeah."

"That happen often?"

"All night, every night. All over Daytona during Bike Week."

"Lovely."

Chapter Thirty-Eight

We didn't wake up till almost ten the next morning.

"So—in the last twenty-four hours, Chad's been arrested, we almost had to sleep on the street, we've had beer baths and pillow fights, and we've prevented a homicide by boobs. What're we goin' to do today?" I asked over breakfast.

"Baby girl, if I didn't know better, I'd say you weren't really enjoying Bike Week."

"Well, it's been a new experience, I'll give it that."

"Let's ride the Loop," Spike suggested. "Give the girls some fresh air and a little sanity."

"That'd be nice," Stacy said. "The Loop?"

"A twenty plus mile run around the area. Great ride, great scenery. Very peaceful. You can't come to Bike Week and not ride the Loop. It's a law. And this time of day, it might not even be real crowded. Lots of folks still sleeping off last night."

"Sounds like a nice change."

We picked up the Loop at its start at Granada Bridge in Ormond Beach and ran down John Anderson Drive. Then we ran into an outdoor Cathedral of overhanging branches. It was glorious. Blue sky peeked through green. No other riders in sight. Peace on earth. Right up until the moment Spike swerved and the Harley Road King came so close to hitting the pavement my heart almost stopped. Chad turned in a half circle and came back around to the Dark Angel.

Spike straightened it up and came to a stop just off the road. His foot hit the kick-stand harder than a place kicker desperate for the winning field goal. He flung himself off the seat and charged into the middle of the road.

"What the fuck, man! You crazy? Just standing there in the middle of the freaking road?"

I looked at Chad. Chad looked at me. We looked back at the road again for confirmation. Nope. Nobody was there. Stacy flung herself off the bike and raced to Spike, grabbing one of the arms he was flinging wildly for emphasis.

"Spike!"

"Help? Buddy, you got a mighty peculiar way of asking for help! I have a lady on the back of that bike, she'd have been hurt if I'd had to lay that bike down!"

"Spike, calm down!"

"He coulda gotten you hurt, Stacy! Anybody that stupid, I'm not worried about him getting hurt, woulda served him right!"

"Spike, you couldn't have hurt him. He's dead."

"No, he's not! He's standing right there—" Spike broke off. "He is standing right there. Isn't he?"

"For you and me, yes. For Chad and Ari, nope, they can't see a thing."

Spike looked over at us, eyebrows raised.

"Guys? C'mon, you see him! Don't you?"

Chad laughed. "Nope. But that's okay. Because I can finally tell you—Welcome! To the world of magic! Always knew sooner or later you were gonna turn it loose. Guess our own little private coven's growing."

Spike backed slowly away from the dead man only he and Stacy could see. He shook his head.

"No. Mom always said I had it. I never did. I don't. I don't want it."

Stacy leaned her head against his shoulder in sympathy.

"Darlin', some things—you just don't have a choice about."

"But you see him? That's your thing? Like Magic Man and Ari just know things?"

"It's one of my things. We all have kind of a mix of things. So do you. And now that you're open, you'll start finding out what your other things are."

"And you've been seeing dead people how long?"

"All my life, darlin'. Don't remember when I didn't. And we see them for a reason. Now, this guy needs help. So let's go help him." She called over to us. "Y'all excuse us a few minutes? We need to have a talk with our visitor here."

"Take your time. We'll be right here."

*　*　*

Chad pulled completely off the road by the Dark Angel. Spike and Stacy stood on the opposite road shoulder having their conversation with the dead man we couldn't see.

"What's his name?" I asked.

"Whose name?"

"The missing-in-action agent you're supposed to keep an eye out for. Because you know damn well we just found him."

"Yeah, poor son-of-a-bitch. Damn it."

"Who is he?"

"Name's Blake Stanton. Undercover as Buck Johnson. His handle was Badass Buck."

"You're kiddin' on that, right?"

"Badass?" Chad smiled faintly. "No, I'm not kidding but he wasn't enough of one. Obviously."

"What's her name?"

"Whose name?"

"The woman who didn't recognize you in the jazz club last night. Yes, she did. You recognized her, too."

"Baby girl, I told you I didn't."

I cocked my head and speared him with a stare.

"I know what you told me. And you disappoint me. Your first outright lie. Had to happen sometime, of course. It's just I never really believed you would. Flat-out lie to me."

"Baby girl—"

"Drop it if you don't want a full out throw-down right here, right now."

"Yes, ma'am."

I looked back at Spike and Stacy, still in earnest conversation with thin air. I caught a movement back in the tall grass just off the shoulder.

"Oh, shit!"

"What?"

"Look in the grass behind them. Wait a minute—there!" A flash of black tore through the grass and back into the trees. "Micah. Hell. Now we're really in trouble."

"Honey, I told you, that's not Micah."

"I know what you told me. You told me it wasn't Micah in Savannah, either, and look how that turned out!" I whipped out my cell phone and hit Buddy's number back at Pine Whisper.

"Buddy? Hey!"

"Miss Ariel, you ain't got nothin' better to do in Daytona than call and check up on an ol' man?"

"Stop that, you're not an ol' man. Don't know what we'd do without you. Just wanted to check on the animals. Thor miss us?"

"'Course he does, you know better'n that. 'Bout kicked me off my own bed last night, he was sleepin' real restless. But he's fine. Listenin' to your voice now, got his head anglin' toward the phone."

"Hey, baby! We'll be home soon, you be good for Buddy, okay? Buddy, when's the last time you know for a fact you saw Micah?"

"Micah?"

"Micah. You know. My cat. The big black one."

"*Wellll*—you pin me down to it, I guess—last time I'm certain sure is about five minutes after y'all pulled out and hit the road."

"You didn't see him eat supper with the other cats?"

"That cat's a law unto his own self, Miss Ariel, you know that. I put some food on the deck for him, too, but he hadn't eaten it as of this mornin'."

"Figures. Do me a favor and call me if you see him, okay?"

"Okay. But you know he comes and goes as he pleases, he's fine. That big boy can take care of himself, you don't need to worry about him."

"Oh, I know. I'm just trying to keep an eye out for what else he's planning to take care of."

"Ma'am?"

"Don't mind me, Buddy. Give Thor an extra chew bone tonight."

"Sure thing. Y'all have fun and be careful."

"Thanks. See you soon." I hung up and turned back to Chad. "Guess you heard all that." Buddy's wasn't the quietest voice on the planet.

"Yeah, but Micah could be anywhere on Pine Whisper. He only stays around the house when you're there."

"That's because when I'm not there, he's staying around where I actually am."

"He's not—"

"Savannah."

"Got a point. Guess the conference is over, here comes the Ghost Squad."

The Ghost Squad walked across the highway and joined us. Spike looked more than a little shell-shocked. I sympathized. Realizing one was a "person of power" wasn't the most calming experience of one's life.

Stacy took the lead.

"His name's—"

"Blake Stanton," Chad said.

"Yes. And he's your—"

"Missing in action undercover rider with the Dark Rulers."

"Didn't think that'd surprise you."

"Dark Rulers?" I raised my eyebrow. "Funny. That was the name on the jackets last night, those folks you didn't recognize who didn't recognize you. Don't suppose you'd care to share the name of the gang you rode undercover with all those years ago? And of course it couldn't possibly have been the Dark Rulers."

"You're being sarcastic, aren't you?" my husband asked.

"So glad you recognized that, I was sure as hell trying hard enough."

Stacy glanced back and forth between us, surprised at the tension. Spike reached down and took Stacy's hand. I was pretty sure he didn't even know he'd done it. I was equally sure she didn't realize she'd tightened her fingers around his. The crimson aura around them danced and pulsed.

"So what do you want to do now, Magic Man?" Spike asked.

"What does our friendly ghost want?"

"He wants the job finished. He wants the Dark Rulers taken down. And he wants his colors buried. His real ones, that is. Left 'em with the club. He's a DragonHawk out of Washington state. I mean, in his real life, not his undercover. Told him I'd call his club, at least we can do that much for him."

"Poor bastard came a long way from home to die." Chad's eyes had that cold, far-away look they always had on the hunt. "And you can't take the Dark Rulers out. You can chop 'em down, at least the big boys. Over and over again. Just like you can with the other gangs, with the cartels. With any organized crime. Don't matter. Don't mean a damn. They just—come back. With new big boys. Sometimes even with the ones you already took down."

"Yeah."

"Well," I said, "we can make sure he gets buried, can't we? Him, I mean, not just his colors. Surely he told you where his body is?"

Spike and Chad grimaced.

"*Welllll—*" Spike started and hesitated. "Thing is—"

Chad took over. "The thing is, he's not buried. Exactly. Is he?"

"No. He's in pieces. In the swamps by the Loop. Or he was. At first."

"At first?"

"Baby girl. This is gator country."

"Oh. I see."

"I was afraid you would."

"So what now?"

"Now," Chad chewed the inside of his lip a bit. I'd never seen him do that. "Now I think I need to do some cruising up and down Main Street. By myself. I think you girls need to have a leisurely afternoon. Work on your tans out by the pool. Walk the beach."

"And where would I fit into this peaceful little scenario?" asked Spike.

"You stay with the girls, make sure they don't get mistaken for Spring Break girls. Keep the predators at bay."

Fury coiled within and threatened to erupt from my skull. I wasn't the only one. Spike exploded.

"Fuck that shit, man! When hell freezes over. You're not fooling anybody, Magic Man. You're going cruising for Dark Rulers. Who already know you're here! Don't you give me that look, Ariel says they recognized you, then they recognized you, guess you're not as different now as you thought you were. And you wanta go by yourself because you don't wanta pull the respectable doctor into it! You think I've lost it, Chad? Can't handle myself anymore? *Shiiit.* You don't remember how I turned into Spike? Okay, you've saved my ass more than once. But I've saved yours a few times, too. You're not cruising Main Street alone. Are we clear on this?"

"The girls—"

"Definitely do not need to be with us while we're hunting. But they don't need a babysitter at the pool, either! Damn, Chad, give 'em some credit! They're not little girls."

As one, Stacy and I raised on our tippy-toes and kissed Spike on opposite cheeks. "Thanks for noticin'," Stacy said. "But since it's established we're not little girls, why can't we go with—"

"Because you'd put us all at risk, honey," Spike said.

"Spike, damn it—"

"Chad. Don't insult their intelligence. Tell 'em the truth."

"He doesn't have to." I took over from Stacy. "Like you said, don't insult our intelligence. They see us with you, we're targets. Weak links. They saw us last night, but we coulda just been pick-ups. They see us with you today, that'd make us targets for sure. And y'all need to be concentrating on them, not us. We'll stay at the hotel."

"Thank you. For not arguing."

"One condition."

"Knew it was too good to be true."

I whipped my phone back out. "Give me a contact number."

"A contact number?"

"The agency. Whatever agency it is. For backup."

"I can't—"

"Sure you can. And you will."

Chapter Thirty-Nine

Stacy and I hopped off the Intimidator and the Dark Angel as soon as they roared back into the hotel parking lot.

"Go!" I shouted over the revving engines and waved them off.

"You're sure you'll be okay?" Chad shouted back.

I answered with my Medusa stare.

"*Okaaaay* then," he shouted. "No need to get nasty about it."

I felt nasty and I was glad. Because guess what? Rage blocked the mind connection. He couldn't read me. And man, was he pissed. I could feel his frustration every time he hit the brick wall around my thoughts. Usually it took effort to block the other out. Not this time. And even better, I could still read him. Not because he wasn't trying to block me out. Oh yeah, he was trying. To a certain extent, it worked. But not completely. He was too fragmented. Too many emotions, too many memories, racing through his brain to block me out entirely.

Apparently they didn't plan to pull out until they saw us head to the room, so I headed for the room. I cleared the steps onto the second floor before I saw them back out on the open road, headed into town. Stacy already had her cell phone out.

"I'm thinking taxi," she said. "Parking's gonna be a bitch if we rent a car. Whatcha' think?"

"I think you're a genius."

* * *

Following instructions, the taxi pulled to a halt at the start of Main Street.

"Are you sure this is okay?" the driver asked. "I can get you further down the street."

I looked at the parade of bikes moving maybe a tenth of a mile an hour, at the sidewalks and the bikes parked cheek-by-jowl.

"Thanks, this is fine." I handed over the fare with a generous tip and we hopped out and started walking down the sidewalk.

"Okay, what now?"

"Don't know. Exactly. But I will. Be on the lookout."

"For them?"

"For Micah."

"The cat?"

"Yeah."

"You know you could find out exactly where they are. You just have to connect to Chad, I know damn well you're blocking him."

"Yep. Damn sure am. And he's trying to block me but it ain't workin' real good. Got too much on his mind. But it's working enough that I'm not reading him clear. Why don't you see if you can connect to Spike? He's so rattled by all this he'd either not notice or not believe it, think it was his imagination."

"Me? Connect with Spike? Why the hell you think I could do that?"

"Oh, *puleeezzeee!!* Don't even go there."

Her face reddened and she side-stepped neatly. "Why are you so mad at Chad? This past undercover thing—it was way before you ever met."

"Because he lied to me. To my face. Last night and today. He recognized those bikers. The Dark Rulers. Last night in the club. And he knew damn well they recognized him. We should have been back on the road this morning, headin' home. Which we still could have done even after y'all's little visit with the ghost biker. Especially after y'all's little visit with the ghost biker. I</p>

280

didn't even bother to suggest it, knew he wouldn't consider it. Oh, no, brother biker's dead, he's chargin' right on into the Dark Rulers, knowing damn well they're on the look-out for him. Gotta have justice, though. Even if it kills him. Which this time, it just might."

"And you really think your cat's goin' to show up?"

"My cat's already shown up. And he'll show up again. So be on the lookout. Now try and see where Spike is."

"I can't—"

"Bullshit. There's an actual highway running between the two of you, for God's sakes. Started out pale pink. Been crimson since last night. It actually pulses when y'all look at each other. "

She sighed. "Okay, let's go in someplace for a soft drink and sit a minute. I've never had a connection before with anybody but you. I'll need to concentrate."

* * *

I sat across the table watching my little sister concentrate on this new connection of hers. I loved Spike myself. She couldn't fall for a better man. But Vegas, damn it. Of course, with me being in south Georgia and her being in Macon, we were several hours apart anyway. But Vegas was damn near clear across the country. Handwriting was definitely on the wall about that, though, unless Spike decided to relocate.

Stacy's face settled into a blank expression, her eyes closed. She sat for a few moments and then opened them.

"I don't know, Ari. They're moving in and out of the bars. And Spike's so damn mad he's 'bout to bust a gasket himself. I don't know why, exactly. Part of it's what you said, that we should be on the road home, but there's something else, too. Something deeper. From before. Really strong, but real mixed-up. I can't get it."

281

I shrugged. "Well. We'll just have stay alert till we do get it. Or see them. Let's play Biker chicks. Cruise the shops."

We walked down the street, taking in the crowd. Black leather, tight denim, feathers, sweatbands, shaved heads, long hair, tattoos, body piercing. Bare butt cheeks peeked out from short short cut-offs. Cleavage overflowed halter tops. Muscle shirts. Lots of muscles. Lots of used-to-be muscle that wasn't quite anymore. Full mountain man beards, trimmed beards, scraggly beards. Head bandanas. Foot gear ran the gamut from flip-flops to biker boots to six inch platforms and/or spike heels. Pretty much what I'd expected at Biker's Week. Can't say as I expected what walked toward us, though, and I wasn't about to risk accidental contact with that particular fashion accessory. I stepped back towards the shop fronts and pulled Stacy with me.

"What?"

I pointed.

"No. Way."

"Way."

A tall biker came down the street toward us. Shoulder muscles rippled as he walked. The long length of the spotted boa constrictor wrapped around his neck rippled, too. The big head raised and lowered as it swayed back and forth, taking in the sights. Its tongue flicked out occasionally, tasting the air and any by-passer brave enough or drunk enough to pass close enough.

Stacy stepped back even further, crowding the shop's doorway, pulling me with her. The duo passed by. Almost. Just when I thought we were in the clear, its massive head swiveled toward us and its long body undulated. It bunched its muscles and lunged straight at us. The long tongue flicked. I cringed and cowered back. Not far enough, though. It got me square on the cheek, licking rapidly.

Its owner grabbed it close to the head and pulled it back.

"Cyrus! Where yo' manners, boy?"

Cyrus flicked his tongue harder.

"'Scuse us, pretty ladies, but got to admit, the boy's got good taste! You two mighty pretty things!" Cyrus lunged toward me again. "Cyrus! I said behave yo'self, now! 'Course she tastes good, bound to, way she looks, but you just can't go 'round tasting all the ladies!" The biker reeled Cyrus in like the line on a fishing rod, waved cheerily, and continued on his way.

I leaned my back against the store wall and slid down slowly all the way to the ground.

"You okay?" Stacy knelt beside me. She grabbed my hands and rubbed them like she was reviving a shock victim. Mostly because I probably looked like one.

"If I can sit a minute. Rubber knees."

"Guess I'll let you get by with it this time."

"Gee, thanks."

"I'da died. Was it as icky as it looked?"

"Actually, it felt like gettin' licked by a happy puppy. Real soft tongue, like a human tongue, almost. Thank God, 'cause I'da had a heart attack for sure if it felt as icky as it sounds."

"*Meoooowww.*"

Micah rubbed against my thighs and paced impatiently back and forth across my lap.

"So now you decide to show up. Where to, big boy?"

He took off down the street, glancing back to make sure we were still behind.

"What's the deal with the cat, Ari? Give."

"Wish I knew. I just know he—shows up. When I need him."

I grabbed the hand Stacy extended to help me up and Micah darted on down the street, looking back to make sure we followed.

We increased speed to keep up. Must be the heat and the press of the crowds. The after-shock from the snake smootch. Maybe I needed to eat. Nausea roiled up from the pit of my stomach and dark spots started dancing in my line of vision.

"Ari!" Stacy's voice was muffled, hitting my eardrums through some barrier that distorted and slowed the vibration of her voice. "*Arrriii!*" And then I didn't hear her anymore. Because I wasn't there. I was somewhere else.

* * *

It was night. I was on a motorcycle. A big one. Not as a passenger, as the sole rider. Riding with a pack. The pack pulled off the road and into a building. A warehouse. That was it. A warehouse. Somewhere. I didn't know where. Sound echoed and bounced off the metal walls as the riders cut engines and dismounted.

"Damn fine work tonight, men! 'Specially from the Snowman! Celebration time!"

A sound system blared. Heavy metal. Beer cans popped, liquor bottles splashed. Bodies gyrated in the center of the floor.

"Snowman!" A huge bearded biker thrust a woman toward the rider called Snowman. "Here! You deserve the best tonight!"

Snowman moved into my sight. Red hair and beard. Tight spiral curls halfway down his back. He grinned as the woman threw her arms around his neck and snaked her body up and down his. He didn't like it but he did. He wasn't one of them but he was. He was their brother. Except he wasn't. Two men. Outlaw. Law enforcement. At war with each other, each vying for survival.

"Doan min' if I do."

* * *

284

I whispered. "Except they did."

"Ari, don't do that! You scared the crap out of me!"

Stacy shook my arm. I was sitting on a bench in front of a souvenir store.

"You almost fell flat on the sidewalk! I barely got you over to the bench! What happened?"

"A flashback. I think. But not mine. Chad's. And it was them. At least, the woman. And one of the men."

"Who was them?"

"The bikers in the jazz club last night. They did recognize him. I knew it."

Chapter Forty

"Meeeooowwww!"

Micah curled around our feet, displeased with the delay.

"Well, excuse me to hell and back," I said. "Hard to keep movin' when you're passin' out."

"Hsssssssssssss!"

I stood up and waved my hand in an "over to you" gesture.

"Lead the way."

He tore off down the street. We took off after him in hot pursuit, trying to keep him in sight in the press of people. A crowd coming out of a restaurant cost us several seconds while we negotiated through them and when we emerged from the throng, he was gone.

"Damn it! If he wants us to follow him so damn bad, he's goin' to have to make allowances for this freakin' crowd!"

"Don't waste time complainin'," Stacy said. "Just keep goin'. We'll catch up with him."

There! Further down the street, almost to the next block. We put it in high gear. At least until the world went out of kilter again.

* * *

The Alabama Snowman—I couldn't think of him as Chad—slouched in the corner of the dark parking lot, watching the doors. A roadside biker bar. I didn't know where. The flashing neon sign, missing half its bulbs, spelled out "Hell on Wheels".

He had a cell phone to his ear. A relic from another time, a time when cell phones small enough to carry were just coming into common usage. Cell phones huge by today's standards. A call he didn't want to make. A call he couldn't wait to make.

"Highway 47. Mile marker 16. Tomorrow night, 0200 hours."

He paused and listened.

"Just be there."

He pocketed the phone and walked toward Hell. Hell on Wheels.

* * *

"Ari!" Stacy was making a career out of shaking my arm. "At least this time you didn't almost fall down. Where you been?"

"Listenin' to the Snowman set up the Dark Rulers. Something he didn't want to do at all. Something he wanted to do more than anything he'd ever wanted in his life. Where's Micah, can you see him?"

She pointed. Micah stood at the end of the block. He'd waited on us, but he sure hadn't liked it.

"*Hsssssssssss!*"

"Not my fault," I told him. "I'm doin' the best I can."

He turned his head sideways and shot me a glare, clearly telling me my best wasn't good enough before he moved on down the street.

He stopped in front of one of the myriad bar-restaurants lining the street. Cyanide.

"You're kiddin', right?"

"*Meeeoooowww.*" He didn't budge. He turned in a circle and sat down in front of the door.

"We're supposed to go in there?"

"*Meeooowww.*"

Stacy looked at the name on the window.

"Lovely," she said. "How appetizin'."

287

The door burst open before we could enter, spilling a mass of flailing arms and fists onto the sidewalk. Micah shot threw the opening and into the bar. I started after him and Stacy pulled me back.

"Not a good idea," she said.

"Can't help it," I said. "Follow that cat!"

* * *

"Oh my God!" Stacy rushed across the room, pushing big biker bodies aside like rag dolls. Spike lay flat out on the floor, unconscious.

In the pandemonium of flying fists and bodies, we knelt by Spike. Stacy cradled his head on her lap and tapped his cheeks.

"Spike! Wake up! Wake up, damnit!"

I grabbed a glass of water from a neighboring table, miraculously still standing upright in the melee, and sprinkled droplets on his face.

"*Whhaaattt...*" He bolted upright, coming from stupor into full consciousness in the space of a heartbeat. "Why that—*owwww!*" He rubbed the side of his head. I could see the knot already formed there. And wondered how hard a hit it took to knock Spike out.

"What the hell happened? And where's Chad?"

"The son-of-a-bitch tried to ditch me! Like a freaking novice. Like a rookie. And when it didn't work he cold-cocked me! Son-of-a-bitch!"

"How 'bout you cuss him out somewhere else?" Stacy suggested. "Like somewhere not here?"

"Good idea, babe. By the way, I love you. And you're absolutely gorgeous."

He raised his head and kissed her. As first kisses go, it wasn't a real long one, circumstances being what they were and all, but considering it was in the middle of a bar brawl, not bad. Not bad at all.

"Love you, too. Can you stand up?"

"Really?"

"Really. Can you stand up?"

"Babe, after that, I can do anything."

He got to his feet but I stopped him before he straightened to his full height. "Maybe a crouch would get us out of here a little less conspicuously," I suggested.

"You might be right." We formed a tight line, hunched over, and wove our way to the door. Micah waited on us right outside.

"How the hell did he get back out?" Stacy asked.

"How the hell does he get anywhere?" I countered. "Might be a good idea to get a little further away from here." More bodies flew out the door.

"I'd say so," Spike agreed, and we moved down the block, headed to a group of outside tables sporting colorful umbrellas.

A waitress in a halter-top two sizes too small and years too young for her scraggly bun of white hair appeared about two seconds after we sat down.

"Gettcha?" she asked, making it completely obvious that she wasn't wearing dentures. And that she needed to be.

"Just a soda," Spike said.

"For everybody?"

"Yep, all around."

"*Jezzzz.* Why'd y'all bother to come to Bike Week at all?" She shook her head sadly and moved off. Stacy's eyes widened as she walked away. I raised my eyebrows in silent question. Stacy pointed down at Granny's feet as she walked away.

She was wearing flip-flops and no wonder. Her toenails, painted hot pink and shaped and filed to perfection, poked out at least an inch over the tip of the open shoes. The crowning touch. A true poster child for Bike Week. We howled like hyenas.

"Oh, oh, oh—damn, that hurts!" Spike exclaimed, holding his head.

"What'd he hit you with?"

"Beer bottle. Out of the blue. Musta gone out like a light, never saw the rest of the fighting start. He knew that'd do it. Fights break out every five minutes somewhere or other, nobody'd give it a minute's thought. And now that I'm focusing a little bit more here—what in the hell are you two doing here? We told you to stay at the hotel! Where you'd be safe!"

"We very seldom do as we're told," Stacy said. "Either of us. Especially me. Is that a problem?"

"I'll work around it."

Toenail Granny returned with our drinks. Our not terribly large drinks. "That'll be fifteen bucks." Welcome to Bike Week. Spike handed over a twenty.

"You need change?"

"No, ma'am, have a great day."

"Don't guess you need any connections, not with the lookers you sittin' with, but they don't treat you right, come back and see me. I'll hook you up."

Granny moved to new customers. And I moved back into darkness.

* * *

Highway 47. Mile Marker 16.

"You're surrounded! Hands in the air!"

"Sonofabitch! What the fuck?! Break! Break!"

Cycles spun and swerved and gunned. Riders tore off into the darkness. Some made it, some didn't. Metal screeched as bikes hit dirt. Sound of gunshots. Shrieking sirens. And faintly in the distance, the roaring engines of the bikes that made it out.

The Alabama Snowman hung back from the escaping pack, falling behind. When the last rider in his sightline rounded a curve, he pulled over to the side, punching viciously at the keypad of that dinosaur of a cell phone.

"What the *fuck?!* Are you guys completely insane? That wasn't a take-down, at least half of 'em are on the road! Best guess is the third safehouse. "

He shoved the phone back into his jacket and tore off into the night.

Rush of wind. Light drizzle of rain. Another warehouse. Where, I didn't know. Not the same one. Sanctuary. Safehouse. But not for the Snowman.

The biggest rider—the Prez? Ripped his helmet off and slammed it down on the concrete floor.

"Set up! Fucking set-up!" The Prez turned. "Snowman? Where the fuck you disappear to all the time?"

A hand flashed. The Snowman's t-shirt ripped downward from the neck, bringing the zipper of the leather jacket with it.

"Wired! You're fuckin' wired, you bastard!"

Chapter Forty-One

"Ariel! Earth to Ariel! Where the hell'd you go, honey?"

Spike shook my arm and Stacy reached over to stop him.

"Been happenin' all afternoon. Flashbacks. Not hers, Chad's."

"Not Chad's either," I protested. "The Alabama Snowman's. Haven't seen you in 'em yet, but I know you were involved. How?"

"Wasn't really involved. I just—helped end it."

"You wanta explain that?"

"Nope. Not really."

"Didn't think so. So what happened after the—Prez? Is that what they call it? Fingered the Snowman?"

"Flashbacks that good, are they?"

"They're makin' progress, yeah. Just not quick enough. So fill me in." But he didn't have to. The damn flashbacks, once started, had a time-table of their own, accelerating with light speed.

* * *

The Prez whipped out his own dinosaur of a cell-phone.

"Snowman's a plant. Put the word on the street."

Wail of sirens. Blare of loudspeakers. Most telling of all, the click of automatic weapons at the ready that sounded from the shadows. From the inside shadows.

'Best guess is the third safehouse.' Good guess, Snowman.

"You're surrounded! Come out with your hands up!"

The Prez looked at Snowman with reptilian eyes. "Judas."

One of the armed agents laughed as he stepped forward out of the line. "Wow, I'm impressed, douche bag, you know your Bible."

The Snowman's right hook flashed out and the agent hit the floor.

"You stupid sonofabitch!"

"What the hell? Your cover was blown, they'd seen the wire—"

"And you couldn't come out before he made that call? My family's dead, you bastard! And you just helped kill them!"

Snowman raced to the lever opening the warehouse and cranked it. He ran back to his cycle and revved out into the crowd of waiting law enforcement.

"Stop! We'll shoot!"

"Hold your fire! Hold your fire! One of ours, let him go!"

Racing wind. Whirling maelstrom of dread. Faster. Faster. Down country highway. Onto small town streets. Onto the street. The street lined with fire trucks.

The cycle hit pavement when the rider jumped off, no time wasted to set the kickstand.

"Mom! Dad!" He charged toward the flaming house.

"Stop him! It's suicide!"

It took four firefighters to tackle him down.

"No way in! Not even when we got here! No way anyone was alive in there! No one! You hear me, son?"

And the flashback faded away, leaving me with the smell of smoke in my nostrils and the sound of Chad's weeping in my ears.

* * *

I shook my head and wiped the tears from my own eyes. Stacy had vacated her chair and stood leaning over me, holding me tight in her arms.

"Oh, God, will you stop that? That was the longest one yet, the look on your face—"

I looked at Spike, who stared at me with dread. "Give," I ordered.

"Honey—"

"Give. What's your connection with Chad really? The one that let you help end it?"

"I was in the foster system. Chad's parents took me when I was thirteen. Chad was sixteen. And from the first day, they didn't make me feel like a foster anything anymore. I was their child. I was Chad's brother."

"Where were you? When it happened?"

"Nevada. My mother was from Nevada originally. Dad—Chad's Dad. My Dad. The only man I ever called Dad—he'd found my grandparents for me. My high school graduation present, a trip to meet them. And when I did, I found out Nevada had a medical program that let you combine some undergrad with medical school, shorten the time a bit. So I stayed. And after Mom and Dad—I never came back. Not for good."

Stacy looked from one of us to the other. "So nice to be in the loop. Let me guess. Chad got busted by the Dark Rulers—"

"The Alabama Snowman," I corrected. "They're not the same person. Just the same man."

"Makes perfect sense." Stacy nodded. "I even get it. And when they found out, the Dark Rulers killed his—your parents?"

"Only parents I ever had, yeah. Chad's always blamed himself. And it's true in one sense, he hadn't ever gone undercover, they wouldn't have been in danger. But if it'd been handled right, they still wouldn't have been in danger. Stupid, stupid mistake, the whole bust from the git-go. Should have had 'em all. Should have had protection on Mom and Dad soon as they knew they didn't net the whole group."

"But still—sooner or later wouldn't the Dark Rulers have tracked them down?"

"Oh, honey! They loved it. And they were all set. In position to go into a—witness protection program, sort of. In Vegas. It was all a big adventure to Mom. Said not everybody got to re-make themselves and she was gonna be a Las Vegas blonde this go-around. Man, did she love that. And I'm so damn sorry I never got to take her to a Vegas show. She had a real thing for Wayne Newton."

Spike's eyes looked suspiciously wet. Then they widened suddenly as he looked past me.

"What now, man?" he asked the seemingly empty air.

"The ghost agent from this morning's back, isn't he?" I asked Stacy.

"Yep. Don't be rude, Spike, invite him to sit down. Oh, never mind, he just did."

"Thanks for keepin' me in the loop," I said.

"No problem. Now hush."

I sat back and hushed.

"Aw, man, so when is this supposed to go down?" From Spike's expression, whatever it was couldn't be good. "Okay, now I got a question for you. You seen my buddy around, the one with me this morning? Rides the Honda? Hey, come back here!" Spike banged the table with the flat of his hand. "Damn it! Ask 'em something they don't like, they just disappear on you!"

Stacy reached over and took Spike's hand. "Yeah, the dead are a flighty bunch," she commiserated. "Ari, it might be time to call that number you coerced outta Chad this morning. The one for whatever damn Agency this poor guy was working for."

"Because?"

"Looks like the Dark Rulers have branched out from just drugs and weapons," Spike said. "Seems they're having a private auction tonight. Involving human merchandise."

"White slave trade."

"Bingo. Great time for Chad to go poking around looking for 'em."

"You know it. Well, here goes nothing." I pulled out my phone and punched in the number I'd forced out of Chad. I got an answer after two rings. Not the one I was expecting.

"Luigi's Pizza!"

Spike waved at me furiously. I covered the phone with my hand.

"Leave a message!" he mouthed. I raised my eyebrows. "Message!" he mouthed back. "Leave one!"

"This is Ariel Garrett," I said. "Chad Garrett's wife. Understand there's a party goin' on tonight, please have the caterer call me back. On this number, not on Chad's. Thank you."

I hung up and looked at Spike.

"Good job, honey. I should've thought of it before you called but that was damn quick thinking."

"Luigi's Pizza?"

"Honey. You think they're going to answer the phone 'Search and Rescue for Agents in Trouble'?"

"No, guess not."

"No, of course not. Turn your ringer up so we won't miss a call back."

"If we get one and he didn't just give me a wrong number."

"There's that, yeah."

"Think he did?"

Spike shrugged. "Six of one, half a dozen of the other."

"How comforting. Well, nothing's gettin' done, us just sitting here. Time to do—something."

I started to my feet but sat back down abruptly. Surely I knew all I needed to know by now. Would these damn flashbacks never quit? Well, not yet, anyway.

Chapter Forty-Two

A garage. Not a warehouse. A regular, ordinary house's garage. Chad—no longer the Snowman—stood at a work counter, glass bottles lined up in front of him. Corks, already threaded with long pieces of cloth, stood in front of each bottle. The smell of gas permeated the air, laced with a hint of alcohol. Ah, of course. The strips of cloth, the wicks. He'd soaked them in alcohol. He worked methodically, pouring gas into the glass bottles, corking them firmly, and storing them in the leather saddlebags.

The kitchen door leading from the house into the garage slammed shut. He turned his head.

"Squirt. What're you doing here?"

A younger Spike—no, he wasn't Spike, not yet, he was Squirt, twenty-two or twenty-three, tops, walked toward him. No beard. His shoulders and chest hadn't grown into their massive promise quite yet.

"Got in about nine tonight. Expect me to stay in Nevada when I knew tonight was it? Been chasing your ass ever since. They wouldn't let me near the house, either."

"I didn't see you there."

"Got there after you left. Said you'd been there. Well, didn't say it was you. Pretty unmistakable from the description."

Squirt moved to the counter and started filling bottles with gasoline.

"What the fuck you think you're doing?"

"Going with you."

"Like hell you are."

"Try and stop me. My parents, too. Even if they didn't have to be."

"You'll get yourself kicked out of school."

"So? You're 'bout to get yourself kicked out of organized law enforcement."

Chad snorted. "Yeah. Some organization, huh?"

Between the two of them, every glass bottle stood full. Squirt walked over to a cycle I hadn't noticed parked on the side of the garage and wheeled it over, opening the saddlebag and loading up. Obviously his, stored at big brother's house.

In unison, the brothers by choice, that bond so much stronger than blood, fastened their jackets and mounted their cycles. Helmets? *We doan need no stinkin' helmets.*

"You ready, Squirt?"

"Let's do this thing."

Chad reached into his jacket pocket and pulled out a gun. A Glock. He handed it to Squirt.

"Don't take it if you can't use it. Don't come if you can't use it."

"I can use it."

Revving engines. Billows of exhaust. The garage door opened. Riders armed, ready to make their own storm. Self-appointed Enforcers of the Code of the One Percenters. Do unto others exactly what they did unto you.

Rushing wind. Twisting turns. Hint of red foretelling fiery dawn. Narrow streets. The wrong side of town. The lairs of the Dark Rulers. Off the streets and onto sidewalks, down walkways to run-down houses, off into the yards. One rider toward the front windows. One rider toward the back windows. Hands flashed down to saddlebags, grabbing bottles. Lighters flared, cloth wicks soaked in alcohol grew blossoms of red. Crashing glass in front windows. Crashing glass in back windows. Screams and shrieks. Dante's Inferno, One Percenter style. And off to the next target, and the next.

At a four-way stop, Chad leaned closer to Squirt.

"Word's out on the street now. They know we're coming."

"Yeah."

"We got one good hit left. But they'll be waiting for us. Spike'll be at this one. Keep your eyes open and your head down."

"Spike?"

"Handle's from his weapon of choice. Railroad spikes. Polished and filed, uses 'em like throwing knives. Razor sharp. Eyes open. Head down. Ride low."

"Got it."

"Be damn sure you do."

Into the next yard. Their heads weren't down low enough. A fine link chain jerked itself taunt out of the grass across their path. Cycles crashed. A Wild Man of Borneo—Spike—facial features hidden under the bush of hair, jumped from the shrubbery. His arm drew back, sending a heavy metal projectile whizzing through the air. Squirt rolled and the railroad spike, sharpened to a stiletto point, buried itself half-way in the dirt.

The attacker threw himself on top of Chad, his weight knocking him back to the ground.

"Bastard! You were our brother!"

His arm flashed upward, silvery gleams coming off the polished spike in his hand in the dawn light. Striking position.

Squirt grabbed the handle of the dirt-bound spike protruding from the ground. He yanked it free and hurled himself forward as the biker's arm began its downward arc. Loud, wet smack as the stiletto point of the dirt-coated spike tore its way through the flesh and bone and tendons of the hand wielding the spike intended for Chad's heart. A dark geyser of blood exploded into the reddish rays of the rising sun. Screams of agony drowned out the faint wail of approaching sirens. Chad's body surged upward, flipping the screaming biker's body off and pinning it under his.

"Think you just lost claim to your handle, ass-wipe!" His fist connected hard with the biker's jaw. The head lolled as he lapsed into unconsciousness.

"Chad, the sirens are getting closer. We stay or we go?"

Chad stood.

"We go. Don't trust those ass-wipes either. Bikes rideable?"

"Think so." The man who'd started the night as Squirt lifted his cycle and mounted it. Chad raised his own bike.

"Then we ride. Guess you didn't need that gun after all. Spike."

* * *

The real world came back into focus. And surely, please God, surely I was done with these heart-wrenching rides down a memory lane not my own.

I looked at Spike and Stacy, watching me with worried eyes.

"Where you been, baby?" Spike asked gently.

I smiled. "Watching Squirt's long night's journey into Spike. No wonder you and Chad don't advertise you're brothers. You probably shouldn't have even stayed in contact. At all."

"Well, that was mentioned to us, yeah. We didn't pay that much attention. Though even we knew it wouldn't be a good idea to broadcast the relationship. It just got to be habit not to."

"What's your real name, darlin'?"

"Stuart. But nobody's called me that since Mom and Dad died."

"Battle trophy."

"Yeah."

Stacy coughed. "Hello? Another person at this table? Anybody notice?"

"I'll tell you all about it, darling, I promise. In more detail than I'm sure you'll want. But I don't think we got the time right now. Ari? Ideas? What now?"

"I don't know." I was exhausted suddenly. I understood now, and understanding carries its own forgiveness. He'd ridden with the Dark Rulers, walked a line few men ever walk, a dangerous line between two worlds that of necessity blurred together, leaving no clear-cut path of righteousness, only varying shadows of gray darkening into deepest black. No wonder he hadn't wanted to share it, any of it, and I hadn't had any right to expect him to. It'd cost way too much. His parents' lives.

"Well, well, look who's back," Spike said, raising his glass and toasting toward an empty chair. Ah. Our friendly ghost. "Be nice if you had a little more concrete information this time." He leaned forward. "Really? You don't say?"

My phone shrilled loudly. The ringtone announced an incoming call from a number not programmed in.

I grabbed it halfway through the first ring and hit speaker. We all leaned in close.

"Hello?"

"Luigi's Pizza. This is the caterer. How big a party are we talking about tonight?"

Chapter Forty-Three

"I'm not sure," I said.

Spike looked at the empty chair and took over. "At least fifteen or twenty if we get there early enough. After that, all bets are off, they've got more guests invited."

Long pause. When the voice spoke again, it didn't sound happy.

"Dr. Forrester. I assume it is Dr. Forrester now? Sure hope so. We expended a lot of effort to keep you in medical school after that little night ride of yours. Almost as much as we expended keeping you and Garrett off the Most Wanted list."

"Yeah, that really made it up to us, that little slip of yours that got our parents killed."

"*Touché.* Any idea where this little party's going to be?"

Spike looked back at the empty chair. "One of the empty warehouses back off the old Florida Railroad tracks. The ones the Florida East Coast line don't use anymore."

"Lots of empty warehouses back off the old tracks."

"Yeah, well, it doesn't have big street numbers plastered on the front. I know which one it is."

"And you intend to show us, not tell us."

"Give the man a cigar."

"You don't trust us?"

"You think?"

"Garrett had any luck locating that missing cook of ours?"

"Depends on your definition of locating. He's not gonna be catering any more parties."

"Well. We figured as much."

"Which bothers you not a bit, does it, you son-of-a-bitch?"

"Language, Dr. Forrester, language. It goes with the territory. Where's Garrett?"

"In the middle of the party. And if he doesn't make it home tonight, you'll be a lot less fond of me than you are now."

"I need to organize the staff. When are the other guests arriving? And what's the entertainment?"

"Probably got an hour. Don't know how much longer than that. Believe an auction's planned. Not a charity event."

"We'll call in an hour."

* * *

Stacy reached over and took my hand. "Ari—"

"I know. They've got him. Our friendly ghost told you."

"But he told us where they are, too. So let's move it."

"But—you've got your cycle. I guess the Intimidator's still there, too, but I can't freakin' ride it alone!"

"Where there's a will, there's a way. Let's go." Spike stood up and started looking up and down the rows of bikes.

"What the hell are you lookin' for? I can't ride a cycle, even a small one!"

"Not looking for a small cycle." He grabbed Stacy's hand with his right, my hand with his left, and started moving down the sidewalk so fast we had to trot to keep up.

Down one block, onto another, Spike's eyes moving non-stop over the crowd.

"There! Desert Troopers out of Vegas!" He charged over to a group of bikers in the same club colors. "Guys! I'm—"

"Wait a minute. I know you. Never forget a face. Dr. Forrester? Yeah! Dr. Forrester! My grandson's baby doctor! You're a biker? I'd known that, I'd have been after you to come ride with us! What's your club?" The man inspected Spike's jacket, looking for club affiliation.

"Yeah, life-long biker, but my brother and I tend to ride alone. And thing is, my brother's gotten himself in a little jam down here and I need to get to him. But I've got my sister-in-law and my lady here with me and neither of them can ride alone. Any chance one of you have a bike with a sidecar?" He pulled the Dark Angel's keys out of his pocket. "Lot to ask, but here's my keys. Black Harley Road King with Nevada plates, M99, parked in front of Cyanide. I'll take full responsibility if I could possibly borrow—"

"Hell, man. Know you wouldn't recognize me, but I sure as hell recognize you. Saw you in the waiting room at the Children's Hospital. When you came out and told my son and daughter-in-law my grandson was gonna be fine. Meningitis. We damn near lost him. You saved his life. Where's Moondog? Moondog!"

"Sure thing." One of the other bikers stepped forward and handed over a set of keys. He pointed down the row of bikes. "Right down there, the dark red Harley. With the sidecar."

The Brotherhood of Bikers, Lord bless 'em. And they weren't done yet. The Desert Trooper Spike had first approached held us back a moment.

"Doc!" He whipped a card out of his wallet. "Take this! My cell number's on it. Lots of us down here. And we're not the only Vegas club here, either. You need us, you call."

"Thanks, man. We really appreciate this."

"Yeah, well, I really appreciate my grandson still being with us to have his last birthday party, too. No joke, doc. You need us, you call."

A grin split Spike's mountain man beard. "You know, I might just do that."

* * *

We charged down the street to the dark red Harley with the sidecar. Now how in the hell did one fold oneself into a sidecar?

Spike straddled the bike. "Stacy, get on back. Ari, just pretend it's a canoe."

"Okay, but you should know I can't swim."

"Just consider me your life preserver, sweetheart."

Spike maneuvered into the Main Street traffic and inched his way down the street. He turned into the first alley and started working his way back toward the old, unused tracks of the railroad system, cutting across city streets when the alleys ran into them. I was totally confused in a matter of minutes. Not Spike. Less and less traffic moved on each succeeding street we crossed, until finally, Spike turned back onto main road and let our borrowed Harley loose.

We ran down into the back streets of the industrial district, and further back into streets lined with dilapidated warehouses. Probably only street people knew these warehouses now. The street people and the One Percenters.

Spike pulled over into a weed-filled lot between two of the ramshackle remnants and ran up close to a wall before cutting the engine.

"There." He pointed down to a rusted warehouse standing alone, its companion buildings having fallen victim to years of disuse and neglect. It looked rickety on the surface, but on closer inspection, it seemed— sturdier—somehow than the rest of the remaining structures. "They've fortified it a little bit. Put up some pinning on the inside."

"How do you know?" I asked. "That it's the one or that they've put up any pinning?"

Stacy pointed to the shadows. "Him. Our ghost. We all got our own little sack of magic rocks to tote around. He's been floating in front of us the whole time. And him. Your little sack of magic rocks to tote around." She pointed over to a clump of weeds near the front of the lot. Micah stood up and stretched. Then he looked over at us, arched his back, and swished his tail, obviously asking what took us so long.

"Oh," I said. "Them. Of course."

My phone shrilled. Shit! I grabbed it and hit the button to switch it back to vibrate as I answered. We were pretty far from the warehouse but there wasn't a lot of city noise down here, either.

"Luigi's Pizza. Put Dr. Forrester on the phone."

I handed the phone to Spike. Luigi had no manners, but this wasn't my world. It wasn't really Spike's either, but he sure had a better acquaintance with it than I did.

"Yeah?" Spike didn't put the phone on speaker for the same reason I'd hit the vibrate button, I was pretty sure. I couldn't distinguish the words, only the curt tone. But Spike didn't look happy. "You're shitting me, right?" I mean, he really didn't look happy. "Tell you what, Luigi. You take your bureaucratic red tape and you shove it right up your ass." He clicked the phone off and handed it back to me.

"What?"

"They're having administrative difficulties getting approval to move on this. It'll be several hours before they'll be in position to move in."

"Say what?"

"They're fucking bureaucrats. The same kind got Mom and Dad killed. Now, it's one of two things. They called to double check the GPS fix on your phone. In which case, they don't want to deal with us, talk with us, argue with us, or try to pull Chad out first. They're gonna come barreling in with all guns blazing and to hell with him if he's in the line of fire. Or they really are tied up in red tape with one hand not knowing what the hell the other is doing and won't move until Mother May I says yes they can. Which will be God knows when. And Chad aside—they're starting an auction at ten p.m. tonight. Young, scared girls. Up on the block. To middlemen who're gonna take 'em God knows where and do God knows what with 'em. And that's probably the plan. To wait till the auction's in full swing so they can take down the buyers. Which puts those little girls right in the middle of it but hey, who cares about that?"

I wanted to throw up.

"So what are we goin' to do? Did our ghost tell y'all how many Dark Rulers are even in there?"

"Yep. Too many for us."

"So what are we—"

Spike pulled the Desert Trooper's card out of his pocket.

"We're calling in the Calvary."

Chapter Forty-Four

Spike punched in the number.

"Jack? Spike Forrester. I got a situation."

Stacy and I crowded close to the phone. Jack kept his volume up high. We didn't have any trouble overhearing this conversation

"I got bikers. What's your situation?"

"If I tell you, there's gonna be people want to kill you."

"Hot damn! The best kind of situation. Lay it on me, man."

"Tell you up-front. My brother's gotten on the wrong side of an OMG. The Dark Rulers. And it goes way back. One of the reasons we both ride solo. You still in?"

"Like super glue."

"'K. Years back, he put the hierarchy of the Rulers away. For awhile.

"You mean your brother—" One thing Jack wasn't was dense. You could hear understanding in his voice.

"Yeah. I do. But they're out. And they recognized him. They have him. And they've branched out their old OMG operations, too. To include merchandise of the human kind. Merchandise they intend to sell tonight. You following me?"

"Damn sure am."

"And seems like the people ought to be helping are too tied up in red tape to move fast enough to do any good."

Jack snorted. "Figures. Where you at, where are they, and what's the plan?"

Spike ran it down. Except for the plan part. Seeing as how we didn't really have one.

"I'm calling in all the Vegas clubs down here just as soon as we hang up. But we don't want to roar in a big group. Gonna send 'em in couple at a time, I'm thinking. And I'm making a side trip to an industrial supply house."

"Good man. What's your side trip?"

"Didn't you read my card?"

No, actually, except for the first name and the number, none of us had. We did now. Jack Hudlin, Ph.D. Chemical Engineer. Hudlin Technology, Inc.

"Some damn," said Spike.

"You betcha' ass, son. Gonna be some smoke bombing in the old warehouse tonight. Among other things."

* * *

We waited. Shadows formed and re-shifted.

"Ari, you know I need you to go in, right? Ghostman's pretty good but I need you to see the layout. From Chad's eyes."

"I know."

I didn't want to. Because I'd already dipped a toe in the water. Water dark and cold as the River Styx. Water of memory. Of hate and hurt. And betrayal. His of them. Them of him.

I took a deep breath, rubbed the big diamond of my engagement ring, that magic talisman that deepened our connection, and dived in.

* * *

His jaws hurt. Both sides. Which meant mine did. And it was hard to focus through eyes swollen almost shut. Hard to breathe through the bloody nose, too. They'd worked him over pretty good. Shoulders hurt, but that was mostly from bouncing around on the floor of the crash van they'd tossed him into when they'd jumped him in the alley back of Cyanide.

He was on the floor, his back against a wall. Not tied to anything, we weren't that lucky. Chained. And on second thought, maybe that was lucky. The wall he was bolted to wasn't all that sturdy anymore. Enough pressure and the bolts should pop right out. I counted fifteen Dark Rulers, including the Prez. And a bushy wild man from Borneo. The original Spike. Until our Spike had claimed his handle, anyway. I wondered if they still called him Spike. Then he moved and I saw it. The hook that replaced the hand. So. They'd had to amputate. I'd bet Pine Whisper Plantation they called him "Hook" now. And there was the woman from the bar. I was right. One and the same as the woman from the flashback. Snowman's reward for a job well done.

She came over and squatted in front of him in a modified version of that favorite Bike Week pastime, death by boobs.

"Used to love these, Snowman, remember?" She ground against him. "Betcha never found anything like 'em since!" She ground forward hard again, pushing his head back against the wall before she relented and backed off.

He gasped for breath by the time his nose and mouth was clear.

"No, Iris, I never found anything like 'em since. Silicone that hard's not all that common, thank God."

I winced. The man never would learn when to shut up. The bikers laughed and cat-called.

"Hell, Snowman, you always did call 'em like you saw 'em! Damn sho' right about that, now!"

The woman—Iris?—slapped him hard and blood trickled from the corner of his lip.

"Shut your fuckin' mouth! Don't you talk to me that way!"

"Back off, bitch! Can't take the heat, don't play with the fire. You knew he was a smokin' gun. Always was."

"You defending that—that Judas!"

"Oh, hell no, bitch! Just want him alive and conscious for tonight's finale after the auction. The motorcycle pull." The Prez grinned. If I'd actually been standing there, I'd have fainted. The image in his head was that clear. The image of Chad, each limb chained to four revving motorcycles. Motorcycles tearing off in opposite directions.

Baby girl! Pull it together! Chad's voice echoed through my brain. *Ain't gonna happen. You're here now. The Coven's here. And everything's gonna be just fine.*

Glad you think so. Have you seen the girls?

No, but they're in the back, behind this wall. Drugged to the max. They won't be targets. And they're really cocky. Got a lot of cops on the payroll. No lookouts, no guards. Not now, anyway, there will be in about an hour when the buyers start coming in.

Good. Don't know yet exactly what's happenin'. Be ready for anything. Probably gonna get confusin'.

I'm always ready for anything. Thought I told you to stay at the hotel with Stacy.

Oh, bite my ass!

Love to, darlin'. Anytime you say. Let's just get out of this mess first, how 'bout it?

Just be ready. I disengaged and went back to the waiting members of our little family Coven.

* * *

"Well?"

"Well, we get him out or he's tonight's finale at the motorcycle pull."

"That I already know. Where's Chad? Position wise? And the girls?"

I ran down the layout. "Didn't our friendly ghost tell you already?"

"Yeah, but one thing I've already found out. The dead don't always have the same perspective of distance we do."

311

The first Calvary reinforcements pulled up, three riders wearing the Desert Trooper Colors. One of them rode a very familiar cycle.

"Hey, Doc! Damn, this roadster rides smooth! Might have to go visit the dealership when we get back to Vegas."

"Moondog, my man, what you've done, what all of you are doing—hell, I'll give you the roadster."

"Mighty generous, Doc, but that wouldn't be right. Brotherhood's gotta stick together. Us against the world. We're gonna have a good many riders pulling in here. What the Jackster thought was, the three of us get here first, you show us where. And we ride out to meet the incoming and keep 'em further back till we hear the signal, keep the noise down. That work for you?"

"What's the signal?"

"Well, knowing the Jackster—I'm thinking it's gonna be loud. He oughta be right behind us."

Sure enough, Jack Hudlin, Ph.D., Chemical Engineer, rode in quietly. Or as quietly as his Harley ever ran.

"Moondog, you take Darrell and Stan and go greet the guys a couple of blocks back up. Hold everybody there. Keep your phone handy, I'll call you when we're sure what we're doing." The trio obediently rode back out toward the incoming riders. "So, Doc. What's the situation?"

Spike pointed down toward the old warehouse. "The Dark Rulers have my brother chained to a wall. They've got their merchandise drugged out of their minds in the back units. Fifteen Rulers right now. Most of 'em got history with me and my brother. And they don't like us much. But they're cocky, no look-outs, at least not till the party starts."

The Jackster looked us over. "Pretty good recognizance there. You just pull all that outta your ass, did you?"

"No. Did some scouting."

"I'd say so. Them windows pretty high to be showing all that. And I don't see a ladder. Or any scaffolding."

"No, you don't."

"But you're sure of your intel?"

"It's golden."

"Gotta share that with me sometime. Whatever technique you're using, it'd bring a high price on the market."

"Not anything you'd call marketable."

"Didn't much think so. Well. Here's what I'm thinking. Especially now that I'm sure it's a free-standing building." He lifted the top of his bike's saddlebags. And proceeded to tell us what he thought. "So whatcha' think?"

"You're a genius," I said. "And I'm goin' to find a bumper sticker that says 'I love chemical engineers.'"

"Well now, I wouldn't go that far. But I think it's about the best we're gonna do. So. Let me call the boys, tell 'em to start moving the formation in slow so they can be ready to rush when the noise starts. And then we'll all move into position. Let's get ready to rock and roll!"

Chapter Forty-Five

Stacy and I slung the bags holding our ammunition for Phase One over our shoulders and the four of us moved into position. Spike and I headed for the third window down from the doors on the right side of the building, Stacy and the Jackster to the third window down from the doors on the left.

Spike bent forward slightly, turned his hands and laced his fingers together to make a ladder for my foot. I stepped up, grabbed the top of his head and swung myself up onto his shoulders. None too gracefully, I might add. Stacy'd probably done the same thing on the other side of the building with the speed of a gazelle when she'd bounded up on Jack's shoulders. There was method in our madness. I was shorter than Stacy by several inches, Jack was shorter than Spike by more than several inches. This pairing gave us about twelve feet of height on both sides of the building, more than enough to reach the high windows with their broken panes of glass. Always provided I could manage to pull off the next move, of course, which was to actually stand up on Spike's shoulders.

"*Owwww!!*" Spike breathed. Oops. I was pulling his hair, trying to hold on and maintain my balance while he moved closer to the wall, so I could brace myself against it as I stood up.

"Sorry!" I hissed back. I shifted, took a deep breath, and made my move. Okay, one foot up on one shoulder. Spike's hand moved up and grabbed my ankle to steady me. Then the other foot was up, and Spike was bracing me with both hands while I braced myself against the wall. I straightened. We were right about the height. An empty pane in easy reach just begged to be useful. So I used it. I pulled one of the Jackster's glass bottles out of the tote around my neck and lobbed it in. It hit the concrete floor with a satisfying *crrraccccccckkkkkk* as the glass shattered. Two seconds later, Stacy's glass bottle shattered behind it.

Yep, the Jackster knew his stuff. And he was right. These weren't ordinary smoke bombs. Wafts of smoke floated out of the broken panes of the high glasses. But he'd told us to toss in two more each, to be sure visibility inside was pretty much zero and one thing about me—I was really good at following instructions. When I wanted to, of course. So was Stacy. *Crack! Crack! Crack!*

"What the fuck?!"

"Sonofabitch!!"

Time for Phase Two. I grabbed one of Jackster's little metal canisters from my magic tote bag of chemical engineering marvels and lobbed it through the window. It launched World War III inside the warehouse.

Ratatatatatatatatatatatatattatatatatatatatatatatataat atat. Stacy's little canister joined the party seconds after mine. Machine gun fire echoed loud in the metal walls and bounced off the concrete floor. Not really, of course, these were the Jackster's special noise makers. But if I hadn't known that, I'd sure be diving for cover. And from the sounds coming from inside, that's exactly what the Dark Rulers were doing, too. Bodies thudded into walls, onto floors. Ah! That had to be a whole line of cycles crashing down onto concrete. Sweet! I waited for a lull in the cacophony that indicated the first canisters were running low and lobbed another. From the other side of the building, Stacy did the same.

"Get down!"

"Get down where?! It's coming from everywhere!"

"Where the fuck are the bastards?"

Ah! I heard the sounds of Phase Three approaching. Time to really get this party started.

"Ari! Chunk the last canisters! We need to get to the doors!"

"Right!"

I lobbed the last two machine gun nests in my arsenal. I slid my hand down the wall till I could reach Spike's hands where they braced my legs. I sat down on his shoulders and he swung me to the ground.

We raced to the front doors just as the four wheel drive trucks Jackster'd commandeered pulled in front of the warehouse. As one, the three of them braked to form a line, shifted into low gear, and revved the powerful engines. Bikers swarmed onto the lot and circled the perimeter, riding fast. Truck engines revved one last time and lunged forward. The rusted metal doors flattened like pancakes. Smoke billowed out in waves. And so did the Dark Rulers. Coughing and gagging and throwing up in the weeds.

I raced into the smoke toward the interior wall where Chad was chained. I found the wall with no trouble. By running straight into it so hard I knocked myself flat on my butt.

"You always—did—like to—make an—entrance," Chad ground out between coughs. I squinted and peered through the fog. Jackster was right. He made a serious smoke bomb, but they cleared out quick. Enough so that I could see Chad's outline. I threw myself down on the floor beside him and hugged with everything I had.

"Hey, ease up, I'm okay," he got out before coughing again.

And then Spike loomed out of the smoke like a murderer in a horror movie, rapidly snapping the teeth of a big bolt cutter back and forth. "Think these might be useful?"

"Do it, son."

Spike snipped twice and the chains fell from the wall. Spike reached down and took one of his hands, I took the other, and we hauled him to his feet and out into clear air. The Dark Rulers sat in a circle on the ground, tied securely together. Bikers surrounded them. They weren't going anywhere.

"You okay?" Chad looked horrible. How much of that was nausea from the smoke and how much was simply due to his bruised and battered face, I didn't know. Then he hunched over a nice pile of weeds. He looked much better when he stood back up. Nausea then.

Jackster walked toward us. A biker wearing colors I didn't recognize walked with him. The ornate script made the Club name hard to read. "Doc, happened to find another doctor down here, he wanted to come along for the ride, case anybody got hurt. Figured it'd be a good idea, knowing those poor girls were in there and all. He just checked on 'em. Mike, you wanta fill 'em in?"

"Sure." Mike stepped up and smiled at us. "Well, way the building's set up, they were in a completely different section. A little smoke got back there but not enough for 'em to even notice, high as those bastards have 'em pumped up. They don't have a clue what's going on, so they're not scared or hurting or in any immediate danger. So I'd recommend we just leave 'em right where they are until the authorities get here and call in ambulances to take 'em where they can get detox treatment."

He turned and looked directly at me. I stared into beautiful green eyes, dark as moss. As I watched, they narrowed and tilted and took on a yellowish cast. The pupils contracted in from the sides in an oval, turning into vertical slits. Like cats' eyes. My own eyes widened. He saw the dawning comprehension and shook his head slightly. And winked at me.

"The authorities will be coming, I'm assuming?" asked Jackster.

"I'm pretty sure the authorities will be making an appearance very soon now," Spike said. "And I'm pretty sure they're not going to like it, us barging in without them."

"Because they wanted the guys coming to the auction, didn't give a damn if the girls or your brother got dead in the cross-fire."

"You got it." Jack Hudlin, Ph.D., was one smart man. Not just book smart. Street smart. Then again, they didn't hand out Ph.D.'s in chemical engineering to dummies.

"Time for us to go then, I think."

"Yeah. Man, I'll never be able to pay you back—"

"Look us up when you get back home, Doc. Be a Desert Trooper jacket waiting for you, anytime you want it."

"I'll be there to get it. Soon as I get back and settled."

"Here's the keys to your Road King, you wanta give me back the keys to Moondog's cycle, we'll pick it up on the way out. And here's the keys to mine. For your brother. Don't think you'll wanta be asking for any favors from the authorities when they get here. I'll ride back with one of the trucks. Call me in the morning, I'll get my cycle back."

"Man, you think of everything." Spike handed over the keys to Moondog's cycle.

"Troopers! Let's move out!"

I called after the doctor in the unknown club colors. "Mike! Don't recognize your colors. What's your club?"

He turned and looked back. "The Guardians." He waved and turned.

Naturally. What else? I whipped out my phone and punched "micah as angel" into the search engine. It took two seconds to come up. "Angel of the Divine Plan. Micah watches over spiritual evolution, seeking every opportunity to reveal God's Divine Plan and reveal the next steps of our Life purpose."

I looked back up from my screen. Jackster was climbing up into one of the big trucks. I didn't see Doctor Mike anywhere. Just Micah's sleek, black body disappearing into the weeds by the side of the next building. That sneaky little devil. Angel. With him, I wasn't sure there was too much difference.

"See you at home, Micah!" I called. I knew he'd be waiting on the porch railings when we got back.

"The cat?"

"Sometimes."

"*Okaaaay.* If you say so." Chad looked better by the minute. He watched our Cavalry ride out. "How in the hell did you pull all that together?"

Spike snorted. "Think you're the only cloak and dagger man in the family?"

"Thought I was the only one stupid enough to make a habit out of it."

"If you didn't still look so green, I'd knock you down, but I'm afraid you'd puke again. This time on me."

"You're pissed 'cause I knocked you out in Cyanide, huh?"

"You're unbelievable, you know that?"

I shook my head. How had I ever missed they were brothers? "Anybody notice there's a helicopter circling overhead?" I pointed upward. "Or hear that car door slam? Or see the guy walkin' toward us lookin' really pissed?"

The man was stiff as a ramrod and wore a suit that just screamed "government man".

"I'm arresting all of you for obstruction of justice!"

Spike and Chad moved forward together at the same time. I stepped between them and held my arms back in a blocking motion.

"I got this one, boys." I turned to the agent and smiled. "Luigi, I presume. How nice of you to join the party after we wrap the presents for you."

He ignored me. "Garrett, you and your brother been nothing but trouble for us for years! Now we'll never get the buyers who were going to be at that auction! That's three years of work wasted because Forrester couldn't wait! You're done, I'm through covering your asses—"

Damn. Nothing makes me madder than being ignored. I stepped in front of the ranting agent and stared straight into his eyes, pouring power from mine into his.

"Luigi! I don't think you understand the situation. Chad Garrett's not even here. Neither is Spike Forrester. You haven't seen them in years. None of us are here. You won't even see us leave. A rival gang busted the Dark Rulers before you ever got here. Now, do you understand me?" I held his stare and poured more power through. "I said, do you understand me?"

He turned around and stalked rapidly back to his car, barking furiously into his phone.

"Damn it to hell, get me some ambulances out here for the girls! Place is cleaned out, they're just tied in a circle waiting for us! Must've been at war with another gang!"

"Baby girl, you rock."

"Yeah, I do, don't I? How you feelin'? Think you can ride that Harley?" I pointed at Jackster's Roadster, patiently waiting beside the Dark Angel.

"I gotta be dead not to able to ride a bike."

"Then I think it's time for us to cruise. In just a second." Spike dropped to one knee in front of Stacy. "Anastasia Anson, before any more outlaw gangs try to kill us or another Luigi clone tries to arrest us, you are going to marry me, aren't you?"

"You goin' to teach me to ride a bike by myself and buy me a Harley?" I shook my head. My sister. The family athlete. The she-devil dare-devil.

"I can do that."

"Then I think we can come to terms, yeah. As long as we can do it at the Tunnel of Love Drive-Thru on the Dark Angel."

"Mom's goin' to have a shit-fit, you cheat her out of her last chance at a weddin'."

"Can't let you and Chad have all the fun."

"Works for me," Spike said. He stood up and cupped his hand around Stacy's jaws for a short, forceful kiss.

"Okay, are we ready now?" Chad revved the engine of the borrowed Harley.

The Dark Angel revved back. And the newly formed Garrett-Forrester Coven, forged in bonds of blood and love and marriage, roared off into the falling night. On Harleys.

Chapter Forty-Six

If there's one thing this past year has taught me, it's that there's an underlying power, a Grand Conductor, leading the magical symphony of the universe. Everything and everyone is connected, intertwined. And in that connection lies the ancient, universal truth, lost and twisted and forgotten through the ages. The truth? There's a little bit of magic in all of us. Lots more in some than in others, of course. And that magic in and of itself is neither good nor evil. It's an either/or situation, and depends on the person possessing it.

And that's where the Guardian Council comes in. Sometimes a lot more forcibly than others. I knew about the Guardians, of course, they had Chad on speed dial. Chad's contact G, a/k/a Gabriel Smith, was one of the head haunchos. Since my first encounter with him during our little Resurrection Society adventure, I'd learned that the Guardians, complete and proper name being The Galactic Guardian Council, patrol every aspect of the magic world, up to and including some parts of it nobody would ever think of. Specifically, they keep an eye on magic turned or turning dark. Everywhere. As in *everywhere.* Nobody'd ever come right out and said so, but let's be real here. Any entity that can do that—well, they're not entirely normal humans, now are they? I wasn't sure exactly what they were yet, mind you, but I definitely went on high alert with every new contact. And I never forgot the elusive doctor with the gorgeous green cat eyes who'd shown up during our take-down of the Dark Rulers wearing *The Guardians* biker jacket. That just took coincidence too far.

So far, I'd learned that the Council was a very convoluted organization with three major divisions. MeanStreet LLC, FlyingLow, LLC, and SassyWings, LLC. Gabriel heads MeanStreet. So called because they patrol some mean streets. Who heads the other two? We'll get around to that. Why LLC? That's very simple. Limited. Liability. Corporation. Because even the Guardians can't absolutely guarantee they can protect humans, magical or not, against their sometimes almost unlimited stupidity. Or even against their own stupidity. Just because Guardians aren't entirely normal humans doesn't mean they can't be stupid. I was about to learn a lot more about them than I'd ever wanted to know, but not all at once and not in any shape, form or fashion that could be classed as straightforward or logical, so I can't give you a first-hand account, I'll have to piece it together for you, in as chronological an order as I can get it from all I was about to learn. But this, I'm told, is how it all started.

* * *

The Grand Conductor sighed as the dark crept out of the edges of brightness and shadowed the earth. Obviously, some sort of check and balance system had to be put in place. Tricky thing to do. That free will factor. Enough to make a Grand Conductor shout out loud.

"Did I give you a brain? Is it still in your head? Is your head with you today?" Still, how boring life would be without it.

What to do, what to do?

Good needed a Guardian. More than one, in fact. A Council. A Council of Guardians. Hmmm. Couldn't be fully human, of course. Couldn't be just pulsing energy like the Grand Conductor. More a combination of both. Couldn't be too many of them, either, certainly not enough to patrol the streets of humanity all by themselves. That much power in one place...no, not a good thing. Enough for supervisory positions only.

The Grand Conductor concentrated. Pulsing particles, rainbows of light. The music of creation. Flash of lightning, crash of thunder. There! Done! Enough to start with, anyway. He could always make more later.

"Gabriel. Michael. Raphael. Welcome, boys! Have I got a job opportunity for you or *what?*"

They'd need help. From the humans themselves? That was a thought. A reward. Exemplary lives deserved exemplary rewards. A magical being who never succumbed to the temptation to misuse magic in life wouldn't misuse it in death. Especially if they weren't really dead. Just—transformed. And of course, there was transforming and then there was transforming. No need to limit the form they could operate in. Human form might not work as well sometimes as say, a cat. Or dog. Or whatever. And then there were those who walked a tightrope between good and evil, balancing delicately between the two. If they hadn't proved themselves in life—well, maybe they deserved a second chance after death. No point in wasting all that magic.

And speaking of wasting magic, well, hey! Plenty of living magical folks walking around all the time, too. Powerful, some of them. Already utilizing their magic to protect the innocents. So why wait till they were dead to recruit them? Definitely. Gotta pull the humans in. Human resources, that was the ticket! The Grand Conductor smiled.

"Oh, yeah, boys! We're cooking with gas now! Don't just stand there and flap those wings at me!" Then the Grand Conductor frowned. "Can't have you walking and talking down there looking like that, you'll stand out in the crowd." Wave of hand, problem solved. "Don't worry, guys, you'll have 'em if you need 'em. Now hit the streets. There's some mean streets down there need patrolling."

Chapter Forty-Seven

"You want to explain yourself?" Gabriel, also known occasionally as Gabriel Smith, glared over his desk at the long figure lounging in the hot seat. At least, most individuals sitting in the chair in front of his desk considered themselves in the hot seat. Not this one. Never had, never would. Damn it.

"I look like a psychologist to you, O Fearless Leader?"

"Your vocabulary has four syllable words in it? I'm impressed."

"Well, you know how it is. I have so little time when I'm not stuck with *meooowwww* and *hisssss*. Unless of course I'm using *woof* and *grrrr*. Like to expand my horizons when I can."

"And whose fault is that? That you're—what was that you said, now? Stuck? I want to be sure I've got it right because stuck implies you're stuck. Fixed, immoveable, unable to alter your situation by choice. When in fact, how many promotions have you refused? This was supposed to be an interim assignment. Just to be sure you had the proper dose of humility. Empathy. Wouldn't get the big head. 'Cause that has happened, you know. Nobody ever intended you to make it your eternal career choice! Face it, Micah! It's way past time for you to move on!"

"But you can't make me, can you?" Micah grinned. A Cheshire cat grin. "Yep, that 'free will' thing. It's a real bitch sometimes, ain't it?"

"*Squawk*...real bitch...real bitch...squawk...hot mama gimme some..*squawk!*"

"Harold! Can it!" Micah and Gabriel shouted in unison.

The parrot sitting on the perch under the framed office logo blinked and ruffled his feathers.

"Well, 'at's the last time I attempt to interject some humor in the situation, what?"

"What are you doing here, anyway? Aren't you supposed to be keeping an eye on that magic act in Vegas?"

"Everybody's entitled to a spot o' R&R now an' a'gin, mate! Pip, pip, cherio an' all that. Besides— 'achoo! 'Scuse me, mates. 'At damn rabbit's got me sinuses all clogged, it's allergic to 'em I am, but does anybody care? Why'd I get tagged with 'at one anyway?"

"Because it takes a con to know a con, Harold. And in your day, you were the best."

"Flattery and a dollar'll get you a cup of coffee, mate. Maybe."

Gabriel glared at Harold. "And you just can't wait to get back to that perch beside the rabbit, can you, Harold?"

"Pretty bird...*squawk*...Harold wanna cracker...Harold don't want no stinkin' rabbit...*squawk*..."

"Then Harold best be putting a clamp on that smartass beak." Gabriel turned back to Micah. "Now. Back to you. What in the hell possessed you to show yourself in human form to one of your charges on that last assignment?"

"The devil made me do it?"

"Not funny."

"Oh, lighten up, G! She saw a guy. That's all. For just a minute. And the next time she looked a black cat was walking off." Micah shrugged. "No big."

"A guy in a leather jacket with a logo reading *The Guardians.* You don't think she had that cell phone whipped out in two seconds flat looking up angel names on the search engine?"

"Did she?"

"She did."

"You saw that?"

"It's in my job description."

Micah waved a casual hand in dismissal. "We're talking about Ariel Garrett here, G. The lady who named the stray cat Micah right off the top of her head. I never told her in cat-speak that was my name. She just knew it was. She's not your ordinary witch and she was about two centimeters away from figuring it out anyway. Now, you gonna just keep me here chewing my ass or you got a new job for me? 'Cause you can't fool me. You're trying to work me to damn death to make me take a promotion. Ain't happening. I like what I do. I like humans. Used to be one."

"I can't work you to death. You're already dead. Sort of. And you sure are throwing 'ain't' around a lot lately."

"I've been in the south a lot lately, remember? That assignment by the name of Ariel Garrett you're yelling at me about? Very handy word. So is y'all. Rubs off on you. New job?"

"There's a particularly nasty group of wannabe black wizard badasses in Philadelphia. You know the drill. Working their way up the 'oh, let's summon the dark master and gain eternal youth' chain. Progressing rapidly up the ladder from sacrificing white cocks—"

"I do 'ope you're talking about the chicken kind of cocks, mate! Makes me cringe if you're not."

"Harold, you're a bird. Remember? Sacrificing the chicken kind of cocks should make you cringe. But yes, the chicken kind of cocks. And they're moving up the animal chain. We have intelligence they may actually be planning a human sacrifice tonight. Of the infant kind."

Micah grimaced. "Never ceases to amaze me I can still be amazed at these sick sons-of-bitches. You'd think I'd be used to it by now."

"Got two different addresses for you. Apparently they alternate. Both addresses high-end." Gabriel scribbled furiously on a notepad and tore the sheet free.

Micah snorted. "Big surprise there. Poor people too busy trying to live this life to worry about trying to stay young and beautiful forever."

Gabriel's cell phone rang and vibrated simultaneously. "Here." He handed over the sheet of note paper. "And don't forget about the Vegas magic act, either. Harold, you've R&R'd enough, how 'bout you get your little tail feathers back where they're supposed to be?"

The desk phone buzzed loudly. Gabriel grabbed it with one hand and picked up the cell with the other, bracketing his ears.

"Yo, whut up?" Two for the price of one. "Hold a minute, please." He lowered both phones and glared at Micah. "You still here?" He flipped the glare to Harold. "And you didn't fly the coop yet either?"

"We're on it, G. Don't have a heart attack." Micah headed toward the door.

"I can't have heart attacks. What I can and do have are exasperation attacks. Frequently. Priority to the Philly thing."

"You think?" Micah shot back over his shoulder.

"Smartass angels," he muttered. "Gonna be the death of me yet. If I could die, that is."

* * *

Two figures, dressed in black and gray to match the darkness, crouched in the shadows of the gated mansion gardens.

"That's it, little girl. Right there. That's our pay-off."

"I've heard that before, Daddy."

"But this time it's the truth, sweetheart! I swear! No more shadows. Money for training. You could be a world-class gymnast. You should be a world-class gymnast. Not swinging from ledges and tree branches and climbing in windows! I know it's my fault. Know I'm no kind of a father at all, using his little girl to help him rob folks. And I'm so sorry, Mia, so—"

"*Sssssh.*" She pressed her finger against his lips. "It is what it is, Daddy. We are what we are. You have your specialty, I have mine. Time to move." She adjusted the ear piece in her ear, checked the position of the microphone pinned to the neckline of the sleek body suit she wore on the job to afford maximum flexibility and movement. She reached over and did the same for her father. "Go take out the alarm system. I'll be in position when you give the word."

"I love you, baby. Last time. Swear to God. After this, you can be a normal teenager again."

She didn't have the heart to tell him she'd never had the chance to be a normal teenager.

"I know, Daddy. Love you. Now go."

"Remember, Mia. Just because the owners are in Europe—"

"Doesn't mean the house is empty and we don't know where the staff is or when they might walk in. 'Cause the butler might want to bang the maid on the boss's bed."

"Mia! Good lord, girl, where do you come up with such things?"

Mia Fiori laughed. Her father genuinely believed he'd kept her sheltered. Other than making her his partner in burglary, of course. Not that that was his fault. She'd insisted. And to him she'd always be his little girl. Well, she'd always be his girl, just not so little any more.

The figures separated and took opposite directions into the darkness.

She moved in and waited close to the wall under the second floor window targeted for easiest and closest proximity to the safe in the Master Suite. Poor Daddy. That one lapse in judgment, that one time he'd given in to temptation—well, sometimes one time was all it took. Nobody'd known the alarm systems marketed by the security company he worked for better than Tony Fiori. And it hadn't taken much effort for that big league bank robber to find that out. Or to leave Tony holding the bag for the entire heist, though that hadn't worked out as well as the robber'd planned. Tony'd plea-bargained himself down to a few years in the pen and a few more on probation by giving up a shit-load of information the master-mind didn't even know he had. Which just went to prove the value of insurance. Still, the damage was done. He'd never worked a decent paying job again, certainly not one that carried health insurance. Mia'd been 13 when her Mom got sick. And no way in hell was Tony Fiori consigning her to what he called "the charity wards".

Neither was Mia. Nor was she about to let Tony try this with any partner who couldn't be trusted. Which meant any partner other than her. She didn't need her Mom dying and her father in jail. It'd been hard to convince him what a valuable tool she could be, but she'd finally managed to talk him into giving her a chance.

The rest, as they say, was history. Anna Fiori hadn't died in a charity ward. She hadn't been buried in a pauper's grave, either. But it took damn near every penny of every job Mia and Tony pulled to make sure of that. With nothing left, Tony planned this. The big one. The last one. The one to end it all. Goodbye Mean Street, hello Easy Street. Or so Tony said. Mia'd heard a lot of broken promises in her life. Though never because Tony hadn't tried to keep them. She smiled. Not the smile of a teenager. The smile of a woman who'd walked through fire on more than one occasion and still lived to tell about it. Even if she sported a lot of scars.

"Okay, baby! Mark and move."

She jerked in surprise and her elbow slammed into the stone wall. Damn. What she got for giving in to old memories. Served her right. She straightened up and backed away from the wall a bit, looking up at the target window. Nice ledge. Just perfect for a grappling hook. If she'd needed to use one, which she didn't.

She crouched, jumped, and caught the first branch of the big oak situated right outside the bedroom. Made for great shade, she was sure. It made a great ladder, too. Her gloves gave her the grip needed to start the swinging arc to loop her legs around the next branch and pull herself up. She reached for the next branch, and the next, and there she was. She maneuvered over and shoved at the window. It'd be locked of course, but you never knew. Sometimes alarm systems gave a false sense of security. And this time—unbelievable! This was one of those times. The window slid upwards.

Quick as a cat—and she was a cat burglar, after all— she slid through and into the room. A guest bedroom, just down the hall from the master suite. She moved to the door, cracked it open, and listened. Then she closed her eyes and concentrated to listen beyond her ears. To feel the listening. And something didn't feel right.

No one was in sight, though. And if something wasn't right, she'd best be moving her little cat burglar feet. Strategically placed nightlights cast enough light for a safe walk down the hall, but not much more than that. She moved carefully, staying near the walls, keeping to the shadows. Almost there. She paused. Something was off. Beyond the door to the master suite, the hall made a ninety degree turn and continued on, leading—where? Her skin prickled. No, her nerves prickled. Not the ordinary heightened sense of awareness that came with every job they pulled. More like fingernails on a blackboard. Or a fork scratching across a plate. A subliminal sound abraded her ear drums.

Time to get her butt into that master suite and use those sensitive ear drums of hers on the safe, the way Tony'd taught her. But she couldn't. She kept walking towards that ninety degree angle where the hall turned. The subliminal sound got louder and louder. And then all at once it wasn't subliminal anymore. Low, concentrated, throbbing. Chanting. Someone—no, a lot more than one someone—was chanting. She'd heard it all her life. At Mass. Not that she and Tony went to Mass much anymore. Confession and penance didn't seem like such a good idea, knowing full well they'd be repeating their sins, and sooner rather than later. But Mom had so loved Mass. And even when she'd been too sick to go to Church, she'd loved her recordings of the Gregorian chants.

Mia loved them, too, the feeling of peace, the pulsing power of faith they imparted, but she didn't listen to them anymore. She felt unworthy, undeserving. This, though. No, this was different. The key? The language? Yes. But that still wasn't it. This chant didn't soothe. It irritated. More than that, it crawled through her brain, buzzing like a nest of angry hornets, burning her ears, burning her brain, burning her skin.

If she had the sense God gave a goat, she'd turn and run. In fact, she tried to do just that. She couldn't. Something wouldn't let her. Something she couldn't control.

She made the ninety degree turn with the hall, into a shorter corridor running into double doors. Light spilled faintly underneath them. The chanting increased in volume. Dark. Commanding. Unholy.

She tried again to turn and run. Her feet wouldn't move in any direction but forward. Something unlike anything she'd ever experienced before wanted her to see what was beyond those doors.

She put her hand on one of the handles and slowly—oh, so slowly—turned. She pushed inward millimeter by millimeter until one eye peered into the flickering candlelight. Candlelight from the rows of black candles flanking the upside down cross above the perverted altar. Robed figures in a semicircle bent and swayed with the chant, and settled into a pulsing monotone. Above the chant, a piercing wail speared

Mia's heart. A baby. Her eyes flew back to that hideous altar. They had a baby on that altar. And every robed figure held a knife. Knives with twisted blades.

How much time did she have? And time to do what, exactly? If she rushed in and grabbed the baby, they'd kill her. No question. Problem was, then they'd kill the baby anyway. Because nobody'd know it was happening. And she never carried a cell phone on the job. No pockets, no room, no need. Just extra baggage. She closed the door and backed away from it. Whatever power made her walk down that hallway and open the door in the first place had better make sure she had enough time to get it back open again, that's just all there was to it. She pulled the neckline material to move the microphone as close as possible to her mouth.

"Daddy!"

"Mia, good God, girl, I was just about to come in after you—"

"Daddy, you have to call the cops and get them here. Now! I don't know how much time we've got!"

"You've lost your mind—"

"Listen to me! There's a—cult or something! In a big room up here! They have a baby and Daddy, they're about to kill it, now call the cops! Now!"

"Mia, you get your ass out—"

"This is bigger than us, Daddy, just do it!"

The cadence of the chant changed. Surged. Moved to climax.

"Do it!"

Mia ran through the double doors just as the knives began their downward descent and flung herself over the wailing infant.

* * *

A black cat leapt branch to branch up the massive maple tree. Not just any black cat. A cat with an angelic disposition. Micah. His ears quivered, his nerves screamed. That chant. The cadence was changing,

changing too fast for cat mode to keep up with. Why the hell hadn't Gabriel sent him out sooner? Not like G to cut things this close.

No help for it. Psychic hooks shot out from his brain, searching for the pulsing energy that powered the Universe. Got it! He reeled it back in and black cat became a glowing orb streaking the last few feet toward the window at light speed.

The orb burst through the glass. Blazing pure, golden power overshadowed the dark blackish-red shadows of the mini-hell on earth created by the robed figures. The power attacked, shifting form into a massive shadow of a human figure sporting wings. The wings beat furiously. High winds buffeted the room, bouncing back and forth, one stream merging into another and another until they converged and shot full-force toward the target. The robed figures shrieked but the wind didn't care. It lifted them off their feet and sucked them into the whirling vortex, and as suddenly as the raging energy appeared, it departed. The room held nothing but the giant shadow of the winged human figure. And a teenage girl, thirteen twisted knives protruding obscenely from her bleeding body as it sprawled over the wailing infant.

Sonofabitch! This wasn't a rescue mission. It was a harvest. Gabriel could've told him, damnit!

Glowing light covered the girl's body, rising, rising, into human shape. The figure of a teenage girl. Confusion radiated out from the light. Micah pulled his energy in tight, forming the compact figure of a human male in his prime, wings now in proportion to the human size. He swooped over to the radiant shadow above the body and gathered it into his arms, hugging tightly, rising upwards.

"Whaa—where—what's going on? What's happening to me?"

"Don't worry, sweetheart. I've got you. I've got you. You're going home."

Chapter Forty-Eight

Lights, camera, action! Well, okay, no camera, this was a live show. Harold sat on his perch on the Vegas stage and squawked. So far, just a show like any other. Like all the past four performances. Nothing out of the ordinary. Maybe Gabriel was wrong about this one. Harold hadn't seen anything to bend his beak out of joint yet. Even if the magician's name was Damien. And even if Damien's obligatory lovely assistant gave new brilliance to the sheen of the gold-sequined body suit.

"*Squawk*...hot mama gimme some..." Ooops. Inappropriate but Harold just couldn't stop himself when the stage lights shimmered off those gold-tinted stockings showcasing those legs that just didn't bloody stop.

"Volunteers? Volunteers from the audience?" The handsome magician, appropriately dressed in dramatic black with whirling cape, twirled his handlebar black mustache. "Can't close the show without some volunteers! Take a tour through Magic Land you'll never forget on our Magical Carpet Ride! Sights never seen by the human eye! How 'bout you?" He pointed to a table in the far corner, a young couple, newlyweds at a guess, one of many such couples taking advantage of the ease of Vegas weddings. They giggled at the attention. Neither of them felt any pain, that was certain. Drunk as skunks.

"Sure! We're game!" The guy stood up, swayed, and grabbed for the back of the chair. He extended his hand to his lady and they made their shaky way to the stage, holding onto each other for support.

"Observe, ladies and gents!" Damien opened the doors of the large black box. Persian carpet lined the back, sides and flooring. He tapped the sides, roof and floor with his cane. "No hidden doors, no way out! And in you go!" His black cape swirled and twirled as he and his obligatory lovely assistant herded the couple inside. "Off for the ride of your lives! Wave goodbye to the audience as you leave!" The box began a slow turn, moving in a circle, door still partially open. The magician slammed it shut just as it began to accelerate.

Harold perked up and focused. Of course the box was on a pedestal that revolved, that wasn't new, but it'd never turned that fast before. Blimey, it was spinning like a top! Making his stomach lurch, it was, and didn't Damien remember those two were fairly pickled? Better have a carpet cleaner handy, that box was surely going to need one.

And was it—Harold's eyes widened. "*Squawk! Squawk!* Shiver me timbers...fire in the hole...fire in the hole!!"

The bloody box bloody lifted! Off the floor! One foot in the air, two feet in the air...of course, nothing magical in lifting a box off the ground. You only needed a rope and pulley system or some version of it employing thin wire that seemed invisible, but with the box moving at that speed—and anyway, it'd never done that before.

The box started coming back down, the spinning revolutions slowed. Damien stepped up to the doors. He grasped the door handles, pulled the doors open, and swirled his cape. Empty box. Of course. It always was. That was the whole point. But this time—no, this time, Harold wasn't a happy bird about it.

The audience clapped and called. Damien stepped to the front of the stage with Assistant Golden Girl. They clasped hands and bowed.

"Thank you! Thank you, one and all!"

Harold looked over at the sides of the stage. At previous shows, the "volunteers" waited in the wings, ready to come out and take their own bows. Not this time. Nobody was there.

"*Squawk*...no fire in the hole...no fire in the hole...whassup doc!"

* * *

Backstage in the dressing room, Damien threw off his cape and stretched.

"I love it when we finally get moving!"

Golden Girl unzipped the side zipper of the gold-sequined bodysuit and burst out of it.

"*Squawk*...what a pair...what a pair..." Best part of the show. Harold never could stop himself when that zipper unzipped.

"Damn parrot. You'd think he actually knew what he was saying." Golden Girl reached for her dressing gown and slipped into it.

"Maybe he does. Seems to be the usual male reaction."

"Sure he's a male?"

"No, actually, I'm not. Never checked."

Harold's eyes widened. *And you'd bloody well better not try either, mate!*

"Did you get confirmation? That the package made it through?"

"Not yet."

"And you're sure that couple won't have anybody checking on them?"

"Yes, I'm sure that couple won't have anybody checking on them. At least not for a few days. Told you, they're here alone, not with a group, not with friends. Spur of the moment elopement, didn't even tell anybody where they were going. Heard 'em in the lobby when they were checking in, laughing over their grand adventure. And about damn time, too, seems like everybody in Vegas is here with some group or other this time."

"Good pick."

"Oh, yeah. All that sexual energy just busting out from the seams. All we need is a few more like that and then the finale. Which needs to be Saturday night, I don't wanna stretch it any further, that's cutting it too close. Yeah, Saturday we're outta here. We'll go for the power at that show. Won't matter if they're alone or not, we'll be long gone."

"Speaking of seams and busting—this skin's getting horribly tight."

Harold's eyes bugged. Was that a tentacle waving out of her hair?

"Up to you. But you know human form feels even worse if you break out of it and have to go back in than it does if you just stay in it in the first place."

Blimey and holy hell, that wasn't just one tentacle waving out of her hair, it was three! And counting!

"I know." Golden Girl shrugged. "But you know what? I don't care. Got to have a break!"

"*Squawk*...invasion of the body snatchers...invasion of the body snatchers...whassup doc...*squawk!*"

* * *

While all this was going on, I was half a continent away in our home at Pine Whisper Plantation, packing. Stacy'd joined Spike in Vegas within a week of our return from Daytona and the wedding was set for this coming Saturday, to be held in Vegas at the Little White Wedding Chapel's Tunnel of Love Drive-Thru. On motorcycles. Can anybody say "copycat"? But I had to admit, considering the circumstances and all, nothing could be more perfect. And after all, I'd started the family tradition.

I almost closed my suitcase but didn't. Something—I needed something else. What?

"Baby girl, you been staring at that thing for five minutes. Want me to go pull the sink outta the kitchen and throw it in there for you?"

"Nobody likes a smart-ass warlock."

"You do."

"Not always. Always love him though."

"Care to prove it?"

"Not right at the moment. I need to finish packing. You think there's any chance at all we can have just a normal trip to Vegas this time?"

"I gave up hope several lifetimes ago anything we do or any trip we take's gonna be normal."

I sighed. Yeah, "ordinary" waved bye-bye to us long ago.

"Stacy said Mom and Daddy's flight ought to get in at more or less the same time ours does. And Mom still hasn't given her any flack over anything." My mother'd never forgiven me for my own wedding and I doubted she ever would. I hadn't thought she'd be any fonder of Stacy's wedding plans, either, but at least Stacy did give advance notice. And give her a chance to actually get there. I grinned and tried to resist, but I couldn't. "She always did like Stacy best."

"Missed one daughter's wedding, doesn't want to miss both of them. But does your Dad actually know how to ride a motorcycle?"

"Oh, c'mon! It's a drive-thru, doesn't have to be on a motorcycle. Spike said he'd put them in his Beemer. Mom'd probably forgive either of them anything. I mean, after all, Stacy's marrying a doctor. He drives a Beemer and everything. Even if he does live in Vegas."

"Far cry from a disreputable PI, for sure."

"She's warming up to you, Magic Man. Though I'm not surprised. That magical charm of yours."

"I resent that. I would never misuse power just to make your mother like me. It's natural charm, pure and simple."

I laughed and walked over to my dresser. I hesitated a minute and then pulled open a drawer. I licked my lips in indecision. But I couldn't fight it. Yeah, this needed to come with me. I walked back to the bed and placed the case firmly in the top pocket of the suitcase and slammed the lid shut.

"There! All done!"

"The Tear? You're taking the Tear of Isis to Vegas? Why?"

"I don't know why, okay? I just know—I need to take it."

Chad stared at me. "Baby girl, remember what I told you at the start? That persons of power are usually a mix of talents, some a lot stronger than others?"

"Yeah."

"And you're such a strong telepath it hasn't even occurred to you yet, has it?"

"What?"

"That a latent talent for pre-cog's been getting stronger and stronger with you."

"No, it's not. Both of us just know things. Knowing things is our thing."

"This is different. Telepathy is looking at other people and knowing them for what they really are. Inside. Pre-cog is a premonition of things to come."

"Other than the fact that it'll be a miracle if this wedding goes off without getting some or all of us in trouble, I don't know nuttin' from nuttin'."

"Yes, you do. Because you know you have to take the Tear of Isis with you. You don't know why, but you know you do."

"Maybe I just think it'll look good with that slinky black sheath I bought for the Vegas shows. The one with the plunging neckline."

"Now you're talking magic. You done with that suitcase?"

"Yeah. Why?"

He lifted it off the bed onto the floor, enveloped me in his arms and fell backwards onto the spread.

"Got another use for the bed right now."

"Do you now?"

Good thing I didn't have a clue what was going on at Command Central, MeanStreet Division of the

Galatic Guardian Counsel. I wouldn't have enjoyed that interlude nearly as much.

* * *

"Yo, whut up?" Gabriel barked into the mouthpiece of his desk phone. He cocked his head, listening intently. "That's impossible. Nothing like that's happened in millennia." He frowned. "Definitely. We definitely need a meet. How 'bout four o'clock?" He frowned harder. "No, not Eastern Standard Time. Get with the program! Universal time. This is a universal problem. Of extremely universal consequences. You calling Raphael or do I need to?"

The wall of Gabriel's office dissolved into a blaze of light. A mini windstorm blew into the room on a flurry of beating wings, sending papers swirling off his desk. The wall reformed and Micah, in compact angel form with wings high and proud, blew into the room, cradling an unconscious body. He flew lightly over to the couch and gently deposited his cargo on it, positioning a couch pillow carefully under her head. Poor baby. She'd be awake pretty quick but that first out-of-physical body trip was a killer. Knocked everybody out.

He compacted his wings tightly, stalked over to Gabriel's desk and slammed a fist down on the wood.

"Good. I'll see both of you then," Gabriel said into the phone. He hung up, leaned his chair back and propped his feet on the desk. "And what's got your feathers in an uproar?"

"You! You set me up! This was never a preventative mission! It was never about the baby! It was a harvest! Of a new angel!"

"And your point is?"

"You lied to me, G!"

"I did not! I never told you a damn thing that wasn't true. You're the one who assumed your assignment was to save the baby. And you still don't have it right. Exactly. She's not an angel. She's a second-chancer."

"What did you say?"

"Second-chancer. Not full angel. But she deserves a second chance to be."

"The hell you say!"

"Micah. She's a teenage cat burglar. Look at her clothes. Look where you found her. What you think she was doing in that mansion? Looking for gumdrops? She and her Dad have been pulling jobs for years!"

"And just why do you think they—and more specifically she—was doing that?"

"Okay, so the Dad had his back against the wall trying to take care of her Mom. And she did it to take care of her Mom and keep her Dad out of trouble. Shoulda known you'd pull that out of her essence on the way up. Still doesn't excuse it."

"You sonofabitch."

"Hey! That's an insult to the Grand Conductor, not just me!"

"You can't take the heat, get outta the kitchen! She is not a second-chancer! She shouldn't even be dead! She's a baby herself! Why the hell couldn't you just let me handle the cult and take care of the baby?"

"It was her time, Micah! Free will only goes so far. It was her time and this was her way. Or would you have preferred we leave her on earth until all the innocence and good she had leached out of her soul? What then? Where would she go when that time came?"

"Innocence and good would never have leached out of that girl's soul! She took thirteen knives in her back to save that baby, G! Thirteen!"

"She reminds you of somebody, doesn't she? Like Hannah?"

Micah's face twisted and darkened.

"Don't talk about my little sister!"

Gabriel's face softened. "Look, Micah. I know you've never understood why Hannah didn't come up with you. But some humans are born to be repeaters. Living many lives before their harvest. Not because they're inferior. Because they're on a different path. A path through many lifetimes, touching many people. As humans."

"Then why didn't I have the choice to repeat? To go back into other lives with her?"

Gabriel shrugged. "I'm not the Grand Conductor. I can't answer that. One more time. Free will only goes so far."

"That girl is not a second-chancer!"

"That's not your call."

"How many promotions have I turned down?"

"How many—what the hell's that got to do with this?"

"How many promotions have I turned down?"

"A lot."

"And promotions are rewards, right? An acknowledgment of a job well-done?"

"Well, yeah. But admit it, Micah. To yourself, if not to me. You've never taken a promotion because you think somewhere, someday, you'll find Hannah again. Whoever she is. In whichever life you find her. Don't you? And for what? Have you ever, one time, come close?"

"None of your damn business. Okay, it's reward time. And I'm calling 'em in, all of 'em. All the rewards I never took."

"What?"

"She has full angel status. That's what I want. For all the promotions I never took, all the rewards I never claimed."

"I can't—"

"Sure you can."

"I don't have that kind of authority!"

"So negotiate for it. Do this one thing for me. I've never asked. Once. This time, this time, G—I'm asking."

Gabriel sighed. "Shit. You drive a tough bargain. Okay, okay. Somehow I'll fix it. But you gotta train her."

Over on the couch, Mia moaned slightly. Her eyelids fluttered.

"Agreed. So fix it. Priority."

"Priority."

Micah moved to the couch and kneeled beside it, smoothing her hair back as she struggled back to consciousness.

"Where—where am I?" She sat up abruptly and groped behind her back, feeling for—feeling for what? She wasn't sure. "The baby! Is the baby okay? Oh, my God! I'm dead! Aren't I?" She stared into Micah's eyes. "But you—you saved me? Didn't you?"

"The baby's fine, sweetheart, I promise. Now about the rest of it—I guess that depends on your definition of a couple of words. Like dead and saved. We need to talk."

The office wall shook. Harold, his small parrot body blazing golden light, shot in through the wall.

"*Squawk*...invasion of the body snatchers...invasion of the body snatchers...whassup doc...*squawk!*"

Mia gasped. "What's—who's—that? Them? And oh my God! Your back! Are those wings? What's going on?"

"Damn," said Gabriel mildly. "Talk about second chancers and in one flies. Whut up, Harold?"

* * *

The phone rang in an office very similar to Gabriel's. Except for the lighting, a peculiar shade of blackish-red. Probably had something to do with the upholstery on all the furnishings. And the curtains. And the lighting itself. And the impossibly black wood of the big desk. Or maybe from the reddish glow emanating from the eyes of the desk's occupant.

The intercom buzzed on the desk phone.

"Yes?"

"He's here."

344

"Let's not keep him waiting. Show him in."

The man behind the black desk leaned back in his chair and propped his feet on the scarlet desk blotter. He laced his hands behind his head. Like Gabriel, he was long and lean. On first blush, even handsome. But there was something there, something behind the regular features. Something feral. Waiting to escape.

The door opened.

"Well, well. Long time no see, brother. How've you been, Jerahmeel?"

"I'm not your brother, Lucifer."

Lucifer smiled. Very pleasantly. Except for that slightly pointed edge to all his teeth.

"Not in a long time. But seeing as how you're here, I'm thinking you're ready to renew the relationship."

* * *

"Harold, calm down! We can't understand a damn thing you're saying with all that squawking!"

"Invasion of the body snatchers...invasion of the body snatchers! Does anybody bloody listen to me or am I alone on this planet?! *Whoo*, and hello, pretty girl on the sofa! Where'd you come from?"

"Newbie. Formal introductions later. Who's a body snatcher?"

"That bloody magic act in Vegas! Why do I get stuck with all the shit jobs?"

"Got two words for you, Harold. Second. Chancer. Remember?"

"Right. Okay, so I'm sitting there on my perch on stage, weather eye on the horizon and all that bullarky. Magician dude makes this couple from the audience disappear in his magic box."

"Not that uncommon for magicians."

"They bloody well didn't come back, mate!"

"At all? You know magicians send the audience volunteers—"

"Out from the back of the stage or under the stage or whatever floats his boat, but I'm telling you, mate, this couple's gone! And the magician and his assistant? *Squawk*...what a pair...what a pair..."

Gabriel sighed. "Why do I think that's actually not a reference to the magician and his assistant?"

Micah laughed. Mia looked from one to the other. She tugged Micah's hand and shook her head.

"Really, where am I? I'm dreaming. This can't be happening."

"Sorry, darling, yes, it is. I'll explain in a few."

Harold squawked again for attention. "Oh, she's got a pair, mate! Problem is, they aren't really hers!"

"We're not really concerned with cosmetic surgery, Harold."

"You'd better get concerned, mate! 'Cause they've snatched some other bodies somewhere! To wear! You twig?"

* * *

"So tell me about it. My guess is you've finally figured out you can't save humans from themselves. So you might as well use 'em." Lucifer opened an ornate box and lifted a cigar out reverently. He sniffed it and sighed in satisfaction. He cut the tip, struck his fingertip against a rough stone paperweight, and lit it. He waved his hand casually toward the box. "Join me? Cuban. Finest of the fine. Hard to get without—connections."

"I'm tired of being a flunky. The big three get all the attention. You get more attention than me. Nobody even knows my name."

Lucifer guffawed. He choked and a stream of smoke streamed from his nose and mouth.

"Oh, this just keeps getting better and better! Not even disillusionment! Jealousy, pure and simple! Just go ahead and say it! Repeat after me, now! The Grand

Conductor likes them best! Oh, this is just icing on the cake! Cream cheese icing at that!"

Jerahmeel glared across the desk. "Glad I'm such good entertainment."

"Little brother, I haven't had this much fun since Nero fiddled while Rome burned. But okay, whatever. Never look a gift horse in the mouth and all that. And of course, the more ignoble the reason, the better. Now. What about your staff? It's not impossible to stage a coup alone, and you don't want too many noses sniffing in the business but it's a lot easier with at least one other—team member, as it were. Got anybody?"

"Of course. What kind of fool do you take me for?"

"The jealous kind. Duh."

"Remember my head honcho? Seraphim?"

"Goes by Sera. Transformation form of choice is a black cat. Not terribly original. Always struck me as a bit of copycatting there. But then, she never was especially bright."

"She's a bitch. Hell to live with. And that's another thing. Gabriel gets a head honcho like Micah? Certified hero and all that? And I get a bitch who choked to death on a fishbone? Or her own spleen, more likely. I mean, how fair is that? Woman never should have been an angel to begin with, let alone assigned to one of us! How'd that happen, anyway?"

Lucifer waved his hand in dismissal. "Grand Conductor owed her grandmother a favor. Or so I've heard. You ought to be glad she's a bitch. And a stupid one. You had a Micah, you wouldn't be here right now talking to me. Because he'd know it. And so would everybody else on the Guardian Council. Why's she willing to throw in with you? Big reward, but big damn risk."

"General piss-off. Got the hots for Micah and he won't have anything to do with her. What do you want out of this?"

"MeanStreet. I want Gabriel's third of the Guardian Council."

"MeanStreet? Michael was the one tearing after you with fire and fury, as I recall. Gabriel pretty much stayed out of it."

"Exactly. At least Michael had the courage of his convictions. Gabriel? Ran away to earth and waited to see who won. Playing both sides against the middle. You're either with me or against me. Neutrals not allowed."

Jerahmeel shrugged. "Works for me."

* * *

"So she actually—unzipped? Like—her skin? And stepped out of it? New one on me." Micah looked over at Gabriel. Who'd actually dropped his casual feet-on-desk pose and leaned forward in his chair. "But not, I'm thinking, a new one on you, G. Your poker face is slipping. And it's saying you've heard of this before and you don't much like it."

Gabriel relaxed his frown and resumed his signature casual posture. "Sounds like a dimensional break. Demons from an adjoining dimension. Happens. Very rarely. Nothing to worry about, I'm on it. Harold, from what you heard, got a guess as to a time frame?"

"Saturday night, mate! Didn't I just say so? Nobody bloody listens to me!"

"No, you didn't just say so, that's why I asked! Okay, that's a little time, anyway. Now fly on back and keep tabs like a good little parrot. Keep me posted. Especially if there's any change in the time schedule. And don't blast the wall again on your way out."

"Hmmph. 'At's all the thanks I get?"

"Want a cracker?"

"Bite me tail feathers, mate."

"Watch it, Harold, don't get cute. Or I'll tell Micah to eat you next time he's in cat form."

"Cat form?" Mia whispered.

"I'll pass, thanks. Gives me indigestion just thinking about the feathers."

"Harold, you still here? Micah, give the newbie the tour, I've got a meeting in just a few. Mia, welcome. To MeanStreet, LLC. Hope you like us. 'Cause it's not going to be a short-term relationship."

Chapter Forty-Nine

"Well, hey, good-lookin's! What'll it be, boys?"

Michael glanced up from the menu. Oh, yeah. This barbecue shack knew how to hire waitresses. Knew how to dress 'em, too. Not every figure could handle halter tops. Too much equipment lost the "come hither" effect. Too little, on the other hand—well, who wanted to play "hide-and-seek"? And the cut-off blue-jean shorts! Ah, that fringe at the bottom! The perfect combo.

"Well, hey yourself, little darling! We're expecting one more. So just bring us a couple of drafts to start— oh! There he is. Coming in the door. Bring us three drafts and check back with us?"

"You got it!" Miss Perky Halter Top watched the figure approach the table. "You guys brothers? Sure look a lot alike."

"Yes, ma'am, Miss Eagle-Eye. You pegged us. I'm Mike, this is Rafe, and here comes Gabe. Smith."

"I'm Jenny! Smith! Think we're related?"

"Oh, I doubt we're that lucky, Miss Jenny."

Be right back with those drafts!" Jenny headed toward the bar. And man, did those high wedge sandals put the right sway in that backside!

"Boys, we got to get down here more often! Man, what a pair!" Michael looked longingly after Jenny.

"I wanta hear that, all I got to do is call Harold in to report. Don't need to hear it from you."

"Man, lighten up! Take some pleasure in life! Listen to the music!" Hank Williams wailed from the speakers. "Classic country, you can't beat it."

"I can listen to the original anytime I want."

"Yeah, yeah, we know," Raphael quipped. "Heaven's got a hell of a band."

"Damn straight." Raphael and Michael high-fived.

"Are you two ever serious about anything?"

"Here you are, boys!" Jenny returned with tall frosted mugs as Gabriel settled in his chair. She plopped them down cheerfully. "Special today's the baby-back ribs. With fries and coleslaw and Texas Toast. Sauce is out of this world!"

"Three specials," Gabriel said. "Heavy on the sauce, extra Texas Toast."

"You got it!"

"Damn, Gabe, you might give us a chance to order for ourselves. Free will and all that, remember?"

"You're in a barbecue shack. What the hell else were you gonna order?"

"Baby-backs, but that's not the point. The point is—"

"The point is you're right. And we're in serious trouble. Just got word of a dimensional break in my division. Not one of the occasional cracks we all have that drives us nuts 'cause it's gone by the time we know it's there, a full-blown breach, an open conduit. That means there's a breach in all three divisions. And that means—"

"Damn. We really do have a broken arrow."

"Yep. Another archangel's fallen."

* * *

Vegas's Rainforest Café catered to families. Especially families with kids, even though no Rainforest Café ever forgot the grown-ups. It was always full of children's voices, but these voices had a specific target.

"Dr. Spike! Dr. Spike!" Stacy laughed as three children, ranging at a guess from six to barely toddler-size, charged them as they maneuvered their way out the doors.

351

"Dan, my man! Gimme some skin!"

Small hand smacked giant hand and performed a convoluted series of hand movements ending with bouncing fists.

Not to be outdone, Dan the man's little brother tugged Spike's sleeve and waved his video game. "Dr. Spike! Look! I got a new army man game!"

"Awesome! Wow, how cool is that? You gonna let me play it?"

"Sure!"

Little sister, somewhere between one and two at a guess, toddled up and grabbed his pants leg.

"Up!" she demanded.

Spike complied. "Lily, you cutie-patootie, you keeping these big guys straight?"

Lily tugged the beard Stacy'd convinced him to keep after Bike Week. "New?"

"Sure is. You like it? I'll shave it right off if you don't, got to keep my princesses happy."

"Like!"

"Dr. Forrester, I'm so sorry!" Their mother rushed up to corral the three. "We were coming in when you headed out and they're just so fast!"

"No problem, Mrs. Lindstrom, you know I always love seeing my kids. Guys, this is my lady, Stacy Anson. Stacy Forrester this coming Saturday, in fact."

"Unless your patients run her off first," Mrs. Lindstrom retrieved baby Lily and smiled at Stacy. "The kids just love him. Not just mine, all his patients. So get used to it. My friends tell me their kids do the same thing if they see him. Congratulations."

"Thank you. Lily, that's such a pretty dress! And your brothers are so handsome."

"*Icccck.*" Lily said, and pointed to her brothers.

"Lily, that's enough! C'mon, guys, say good-bye and let's go get our table."

Stacy watched the retreating fan club before turning to leave.

"Wow. There's something really special about a man when dogs and kids love him, you know." She hooked her arm under Spike's.

"Really?"

"Really. My mother's always said so. Never did ask her why she married Daddy, dogs hate him."

"Seriously?"

Stacy laughed. "No, in fact they've got four and I've never seen a dog who didn't like him. They were so cute."

"The dogs?" They cleared the hotel doors and turned left, strolling down Las Vegas Boulevard.

"The kids. You really do have a natural talent for kids, don't you?"

"And hence the specialty choice of pediatrician. As opposed to say, pathologist."

"Bad example, circumstances being what they are and all."

"Damn sure is. Didn't think before I spoke. Good thing I didn't want to be a pathologist, though. Not a good choice at all for a ghost whisperer. I mean, autopsying somebody when you're watching 'em watch you do it?" He shuddered slightly.

"Okay, have we figured out how we're goin' to show Vegas off to Mom and Dad? And Ariel didn't get to see too much of it when they were out here, either."

Spike and Stacy were in agreement on most things. One of them was no honeymoon. At least not right now. They'd do that in a couple of months. They lived in Vegas, after all. Exotic enough to a southern girl like Stacy, and still very new to her. She couldn't wait to show Vegas off to the family.

"Honey, don't try and plan too much for your folks. Let's just cruise the Strip and let 'em pick. We'll go in wherever a show hits their fancy. And if we can't get in one they want one night, we'll get reservations for the next night."

"Works for me. But one thing you can count on."

"Which is?"

"Magic shows."

"We don't got enough magic of our own? We have our own little private family coven, remember?"

"Not that kind of magic. Mom's got a thing for magic shows. Oh, look!" Stacy pointed at one of the large casinos. "There's one!" She reached in her pants pocket for her phone to take a photo. "This way we'll remember all of 'em."

"She does? I've never asked but—your folks, are they, well, magical themselves? Seeing as how you and Ariel—"

Stacy slowed her pace and pursed her lips in thought. "I honestly don't know. I don't know where Ariel and I came from. Our magic, I mean, of course I know where we came from, don't even."

"Damn. Temptation shot down. That was almost irresistible, you know."

"I know. But honestly, I don't know if magic's inherited or just inherent in each new little soul. Or old little soul, as the case may be. I'm pretty sure Dad doesn't have it. If Mom does, I don't think she knows it. I mean, she never tried to explain anything to us about it. And about freaked out over what she called my imaginary friends. Child psychologist freak out. Wouldn't a parent with power try and help their kids understand theirs instead of running for the child psychologist?"

"You'd think, yeah. Hell, Mom, tried to help me. I just wasn't having any of it. I figured the magic in that family—and it wasn't just Chad, looking back, Mom just—well, she glowed. Kinda like you and Ariel do. Anyway, there was a lot of magic in that house. And being a foster child, no blood connection, I figured I was out for the count. And then came you. And Daytona."

"Well. Anyway, whether Mom does or doesn't have magic, knows or doesn't know she does—she loves magic acts. Always has. And look! Another magic show!" Stacy pulled out her phone again. "Oh, yeah! Mom's goin' to love Vegas!"

"Hate to say it, but actually—I'm glad." Michael took a long swig of his beer.

"You're glad we're gonna go through all this shit again?"

"I'm glad you've got a breach in your division. You kept insisting it was impossible and since I know damn well I got one and Rafe knows damn well he's got one—"

"Rafe's sitting right here, you know." Rafael took a long draw from his mug, too. "And he can talk. You're always trying to take over, Michael."

"Well, just excuse me to hell and back!"

"Wait a damn minute here! Back up! Are you saying just because I wasn't sure I had a breach, you thought I knew damn well there was one? And thereby might be the broken arrow? Me?!"

"Guys! Can it!" Rafe hissed. "Incoming waitress."

"Here you go, boys! Y'all must be hungry, never saw such scowls! Don't worry, this'll fix you right up! Anything else?"

"This'll do it, honey, thank you."

"Y'all save some room for desert now, hear?" Jenny headed back to the kitchen.

"Man, what is it about southern girls?" Michael shook his head as he watched her rear retreat. "Aren't they just the best?"

"You just told me you thought I was the broken arrow and you're sitting there now stuffing your face and watching a waitress's rear-end? I don't believe you, man!"

Rafael reached across into the bread basket for a piece of toast. "Gabriel, calm down. He's still bent out of shape 'cause you opted out of the last brouhaha and decided to stay down on earth a while."

"Call it like it is, brother." Michael sucked the last morsels of meat off his first rib and licked his fingers. "He ran away to earth."

"Somebody needed to be looking after the humans while all you assholes were having a pissing contest! You ever think of that? Maybe spilling your brother's blood got your rocks off, Michael, but it didn't hold the first damn bit of interest for me! I loved Lucifer as much as I loved you!"

Light shot from Michael's eyes and the beer left in the mugs bubbled. Rafael slammed his arm across the table between the two.

"Enough! Don't cause a scene! And I get damn tired of refereeing you two! Now we have a problem here! Agreed? So what are we going to do about it? I don't even know where my break is! Neither does Michael!"

Michael and Gabriel both settled back in their chairs.

"No worries," said Gabriel. "I know where mine is. Vegas. And I know who's going to be there. Tomorrow. If I can just steer 'em to the right place."

* * *

I frowned as I settled into the front seat of the SUV. So far everything had run smooth as silk. We were flying into Vegas from Jacksonville, Mom and Dad would arrive about the same time from Atlanta. But something was wrong. Something was missing. I did a mental run-down of the checklist. All luggage loaded? Check. All pending War-N-Wit, Inc. jobs done? Check. Pine Whisper Plantation's caretaker par excellence Buddy McAfee all set to look after all the animals while we're gone? Check. And for us, that just wasn't normal. What was missing? Oh, yeah! Ringtone signaling incoming trouble—magic world, Chad's past law enforcement affiliations, whichever. Sometimes both, but gotta have at least one. And there it was, coming in loud and clear from the dash. Check. The nerve-pinging tingle from the theme for The Twilight Zone.

"Knew it was too good to be true," Chad said. "Answer it."

"Hello?"

"Yo, whut up?"

"You tell us, G."

"You don't have to sound so cautious, I don't bite."

"Much," said Chad.

"I resent that. And besides, I was just calling to wish you a good trip. And send good wishes to your brother and sister. Glad Spike finally broke out of the closet. Been meaning to call and suggest you introduce him to us but I just haven't had a chance. We can always use some more of the good ones, Spike and Stacy'd be welcome."

"We'll be sure to relay the message," I said.

"Have a great time in Vegas, do the Strip right. Oh, and while you're there—"

"I knew it." Chad shook his head mournfully.

"Hey, it's nothing! We just got wind one of the magic shows playing right now might be using some low-level magic to con some of the audience. Nothing big, just since you're there anyway—"

"I hate magic shows. Remember?"

"That's a hell of thing for the guy so many people call Magic Man to say."

"G, you couldn't pay me enough to go near a magic show."

"Uh, honey?"

"What?"

"Sorry to tell you this, but Mom loves magic shows. There's three playing on the Strip right now. Stacy's already told her about 'em."

"Should I groan now?"

"'Fraid so. She's planning to hit every one of 'em. Which one's using the low-level magic con, G?"

"Magician by the name of Damien. So you'll keep an eye open for us?"

"Sure," I said. "No problem."

I hit "End" and settled back in my seat.

"You don't have to go to the magic show. I don't much care for 'em myself, never have, but since Mom does, we'll kill two birds with one stone."

"How so?"

"Stacy's Bachelorette Party. Such as it is. I mean, if a girl's getting married with a big traditional wedding, they have last-fling parties too, you know, can't let you guys have all the fun. But since all of Stacy's close friends are like—not in Vegas, we decided we'd just do it ourselves. Stacy and Mom and me."

"You didn't have a Bachelorette Party."

"I was runnin' from Mom and big planned weddings. Didn't give Stacy the chance or even option of coming." And in retrospect, that'd been a damn good thing. "But since we're having a modified girls-night-out, we'll just do the magic show then. Mom'll love it. And you won't have to suffer through it."

"Don't know as that's such a great idea. G said some low voltage magic was going on, you know."

"Thought I was some high voltage magic. You don't think I can handle a magical con by myself?"

"You're high voltage everything, baby girl. Period."

"Glad you agree. Then that's settled."

"Okay. I guess."

Ignorance is such bliss. If I'd known then what I know now—I'd have done the same damn thing, I'm not even going to lie about it.

* * *

"Right this way, madam." The waiter ushered the raven haired beauty in slinky black to the corner table. "Mr. Smith's already ordered your cocktail. I'll be back with you in a few minutes."

"Thank you, that'll be lovely." The madam in question slipped fluidly onto the proffered chair.

"Sera, my dear. Turning as many heads as always, I see. I love to see the looks on all the men's faces when you walk in a room."

"I don't know why you still use Smith." Sera picked up her Marguerita and licked the salted rim delicately. "None of the 'Smiths' would piss on you if you were on fire."

"Sera! No need for crudity. Doesn't go well with that elegant demeanor. I use it because they use it. And like it or not—and I know they don't—we're still brothers. They can't deny me. They took a lot. Can't have the name back."

"Still don't know why you'd want to use it."

"Because it's mine. Now, on to business."

Sera frowned. "We're in Vegas, Luce! All you want to talk is business?"

"For now. And we have a busy night. We still have to hit Paris and Bejing."

"The other breaks?"

"Of course. Have to have one in each division. Concentrated attack. Those little whispers of yours in Jerahmeel's ears! Just perfection, my dear! He thinks it's all his idea, just like he's supposed to."

"Male stupidity. Never ceases to amaze me. Why he thinks the head demon from the Razkaal Dimension would ever think to contact him if they wanted to take over earth I'll never know. I mean—who even knows his name? Here on earth even? Let alone in the Razkaal Dimension."

"Well, you know how it is. Pride goeth before a fall. As I know from personal experience. Working from the shadows is much more effective, but wisdom comes with experience. That's the beauty of little brothers. Still bothers him, that nobody knows who I am thing."

"And that means even whatshisname—'cause I'm not even going to try to pronounce it—thinks all this is just his idea, too?"

"Kaxchotx. Ka-chat-x. Don't offend our allies. Yes, of course he does. It's all his idea and he and I together will rule a new dimension created from his and mine. Just like Jerahmeel thinks all I want out of this is the MeanStreet Division, like I'd just hand over the other two."

Sera laughed. "Talk about having your head up your ass! That's some kinda stupid. Both of them."

Lucifer sighed. "So true, my dear, so true. But then again, a Razkaal's demon's ass is a bit hard to find. Very odd shapes they have. But you're not any kind of stupid, are you?"

Sera licked more salt from the rim of her fine crystal stemware. "Not hardly. Give me designer clothes—it gets really tiresome running around in that cat fur all the time—fine crystal, good china, a few diamonds and a penthouse apartment. Oh, and a Lamborghini, of course. I'm good."

"A wise woman's worth is above rubies."

"Don't think that's exactly how it goes."

"Close enough." The band swung into That Old Black Magic. "Oh, just listen! They're playing your song, dear. Let's dance."

* * *

"So let me get this straight. I'm dead. And I'm an angel?" Micah led Mia through the halls of MeanStreet, LLC.

"In a nutshell. And this is the Intelligence Department." Micah opened a door and ushered her in. Two rows of computer stations stretched its length. The computer terminals rivaled any American corporation in cutting-edge technology. Dings announced incoming emails and fingers flew over the keyboards. "Manned 24/7."

"Who are those guys?"

"Angels, of course. Computer geeks' heaven for sure."

"They don't have wings." Mia glanced over at Micah. "And you don't have any wings, either, not right now. So—angels have different assignments?"

"We don't walk around with our wings spread all the time. Sort of defeats the anonymity thing. And of course we've all got different assignments. Humans have different talents in life. That doesn't change in death."

"And my assignment? What do I do?"

"You're a field angel, of course. You work the streets. All that acrobatic, gymnastic talent. Can't let it go to waste."

"But that parrot that flew in? A parrot angel?"

"Well—thing is, angels aren't limited to one form. We can take any form we need to get the job done. I tend to like black cat form myself. Sleek, supple, blends in well with the shadows. I do use dog form occasionally but humans tend to pay more attention to stray dogs. A cat running around by itself doesn't attract much attention. If I wanna get in close and personal with an assignment, oh, yeah, a dog's the ticket. If I wanna stay low, can't beat a black cat. And Harold—the parrot—well, he's not an angel. Exactly. He's—"

"The other guy—G?—called him a second chancer."

"Yeah. Some folks don't really meet full angel criteria when they actually—well, die. But there've been things in their life or in their death that kinda demand they have a second chance to be. Take Harold. One of the greatest con men ever lived. Bilked folks outta hundreds of thousands of dollars. Never hit the big-time, though. 'Cause deep down, his heart still cared more for others than for himself." Micah led her out the door and back into the hall.

"I'm a thief. Have been most of my life. So why am I an angel and not a second chancer?"

"And moving right along, this is the break room." Micah opened another door. A break room like any other, coffee pots full and steaming. A snack dispenser in the corner, though it didn't have any cover over the front and snacks were free for the taking. A refrigerator, an icemaker, a dishwasher. It took a few minutes to notice the food and water bowls on the floor, the bird perches hanging from the ceiling, the birdseed dispensers scattered about. A block of cheese sat on a saucer on the counter. "Sure is quiet today, nobody's around."

"Nice to know I'm nobody, Micah, thanks a lot!" A gray mouse poked its head around the side of the cheese block.

"Charlie! Sorry, man, didn't see you there!"

Charlie lifted the shard of cheese in his paws to his mouth. "Whole point. Less folks see of me, the better I like it. Way easier to operate that way. Who's the dish?"

"This is Mia. Don't scare her, she's still— acclimating."

"Nice to meet you, Mia. See you around. Good to see ya, Micah, gotta get back!"

"Good seeing you too, Charlie. Hang in there."

"You know it, man!" Charlie disappeared into a miniscule hole under the counter.

"So—angel or second-chancer?"

"Anybody up here in animal form is a second-chancer. They can't change. Until they're ready to move up."

"You didn't answer me. Why am I an angel and not a second-chancer?"

"Because you are."

"You. You did something. I heard you. Sort of. While I was coming to. Arguing with the big guy. About me."

"Mia, the reason you died, the way you died—you didn't have to, you could have walked away, but you didn't. You charged right in without a second thought once you'd made sure back-up was coming—no, you're an angel. Not a second-chancer. Don't give a damn what the big guys say about it."

Mia scrutinized his face closely. "How'd you die?"

"'Scuse you? That's kinda personal, don't you think?"

"Yeah. How?"

"Maybe later. Okay, we've hit the high-spots. I'll drop you by the Ladies Lounge and wait for you to freshen up. 'Cause from the look on G's face while Harold was telling us about those body-snatching demons, I'm thinking your first training mission's gonna be a lot more 'mission' than it is 'training'".

Chapter Fifty

Gabriel swung his chair back around to face Michael.

"Well, that went a lot better than I expected. In some ways, anyway. It rankles, sending them in blind. But they've got to be relaxed enough not to throw out danger flares and scare the Razkaal demons off."

Michael paced in front of the desk. "Guess you did okay, pulling 'em in and stringing 'em along. So what's the real plan?"

"Real plan?"

"You're so damn casual about all this! What is it with you, Gabriel? You run MeanStreet like a luxury corporation! There's no structure, no strategy, no chain of command! You're just sitting back and hoping the humans'll automatically know what to do! Oh, yeah, they'll just save the day! And everybody runs all over you! That break room, for crying out loud! Like a five star resort!"

Gabriel's face tightened. "It's called faith, Michael! Do you even have yours anymore? Or has structure and strategy and command replaced that? I believe in the humans. What do you believe in now? Anything? Why are you so convinced they're inferior to us? We've never had brother against brother, jealousy, greed? We've never torn heaven and earth wide open? Oh, no, we're just one big happy family! Tell you what, brother, if we were going into your territory, we'd run it your way, General. But since you don't have any idea where in the hell your break is—Paris, London, Madrid, Berlin—or even some po'dunk little pub in the back of the Irish beyond—I guess we're doing it my way!"

"There they are." Micah, in human form, pointed to a happy family reunion in the airport terminal. "See 'em?"

Mia studied the group closely. "Yeah. They're—different, somehow. The younger ones, I mean. They—glow, sorta."

"Good eye. Yeah, they do."

"Why?"

"Magic, sweetheart. See the guy with the silver streaks in his hair? Chad Garrett. His term for it is person of power. And those four? Yeah. Loaded with it."

"So you know them? From somewhere else?"

"You might say that. See the girl with dark hair? That's Ariel Garrett. Chad's wife. Bit of a late bloomer. And the tall dude is Chad's brother—well, foster brother—Spike. That's what most folks call him. He's actually Dr. Stuart Forrester. Pediatrician."

"Him? But he's so big! Doesn't he scare the kids?"

"Oh, no. Kids are full of magic, sometimes it just gets knocked out of them while they're growing up. They always recognize it. He's a bit of a late bloomer, too. And the bright-haired girl is Stacy, Ariel's sister. The older couple's the girls' parents. Out here for Spike and Stacy's wedding. Hope that doesn't get interrupted. Too little joy in life for most folks."

"Did you have much?"

"Much what?"

"Joy in life."

Micah laughed shortly. "Had my moments. On the whole? No. Not a hell of a lot. You?"

"No. No, I don't guess I had a whole hell of a lot either."

"Maybe it's a prerequisite for angelhood."

"Wow, Antsypants! Vegas agrees with you!" I pulled out of our patented sister hug, guaranteed to squeeze the meanness out of both of us. Of course we'd had a hug fest all around, unavoidable when southerners meet. Depending on the circumstances, we hug total strangers. A family reunion in the airport? Any fellow travelers with a fetish against touching better steer clear of us. They're assuming the risk if they accidently end up in the family circle. "Look at that tan!"

Stacy laughed. "Heat without humidity! A Georgia girl's dream!"

"Well, I think maybe the company has something to do with it, too." Mom looked Spike over carefully. An impressive specimen, my brother-in-law. "So glad to finally meet you in person, Stuart. You seem to be takin' care of our little girl just fine."

Stacy and I grimaced simultaneously. Especially me. I recognize a not-so-subtle putdown when I hear one. Mom still hadn't come to terms with my new life-style. The private investigator part, that is. She'd never know about the other part of my new life-style. And she didn't think Chad took care of me in the manner in which she'd like me to become accustomed. As in wrapped in cotton and tucked away on a shelf like a china doll.

"Mom, nobody calls him Stuart. He's Spike. And I'm not a little girl and I don't really need to be taken care of. It's kind of a we-take-care-of-each-other thing, you know?"

"Of course it is, dear!" Mom hooked an arm neatly under Spike's and Chad's simultaneously. Never let it be said my mother played favorites. Not so's you could pin her on it, anyway. "Stuart, Chad, I've always had a fantasy of being escorted through an airport on the arms of two handsome men! Indulge an older woman."

Stacy groaned.

"Mom! The luggage?"

"Oh, my! I figured you two liberated women were taking care of that. With your father, of course. You mean you'd like help?"

"Don't bat those eyelashes at us! And drop the delicate southern flower act! Behave!"

Mom laughed and dropped the act along with the clinging vine grip she had on Chad and Spike.

"Busted! Like I'd trust y'all to make sure you had all my luggage?"

Daddy sighed and headed toward the conveyor belts of luggage.

"Welcome to the family, guys. Hope you both got a good sense of humor. You're goin' to need it."

* * *

"Are you sure we couldn't have hit one more casino?" Mom wasn't happy with us. "And we didn't take in but one show, either!"

"Mom, it's already past midnight and we've got a ton of things to do tomorrow! When did you turn into such a party animal?"

We piled into Spike and Stacy's great room—under protest—after a night on the Strip.

It was time to pull out the big guns. "Mom, I swear I'll print those pictures of you dancing at the casino and post 'em in your garden club bulletin if you don't settle down!"

"Really, Ari!" Mom blinked owlishly and enunciated carefully. "No need to resort to threats. If y'all can't keep up with me, just say so!"

"Mom. You're really, really sloshed. You know that? Don't you think it's time to hit the bed?"

"This early? Why do I want to do that? At least let's have a nightcap! And Stacy, I meant to ask—are we putting you out of your room? How many guest rooms do you have, Stuart? There's Stacy and Chad and Ari and us, I don't want to put anybody out."

Stacy rolled her eyes and Daddy put a finger to his mouth and shook his head violently. I hadn't thought even Mom was naïve enough to think Stacy didn't settle into the master bedroom as soon as she'd gotten here but apparently, yes, she was.

"Oh, it's fine, Mrs. Anson," Spike assured her. "We've got four. Guest rooms. It's a five bedroom house."

Bless his heart. Absolute truth. No need to get into who was using which one.

"Oh, good! Plenty of room for the babies when they come. Ari, you and Chad need to start thinking about that, you know. Your little tree house is just a perfect little dollhouse for a couple, but for the babies—heavens, suppose they crawl right off that deck? I could cry to think of what could happen!" Mom blinked owlishly again and tears welled from the corner of her eyes for the unborn grandbabies not even thought of yet. Yep. Sloshed to the gills. "And call me Grace, both of you. Let's not stand on formality." She plunked down, not gracefully, on one of the couches.

Chad moved over to Spike's bar. "Grace, what's your pleasure? For that nightcap?"

Mineral water! I shot the order to him silently. *At this point, she won't know the damn difference!*

"Scotch on the rocks, please. And make it a double."

"Gracie!" Daddy reached breaking point. "What the hell's gotten into you? C'mon, time for us to go to bed. While you can still walk up the stairs!"

"Bobby, don't be such a spoilsport!" Bobby? Daddy was either Bob or Robert. She never called him Bobby. Mom stood up. Then she swayed. Her eyes rolled back in her head and she went limp. Daddy caught her before she hit the floor.

"Just great," he sighed.

* * *

Outside the sliding glass wall leading to the Forrester patio-pool, two sleek, supple cat forms, blacker than the shadows they patrolled, paced restlessly back and forth. Guard duty. Nothing could happen to this little private coven. Not tonight. The world couldn't afford it.

The larger of the shadows moved in close to the smaller and rubbed his head against hers.

You okay?

Fine.

Mia was more than fine. The sensitive whiskers, new fashion accessories for sure, quivered. The new sounds, the new smells, the new awareness! Had the world always been so rich, so full of scent, so full of sound? How much humans missed!

You sure?

Micah, I'm just glorious!

Yes, you are.

* * *

"I can't take it anymore!"

The magician's obligatory lovely assistant shrieked and threw off her human skin. Of course, she did that every night. Harold was used to it. It reminded him of his first wife tearing her bra off as soon as she came in from work. And his second and his third, come to think of it. Must be a girl thing. It didn't even rate a "*Squawk*...invasion of the body snatchers" from him anymore.

"Irene! Keep it down!"

"My name's not Irene! It's Raxchanxchn! Your name's not Damien! It's Xanchoxn!"

"It's one more night, woman! We can stand anything for one more night! Now get your damn skin back on and let's get up to our room. A couple of more humans, that's all we need! To open the breach forever!"

"Don't you dare call me woman! Like I was some—some—human! And we've got enough as long as the other teams are doing their share. Have you checked on them lately?"

"What sort of idiot you take me for?"

"You really don't want me to answer that, do you?"

Harold blinked and yawned. Oh, yeah. These demons were married, for sure. Or whatever passed for it in their little corner of their dimension. Guess some things just didn't change, no matter what dimension you were from.

"One day, Raxchanxchn! One day!"

"One day what?"

"You're going to the moon!"

"Promises, promises."

* * *

Mom came down the steps. Very carefully. Had to give it to her, though, that was the only sign of last night's excesses.

She sat down on one of the kitchen bar stools and smiled brightly. To cover the wince. Antsypants and I looked at each other and nodded. Special treatment coming up. I sat a big mug of coffee in front of her and added a glass of fresh-squeezed orange juice from the carafe sitting on the bar. Stacy cracked more eggs into a small frying pan and popped bread into the toaster.

"Here you go!" Stacy sat the breakfast plate in front of her with a flourish.

Mom turned slightly green. "Thank you, dear, but—"

"Don't even. First sip the juice. Then sip the coffee. Then eat and you'll feel right as rain. I'll even fork over some aspirin, but not till you eat. We've got a lot to do today."

Mom stared at the juice and then picked it up and sipped gingerly. She took a big swallow and switched to coffee. Then she actually picked up her fork and started eating.

"Where're the guys?"

"Spike leaves by seven every morning, he does the hospital checks before he goes to his office. This is the last day he's working for a week, he's covered after that. And Chad took Daddy out for a ride. You never told us Daddy knew how to ride a motorcycle." Stacy opened the dishwasher and started loading the breakfast dishes.

Mom dropped her fork and clutched my arm.

"Your daddy's out riding a motorcycle?!"

"Well, yeah." Stacy bent over and loaded more dishes in the dishwasher. "Didn't know he knew how."

"He hasn't been on one in years! He's goin' to kill himself! Especially on those monster things in your garage!"

"Don't worry, Daddy's on mine. It's smaller."

"Yours?!"

I laughed. "Spike's living up to his end of the bargain, huh?"

"Yes, ma'am, he sure is."

"What bargain?!"

"When he asked Stacy to marry him, she asked him if he'd teach her to ride her own bike, and if they could get married in the Drive-Thru," I explained. "He said yes to all so she said yes, too. It was hysterical, actually."

"You were there? At your sister's proposal? And are you actually riding a motorcycle, too?"

"It was kind of a family affair. Chad and I were both at the proposal. Mom, face it. You just don't have romantic daughters. Well, you do, it's just—our idea of romance is a little different from most. And no, I don't ride alone, don't want to. I really prefer just riding bitch."

"Riding what?!"

"Bitch. Two people on one motorcycle. Drop the act, Mom, it's been called that for years. If Daddy rode, you had to know that. I'd be pretty sure you've done it, even, 'fess up."

Mom sighed. A *why me?* sigh.

"Anyway, Chad and Daddy are goin' to entertain themselves today while Spike's at work and us girls are out doin' our thing."

"What're we doing? I thought there wasn't anything to do for the wedding, not with that ridu— original wedding you've planned. The Drive-Thru thing."

Stacy laughed. "Not that original. Ari did it. Lots of folks in Vegas do it. And no, nothing about the wedding. Well, except your outfit. We have to check on the party details."

Mom perked up like a wilted flower in a spring shower. "Party? You're having a reception? Like norm—like most brides? And I have my dress, dear. I'd already bought it for Ari's wedding and since I never got to use it, I didn't think you'd mind."

The unspoken words hung in the air. *Since Ari changed absolutely everything including the groom.*

"Well, yeah, it's our version of a reception, anyway. And I need to stop by the clubhouse and check on some things."

"Of course! In his profession, Stuart almost has to be a member of a country club." I could actually read all the unspoken words hanging in the air this morning. This time they were thank God.

Antsypants! I projected out. *You're goin' to just let her keep thinking it's a country club?*

One thing none of us were—well, except Mom and by default Daddy because it was easier to humor Mom than cross her—was country club material. The word club had only one meaning for Chad and Spike. And in Vegas that mean the gus who'd saves our asses in Daytona. The Desert Troopers.

Oh, Ari, c'mon! Let her have a few hours of maternal bliss thinking we're kinda sorta half-way normal! Don't bust her bubble yet.

"So first we'll take care of your outfit and then we'll swing by the club in case I need to pick up more decorations." Stacy picked up Mom's plate, scraped it into the trash, slapped it into the dishwasher and closed the door.

"I told you, dear. I have my dress for the wedding."

Stacy smiled. "Not for this wedding, you don't."

* * *

Spike moved from one of his exam rooms to the other. His cell phone buzzed about 10:00 o'clock. Another emergency? Friends and family didn't call him during morning hours. He pulled it out and glanced at the number. Chad. Strange.

"Hello?"

"Only got a minute, Bob's in the men's room. You comfortable with the girls goin' out on the Strip alone tonight?"

Chad and Spike knew the seamier side of the Strip tourists never saw.

"No. Not happy about it a bit. You? And why'd you want to wait till Bob was in the men's room to ask me?"

"Didn't want him to hear why you'll be a lot less happy when I tell you Ari and I got a call on the way to the airport."

Spike groaned. "Not—"

"No, worse than that. Never told you about this, you've just now stopped running from the room screaming anytime anybody mentioned magic. But magic's got some agencies of its own. Including one run by a guy named Gabriel. Smith, if you can believe it."

"Not gonna like this, am I? Cause no, I don't really believe it."

"There's a magic act playing I'm advised is using some low-level magic. Not in a good way. I made the mistake of telling G I hated magic acts, and Ari jumped on that with both feet. Said they'd check it out by themselves on their girls' night out."

373

"So it's shadow time tonight?"

"Big time."

"Nothing good on television anyway."

* * *

Stacy whipped the Beemer neatly into a parking space on Las Vegas Boulevard. It was still early in the day or she'd never have found one.

"Okay, ladies, let's go shop!"

"Dear? Aren't you in front of a—rather strange store?"

"Biker gear, Mom. Biker apparel."

"But—we're wedding shopping, right?"

"Mom. Do you seriously think I'm wearing a long white gown? On a motorcycle?"

"Which reminds me," I said. "Are you riding your bike or you ridin' bitch? To get married?"

"Bitch. It's just more romantic somehow, don't you think?"

Okay, we were laying it on a little thick but it was just so hard to resist. I glanced at Mom's face. Culture shock in action. Maybe we should lighten up a bit.

"Well, I suppose romance is in the eye of the beholder," Mom said gamely and got out of the car. "So if you're not wearing white—"

"I'm wearing black. Biker gear. So is Ari. And so are you."

"Me?"

"Yes, ma'am. You. And you're getting' a new hairstyle and new makeup, too."

"Complete make-over!" I clarified.

"At my age?"

"Mom! Stop tryin' to look your age and just look like you look! You're a size eight, for heaven's sakes! If Ari and I weren't both size six, we'd just put you in some of ours! They'd fit, but it'd be a little uncomfortable. So we have to get you your own." She paused and pointed at the shop window. "Like that! Perfect! "

Horror washed over Mom's face. "You want me to wear that?"

"Yes, ma'am. With a tight black tee. And if you're good, I'll let you pick the logo on the tee. Pretty Mama would work, though, don't you think, Ari?"

"Oh, absolutely! C'mon Mom, if you've got it, flaunt it!"

We reached the door and I grabbed the handle. I froze in my tracks. There. Right there, over behind the big potted plants in front of the show windows. Micah. Not alone this time, either. A smaller black cat stood close to his side. Two of 'em?

"Ari?" Stacy asked impatiently. "You goin' to open that door or not?"

I mentally shook it off and pulled the door open. No point in looking for trouble till it happened. And it was going to happen. Because it always found me. Always. Usually right after a black cat showed up. A black cat by the name of Micah. I hoped to hell two black cats didn't mean twice the trouble. But I wasn't optimistic about it.

* * *

Mom paused for the fourth time in front of a shop window and stared at her reflection. She reached up and fluffed her hair. No more middle-age chin length pageboy. The layers ruffled in the wind. The new golden brown blush thrust her cheekbones into prominence and the golden brown eye-shadow magnified the amber in her eyes.

Stacy tugged at her arm to get her moving. "C'mon, awakened sleeping beauty! We still have to get you a dress for the clubs tonight. My bachelorette party, remember?"

"Oh, but dear! I brought an outfit—"

"No! You're not goin' out in a two-piece tailored suit! Get over it!"

"But y'all have spent so much money already—"

I sighed. "Mom, you ever total the money you've spent raisin' us?"

"That's different! That's what parents do!"

"Well, this is what grateful daughters do! Now hush!" She was getting better at reading facial expressions. One look at ours and she hushed.

"Oh, look!" Stacy pointed at a long champagne colored sheath in the boutique window. Simple, elegant. Boat neckline. Discretely sparkly. Definitely Mom's color, especially with the new make-up. "Perfect!"

"Oh, my God! That dress in that store has to cost—"

"Mom. You're worth it."

Stacy opened the door and shooed her inside. She turned back to me in silent exchange.

You do know there's a black cat following us, right?

Two of 'em, actually.

And I'm sure you're sure one of 'em's Micah?

Oh, yeah.

The other one?

Not a clue.

Double the trouble?

Distinct possibility. And I got an idea it might concern a phone call Chad and I got on the way to the airport. Talk to you later this afternoon.

Just. Great.

* * *

Mom's classy new champagne sheath safely tissued and bagged in the trunk, Stacy turned off Las Vegas Boulevard and headed toward the outskirts of Vegas.

"Last stop!" she announced.

376

"Oh, I can't wait!" Mom pulled down the passenger visor to access the mirror and fluffed her hair again.

"Mom! It looks the same way it looked when you got out of the stylist's chair!"

"I can't embarrass you at your club, darlin'! Just checking."

Stacy slowed, turned onto a state highway, rounded a curve and pulled into a drive sporting a large "Private Property – No Trespassing" sign.

"*Voila!*" She spread her hands in a flourish.

Mom's eyes rounded like an owl's.

"Uh—dear?"

"Ma'am?"

"This—uh—doesn't look like a—uh—country club, somehow."

It damn sure didn't. The low cinderblock building, built for utility and not aesthetics, sat back off the dusty parking lot. Ten or twelve big motorcycles were parked in front, mostly Harleys but peppered with a few Hondas. Underneath the front row of windows stretched a billboard type sign. "Desert Troopers – Ride the Wind, Brothers!"

"I'm sorry, Mom, I didn't realize you thought it was a country club!"

Like hell you didn't! I projected out. *God's gonna get you for that one, little sister!*

Look on her face is worth it, though, huh?

Oh, yeah!

"Oh, look!" I got out of the car quickly and pointed over to the line of parked bikes. Time to get Mom moving before she went into full shock. "Jackster and Moondog are here!"

And so was Micah and his new little friend. Over there, disappearing around a corner of the clubhouse.

On cue, the door opened. A big grin lit the face of the middle-aged guy in Desert Trooper colors standing in the doorway. He spread his arms and came toward us.

"Well, well, both my little Rambo girls! Ari, honey, good to see you!" He swept me up in a bear hug and swung me around.

"Jackster!" I hugged back as good as I got. "Good to see you, too!"

Stacy got her bear hug. "Mom, this is our good friend, Jack Hudlin. Affectionately known as the Jackster. Jackster, this is our mom, Grace Anson."

Jackster thrust out his hand.

"Mrs. Anson, I sure see where the girls got their looks! Welcome to Vegas!"

Never let it be said Mom didn't rise to a social occasion.

"Why, thank you, Jackster. Where'd you meet my girls, if I might ask?"

Jackster looked behind Mom and over to us quickly. We shook our heads violently. Mom didn't need to know the details of our trip to Bike Week, for damn sure.

"Oh, we ran into them and their guys in Daytona. They were having a little—mechanical trouble. Bikers don't leave brothers and sisters in a jam. Now, c'mon in! Place is a mess right now, the younger crew had a party last night. But they're in there now cleaning up and we'll be all set up for the wedding celebrations."

He ushered us in. Yep, the place was a mess. But it wouldn't be for long. Several club members wielded long brooms and several more were walking around with big trash cans. What color Mom's face had regained vanished again at the sight of the old metal washtubs filled with water. The occasional lone melting ice cube bobbed on the surfaces.

"Oh, great!" Stacy said. "Just leave the washtubs out, no point in putting them up."

"Yeah, that's what I figured." Jackster nodded agreement.

"What are they for?" Mom whispered to me.

"For the beer kegs, Mom. And soft drinks."

"Oh, my." I could see visions of champagne bottles and beautiful crystal glasses pouring out of Mom's brain.

Jackster pointed over to the long tables. "And we'll set up a buffet over there with the ribs and steaks and burgers and 'dogs. And all the trimmings. Grill 'em out back, of course."

Visions of elegantly plated finger food on delicate china plates joined the images fleeing Mom's mind.

"It'll look great, Jackster! You sure you don't want me to get any of the decora—"

"Stacy, we're handling all that! Wanna surprise you. The club's wedding present to you and Doc."

Mom's brain started replacing white fluffy wedding bells and white roses with flags waving skulls and crossbones and roaring Harleys.

Stacy reached up and kissed his cheek. "Y'all are just the best! I'm having the cake delivered about 11:00 that morning, somebody'll be here?"

"Oh, for sure! The grilling crew'll be on duty."

"Okay, we'll leave y'all to it then!"

We waved cheerily to everyone. They waved back. Mom made a valiant effort and lifted a hand weakly. I hooked an arm under one of hers, Antsypants did the same from the other side, and we escorted her out of the clubhouse while she could still stand up.

"Stacy?" she asked as we settled her into the front seat.

"Ma'am?"

"They're very nice, but—somehow I'd have expected your new friends to be doctors and professionals."

We laughed and shook our heads.

"Mom, Mom, Mom! What's that you always told us? Don't judge books by their covers. Or people by how they look. Jack is a doctor. The Ph.D. kind. Chemical engineer. Owns his own company."

"Really?" Mom brightened. "I'd never have guessed!"

"Mom," I said. "Get ready for a real shock to your system."

"Why?"

"You've never seen Spike and Chad in biker gear."

"Stacy?"

"Ma'am?"

"The wedding cake topper's a couple on a motorcycle, isn't it? Ridin'—bitch?"

Stacy smiled broadly. "Yes, ma'am, it surely is! How'd you know?"

Mom sighed. "Lucky guess."

Chapter Fifty-One

Wolf whistles sounded as Mom and I walked down the stairs that night, all set to party hearty. Mom looked fabulous in her flowing champagne sparkles. I wasn't bad myself in a long slinky black number, high slit up the left side. Glittering faux-jeweled flat strappy sandals flashed as we moved. We'd discussed it as we shopped. No heels for these gals on the prowl, tonight was for walking and dancing.

The bachelorette herself came out of the downstairs master bedroom, also in slinky black with faux-jeweled flat footwear. Fresh wolf whistles erupted.

Mom stopped on the stairs.

"What?" I said.

"Your sister's coming out of the master bedroom. All the guest rooms are upstairs."

Enough.

"Mom. Drop the shocked mother act. It doesn't go with your new look. You knew Stacy wasn't in one of the guest rooms, don't even lie about it." I pulled Mom on down and we all converged in the great room. "We ready?"

"Got your phone somewhere in that little square thing you're carrying that passes as a purse?" Chad asked.

"Of course."

"Don't be shy about using it if you think you need to." He kissed me quickly and whispered in my ear. "Though of course you don't need the phone to shout for me. And I still don't like you checking out that magic act for G by yourself."

I gave him a hug to whisper back, "I'll be fine. And I've got Stacy, I'm not by myself."

Stacy pointed at the crystal pendant hanging between the long V-neck of the slinky little black number I was wearing. The Tear of Isis. The pendant I hadn't been able to leave behind. Hadn't been able to not wear it tonight, either, though I didn't have a clue why.

"Wow! Ari, I haven't seen that before!"

"Picked it up in Savannah a few weeks after we got married," I said. "Caught my fancy."

"Well, all three of y'all are goin' to catch some fancy out tonight," Daddy said. "Mind Chad, now. Be careful and don't be shy about using your phones if you need it. Don't know as I even feel safe lettin' you all out, way you look. All of you." He smiled at Mom and she smiled back. It didn't happen often, but every now and then, like now, my heart tingled when they smiled at each other.

"Ladies, let's *get this party staaarted!!*" Stacy opened the door and yeah, I'd have to say that's probably when the party started. Several of them. Though I didn't know it at the time.

* * *

Chad checked the front window and watched the tail lights disappear down the street.

"Gentlemen, battle stations!" he called, and the three disappeared into their respective rooms. They reconvened in five minutes flat, dressed for the Strip's nightlife.

"You two sure this is a good idea?" Bob Anson asked. "I mean, don't you think they're goin' to be really—well, upset—if they see us trailing 'em? Like we don't trust them or something?"

"Pissed is the word you're looking for, Bob." Spike led them out of the carport door and over to his black F-350. He'd been driving it ever since Stacy moved to

Vegas, leaving her the Beemer. Besides, he really liked it better anyway. "And yeah, they'd probably be pissed. But I know Vegas too well. It's just not a good idea for three women who look like they do to be cruising the Strip alone. Got nothing to do with not trusting them. It's the rest of the world we don't trust."

"Besides," Chad added, slipping into the backseat. "They're not going to see us. And on that, you can trust me."

* * *

Damien and Irene peeked out the curtains at the crowd filling the tables. He clutched her arm.

"Look!" He pointed at a group of three human females. Obviously a family pod. "Lone females. Check out the young ones. They just freakin' glow."

"Tonight's targets, then."

"Oh, yeah."

* * *

We settled in at a table near the front of the stage.

"Mom, you think maybe you could nurse that one drink a while before you get another one tonight?"

"Ari, what are you implying, dear?"

"I'm not implying anything. You were sloshed last night. To the gills."

"I was not!"

"Were too," Stacy confirmed. "You passed flat-out. Woulda hit the floor if Daddy hadn't caught you."

"Then how did I wake up in bed, might I ask?"

"Chad carried you up. We didn't figure Daddy's back was up to it."

"Excuse me? Now you're implying I'm overweight?"

"You know Daddy's back goes out. We didn't need both of you flat on the floor."

I looked at Mom's face. She truly didn't remember. And obviously thought it was time to switch topics.

"Stacy, your house is just perfect for the babies. Except for the pool area, that worries me a little bit."

"Mom, don't start. It'll be a while. I've been talking to a few law firms out here, haven't decided which one I'll go with, but I definitely want to go back to work. For now, anyway. Spike really wants me to consider going back to law school."

"*Eeeeewwwww*, Antsypants! Think about that real hard. Suppose you turn into an attorney?"

I didn't have anything against the profession. It was the personality change that frequently went with it I didn't like.

Stacy laughed. "I know! And I don't really think I want to. Because yes Mom, at some point there will be babies and I won't want to work while they're little. But I don't want any yet and I don't want to just sit home all day while Spike's at work, either. It's not like I can go to work with him, like Ari can work with Chad. That's all still legal work, just a different sort. I'm not a nurse, or a medical anything, what would a legal eagle do in a doctor's office?"

Mom looked at me. Time to switch targets. "Actually, Ari, you're older than your sister, you know. Almost thirty. So—"

"Drop it, Mom. I don't feel my biological clock ticking. And our profession doesn't lend itself too well to babies right now. With me you've got to settle for fur-grandbabies for way into the foreseeable future."

I glanced up as the last of the audience seated. Something about that man coming down the side of the room to one of the far left tables...mid to late twenties, maybe. The girl by his side seemed a little young for him, but then both Stacy and I'd always looked younger than our ages, too. I took her for late teens, but it was possible she was older. And not any of my business in any event.

The lights dimmed and the curtains parted, pretty much at the exact moment I flashed on a figure walking away from me, wearing a biker jacket. A biker jacket with *The Guardians* stitched on the back, in cursive font so fancy as to be almost unreadable. Was that...hard to tell now that the lighting was so low, but I was almost certain it was the same man. Micah. And if Micah was here, inside the club, in human form, and with a friend, too, because it didn't take much imagination to figure out the friend had to be that extra black cat I'd seen today—oh, hell.

"*Ohhhh....*" Mom focused on the stage and discussions of grandbabies fell by the way side.

Ari? Stacy asked silently.

Yeah?

You sure this is the magic act you're supposed to check out? Seems pretty standard to me.

Me too. So far. Let's hope it stays that way.

Like the parrot, though.

Yeah, he's a hoot.

* * *

Micah did a rapid assessment of the territory as the lights dimmed. Perfect positioning. Up close to the stage, at an angle. The girls were in easy view with a turn of the head. It couldn't have gotten any better, even if he'd been able to pick the table himself. He leaned in close to Mia.

"Be ready."

"For what?"

"Anything."

* * *

So far, so good. The show was your typical Vegas magic act, considerably above ordinary stage magician but nothing on the order of a Copperfield or a Siegfried

& Roy. We weren't at the Aladdin or MGM and nobody expected anything on that majestic a scale.

Damien appeared ready to wind this baby up.

"Volunteers? Two volunteers from the audience? Take a tour through Magic Land you'll never forget on our Magical Carpet Ride! Sights never seen by the human eye!"

Ari? Is that our cue?

Oh, yeah.

"Oh! Me, me!" Mom hopped up from her chair and waved her hands. Crap. Not that I hadn't expected it.

I looked at Stacy. Stacy looked at me. I nodded. We both hopped up with Mom.

"Three volunteers okay?" I called up to the stage. "We're a package deal."

Damien clapped his hands in delight. "And such a trim, slim package at that! Of course you'll all fit on the Magical Carpet Ride! C'mon up!"

* * *

Micah grabbed Mia's hand as the three "volunteers" headed toward the stage.

"Stand up and move over to the side, deeper in the shadows!"

"And then?"

"Change!" Micah ordered. Attention focused on the stage, nobody noticed the true magic transpiring over in the shadows or saw the two black cats replace the humans. On stage, the three volunteers stood close together inside the large black box.

Micah's cat senses tingled. He sent the order silently.

Get ready.

I'm ready.

"And in you go, off for the ride of your lives! Wave goodbye to the audience as you leave!" As at all past shows, the box began a slow turn, moving in a circle, door still partially open.

A collective *oohhh* went up from the audience as the black cats leapt into the open box a split second before the magician slammed the door shut.

"*Squawk*...go Jim Dandy...go Jim Dandy!"

* * *

"Damn strip traffic and drunk drivers!" Chad slammed the door of Spike's F-350 and stalked rapidly up the sidewalk. They'd been stuck in traffic for close to forty-five minutes at an intersection pile-up, completely blocked in by emergency vehicles. "Couldn't you have maneuvered any faster than that, Spike? Didn't I teach you how to drive?"

"Yeah, but I didn't think switching over to the sidewalk and driving on it'd be such a good idea. Cause that might've, you know, gotten us arrested or something strange like that what with those two police cars sitting right there! Which wouldn't do the girls any good, now would it? It's not like we don't know where they were going first."

"I should've gotten out and walked."

"We were way far down the Strip and just walking wouldn't have gotten you there any faster. And you're not dressed for jogging. Not without attracting a hell of a lot of attention. Cops kinda notice when a man's running down the Strip. Usually that's not a sign of something good."

Chad stopped dead still in front of the hotel-casino.

"Shit, damn, hell!! They're gone!"

"What do you mean gone?" Bob asked.

Spike stopped dead still, too. "Yeah, they are. All of them."

The brothers each grabbed a handle of the double doors and charged into the lobby, heading for the club showcasing Damien's Delights.

"Shit!" Chad wove in and out of departing bodies spilling out of the show and stopped a hostess.

"Show's already over?"

"Yeah, Damien cut it pretty short tonight. Manager's not gonna be happy. Probably back there now chewing him out."

"Can we get back to his dressing room? He's an old friend, we promised we'd be here tonight for the show. Hate to have him think we didn't show."

"Well, I don't know—"

Spike pulled out two one hundred dollar bills he'd folded in his pocket for emergencies and let it peek discretely at the hostess.

"Right this way, sir! It's right off the left of the stage."

* * *

"Where—where are we?" Mom clutched my arm. I batted away swirling clouds of bluish smoke.

"I don't know, Mom. Stacy?"

"Here!"

"Where?" I groped through the fog.

"Here!" Thank God. Her hand reached out and connected with mine.

"Somehow that wasn't nearly as much fun as I thought it'd be," Mom said. "Aren't we supposed to be under the stage or something? And isn't that magician supposed to bring us back?"

"That's the idea in most magic shows, yeah. But I'm afraid not in this one."

"And those cats! I almost had a heart attack when they just landed right on top of us while the door was closin'! Where are they?"

Yes, where were they indeed? The smoke dissipated somewhat, still there, but cleared enough to see we were in an enclosure of some kind. Then it hit me. A holding cell. Sort of. It was the closest I could come, anyway. A denseness shimmered beyond the smoke. Like walls.

I looked down. Over on the side, pacing restlessly in the tendrils of fog. Two black cats.

"Micah! Get over here! You gotta lot of explainin' to do, son!"

* * *

The guys paused outside the dressing room door.

"...big idea, cutting a show that short! I get any demands for refunds, it's coming out of your cut!"

"Hostess was right," Spike said. "Manager's raising hell."

"Not as much as we're about to raise. You ready?" Chad raised his eyebrow.

"Let's do this thing," Spike affirmed.

Chad laughed shortly. "First time I heard that, we damn near got incarcerated for life, little brother."

Spike shrugged. "Worked out okay that time."

Chad reached inside his jacket, pulled his gun from the shoulder harness and nodded. Spike threw the door open and stood aside.

"Now what the hell's going on?" The manager turned and glared. He threw up his hands at the sight of the gun. "Whoa, guys! I'm not in this! You want him?"

"Oh, yeah."

"You got him. Damn shyster, knew he was going to get some of you guys on his tail and lead 'em back here. Probably trying to count cards or something! Just don't leave any blood in here, okay?"

Chad's gun pointed steadily at Damien's head, the sights moving to keep the target lined up as the magician backed up and edged toward the wall.

"You got it, man. Thanks."

"No problem."

"Let's be sure it's no problem, okay?" Spike handed over another set of folded hundred dollar bills. Very handy things to have in Vegas.

"Like I said, man. No problem. At all!"

The manager shoved the bills in his pocket and tore out the door.

389

"Vegas. Gotta love it," Spike said.

Chad cocked the hammer back on the Glock. Very deliberately. *Cliiiccck.* Damien's back tried to merge into the wall. He'd backed up as far as he was going to back. The gun sight still didn't waver from the magician's head.

"*Squawk...incoming...incoming...squawk!*"

Spike's gun appeared from nowhere. "Un-huh, sweetheart, I don't think so."

Irene sat back down on the chair she'd been about to lunge out of.

"Okay, buddy. You got to the count of five to tell us where our ladies are."

"Uh, mate?" Harold piped up from his perch. "Little more here than meets the eye. You might want to unzip 'em, you twig?"

"Unzip?"

"Like their skin. It unzips. They're demons. B'lieve they called home base the Razkaal Dimension or some such. So I wouldn't be so bloody certain the guns'll work on 'em."

"I'm willing to give it a try."

"You told the manager you wouldn't leave any blood," Spike reminded him.

"I lied."

Bob Anson stared back and forth between the two men his daughters loved. "Who the hell are you guys and where did my girls find you? And that parrot's actually talking to us?!"

Damien threw his arms up. "If you shoot, security'll hear the noise!"

"That's what silencers are for. One," Chad counted. "Three...."

* * *

"Ari, dear, you're talkin' to a cat. People'll think you're strange."

390

Trust Mom to focus on that when we were stuck in a fog bank in the middle of heaven knew where. I was pretty sure wherever we were, it wasn't earth, not as we knew it. And equally sure Mom's definition of "strange" was about to undergo a major overhaul. I didn't think it likely the starship Enterprise was standing by to beam us up, either.

I inspected that denseness shimmering beyond the smoke. It seemed to be lightening, somehow. Lifting.

Garbled noise flowed toward us, at first barely audible, gradually increasing in volume.

Xaztha caxpthalz...rathax nax zathax..qzokatl vichilx...

What the hell? As soon as I asked myself that, I decided it probably wasn't a good choice of words. The noises had a cadence like speech, but nothing like I'd ever heard before.

Figures emerged from the fog, moving toward us. Stick-like figures with an octopus in place of a head. And an octopus where each hand would be on a human. Approximately, anyway. And speaking of octopuses—or octopi or otopodes, for some reason I wasn't thinking in terms of grammatical correctness at that point, go figure—an octopus sprouted at the ends of the stick figures' leg appendages, too. All three leg appendages.

Stacy had to say it, of course.

"Take me to your leader."

One of the figures stepped forward, away from the others.

"Human slaves. Obey or die. You will follow us."

As greetings go, it'd never win the Nobel Peace Prize. But it was English. That had to mean we weren't the first humans these octopus creatures ever had contact with. Which raised all sorts of other alarming questions, such as—where were the other humans?

Stacy'd been a paralegal for years. She knew she had the right to remain silent. She just didn't have the ability.

"Who the hell you think you're talking to, buddy?"

"Silence, human! You will learn!" The creature's hand octopus shot toward her face like a Cat O'Nine tail. A ferocious rush of power tore past me and hit Octopus Man square in the chest. He flew backwards and into the three Octopodes behind him. They all crashed to the ground in a tangle of flailing tentacles.

"Way to go, Antsypants! I've been wondering when another power or two was gonna pop out with you!"

She shook her head. "But I didn't do it!"

"You didn't? Then who—"

We both stared at Mom. She stared back, wide-eyed in wonder, like a child who'd single-handedly demolished a whole house.

"Did I do that?"

* * *

"Five!"

Pfft. Shards of drywall exploded over Damien's shoulder. "Next one takes your hand off, buddy. And you got lots of body parts after that."

"Okay, okay!! Don't shoot again!"

"Start talking!"

"They're not here!"

Pfft. Another bullet exploded from the silenced gun. Damien's hand turned into a mass of waving tentacles and tentacle parts. The parts gushed fishy-smelling green slime. Damien squealed.

"Wuss!" Irene spat. "You sound like a sissy girl!"

"Well, blimey!" Harold blinked. "Guess bullets work after all."

"Tell me something I don't know, Demon Boy. I got lots of bullets."

"I sent 'em through! They're in my dimension!"

"Bring. Them. Back."

"I can't! I would if I could but I can't! The other side's got to do it!"

"Then send us through."

"Uh, mate?" Harold flew over and landed on Chad's shoulder. "Maybe you should check in with the big boss first? I know we haven't been formally introduced but Harold's the name, the Council's my game, you twig?"

Over by the door, Bob announced to nobody in particular, "This isn't happening. I know this isn't happening."

"Oh, I twig, all right! This has Council written all over it." Chad switched to a one-handed gun hold and reached down to his phone clip. "Don't try anything, buddy. I'm real good at multi-tasking."

He glanced down at his phone. Damien lurched forward and two *pffts* sounded simultaneously, one from Chad's gun and one from Spike's. Tentacles and tentacle parts gushing that fish-smelling slime waved around in place of Damien's other hand. Damien howled.

"Told you I was good at multi-tasking. But thanks for the extra cover, little brother."

"Yeah, I'm good at multi-tasking, too. *Un-huh-huh*, sweetheart," Spike warned Irene. "Gun was only off you a split second. It's right back on target now."

Chad hit the phone screen. One ring and the call went straight to voice mail.

"Yo, whut up? Outta pocket right now, leave a message and I'll get back to you."

"Shit, damn, hell, fuck!" Chad fumed as the automated answer program wound its way to the requisite beep. "G, you son-of-a-bitch! You set us up! You knew damn well this thing wasn't some low-level magic con! They've got the girls, G! They're in some damn demon dimension! Now you get your ass in gear and answer this!" He shoved the phone back onto its clip and turned back to Damien.

"Okay. Now you get your ass in gear and send us through!"

Gabriel and Michael moved through darkness, backlit by a reddish glow that erupted now and then into full-blown flame.

"Where the hell's Rafael? Stupid idea, him splitting off like that! Why does he think he can find the back way in if I can't?"

"You're so damn full of yourself it's a miracle you got room to breathe, Mike, you know that? Rafael's in the same hell we're in. And he might find the back way in when you can't because you've got no damn patience! For you, it's full battle attack mode or nothing. Shit!" Gabriel came to a full stop and grabbed at his shirt pocket. He pulled out his cell phone and groaned. "Damn! I didn't feel it vibrate till it'd already gone to voicemail!"

"We're on a freakin' stealth mission and you're gonna stop and listen to a voicemail?!"

"I am this one. Damn straight. Deal with it."

Gabriel held the phone to his ear. Chad's voice blasted into his eardrum.

"Oh, hell!" Gabriel's face paled. He hit the call-back button and muttered impatiently as he waited. "C'mon, c'mon, c'mon!!"

"G! 'Bout damn time, you double-crossing son-of-a—"

"*Squawk*...wasting time, mate, get to it!" Harold's voice cut in. Chad obviously had the phone on speaker.

"I never intended the girls to go through alone! I can't believe you actually let that happen!"

"Wouldn't have if you'd played straight with me, G. I should've known better but it's a mistake I'll never make again. Can't even trust the Guardian Council. We deserve better than that."

"Yeah, you do. I'm sorry. So the first thing is to get to them. Ari and Stacy went through?"

"And Grace. You know, Mom."

"Their mother?"

"Ah, the light dawns!"

"Oh, crap! Well, that might work out better'n you think. Grace's been in denial her whole life. The three of 'em might be more than the Razkaal demons banked on. 'Cause if there's one sure-fire way to bring a person of power out of the closet, it's a threat to somebody they love. Look at Spike. He didn't surface till he met Stacy. And the girls are Grace's babies. Oh, yeah, she might kick ass."

"Grace? What does she do?"

"Grace. She's a very powerful telekinetic. She can move things with her mind. She just doesn't know it. Ari's mind control's a variation of that, I'm hoping to hell Stacy got some variance of it hidden in there somewhere. Harold, you know where Micah and Mia are?"

"Go Jim Dandy...*squawk!* Oh, yeah, they jumped straight in that magic box with 'em right 'afore it slammed shut."

"First good news I've heard all day."

"Micah?" Spike cut in. "The magic cat from Daytona?"

"Ari's never thought he was just a cat, magical or otherwise. Right now, I don't even think he's always a cat."

"Everybody needs to stop talking over there and give me a minute to think!"

"Too bad. I've already thought, G. Demon boy's gonna send us through before he finishes sliming to death. Now you know where we'll be so some back-up would be nice if you think you can handle that!"

"Magic Man, wait just a damn min— " The phone clicked off.

"Well," Gabriel said as he pocketed the phone. "That coulda gone a lot better."

Rafael's voice cut through the darkness. "Gabe! Mike! Found a way in! Move your damn wings and let's go have a talk with brother Lucy!"

"Okay, Demon Boy. How'd you send 'em through?"

"The box! The box on stage!"

Bob Anson finally broke out of his shock.

"Wait just a damn minute here! Parrots that really talk, magic cats, demons dressed in human skin?! Demon dimensions?! Persons of power?! Like magic power?"

"Yes, sir."

"And Ari and Stacy—"

"Are extremely powerful witches, sir. We're both warlocks. Sorry to break it to you like this."

"Well, damn. That explains a lot. Especially about Grace."

"Sir?"

"Explains why every time she gets really pissed at me, all the pictures fall off the wall. All the picture frames have that plastic stuff. None of 'em have glass. We damn near went broke replacin' picture frames the first couple of years we were married."

"Glad we cleared that up for you, Bob." Chad turned back to Damien. "Now, before we head to that box I need some answers. Why'd you send 'em through? And how many have you sent? What does your kind do with humans?"

"They—"

"Human slaves power our world," Irene spat out. "And if you go through, you'll die!"

"I wouldn't make any bets on that, sweetheart. Power your world? How? What do you do with them?"

"The weak-minded work the mines, good for nothing else. That's most of them. The stronger ones—"

"Irene, shut up!"

"You shut up or I'll shoot you in what passes for your balls. Might not be the right spot but I'll keep trying till I hit it. Keep talking, Irene."

"Irene! Don't be more of a damn idiot than you usually are!"

"My name's not Irene! It's Raxchanxchn! Your name's not Damien! It's Xanchoxn! And don't tell me what to do!"

"You two really are the love story of the century, aren't you? I'm waiting, Irene. What do you use the stronger ones for?"

Irene shot a sideways glance at Damien and shut down the information pipeline. "For something else."

"What?"

"To work some other power source, I don't know the details! I'm not one of the techno-geeks!"

"How many? Over how many years?"

"Do I look like a history professor? I don't know how long. Forever. Back to the beginning. How many? No idea. A lot, I guess, I mean, it's been going on forever. We don't take many at a time, not even enough for anybody to notice. I don't know what the big deal is. Humans are so selfish."

Chad's jaw muscles twitched. So did the muscles in the hand holding the gun. He reached into an inside pocket of his jacket and pulled out two rolls of duct tape. "Spike, I got both of 'em covered. Hand your gun to Bob and do the honors on Demon Girl. We don't need her out there with us, he'll be enough to handle. Besides, I think she's more dangerous than he is."

"Coulda' used that back in the day." Harold peered down from Chad's shoulder. "Travel-size duct tape!"

"They make travel-size everything these days. Much easier to carry than cuffs."

"You know, mate," Harold observed while Spike secured Irene. "She's got those same slimy wavy tentacles he does. Only seen 'em sort of unzip themselves and hang the skins up, but wouldn't surprise me much if they could just bust straight out of it, you twig? Don't quite think even duct tape'd hold her then."

"Voila! Done!" Spike stepped back and checked his handiwork.

Chad motioned for Damien to walk in front of him. "Okay, move it. Wouldn't surprise me either, Harold. And that's why she's taking a little nap while we're conducting business. Goodnight, Irene." The gun butt connected with the back of Irene's head and she went out like a light.

"Wait a minute! He's dripping slime. Cover me." Spike stripped a couple of pillowcases off the pillows on the dressing room's day bed, slipped them over the smelly mass of shredded tentacles and duct-taped them to the magician's forearms. "Okay. What if a cleaning crew's already in the club?"

"Won't be, mate. Besides, curtains'll be closed."

"Harold, you're a good man to have around. Let's move."

Chapter Fifty-Two

Stacy and I stared at our mother. Some damn.

"So that's where we came from!" Stacy exclaimed.

"Yeah, well, while the octopodes are over there untangling themselves, we might oughta move our asses somewhere else!" I pointed over to the tangled mound of tentacles, tugging and pulling on each other as they tried to unknot.

"*Meowwwwwwwwww!!!*"

Micah wound rapidly around my legs and then shot straight out into that bluish swirl of smoky fog that seemed to stretch for miles, the smaller cat hard on his tail.

"Okay!" I called after him. "But you've still got a lot of explainin' to do!"

"But Ari, dear, what do we do now?" Mom asked.

"What I do best, Mom. Follow that cat!"

* * *

Bob Anson measured the magic box with his eyes. "Well, it'll be tight, but I think all three of us can fit in."

"Bob, you can't go through with us," Chad said.

"What the hell you mean I can't go through? My girls and my wife went through! You think I'm too old to be any use over there?"

Spike put a hand on Bob's shoulder. "You're too pissed to think straight, man. Use your head. Somebody's got to watch him while we're going through. Afterwards, too, and the other one's not gonna stay out all that long. You might not have noticed but Harold over there can't exactly hold a gun on 'em. No hands."

Harold flew off Chad's shoulder and landed on Bob's. "'E's right, mate. 'E also serves who only stands and waits and all that rot. That's you and me, mate. Guard duty."

"One of you can—"

"Bob. I've done this sort of thing my whole life. And I need Spike with me, he's not your ordinary doctor, he had a whole 'nother career before and during med school. We need you and Harold to take care of this side and each other. Harold, you understand what I'm saying?"

"*Squawk!* You can count on me, mate! Bob's in good hands. Wings. Whatever. *Squawk!*"

"Shit. Yeah, okay."

Chad reached down to his ankle and pulled out his back-up gun. "Here. You know how to use it?"

"Damn, how many of those things you got? Yeah, don't travel in your circles, but I know how to use a gun. Pretty good shot, actually."

"Good. Use it if you need to. So let's get this show on the road." Chad and Spike got in the box. "Demon Boy?"

"Enter the box and take a magical carpet ride—"

"Can the crap and just do it!"

"Okay, okay!"

Damien moved close and hit a button on the side of the box with his elbow. His hands weren't much use at the moment. The box just sat there.

"I still got the gun, Demon Boy!"

He raised his elbow again and jabbed at the button. "I'm trying! Maybe my elbow's too big to push it in right!"

"Show it to Bob!"

Bob moved over, gun carefully aimed.

"There! Right there!"

Bob reached out and felt the side. "Yeah, it's a button. You'd never know it was there if you just didn't know it."

"Just push it! Like an elevator button! That's all there is to it. This is just an elevator between the worlds."

Bob pushed. Again. And again.

"I can feel it going in. It's just not doing anything."

"Demon Boy!"

"I don't know anything else to do! It's not moving! The door must still be open on the other side."

"Why would it still be open?"

"I don't know! They unload the cargo, they close the door, it's ready for next time. That's all I can tell you, I'm not a freaking scientist, for crying out loud, I don't know how the damn thing works!"

"Shit, damn, hell! Okay, out!" Chad and Spike got out. "So if the door's not closed—"

"It means the girls are out of the damn thing on the other side," said Spike. "But the locals haven't closed the door. Probably because they can't."

"Because the girls didn't work out quite like they planned."

"Hell, no. They don't play well with others."

Spike laughed. "And that's just Ari and Stacy. If something happened to trigger Grace, and she's as powerful as your man Gabriel claims—"

"Furniture's flown across the room a few times," Bob volunteered. "But she's got to be really pissed for that to happen. And usually hungry, too, come to think of it."

"A pissed, hungry witch is not a good combination. That was Ari's trigger for the mind control thing the first time."

Bob smiled. "Tell you what, guys. They tried to lay a hand on one of Grace's girls—I'd say those demons are getting a new definition of Hell."

"Okay, back to the dressing room. Move it!"

"Let me!" Bob stepped forward and motioned Damien forward with his gun. "Start walkin', bud."

Spike leaned closer to Chad's ear as Bob moved in front of them. "Lot to leave Bob with, watching both of them, don't you think?"

"You know damn well I was gonna blow Damien's head off before that door closed and Harold was gonna get Bob out and away from here. Wanted to blow Irene's off back in the dressing room but I didn't want to freak Demon Boy out of his mind."

"He'd of probably thanked you. But nice to know you haven't gone soft on me. I was beginning to wonder. What now?"

"Damned if I know. Let's get back to the dressing room and see if we can get Demon Boy to tell us something about the other side before we try again."

* * *

I grabbed Mom's right hand, Stacy grabbed her left, and we charged out into that swirling blue fog like Olympian runners. Demons weren't yapping at our heels at the moment, but they would be soon enough. Flashes of black raced in front of us, setting the course. The fog began to lighten, and I saw we were running on stark and barren ground, like the backdrops on old episodes of The Twilight Zone, the sci-fi ones set on alien planets. Outcroppings of bare boulders decorated the landscape and hills loomed in the distance. So this was a flat plateau, surrounded by hills. Not mountains exactly, but not small, either. Foothills. Good battle terrain, if we could get to the top. And how the hell did I know that and where did such crazy thoughts come from when one was running for their life? Of course. Livia. It'd been Livia's subconscious memories who'd made me stop at that display of faux-jeweled sandals, styled after the old Roman sandals, that now shod our feet, I'd bet Pine Whisper Plantation on it. I shuddered to think of this run in spike heels or backless shoes.

The flashes of black veered to the right. We followed and the ground began to incline, not much at first, then increasing at a steep angle, winding into the rocks. A natural stairway into the hills. The hills we needed for tactical advantage. I wasn't in bad shape, Mom jogged every morning and Stacy was a natural athlete, but even she was beginning to pant by the time we gained the sheltered circle of rock at the top of this foothill. A natural clearing opened out of the rock, sheltered from view but affording a vantage point over the plateau and the surrounding foothills.

Micah and friend perched on rocky seats, waiting for us.

"Meooooowwww!"

Enough.

"Nope, sorry, son. That *meoowww* is out of business. Give. Right here, right now. Change your ass back to human—or angel—or whatever the hell it is form you really are and start talkin'. In English."

* * *

Lucifer frowned and looked up from the paperwork on his desk. New contracts were a bitch to review. What the hell was all the commotion coming from his assistant's desk out front?

"You can't just barge in here without an appointment! The boss is a busy man!"

"Watch us."

The door swung open and the Smith brothers sauntered in.

"Yo, Lucy! Whut up, dude?"

"Well, well, long time no see, huh, Lucy?"

"You still loosey-goosey, Lucy?"

"Don't call me Lucy! I hate it when you call me Lucy!"

"Stop grinding your teeth, Lucy, you know that causes all kind of dental problems." Rafael smiled and sat down in one of the chairs in front of Lucifer's desk, draping his left leg casually over the arm.

Gabriel plopped down in the other chair and draped his right leg casually over the arm.

"Well, that's just rude, you guys taking both the good chairs." Michael pulled up a straight-backed side chair, twirled it around, and sat down with his feet draped around the sides and hands across the chair back, chin resting on his folded hands.

"How'd you get in here? This is my turf. The Grand Conductor brother-proofed the boundaries so we couldn't cross between your territories and mine. But since you did, you know you broke the treaty and I'm not bound by any of its terms, right?"

"Listen up, bro," said Gabriel. "You broke the treaty. And we know it. We found your little back door, we've always known you had one. You've been using it for years. You really thought you were slipping that over on us? So all rules are off already."

Lucifer leaned back in his deluxe desk chair. "Really? So if you've always known, why wait till now to do something about it?"

Rafael laughed. "Because you're just so damn cute when you go out in disguise, Lucy! I mean, some of those outfits! Really? But this one—this one we can't let pass for ol' times sake, bro, sorry. So spill it."

Lucifer raised his eyebrow. "Spill what?"

"That damn raised eyebrow was always your giveaway, Lucy." Michael stood up and flipped the chair away. He walked up to Lucy's desk and slammed his hands down on the surface. "We know about the inter-dimensional breaches. All three of them. Inter-dimensional breaches only happen when one of us fall. You already been there, done that. So who's fallen? And why'd you want him to?"

"Aren't you giving me too much credit? Why'd you think I wanted anybody else to fall?"

Rafael stood up and slammed his hands down on the desk. "Because we got long memories, Lucy. About you and that Razkaal head hauncho. And how well you got along. About how similar the Razkaal dimension is to your turf. About how fond the Razkaal demons are of humans. And why."

Gabriel joined the circle of slammed hands on the desk. "You and the Razkaal man? Marriage made in Hell. But you can't really get together without another breach. And you can't make one big enough by yourself. Not again. So you need somebody else to. We're pretty sure we know who. But being the good guys just sucks sometimes. Can't just go around accusing falsely, you know."

"And you think I give a damn about your little ethical dilemma?"

"Oh, hell no. You don't give a damn about anything or anybody except your own little deals. And we're about to put *toot finite* on one of those deals, 'cause we know damn well it involves those breaches. And we're about to seal them. Permanently. You might have cooked your goose with the Grand Conductor on this one, bro."

"Oh!" Lucy clutched his heart. "I'm scared! Stop!" He laughed. "I'm safe as Fort Knox, bro. Remember last time? Even the Grand Conductor said it. There has to be a balance between darkness and light. And I'm it. My whole *raison d'être*. Without me, there's no balance. Know what that means? You can't touch me!"

"Oh, c'mon, Lucy, finish it out! Go ahead, say nanny nanny boo-boo, why don't you? But you know what they say. He who laughs last, laughs loudest." Raphael shrugged. "Or something like that."

* * *

"*Meooooowww!*"

"I said enough of the meow thing. Human form. Front and center. Now!"

And in the blink of eye, there he was. Micah. My Micah. The doctor-biker in Daytona, the man I'd seen in the club right before the show started. The teenage girl I'd seen with him in the club was lovely. Eighteen, maybe, I thought. Possibly nineteen. Certainly she wasn't twenty yet, though her eyes spoke of ancient wisdom not commonly possessed by girls her age.

"That's not fair," I said.

"Not much is, sweetheart," Micah confirmed. "What in particular isn't fair?"

"Her." I pointed. "She's too young to be an angel."

"You know, that's exactly what I told G. Didn't make any difference, though. Ari, this is Mia. Mia, this is Ari. And I believe you should do the formal introductions for your Mom and Stacy, don't you?"

"Can I get a hug first?"

"Thought you'd never ask. You're one special lady, Ariel Anson Garrett."

"You're one special cat, Micah. Angel of the Divine Path."

"The internet knows that?"

"Technology's a wonderful thing, huh?"

We hugged. I felt the power flowing from him, greater than any force I'd ever felt. What a wondrous creation an angel was.

I wiped my suspiciously moist eyes and turned to my family. "Mom, this is Micah. And his friend, Mia. Micah, Mia, this is my Mom. Grace Anson."

"The cats who jumped in the box with us?"

"'Fraid so, yeah."

"Well, I'll just be damned."

I laughed. Mom never ceased to amaze me. What a trooper.

"I doubt that sincerely. Don't you, Micah?"

"Not in a million years would a soul like yours be damned, Grace. Even your name would never allow it."

"Stacy, meet Micah and Mia. In the flesh, so to speak, seeing as how y'all already sorta met in Daytona. Micah, Mia, this is my sister Stacy Anson, soon to be Forrester."

"Please to meet you both. In the flesh, so to speak. Let's not stand on formality here." Stacy reached out for her own hug. I believe I've said before us southerners are huggers. We hug everybody. As they embraced, force waves rolled off them and washed over me, almost knocking me down. They separated. Micah's face was white.

"So it's true," Micah whispered. "I'd hoped—back in Daytona—I'd thought maybe—but I couldn't be sure without touching."

"What's true?'

"She's not just Stacy. She's—she was—Hannah, do you feel it, too?"

Stacy's face turned as white as Micah's.

"Micah? Micah! Oh, my God! I never thought I'd see you again! Even if I didn't remember!" She threw herself back into his arms. He picked her up and twirled her in a circle. Both of them cried and laughed at the same time.

"Oh, dear!" Mom tugged worriedly at my arm. "They do seem to know each other, don't they? Really well."

"Yeah, they do. But I don't think it's quite what you're worried about, Mom."

Micah put her down and I moved between them. I held out the Tear of Isis, that ancient crystal I'd found myself the unwitting guardian of, the crystal pendant I'd brought to Vegas and worn tonight, having no idea why.

"Okay, you two. Attention! Look into this!" I held the Tear up and out by the chain and gazed into it with them, exercising the power of the Seer of the Tear of Isis, to share in the re-living of memories. The memories of reincarnated souls unleashed by the power of the Tear.

* * *

Hills. Rocky hills. Barren hills. Baking heat of the Middle East. The Negev, that was it. The Negev Desert. Guerrilla warriors entrenched in the rocks, bound for Betar where Simon Bar Kochba held off Hadrian's Roman Legions. It wasn't the first time the Hebrew warriors grew fangs and revolted against the invading foreigners determined to rock the foundations of Judaism. This crop of rebels learned much from the failures of the Maccabee Rebellion, finally quelled in 70 AD, 70 CE if one wanted to be politically correct as to the measurement of years. Bar Kochba's Second Jewish Rebellion, beginning in Judea in 132 AD/CE, established an independent Jewish State that held for two years.

Rome answered with six full Legions. Over the months, the sheer force of numbers took their toll on both sides, a toll so great that Hadrian changed the traditional greeting of Emperor to Senate and did not say, "I and the Army are in health." The Army wasn't in health but Rome had one thing the Jewish rebels didn't. A steady flow of bodies to replace the bodies that fell.

Now, three years into the Rebellion, only small bands like this band of twenty remained, bands that struck with lightning speed and the fury of thunder and disappeared back into the interlocking caves of the Judean hills, almost impossible to track and destroy. The end was near, though, and they knew it. Fifty fortified towns and almost a thousand villages burned to the ground, the landscape littered with bodies. Only Betar, that last fortress in the Judean Highlands, remained. And without reinforcements, Simon Bar Kochba wouldn't hold it much longer.

The two men who led this band moved away from the group to look out and down from the rocks at the Roman forces spreading out in front of them.

"They're flanking us, Micah. We have to move before there's nowhere to go."

"Aaron, there's already nowhere to go. You know that. There aren't any caves near."

A third rebel slipped between the two. A woman, too thin. These years in the hills had taken their toll on them all. "Then we fight."

"Hannah—"

"*Ssssh.* I know, you don't have to tell me. It's a good day to die. A good way to die. Between my brother and my husband." She reached over and hugged the rebel on her left tightly. Then she reached over and up to the rebel on her right, put her hand around his neck to pull him close to her and kissed him fiercely. Aaron raised his head and locked eyes with his brother-in-law, confirming the unspoken agreement between them. Whatever happened, she'd never be taken by the Romans. No matter what.

I knew them. I knew them all. As my sister. As Micah, the Angel of the Divine Path. As Dr. Stuart "Spike" Forrester.

The Romans surged up the hills. As one, the two men pulled their short swords and plunged them into the woman's heart. They couldn't take the chance of falling themselves without being certain she wouldn't endure the long, agonizing death of Roman fury. She made no sound, other than short gasps. Her eyes, full of pain, glowed with love. "Love you both. We'll see each other again." And she was gone.

Agonized roars of rage and grief ripped from their throats as they met the Romans. It was short. It was brutal. And at the end of the day, back down in the flat desert at the foot of the hills where they'd made their last stand, five crosses stood in a row. For two of the men on those crosses, this agony paled in comparison with the memory of Hannah's eyes as she died.

* * *

I forced myself out of the immobility of the Seer's trance and wiped the tears running down my face.

"Oh. Dear. God."

Stacy smiled and hugged me close. "It was a long time ago, Ari. We all got our little past lives to tote around with us."

I laughed. "Yeah, but it makes me tired to think about it. How many times we've all found each other. Chad and me. You and Spike. And finally—you've found Micah. Who for some reason isn't reincarnating over and over again like all of us."

"Yeah, that's been a bitch," Micah said. "I asked about it, why I wasn't a repeater—"

"That's what we are? Repeaters?"

"That's the cosmic technical phrase, yeah. But the only answer I got was 'because'".

"Well, ours not to reason why and all that jazz," said Stacy brightly. "And right now ours is to—"

"Figure out why in the hell, pun intended, these demons want humans. And then figure out a way to kick their butts."

"I'm glad all of you seem to know what you're talking about," said Mom. "Because I don't have a clue. And obviously neither does Mia."

No, she didn't. Poor kid looked shell-shocked. "We'll explain later, Mom."

A monotonous droning sound filtered into my consciousness and as soon as it triggered, I realized it had been there for some time, gradually increasing in volume. Equipment? Maybe, but mixed with something else. Something more primitive. Like pickaxes ringing against rock.

"What's that noise? Anybody else hear it?"

"I've been hearing it. Wondered when somebody else was gonna say something, but I didn't want to interrupt whatever little private conversation y'all were having in that little circle while you stared at a piece of jewelry!" Mom rolled her eyes.

"Don't get in a snit, we said we'd explain later. It's coming from over there." I pointed over to the left.

"Hate to leave this little circle, but we've got to shift over some."

We picked our way several hundred yards toward the left, winding through little rocky pathways. The noise increased with every step we took. Finally we seemed to be right over it. I headed to the rocky overhang and peered down.

"Whoaaa, Hannah!" I said.

"Well, that fits, anyway," Stacy quipped and joined me. "Whoaaa, Hannah! For real. It's the Seventh Circle of Hell!"

A cavern yawned in front of us. Crews of humans, rail thin, struggled to lift tools, more or less pickaxes, over their shoulder and then slammed them down against the ugly, rocky walls. Other crews lifted the heavy fragments falling to the ground from the repeated blows and loaded them onto carts, carts pulled by other humans over to a conveyor belt contraption. Octopoids stood over and around them.

The conveyor belt seemed the only thing powered by anything other than sheer brutal manpower. So if they had power to run that, why didn't they have power to mine with something more efficient than humans? What was the damn power source running it? Cable of some sort ran at spaced intervals from the conveyor belt over to the back wall. I followed it with my eyes to little cubicles of some glassy-like substance. The glare made it hard to see inside them. Then a group of octopoids moved and cast a shadow. A human floated in viscous liquid inside the cubicle, wires hooked to the skull on either side. It was a safe bet the other cubicles held the same thing. They were using human brain waves to power that damn conveyor belt.

The octopoids weren't cracking whips. They didn't need to. Those damn tentacles of theirs did just fine. As we watched, one of the men pulling a cart stumbled and fell and two octopoids lashed out with those tentacles from hell. The man screamed and bloody whelps bloomed on his back. But he didn't get up. He was done. The octopoids didn't carry whips, but they did carry something else. Something that looked like laser guns.

One of the demons shrugged—more or less—and motioned to two others. They stepped forward, looped tentacles over the man's arms, and dragged him away from the rocks onto the bare ground. The other demon raised the laser like thing, fired, and the man disintegrated.

"Sonofabitch!" I pulled back from the rocks. "Okay, so that's the reason they want humans. So what are we gonna do about it?"

Micah smiled. A terrible, beautiful smile. "Does the phrase avenging angels hold any meaning for you?"

* * *

"You can't go in there, he's in conference!"

"Raxthan zoranth xchatnaal!"

Michael cocked his head toward the door. "Well, Lucy, aren't you just Mr. Popularity today? That Razkaalan I hear out there?"

Lucifer's office door burst open in a mass of flying tentacles.

"Zanthal xchatnal ranthaz wratkal!!"

"Did you seriously just call him a double-crossing demon from hell?" Rafael laughed. "Oh, that's rich! Didn't you ever hear it was dangerous to make deals with the devil?"

Lucifer half rose from his chair and leaned forward on his desk. Red boiled in his cheeks.

"Kaxchotx, what the fuck are you doing here?! And speak English, damn it!"

"Lucy, Lucy! You're losing your cool, bro! Your little demon pal's upset. He's obviously forgotten foreign languages were never your strong suit. Public opinion to the contrary." Gabriel crossed his ankles and stretched out his legs.

Kaxchotx folded his tentacles across his chest and glared at Lucifer. "What did you send through?"

"Shut up! Shut up right now! We don't discuss our business in front of outsiders, you stupid octopus!"

"What did you just call me?"

"Octopus! And stupid!"

"Class, kindergarten is now in session. Kaxchotx, you just tell us all about it, why don't you?"

"Gabriel, I'm warning you!"

"Lucy, I know this'll come as a shock to your system, but none of us are scared of you. Especially Kaxchotx. Right, old son?"

"Damn straight I'm not scared of him, the double-dealing bastard! I was guaranteed good product! That last batch you sent through! Something's wrong with them! They aren't scared, they talk back, one of them threw my orientation squad clear across the transmitter room! They got tangled up with each other and actually pulled out some of each other's tentacles and now I'm looking at a damn workers' comp claim! And they got out of the chamber before the door re-closed and they're loose somewhere out there, in the hills. Who knows what else they might do?"

Michael whistled. "Sounds like Grace came out of the closet, alright."

"Yep, sure 'nuff," Gabriel agreed. "And Kaxchotx, hate to tell you this, but I'm pretty sure you ain't seen nothing yet."

* * *

"No offense, darlin'," I said, "but you start throwing around full power down there—would that maybe take those humans out of the equation right along with the demons? Revelations and the Acopolypse and all that. And maybe even us. Not to mention can we get back home if you start nukin' the place with angel power? Would that cut us off completely?"

Micah frowned. "Shit."

413

"And here's something to think about. They can use dimensional doors or portals or whatever the hell you call 'em, and they've got lasers that disintegrate targets in seconds. So why are they using something as primitive as humans to mine those rocks?"

"And did you notice they dragged that poor man away from the rock walls before they blasted him?" Stacy added. "So I'm thinking those rocks, after processing, is their energy source. And it's really powerful after it's mined and processed. But before then—"

"Before then it's pretty damn fragile. Easily destroyed. Not the rocks themselves but something in them."

"And anything with concentrated high-power destroys it. Or sets it off, maybe. Soooo—if we got our hands on some of those lasers and started blasting, I'm pretty sure we could do some serious damage."

"And just how do you think we're going to get our hands on those lasers?" Mom demanded. "Really, girls. You think they're just goin' to hand 'em over when you say please?"

Stacy smiled at me. I smiled back. We both turned to Mom.

"Welcome! To the world of magic."

Her eyes widened. "You mean—you don't mean me?"

"We most certainly do."

"That thing I did? When I threw the slime-balls into each other?"

"Yes, ma'am, that's exactly what we mean."

"But I don't even know how I did it! And how does throwing things around get us the lasers?"

"Mom. If you can throw something backward—you can pull something forward. Think about it."

"But—but—"

"Goats butt, chickens cluck, and good little Moms mind their daughters. To paraphrase a very wise woman we know who used to tell us that every time we ever told you 'but'. Close your eyes, Mom. Close your eyes and feel your power. We need you. You're the one with a physical power. Ours are primarily mental. Neither of us can do anything like that."

"Yeah, sorry, Mom, but Ari's right. This time—you de man. Concentrate. Pick up that rock over there and bring it to you."

"I can't—"

"Grace Louise Anson, you stop all that nonsense right now about 'can't'. You can do anything you put your mind to! That sound familiar?"

"Damn. You sound just like me. Okay, okay." Mom frowned and stared at the rock Stacy'd pointed to. She closed her eyes and I could feel the waves of power radiating out. How had she managed to stay in denial all these years? Why had we never known it?

The rock lifted a few inches. Then a few feet. Then it came hurtling toward us. I grabbed her arm and pulled her back out of the way as all of us ducked.

"Oh, dear!" Mom wrung her hands. "Suppose that'd hit one of you? I can't—"

"Mom. Practice makes perfect. Try it again and this time try to float it to you. That one over there." I pointed to a good-size rock.

Mom sighed, closed her eyes, and tried again. This time the rock floated through the air and plopped down at her feet.

"How the hell did you keep that under wraps all those years, Mom?"

"Sometimes—I think sometimes a little of it got away from me now and again. I just—thought I was imagining things."

"Well, you're not imagining a bit of this, Mom. Now. We need a diversion so we can get close enough to be in firing range when Mom floats the lasers out of their hands."

Micah laughed. "Mia, you've been pretty quiet. Think these guys have ever seen any cats before?"

"Wondered if you were ever going to include me in anything. No, I doubt they'd know what to make of a cat. Especially one plastered on their faces."

"And what'll happen if they blast all that angel power with the lasers?" I asked.

"What? Risk hitting moving targets against those rocks they're so careful with? I don't think so. C'mon, we'll all head downhill, get the three of you in position near the bottom."

* * *

"Okay, Demon Boy. Give. Tell me what you do with humans." Chad pointed his gun at Damien's head as Irene stirred and moaned her way back into consciousness.

"You aren't going to kill me. You need me if you want to try again to go through."

"Not anymore I don't. My father-in-law can push that button just as good as you can."

"You showed them?" Oh yeah, Irene was back in the land of the living. "You wuss!" Her features writhed and the skin covering rippled. Masses of waving tentacles burst out of her human camouflage and pulled free of the duct tape. "And I have had enough of all of you!" She lunged toward them, tentacles flailing.

Pfft. Spike shook his head as he lowered his gun. "Damn, octopus brains just ain't very appetizing. Remind me never to order octopus at a seafood restaurant again. Chad, move this along. These silencers are about out of silence. Another shot from either of us is going to be a lot louder and we'll have to get out of here. "

"You never order octopus anyway. You don't like it. Yeah, let's dispense with shooting for now." Chad stepped closer to Damien and grabbed the mangled masses covered by Spike's makeshift pillowcase-duct taped bandages. He squeezed. Damien screamed. "Last

416

chance, Demon Boy. What do you do with the humans?"

* * *

"Okay." We'd maneuvered our way down to the base of the trail and into position. "Mark and move!"

Micah and Mia shimmered. Two black cats blinked up at us in replacement of two angels in human form. Lithe bodies hugged the rocks, enroute to target zone.

Micah leapt onto a big boulder hugging the mine's wall.

"*Hsssss! Meeooooowww!*"

"Xanthall narparzx!?" I didn't speak their language, but I was pretty sure that'd translate out to "What the hell?!" Now, where was Mia? Ah! She leapt up on another of the big boulders.

"*Hssssss! Meeoooowww!*"

I didn't speak cat either, but the meaning couldn't be clearer. *Come and get me.* The guards started toward them, tentacles waving.

"*Hssssssssss!*"

Micah took one, Mia the other. Claws dug directly into faces—such as they were—scratching and clawing. Slimy green goo flew into the air as claws met eyes. The targets shrieked and dropped the lasers as the other guards ran toward them.

"Mom! Now! Grab those two!"

In the flurry, nobody noticed the lasers rising into the air and zooming toward us. Two of the guards raised their own laser guns and aimed them at the black furies.

"Pranthaz!!" Cooler-headed guards lashed out their own tentacles and knocked the raised lasers back down. Didn't matter though. We had two of our own now.

"Now?" Stacy asked.

"Now."

"The walls or the octopus boys?"

417

"The walls. Through a few of the octopus boys, why don't we?"

We stood and fired.

* * *

"So let me make sure I've got this straight," Chad said, increasing the pressure on Damien's mangled appendages. Damien groaned. Slime oozed out of the make-shift bandages and dripped on the floor. "This prazaxhal stuff is very powerful when refined and very volatile in raw state. So you can't use any high-tech equipment to mine it. You use human brute strength?'

"Yes!"

"Something wrong with your own slimy tentacles? They don't wrap around a pick-ax?"

"That's manual labor! You can't pay anybody to do that!"

"And it's so volatile you can't even have any high-tech power around it, so you tap into human brain waves and use that? You actually put wires into human brains?"

"Only the ones with the strongest brains! I mean, why would we use weak brains? They'd run out of power sooner, it's a waste of labor, the dumber ones'll last longer doing the mining."

"You son-of-a-bitch!" Bob started toward him, and Spike reached out a restraining arm.

"Bob. Don't get in the line of fire. Chad's got this."

"Very efficient. Thanks for the intel. And now if you'll excuse us, we have to go try and collect our ladies."

Pfffffttt. This *pfffftt* was quite loud. So much for the silencers.

418

"Man, what a mess." Spike shook his head. "You know, that hostess saw us come in here."

"*Squawk!* No problemo, mate. Hold me out a cell phone with the keypad open, there's a good boy."

Spike held out his phone. Harold pecked at the keypad with his beak.

"*Squawk!* Housekeeping? Harold here. Need a demon clean-up on aisle five *squawk!* Pretty pronto."

Chapter Fifty-Three

Lucifer's receptionist was having a bad day.

"You can't go in there! He's in conference!" Jerahmeel brushed past her without stopping and crashed the door open.

"Oh, what the hell?" The receptionist sat back down at her desk. "Nobody else paid any attention either."

"Jezebel, you're fired!" Lucifer shouted.

"Shit, I ain't that lucky," Jezebel called back. She opened her middle drawer and reached for her nail file. "Besides, you won't fire me, you hate unemployment claims."

Jerahmeel's eyes widened as he glanced around the room. His face blanched. Then he did an abrupt about-face and headed back out the door.

"*Un-huh-huh*, little brother!" Raphael grabbed his arm and pushed the door closed. "Come on in and sit a spell. Don't be shy."

"What the fuck is this? My office is Grand Central Station today?!"

Shrill ringing sounded from Kaxchotx's pocket. He reached in and pulled out a small box. He threw it up to his ear. "Tchatachan?"

"Always wondered what Razkalaan cell phones looked like," Gabriel said.

"Ranchantzal?!"

"Uh-oh! Looks like somebody's getting some bad news," Michael said.

"Xazdhantal pkanthazn swhanthanx!!" Kaxchotx jammed his phone back into his pocket and glared at Lucifer.

"Get them out!"

"Get who out?"

"That last shipment you sent through! They're loose in the mines with laser guns! They're blasting the hell out of the walls! It's an inferno in there! They're about to implode the whole damn dimension!"

Gabriel clasped a hand over his heart and looked upward. "Oh, how I love my beautiful girls! I knew they'd do me proud but this is even better than I expected!"

Loud buzzing sounded, this time from Gabriel's pocket.

"I think that's yours, bro," said Michael.

"This is *my* office! It's not Ma Bell Central! Doesn't anybody turn off their cell phones anymore?"

"Manners ain't what they used to be, no doubt about it," Michael commiserated.

"Sorry, gotta take this," Gabriel said. "Yo, whut up?" The phone wasn't on speaker but it didn't need to be. Chad wasn't happy. Nor was he particularly soft-spoken when infuriated.

"G, you son-of-a-bitch! Did you know what they do to the humans they bring through?'

"Chad, they're fine! Trust me, they'll be home in no time! I'm on it!"

"Trust you?! You're shittin' me, right? And you're damn straight they'll be home in no time, we're trying again, maybe the damn doors are closed by now!"

"No! Do not go through! We're about to get them out of there, I don't need to be worrying about you and your crowd getting stuck! Give me half an hour!"

"In half an hour the girls could have wires stuck through their brains!"

"Not hardly. They're over there with hijacked laser guns tearing the hell out of the place! The Razkaals want 'em out even worse than you do! Half an hour. Or you might wreck everything! Get the hell out of that club and away from those demon bodies I know you're leaving behind and wait to hear from us. "

Long pause. "Half an hour." *Click.*

* * *

Our first blasts punched through the rock walls. Craters bloomed, threaded with veins of white that heated to brilliant red and burst into flame. Within seconds, the mine walls themselves were on fire. Flames spouted out and sheets of rock tumbled down onto the mine floor. As I watched I could see beyond the visible damage to the interior damage. I knew those flames were running inward along those white lines, ready to explode.

Tentacles waved wildly. Octopi rushed madly around shrieking, thoughts of the human slaves the furthest thing from their minds.

I yelled, trying to make myself heard above the roar of flames and explosions.

"Micah! The humans! We need to get them out of here!"

Mom clutched my arm. "Let me try, dear." She closed her eyes and concentrated. I could feel the power reaching out. It gathered the humans in, held them close in protective clasp, and pulled them away from the fiery hell and back towards us, depositing them gently on the ground over behind us and to the left. Except for the ones harnessed to those damn carts.

"Micah! The harnesses!"

Stacy put her hand on my arm. "Wait. I think maybe—"

She narrowed her eyes and stared at the leather-like bindings of the harnesses. They began to fray and with a loud pop disintegrated into nothingness. Mom gathered the freed humans up in her protective gloves and floated them out to the others

"Some damn, Antsypants! That work on the octopuses?"

"Let's see."

She turned her stare toward the few remaining guards. Tentacles began to waver and fade into transparency. Laser guns dropped to the ground. Pop! Pop! Pop! Empty space where seconds before octopi had stood.

"Why couldn't you figure that out sooner? We wouldn't have even needed the lasers!"

"Bitch, bitch, bitch. Just can't please some people."

Stacy's new-found power finished off the remaining octopi in seconds. We stepped into the clearing as Micah and Mia resumed human form.

"What about those poor people floating in those horrible boxes?" Mom pointed toward the wall. Or rather, what used to be the wall. Everything kind of ran together now. "Oh, dear! Oh, girls, the rocks must have crushed them when the walls fell down in all the shooting!"

Stacy and I both put an arm around her. "Mom, I'm pretty sure that was for the best. I can't believe we'd have been able to save them if we'd gotten them out. I mean—they were on like—artificial life support." I shuddered.

Micah nodded. "Very true. Harsh as it sounds, Grace, even avenging angels and kick-ass witches can't save everyone every time."

"I just can't believe it was all so easy," Mia said.

A droning noise crept into the edge of my hearing, moving closer. Like—planes? Everyone's heads raised. Not my imagination then. A group of aircraft like the small fighter spaceships in science fiction shows zoomed in on us over the tops of the rocky hills.

"Mia, you just had to say that, didn't you?" I sighed. Lasers shot out of the noses of the ships like lightning bolts. Heading straight at us.

* * *

Kaxchotx's phone rang again. "Tchatachan?" he barked. Then he smiled. "Xntalchan!" He turned back to the brothers.

"False alarm. That shipment's contained and terminated. Goodbye, boys. Lucifer, you and I need to discuss this when your office isn't so—crowded. Because you owe me a hell of a lot of money in damages. It'll take a mint to get the mines back in shape from all the damage they did before our fighter pilots could mount an airstrike."

"Now wait a damn minute! I don't owe you a damn thing!"

"Except every bit of the damages!"

"Gabriel?" Raphael put his hand on Gabriel's shoulder. "You okay? Those were your operatives."

Gabriel turned to his brother, face white and set, mouth compressed in a hard line. "Those are my operatives. Don't write 'em off just yet."

* * *

I turned to Stacy. "Well, girl, that new power of yours couldn't have triggered at a better time. 'Cause I don't know how long a range these laser guns have. I'm guessing not that far. So go get 'em. Mom, think you could throw those little space junkies around a little bit up here? Better yet, down. Like straight into the ground. Micah, Mia, can you throw angel power but not full force enough to incinerate us, you think?"

Stacy smiled. "I can do that. Mom can do that. And I'm pretty sure Micah and Mia can do their thing, too. But you aren't off the hook."

"I don't have an active power, Stacy."

"You don't call mind control an active power? You can't turn those fighters against each other?"

"I—Stacy, you heard 'em talk. They're demons. I don't speak demon, they don't speak English, I don't know how—"

"Mind control needs words, you think? You sure about that?"

"I—" No, I wasn't sure about that. I'd never thought about it before. I felt the Tear of Isis swing against my neck. I remembered. Remembered the extra gift the Tear brought to its Seer. Remembered that it intensified the Seer's powers.

"Okay, all together now. Angel strikes, Mom's fastballs, Stacy's new pop power. Let's see if y'all can hit with all that while I'm makin' 'em fire on each other. I hope." I turned to the sky. And concentrated.

* * *

Kaxchotx's phone rang yet again. "Excuse me, boys. That's probably final confirmation my world's my own again." He turned his head and answered. "Tchatachan?" His green face took on a decided yellowish tinge. "Ranchantzal?!"

He turned to the Smiths and bellowed.

"Get them out of there! Please! Before I don't have a dimension left!"

Michael grinned. "I love the sound of desperation in the morning. Or afternoon. Or whatever it is down here right now."

Gabriel sat back down in one of Lucy's armchairs and propped his feet on the desk.

"Well, well. Guess that'll teach you to underestimate humans. So, big boy. Things not going according to plan?"

"They're—I don't know how—some of the ships are just disintegrating! Some of 'em are just crashing down like something's pulling 'em. And the others—they're firing on each other! You gotta get them out of there!"

"Well, Kaxchotx, you tell me. Exactly how do you propose we do that? Seeing as how the only way you can get humans in and out are through those cute little elevators of yours. And seeing as how I don't think any of your boys got a prayer's chance in hell of herding those three back into one. Even if any of your boys spoke English. Which they don't."

"I don't know and I don't care! Just do it!"

Raphael smiled. "Well, there is one thing we could try. But it'll cost you."

Kaxchotx's eyes narrowed. "How much?"

"Damn, you must not be as desperate as you sounded. You might have misunderstood. Nothing's up for negotiation here, we'll let 'em run wild over there till there's nothing left to save."

"I didn't misunderstand. I just want to know the price first."

"*Un-huh-huh!* First you agree. Then we retrieve our people. And then we tell you the price. Trust me. It's an offer you can't refuse."

"Okay, okay!" Kaxchotx said. "So go ahead—do your thing! Get 'em out!"

"Okay." The Smith trio headed out the door. Gabriel looked back over his shoulder. "You guys coming? Because it's gonna take all of us."

"Go where? What do you mean, all of us?"

"Look, Einstein," said Michael. "The open breach is at your fancy inter-dimensional elevator. That's not where our people are. And they're not about to head back there. So we have to go to them. And we need all of us to open a breach big enough. We all have to go through to have enough power to hold a breach open long enough to pull 'em out. Lucy, get your ass up from that chair, that includes you. Jerahmeel, stop cringing like a wimp over there, we need your power, too. Such as it is."

"I'm not going anywhere!" Lucifer glared at the group. "Why the hell should I help you?"

"Because we'll make sure before we leave Razkaal Kaxchotx's willing to forego any and all damages he thinks you owe him."

"What?! Like hell I will!"

"Oh? Not as desperate as you say you are? Yet? You want to wait till they work their way back into one of your big cities?"

"No!"

"Then I suggest we start moving. Unless Lucy wants us to disintegrate his office by using it as our departure point."

* * *

The last fighter ship crashed to the ground.

"Another one for Mom!" Stacy cheered. "That had to be hers!"

"You been keeping score, Antsypants?"

"Not particularly but face it—it's easy to tell. Mine just disappear, Micah and Mia's explode, Mom's crash, and yours are always two at a time 'cause they explode each other."

"That's all of them? No more?" Mom scanned the horizon, disappointment in her voice.

"Having fun, Mom? Who'd have thought you were such a warrior princess."

"Anybody who knows you two," Micah said. "You had to get it from somewhere."

An horrendous crash sounded on our left, like a jet breaking the sound barrier.

"*Owwww!*" Mom and Stacy and I clapped our hands to our ears. It didn't seem to bother Micah and Mia much. "What was that?" I turned and scanned the terrain, prepared for another attack. "And who the hell are they?"

A group of men—or so I assumed—stood about fifty feet away from us. Well, five men and an octopus, anyway. I thought I'd caught sight of some extra equipment folding into the men's backs, though. Extra equipment that looked like wings. One of the men stepped forward and held up his hand.

"Yo! Whut up?"

427

"G." I smiled. I'd always wondered what he looked like. He opened his arms.

"C'mon, Ari! Give us a hug!"

I laughed and moved into his arms. Into wow power. I'd thought Micah's angel hug was something but this?

"Gabriel," I said. "As in—archangel?"

"In the flesh. And these guys behind me—"

"Don't tell me. If you're Gabriel, Michael and Raphael can't be far behind."

"Michael." The archangel on the far right raised his hand.

"And Raphael." The archangel next to him waved.

"And the other two?"

"Well, that's Jerahmeel beside Raphael."

"I'm sorry, I don't recognize—"

"The name." Jerahmeel shrugged and sighed. "Story of my life."

"And the other dude you'd know as Lucifer. We call him Lucy. Not with any terribly great affection, I'm afraid."

The octopus scowled. "Can we get this show on the road? And get them the hell out of here?"

I stared at him and narrowed my eyes. *You've stepped into a bed of fire ants, buddy. They're all over you. You're covered in 'em. Havin' fun yet, you slimy bastard?*

He might not know what fire ants were, but he was damn sure finding out what they felt like. He shrieked and started hopping up and down, his three legs throwing tentacles everywhere as his arm appendages slung wildly, trying to shake off stinging marauders who weren't even there.

"Good one, Ari, but stop now, please, we have some final business to conduct with our boy Kaxchotx."

I pulled back and the demon settled down. He glared at me. *Keep glaring, asshole. I can bring 'em right back.* He dropped his head and backed away from me.

Gabriel smiled over my head at the group.

"You did good, guys. Real good. Mia, for a first assignment, you got a doozy. Micah was right, you're an angel to be proud of. Miss Grace, always knew you'd be a force to be reckoned with if you ever cut loose. Figured Stacy'd pop up with some version of that inherited telekinesis some time or other, damn good timing, sweetheart. Now let's get you all home. Before Chad and Spike come after my ass."

"What about them?" I pointed to the humans we'd liberated, lying on the ground close together in the spot where Mom had deposited them after pulling them out of the fire zone. Drained, spent, exhausted, apathetic. They weren't actually dead but their eyes were. They broke my heart.

"We're taking them with us, don't worry."

"The hell you say!" Demon boy Kaxchotx's head shot up at that. "Those are my humans! That wasn't part of the deal!"

"You don't know what the deal was, old son, we haven't told you yet. And part of that deal is we're taking all the humans you have over here. Every last one of 'em!"

"Or what?"

I narrowed my eyes again. *The ants are back, asshole. In your mouth. In your nose. In every hole you got on that body.*

Kaxchotx howled, flung himself on the ground and rolled furiously from side to side.

"I'll take that as an 'uncle'," said Gabriel. "Let him loose, Ari, I still have some business to talk with him."

I pulled back, but Kaxchotx didn't get up. Gabriel leaned over him.

"Now, here's the rest of the deal. You're never going to cross over again. Not even if a breach as big as the Grand Canyon opened up out of nowhere. You're never going to hunt in our dimension. Ever. Again."

"Deal! Deal! Just keep her away from me!"

Lucifer laughed. "Oh, that's rich! And you three gullible fools are just gonna believe him and trot off home!"

"Well, here comes the part about making sure he's not gonna try and collect any damages from you, Lucy."

"Damn straight he's not gonna try! Like he could actually collect any!"

"Oh, he won't have to try, Lucy. You're going to pay up. And then there'll be no need for them to replace worn out humans. Because they'll never need a replacement."

As one, Gabriel, Michael, Raphael and Jerahmeel turned to stare at Lucifer. They raised their hands and lightning bolts sizzled from their fingertips, encircling him in a cage of electric blue.

"What the hell?! Have you lost your freakin' minds?! You can't do this! The Grand Conductor won't let you! He didn't let you last time! There has to be a balance! Between the light and the dark! You need me! I'm the balance!"

"You *were* the balance. But everybody's got a replacement. You supplied your own. When you had Sera whisper in Jerahmeel's ear. See, we don't need but one fallen archangel for the balance, Lucy. And this time—that ain't you. Especially since Jerahmeel's available to move right into your office. You don't seriously think it was an accident he just strolled in right after we did, do you?"

"The Grand Conductor's gonna fry your asses when he hears about this!"

"Lucy, Lucy, Lucy." Michael shook his head sorrowfully. "Whose idea do you think it was?"

"No! He wouldn't!"

"Guess there's a limit for everybody, Lucy. You had your free pass. This second attempt of yours to take over the universe did you in with the Grand Conductor. He's had it. But Jerahmeel's not getting off scott free. He's got to keep Sera with him, can't have her running around loose in public. So to speak."

"I do?! You're kidding, right? Nobody said anything about that! You can't stick me with that bitch for eternity!"

"Guess again, little brother. And that name thing you got going? As in nobody knows yours and how much you hate that? They still won't. They never will. Because from now on, everybody's gonna think you're Lucifer. Forever and always. Deal with it."

"But that's—that's not fair!"

Raphael shrugged. "My heart bleeds, Jerry. You can be Lucifer or you can stay behind here in his place. One fallen archangel's as good as another for this job. So which is it?"

"Sera's not so bad. And Lucifer's easier to spell than Jerahmeel, anyway."

"Yeah, we thought you'd say that." Gabriel bent over Kaxchotx and offered a hand. Kaxchotx wrapped a few slimy tentacles around Gabriel's wrist and pulled himself up. "So, old boy, this close enough to where you need him to be?"

"Yes, but what am I supposed to do for the actual miners? You know, the ones that swing the actual pickaxes?"

"Get all that archangel power hooked up and moving, Kaxchotx, those pickaxes'll just swing by themselves. This is one battery won't lose its charge. So we're solid? No hunting. Ever again. That's the deal."

"Deal. I'll get my men up here to move the cage. It will hold, won't it?"

"Forever. Reinforced with a little extra containment the Grand Conductor came up with. Just for this one special occasion."

"Good enough. Our business is done, then. As soon as you get them out of here." Kaxchotx glared at me a minute and then thought better of it. He turned away and pulled a little square device out of his pocket and punched a button. Demon cell phone, obviously. He began barking orders.

"So, darling. Let's get all of you out of here."

I pointed back to the freed human slaves. "G, those poor people—"

"Kaxchotx, I need to have some staff come pick these survivors up. You'll let 'em in? And back out?"

Kaxhotx hesitated. Then he looked at me. "I'm sure G can always get me back through again, should the need arise." I said sweetly.

He blanched. "Absolutely, Gabriel. Get as big a team as you need. Safe passage guaranteed."

Gabriel grinned and pulled out his cell. "Yo! We need a Recovery Unit over here. Mark my present coordinates, I'm about to be moving. Safe passage in and out guaranteed. And have a big crew of Healers waiting in the ER back at MeanStreet. We're looking at overtime hours here." He pocketed his phone and gestured us to gather in close. "And let's go. I ain't kidding, Chad and Spike gave me a deadline."

Lucifer'd been shocked into silence for a few minutes. His face was parchment white.

"Gabriel, you aren't really going to let them do this to me? Are you?"

"Raphael warned you, Lucy. He who laughs last, laughs loudest. But trust me. I'm not laughing." Gabriel's eyes were bruised with grief. Sorrow lived in every line of his face. "Goodbye, my brother. I've always loved you. I always will."

Gabriel wrapped his arms around me. Michael wrapped his arms around Mom. Raphael gathered Stacy close. Wings sprouted from angel and archangel backs. They fluttered and then beat furiously, forming a rushing vortex. And just like that, we crossed into the No-Man's Land between dimensions, those mighty wings setting a course home. Halfway across the void, flashing lights to our left signaled the crossing of the Recovery Unit, half-a-dozen winged denizens throwing light into darkness. Angels fly among us. Everywhere.

Chapter Fifty-Four

"Okay, that's it! G said half-an-hour, it's been thirty-one minutes. We're going back in."

Chad threw open the door of Spike's truck.

"Wait a minute, son!" Bob reached out a restraining hand. "They might've found those bodies by now."

"No, sir. No blaring sirens, no screams. Harold said it was handled. I believe him. And even if we walk back into a full-scale investigation trying to figure out just what the hell those remains are, we've got to get to that box before anybody moves it."

Spike threw his own door open and swung his legs out. Then he went still. Completely. So did Chad.

"You feel that?" Spike asked.

"Yeah. You, too?"

"Oh, yeah. So you think—"

Cell phones blared simultaneously. Tailored ring tones. Black Magic Woman on Chad's. Witchy Woman on Spike's.

"Thank God. They're home."

* * *

A world and dimension away from last night's visit to Hell, I stood at the buffet table set up in the Desert Trooper's Clubhouse and surveyed the crowd.

Dr. and Mrs. Forrester danced in the middle of the floor. Mom and Dad danced over to their left. I smiled.

"Penny for your thoughts," Chad said in my ear. I sighed and leaned back against him.

"Ever hear of inflation?"

"Okay, I'll up it to a dollar. Might go as high as ten. Whatcha' laughing about?"

"Mom."

"Oh, yeah. Love the outfit. Especially the t-shirt."

Mom decided that morning the black tee with the pink logo "Pretty Mama" was too demure and swiped one of mine. It was a tad tight, but that suited the "Hot Mama" blazing in red across the front. And yeah, she was hot. Black leather biker pants, jacket, boots and all. She'd even turned her nose up at the Beemer for the wedding procession through the Tunnel of Love Drive-Thru.

"Hell, no! You're not sticking me in a car with all those bikes roaring! I'm ridin' bitch with your Daddy!" she'd proclaimed.

"Perfect wedding," I said.

"Yeah, it was. Just like ours, except for the extra hundred or so bikes riding behind."

I laughed. "Yeah, it was a really big wedding."

"Can't say Vegas went as planned this time around either."

"Nope, sure didn't."

"Then again, it sure wasn't boring."

"I'd kind of like to try boring. Just every now and then, for a day or two. Think it'll ever happen?"

"We can dream."

"Until the next one comes around."

Chad's cell phone vibrated against my back from his jacket pocket.

"You didn't turn that off?"

"I don't have to answer it."

"Liar. Yes, you do. It's the next adventure over the horizon. Go ahead. Answer it."

"War-N-Wit, Inc., Chad Garrett. How can we help you?"

The End

Published by BWL Publishing

Vanished
Country Justice
Raising Cain

With Jude Pittman
Mother Shipton and the Sister Witches

Gail Roughton is a native of small town Georgia whose Deep South heritage features prominently in much of her work. She's a retired paralegal who lived in a law office for over forty years, during which time she raised three children and quite a few attorneys. She kept herself more or less sane by writing novels and tossing the completed manuscripts into her closet, most of which have now emerged in published form.

A cross-genre writer, her books range from humor to romance to thriller to horror and she's never quite sure what to expect when she sits down at the keyboard. She usually has a project or two on the backburner but doesn't discuss any for fear of jinxing them. Given her affinity for the supernatural, this should come as no surprise to any reader.

9 780228 627128